HE CLAIMED THAT HE WAS AN ARTIST, A PHOTOGRAPHER FOR THE GREAT MATHEW BRADY. BUT ONE WOMAN KNEW THE TRUTH . . . AND SWORE HER VENGEANCE.

Ruth climbed a flight of stairs and made her way along the corridor. It was still very early, and no one was about. She halted in front of a door and tried the knob. As she'd suspected, it was locked. She lifted her hand to rap on the door, then paused. Smiling grimly, she tapped three times, waited, then tapped twice more.

There were a few moments of silence. Then, at last, Langston Cook, hair tousled, eyes still sleepy, opened the door. He had a blanket wrapped about him.

"May I come in?" she asked.

Langston was speechless for a moment, staring at her. Then he stepped back, clutching at the blanket. She could tell he was naked underneath.

Ruth strode into the room. "I can wait," she said curtly. "Please get dressed."

Langston shot her a puzzled glance. Then he nodded and shut himself into the small bedroom, leaving her alone in his sitting room. She glanced about. He'd left no mark on the room, she saw, as though he didn't live there. Of course, he didn't really live here, she told herself angrily. He was a Southerner first, last and always. She'd been foolish to think photography meant more to him, to believe that he shared Mathew Brady's vision. He was nothing but a sneaking Rebel spy.

Ruth took the pistol from the canvas bag and held the gun in a fold of her black gown. . . .

REBECCA DRURY

A Dell/Banbury Book

Published by
Banbury Books, Inc.
37 West Avenue
Wayne, Pennsylvania 19087

Dell ® TM 681510, Dell Publishing Co., Inc.

ISBN: 0-440-00456-X

Printed in the United States of America

First printing—September 1982

PART I

WINTER 1860-
SPRING 1862

Chapter 1

"Mr. and Mrs. Quincey Valerian request the pleasure of your company at a dinner to be held on March 1, 1860, at . . ." Ruth O'Neill looked up from the invitations she was so carefully copying and stared through the mullioned windows of the Valerians' morning room. Unconsciously, she raised her hand to check the neatness of her chignon. Madame Valerian was always at her about stray curls escaping. "I not only expect," Madame was fond of saying, "I insist on a ladylike appearance in my employees at all times."

Outside, the day was fine and the clear blue sky was dotted with small wisps of clouds. But though the sun shone brightly, a chill February breeze kept Ruth from opening the window. Across the cobbled street, a black slave with a kerchief over her head shook a duster from the upper porch of a large brick house much like the Valerian home. Most Georgetown residences were similiar, tended by slaves who were carefully called servants or the help.

Ruth was used to neither the fine houses nor the slaves. Before she'd come to the Valerians, her home had been on the edge of Washington in Swampoodle, where she'd shared a few rooms with her father and her two brothers, George and Michael. If you were poor and Irish, you lived in a Swampoodle hut. But things hadn't always been that bad. Ruth had grown up

outside of Boston, and though her father had never
been rich, he'd had a job at the foundry and they'd
lived in a snug little house. Ruth sighed as she remembered that house, then straightened her shoulders.
There was no point in mourning for the past. She could
bring back neither her dead mother nor her father's
right arm, lost in a foundry accident. Instead, she
ought to thank God she'd been taught to read and
write. Otherwise she'd never have gotten this fine job,
never be living in this beautiful house.

"I can't imagine how refined Southern ladies permit themselves to be tended by black women." Her
employer had said such things often, and in Ruth's
hearing. Madame Valerian was from Boston too, and
she'd only come to Washington after she'd married a
Southern gentleman. "Negro help is all very well,"
Madame declared, "but not in one's boudoir." Ruth
wrinkled her nose. She didn't particularly like being a
personal maid, although she enjoyed copying invitations to levees and parties and writing notes to accept
or reject the invitations Madame received.

The clop of hoofs and the rattle of carriage
wheels drew Ruth's attention, and she gazed down at
the street. A hired hack stopped in front of the house,
and Ruth stood up to see better, smoothing the grey
wool of her gown. She watched with growing interest
as a young man jumped down from the buggy and
jauntily walked toward the house. When he took off his
hat, Ruth's breath caught in her throat. She'd only gotten a glimpse of him, but he was certainly the hand-
somest man she'd ever seen.

She heard the tinkle of the bell, then a creak as
Ajax opened the front door. "Massa Jeremy!" he exclaimed. "It sure be good to see you. We didn't know
yo' was coming."

"I didn't know myself until yesterday." His voice

was deep and pleasing, and he spoke with a drawl, much like Madame's husband. "How is everyone?"

"Just fine, just fine," the servant intoned.

"I'll go on into the morning room and surprise Cousin Adele," the young man went on.

At this, Ruth hastily sat down and picked up her pen. She heard Ajax try to explain that Madame wasn't at home, but the words came too late. In an instant, the door swung open and Jeremy was in the room.

As he spied Ruth, a puzzled smile crept across his face. "Oh, I *am* sorry," he said, bowing slightly. "I didn't mean to intrude. I'm Jeremy Valerian."

Ruth tried not to stare, but his eyes were as bright a blue as the sky she'd just been admiring. "You're not," she stammered. "Not intruding, I mean. I . . . I work for Madame Valerian." She nervously touched her chignon and, to her horror, felt it give way. Masses of curly black hair tumbled down her back, showering pins to the floor.

Blushing deeply, Ruth scrambled from her chair to retrieve the pins, but Jeremy Valerian was even quicker. She watched in growing embarrassment as he knelt before her, carefully gathering up every last one. When at last he rose and handed them to her, she tried not to look at him. "I . . . you must excuse me," she murmured, trying to edge past him.

He grasped her hand. "I've told you my name, but I don't know yours."

"Ruth. Ruth O'Neill." She knew she must look terrible with her face red and her hair curling every which way. She tugged her hand free, but she couldn't free her gaze from his. She stood still, as if she were rooted to the spot, so close to him that she could see flecks of black in the blue of his eyes. His golden hair curled softly just below his ears, and his chiseled features were like those of the marble statues in the Boston museum.

"I didn't know you worked here or I'd have visited my cousins much sooner," he told her, still smiling.

The spell was shattered. Ruth pursed her lips and frowned, remembering all at once that she was a servant in this house. It wouldn't do to flirt with her employer's cousin. It wouldn't do at all. Quickly, she darted around him and fled up the stairs.

When she had her hair tidy again, Ruth put on her bonnet and shawl. It was her half-day and the clock had already struck one. Madame Valerian allowed her two half-days a week, one on Sunday, the other on Tuesday or Wednesday, whichever suited Madame's needs. On Sundays, Ruth often went home to Swampoodle to see her father and brothers, but the other half-day, if the weather was fair, she usually spent in the fresh air.

She let herself out the rear door and hurried toward Rock Creek, which separated Georgetown from Washington. It was too early for the Judas trees to be unfolding their purplish-pink blossoms, but she'd seen the fuzzy grey buds of the pussy willows around the Swampoodle shacks last Sunday. Spring was on the way, and perhaps looking for its first signs would help her forget what had happened in the morning room.

She hadn't gone very far when she heard footsteps behind her. Then a voice called out. "Miss O'Neill, wait! Wait for me!"

Ruth stopped and turned, only to see Jeremy Valerian striding toward her bareheaded. "I saw you pass the window," he explained, quickly catching up, "and I decided to walk with you." He gave her a warm smile. "After all, my cousins aren't home, and I'd like some company."

Ruth couldn't help smiling back, but she knew she had to make the situation clear. "Madame Valerian wouldn't approve," she said gently.

Jeremy merely shrugged. "We won't tell her. Ajax says she's gone for the day, so she'll never know." He offered her his arm, and bemused and pleased, she took it. "I'm sorry I let the hack go," he remarked as they set off toward the bridge that led to Washington.

"Oh, I enjoy walking." She wondered if he could tell how fast her heart was beating. It was not often that Ruth went strolling with a man, let alone such a handsome one. She'd spurned the Irish lads who lived near her father. None of them really interested her, and besides, she couldn't bear the thought of living in Swampoodle all her life. It wasn't that she was a snob, and she didn't yearn to be wealthy. All she really wanted was enough to "live decent," as her mother used to say. She knew there was little hope of rising too far above her station, and she knew just as well that men like Jeremy weren't for her. Even so, it was wonderful to have him walking next to her, treating her like a lady.

"You're the prettiest girl I've ever set eyes on," he beamed. "Your eyes are like sapphires."

"Thank you." She managed only a brief reply, then struggled to continue the conversation. "You're from the South, aren't you?" At his nod she added, "I've heard the ladies in the South are truly beautiful."

"The South does have beauties, but you notice my Cousin Quincey chose a Northern girl for his bride. Cousin Adele is from Boston, I believe."

"So am I." She said it before she'd thought about how it might sound.

He laughed. "See, you prove my point. Boston must be the home of the loveliest ladies in the country."

By then they had crossed the bridge onto Pennsylvania Avenue. Ahead, up the wide street, was the White House, and beyond it, the gaunt derricks atop the Capitol building. Jeremy paused for a moment to gaze at the view, and Ruth searched for something to say. Was he interested in the Capitol?

"They say the dome won't be completed for at least two years," she ventured. "There's a statue to go at the top called Armed Freedom. I've seen it. It's on the grounds by . . ."

"I know about the statue," he said grimly. "Perhaps the name is more fitting than anyone realizes."

She glanced at his frowning face, puzzled.

Jeremy sighed. "I live in South Carolina." He said the words as though they were enough to explain everything.

Ruth sorted through the conversations she'd overheard at the Valerians'. She knew that the Southern states argued with the North over the right to keep slaves, the right to pursue fugitive slaves into any state. There were even rumors that some Southern states, South Carolina among them, had threatened to secede from the Union, to become separate countries all on their own. But surely that must only be a threat.

As she hesitated, Jeremy's mood seemed to lighten. "Shall we walk uptown to the Willard Hotel and have tea?" he asked. "We can take a hack back to the house so you won't be late."

Ruth was overwhelmed. She'd never been inside the Willard or any of the other grand hotels along the north side of Pennsylvania Avenue. "Oh, yes," she said eagerly. "Id like that ever so much." But her eagerness faded a bit as they neared the hotel. She was painfully conscious of her dowdy grey gown, which had only petticoats to hold out the skirt. Madame had ruled that crinolines were not for maids.

As they entered the dining room, Ruth felt drab and undistinguished, but the waiters seemed not to notice when they ushered the pair to a table, bowing to Jeremy and hovering attentively. In no time at all, Ruth had relaxed. In fact, she felt like a princess, using a silver spoon to stir the sugar into her tea, lifting the fragile china cup as she looked across the snowy linen tablecloth at Jeremy. A princess, escorted by the best-looking man in the room. She scarcely took in the magnificent chandeliers overhead, the velvet draperies at the windows. She was simply too busy gazing into Jeremy's eyes, listening to his voice.

On the way home in the buggy, Jeremy reached for her hand, but Ruth shook her head, folding her hands primly in her lap. "I've never had such a wonderful time," she began, her voice low but steady. "I wouldn't have missed going to the Willard with you for anything. But I . . . I need my job." She looked down at her hands. "Madame Valerian is certain to disapprove. I know my place and I must keep it." She raised her head and gazed sadly at him. "So thank you. I'll always remember this day."

He leaned toward her. "We can be friends. Cousin Adele won't know."

Ruth shook her head. "No, we can't. I'm not good at hiding things from people." She gave him a wistful glance.

He leaned closer, and as his lips touched hers, Ruth closed her eyes against the flood of warmth that rose in her body. She returned his kiss, then gasped and flung herself to the far side of the buggy. "Oh, dear God," she whispered. "Mother Mary, I didn't mean to."

Jeremy raised his eyebrows. "It's not a sin, Ruth."

"But it is . . . it could be. The priest says . . ." She stopped, red flaming in her cheeks. Jeremy didn't want to hear what Father Dunleavy had told her. She struggled to regain her composure. "I'm not . . . not the kind of girl you know in society," she said hurriedly.

"Thank the good Lord," Jeremy laughed.

Ruth looked over at him in anguish, but when she spoke it was with quiet dignity. "Mr. Valerian, I think this must be like a game to you, but it isn't to me." She leaned forward and called to the driver. "Please stop on this side of the bridge." As Jeremy sat staring at her in astonishment, she jumped down from the buggy. She solemnly shook his hand, then turned and made her way off into the fading light of the winter afternoon.

That will be the end of it, Ruth had thought, but all the while she was wishing—wishing what? In the days that followed, she tried to put him from her mind, but she never quite managed to succeed. Despite herself, she strained to hear as Madame and her friends spoke of him. Jeremy was a lieutenant in the United States Army, a West Point graduate, but his assignment to a unit had been delayed because of his father's illness. He was an only son, and as Madame Valerian told a friend, "practically engaged to Rosalie, the belle of the Rhett family. They're in cotton, you know."

Jeremy was not for her. Ruth kept telling herself that, but when she lay in bed at night, reliving his kiss, all she wanted was to be with him again. Even a glimpse of him during the day seemed to set her dreaming. Finally, on her half-day Sunday, she managed to escape from the house. In the afternoon, she set out for Swampoodle, walking along North Capitol Street. I won't let him take over all my thoughts today, she told herself. It's foolishness. Madame's already scolded me for not tending to my duties. No one ought to fall in love with a man so suddenly, just from one kiss.

But when Ruth turned off Pennsylvania to New York Avenue, all her good intentions flew away. There, halfway down the block, stood Jeremy, waiting for her by President's Park.

"I've hired a gig," he shouted. "We'll go for a drive in the country."

"How did you know I'd be coming this way?"

"I asked Ajax. He knows everything. House servants always do."

Ruth felt a slight prickle of unease that Ajax not only knew where she lived but how she got there. "I'm a servant, and I know very little about anyone," she argued.

"You're different." Jeremy offered his hand to assist her into the carriage and she took it, smiling at his enthusiasm. Well, she sighed, so much for good intentions. Once she was face to face with him, there was no way she could resist Jeremy Valerian.

As the days passed, Ruth forgot all about her doubts and fears. She was simply too busy being in love with Jeremy—and too overcome by the thought that he might feel the same way about her. Whenever they met each other in the house, she couldn't help lingering, and neither could he. Their stolen kisses might be sinful but they were also impossible to resist, especially when she knew he was waiting for her, as he was that morning in the library.

"Jeremy," she laughed, pulling away from him, "someone will come. We'll be caught."

"Not in here. No one in this house reads." He took her in his arms and she forgot everything else.

She hadn't dreamed a man's caresses could make her feel as Jeremy's did, as though her bones were melting in the heat of her desire.

Neither of them heard the door open, neither saw Adele Valerian's shocked face.

"Ruth!" Madame Valerian cried.

Ruth and Jeremy flew apart. There was a painful silence, and then Madame drew herself up to her full height.

"Ruth, you may go upstairs to your room and wait. I'll speak with you later."

Ruth hesitated, glancing at Jeremy.

"Go immediately!" Madame snapped.

Trembling, Ruth raised her head and walked out into the hall. She heard the door slam shut behind her. He didn't try to help me, she thought. He didn't say anything to Madame Valerian. Tears gathered in her eyes.

Back in her room, she sat drearily on the bed and waited. It seemed like an eternity before Madame appeared at her door, but when she did Ruth rose to face her.

"Jeremy has left the house," Madame said sternly. "He's returning to Charleston." There was an awful pause. "You'll remain in this room until your father comes for you."

Ruth licked her lips. "My . . . my father?"

"I've had the carriage sent round for him."

That would set tongues wagging in Swampoodle, Ruth thought. She had a sudden desire to laugh, but she suppressed the urge, afraid she'd lose control, laughing and laughing until she cried.

"I shouldn't have expected any better of you," Madame Valerian snapped, turning on her heel, "but I'm deeply ashamed of Jeremy. It's disgraceful. And in *my* house."

* * *

Father, thank the good Lord, wasn't drunk—nor was he entirely sober. But only she could see that, Ruth assured herself as she stood beside him in the morning room.

"I would watch your daughter carefully if I were you, Mr. O'Neill," Madame Valerian said with a disdainful toss of her head. "It's plain to see she can't be trusted around men, and you know what that means. I've done all I can to improve her manners, but obviously breeding will tell."

"I'll be taking Ruthie back with me, ma'am, and I'll be thanking you to mind your own business." Jack O'Neill spoke angrily, meeting Madame's cold stare face to face. "Looks to me like the lad don't have much to brag about as far as manners go. Lucky for him he pulled out before I got here."

Madame's nostrils flared as though she had suddenly smelled something nasty.

Ruth laid her hand on her father's arm. "Da, let's go." She hurried him out of the room and down the front steps.

Jack O'Neill would have nothing to do with Madame Valerian's fancy carriage. Instead he lugged Ruth's heavy bag with his good arm as they walked all the way across Washington. He didn't speak until they were home. Then he tossed the bag to the floor and stood gazing sadly at his daughter.

"Well, Ruthie," he sighed, "you've made a royal mess of things, and I don't rightly know what to do. You've gotten all kinds of foolishness into your head, and I think it's best that you go away for a time. Maybe that'll put some sense back into you." He chucked her gently under the chin. "We'll pack you off to Mary in New York."

"Oh, Da, I don't want to live with her and Tim. They've no room, not with the two little ones."

Ruth's father shook his head. "Your sister Mary's a wedded wife, and she can look after a young girl better than your old da. Of course, you'll have to work. Make no mistake about that. You'll have to pay for your room and board."

"But I don't want to live in New York."

"Be that as it may, to New York you must go. And Ruthie, mind you don't get taken in by another smooth-talking lad who hasn't a notion of marriage in mind."

Tears flooded Ruth's eyes. "I wasn't taken in," she gulped, trying to convince herself that she wasn't lying. "I . . . I never expected Jeremy would ask me to marry him."

Chapter 2

Ruth's purposeful steps faltered when she saw the gilt lettering on the building at Broadway and Tenth Street: National Portrait Gallery, Mathew B. Brady, Photographer. She'd had no idea she'd be going to such an imposing place. All her brother-in-law, Tim Cleary, had told her was that he'd seen an advertisement for a woman secretary in the front window.

She could tell Tim wasn't too happy about having her stay in the already crowded third-floor flat, though her sister Mary was glad enough to have her help, what with two small boys and another baby on the way. Tim was anxious for Ruth to find a job, but no more anxious than Ruth herself. However, staring at Mr. Brady's fine gallery, she didn't think much of her chances. She looked down at her dark blue wool dress and sighed. Mary had done her best to help her perk up the gown, adding ruffles and lending her a crinoline to hold out the skirt, but Ruth still had a long way to go before she looked like the chic women who seemed to fill the streets of New York.

As she hesitated on the sidewalk, an elegantly dressed figure swept past with a swish of skirts and entered the gallery. A customer? Or someone applying for the secretary's position? Ruth took a deep breath, then pushed open the door and went in. She found herself standing on a velvety green carpet at one end of a long room. The walls were emerald green, and the glass ceiling let in a cool emerald light that glittered on the crystal and brass of the chandeliers overhead. Two thirds of the way down the room, by a narrow, twisting staircase, stood a group of women. Applicants, like herself, Ruth thought. She counted nine of them, each one much better dressed than she.

As she slowly advanced, the beautiful green carpet was so soft underfoot that Ruth wished she could kick off her shoes and go barefoot. She tried not to gape at the gold-framed photographs that hung all along the walls. Instead she looked at the long green and gold divans that were placed back to back in the center of the room. She supposed they were there so that customers might sit and enjoy the pictures. Ruth bent and ran her hand over the plush velvet of the seats.

Postponing the moment when she would have to join the other women, she sat down and examined the portraits on the wall in front of her, reading the names underneath. "Edward, Prince of Wales." He looked so young, a boy really, like her brother Michael, standing there solemnly holding his high silk hat. The photograph next to him showed an older man, equally solemn, wearing a wrinkled coat. He had sad eyes that stared from a gaunt face. "Abraham Lincoln," she read aloud.

"A man to be trusted." The voice seemed to come out of nowhere.

Ruth started, rising to her feet, and looked at the slight man with thick-lensed glasses who stood next to her.

"No, no. Sit down," he went on. "I didn't mean to startle you." He spoke with a touch of brogue.

Ruth smiled, reassured, though she remained standing. "I've heard my father call Mr. Lincoln a black Republican," she said, "but I think I'd trust him. He looks kind."

"What's your name?" the man asked.

Ruth was taken aback by his directness, but she was inclined not to be afraid of this mild-looking Irishman with his curly hair and beard, despite her sister's dire warnings about the evil men who lurked in the city, men who drugged women and sold them into a life of sin. "I'm Ruth O'Neill," she replied. "It's been pleasant talking to you, but I came here on business and I must attend to it."

The man merely nodded his head. "I thought you were Irish," he observed. "What business brings you here?"

Ruth thought this was one question too many, especially from a stranger. She drew herself up. "I'm applying for the position of secretary," she answered with as much dignity as she could manage. She glanced down the gallery and his gaze followed hers.

"I'm afraid all those others are too," he remarked.

"Yes." She wished she could simply turn around and leave, but she'd come a long way and she mustn't go away without trying, no matter how futile it might be. She squared her shoulders and started toward the women.

"Wait." The man caught at her arm.

She turned and gave him a puzzled glance. What could he want now?

"I know another way into the gallery," he explained. "There's a special entrance on Tenth Street, a private door for the use of ladies arriving in formal dress. I'll show it to you. Why not use that?"

She hesitated.

"Come, it'll give you an advantage. You can bypass all the other applicants and be the first to be seen."

"I don't know if that's fair."

The man gave her a gentle smile. "And I took you for an enterprising young lady," he said, shaking his head.

"Well, I do need the job. And how wonderful it would be to work in this place. It's so beautiful." Though she looked directly at him, it was hard to tell what he was thinking behind those blue-tinted lenses. But he was still smiling, and it seemed a nice smile. "I'll go with you," she said after a moment. "I just can't believe you're one of those white slavers, waiting to carry me off."

The man wrinkled his brow, and then he began to chuckle. "Oh, my dear Miss O'Neill. I'll have to tell that to Julia—she's my wife. She'll be amused no end to think I was mistaken for a white slaver."

Blushing slightly, Ruth followed him out of the building and around the corner to Tenth Street. Entering the side door, they went up a flight of stairs and into a room where a massive camera sat on a tripod facing an empty chair. As the door slammed shut, a young man in a stained white duster stuck his head out of another door, one marked Do Not Enter.

"Oh, it's you, Mr. Brady," he called. "I'll have the Douglas prints ready in a few minutes." And with that he disappeared.

Ruth turned to stare at her companion.

Mathew Brady chuckled. "Now, Miss O'Neill. Don't be angry with me. I knew as soon as I began talking with you that you were the one I wanted, and I didn't care to run that gantlet of women waiting downstairs."

"I . . . you mean I . . . I'm hired? As your secretary? But why?"

He grinned at her. "Because you're forthright, you don't seem silly or fluff-headed, and you need the job.

And I suppose your being Irish had a bit to do with it." His smile faded and he took her by the hand. "I was once poor, Miss O'Neill. I know how it is. There's something in your manner that says you'll work as hard as I did to succeed. Will you?"

Ruth found her duties easy enough. Mathew Brady's eyesight was very poor, so she read and wrote letters for him. She also made appointments with New York's well-to-do for their portraits and assisted at the sittings. She was surprised to discover that once these eminent people, so comfortable and self-assured, were posed in front of the camera, almost every one of them stiffened up, unable to relax and be natural.

One afternoon, when a small girl burst into tears and couldn't be quieted, Ruth began to sing the child a nonsense song her mother had taught her years ago.

> Oh, the rabbit bit the old brown dog
> And the mouse chased after the cat.
> The dragonfly swallowed the big bullfrog.
> Now what do you think of that?

The girl stared at Ruth, her tears drying on her cheeks.

> "Meow," cried the old brown dog.
> "Bow-wow," complained the cat.
> The dragonfly hopped from log to log.
> Now what do you think of that?

The child's lips curved into a smile. "That's silly," she said. "Sing it again."

Ruth settled the girl back in front of the camera. "You sit here with your mother and be very quiet," she told her, wiping away the child's tears, "and I'll teach you my silly song. Listen very carefully, and after I sing it three times, you try to sing it back to me."

Mr. Brady's portrait of the mother and daughter was an excellent likeness, and Ruth's trick had given him an inspiration. Two days later, he called her upstairs to sing to an austere old gentleman in a silk frock coat.

"But Mr. Brady, what will I sing?" Ruth felt very foolish standing next to the camera with the old man frowning at her.

"Anything," Brady commanded. "An Irish air, if you know one."

Ruth clasped her hands in front of her and nervously launched into "Molly Malone."

> She wheeled a wheelbarrow
> Through streets broad and narrow
> Crying "cockles and mussels alive, alive-o . . ."

After a moment or two, she relaxed. She enjoyed singing, and she'd always liked "Molly Malone." Watching her, the stern man sitting before the camera began to smile ever so slightly. Mr. Brady took a fine portrait, and after that Ruth often sang for the customers.

As the days passed, Ruth grew to love the work more and more. In fact, she would have been perfectly happy had it not been for her memories of Jeremy Valerian. She tried not to think of Jeremy, tried not to hope that he'd walk into the gallery—soon, maybe a minute from now—to tell her he couldn't stay away, couldn't live without her. But she knew it was a dream. She knew she'd never see him again.

Mr. Brady had shown Ruth how to operate the camera, how to fix the wet plates with their solution of collodion and how to process them afterwards. Once she had learned all that, he occasionally took her with him when he left the gallery to take photographs. In June, he told her she was to come with him and Mrs. Brady up the Hudson River to West Point, where he'd be photographing the cadets' graduation exercises. It would be a special outing for all three of them, since they'd be staying overnight and returning the next day.

Mr. Brady brought along a portable darkroom, fixed up in a wagon that was loaded onto the boat along with them. As they left New York, the day was fine, and the breeze that swept across the waves was warmed by the sun. The river seemed to have a life of its own, surging away from the ship in green, brown and white swirls. Seagulls swooped down behind the stern and over the bubbling wake. Ruth stood entranced at the rail for the entire journey up the Hudson.

When they landed at West Point, Ruth stared at the gray stone buildings scattered among the trees. Jeremy had once been a cadet here. She'd be walking the same paths he'd once walked, seeing the same sights. Suddenly she frowned. Stop it, she warned herself. It's over. He never cared for you, despite all his fine words. If he had, he'd have come after you. Leave Jeremy in the past, where he belongs. She directed her thoughts back to her work, watching as Mr. Brady set up his huge Anthony camera on the tripod and racked the great brass-barreled Harrison lens into focus.

"I'll take a few shots of the buildings," he announced eagerly. "Ruth, you look through the lens for me and see if it's properly focused."

Ruth stepped to the camera and bent to put her head under the focusing cloth. She saw through the lens the flagpole and the building behind it. "A clear image," she called moving out from under the cloth.

Brady nodded absent-mindedly, still squinting at the scene before him. "Why don't you and Ruth stroll about for a while?" he asked his wife. "I'm going to wait for the cadets to come past and persuade a few of them to pose by the flagpole. It may be a while."

Ruth was always a bit uncomfortable with Julia Brady. Not that she wasn't pleasant enough, but she gave Ruth the definite feeling that she'd prefer it if her husband hired only male assistants. Ruth smiled a little at the thought. Mr. Brady had never been anything but friendly and courteous. His wife had absolutely nothing to worry about.

As she and Mrs. Brady walked along the paths, Ruth couldn't help noticing how the cadets glanced at her with interest and admiration. She knew her new gown of pink-flowered calico with its crinolined skirt was becoming. And her bonnet, the prettiest she'd ever owned, was adorned with a pink silk rose to match the flowers on the dress. Were all soldiers like Jeremy? she wondered as yet another cadet gave her a smart salute. Were they all deceitful? Heartless? Ruth sighed and turned away.

When the two women came back to the camera and the equipment wagon, a group of cadets was posed by the flagpole, and Mr. Brady, his head under the cloth, was urging them to hold very still. It took a five- to ten-second exposure in bright sunlight for a sharp, clear negative, and any movement would blur the image. Ruth hurried to the wagon and pulled out an apron to protect her clothes from the chemicals. After she'd put it on, she stood waiting until Brady handed her the plate from the back of the camera, then ducked inside the wagon to process it. By the time she reappeared, Mr. Brady had moved the camera. Now he was posing a different group, three men standing beside an old cannon with its pyramid of shining black balls.

"Focus on us," he called to her.

She turned the lens and Mr. Brady sprang clearly into view next to an older officer with a mustache, a younger man in a frock coat, also mustached, and a blond man. Ruth gasped. Could it be? The blond man looked awfully like Jeremy. She pulled her head from under the cloth and stared at the group of men, convinced she was only imagining things. But she wasn't wrong. The man was unmistakably Jeremy Valerian, as handsome as ever in his blue army uniform.

Ruth clutched her hands together, her breathing quickening. He hadn't seen her. What should she do? Walk away? Hide in the wagon until he was gone? No, she must face him. After all, she'd never been a coward. Still trembling, Ruth lifted her chin and waited.

When Mr. Brady stepped back, the three men faced the camera, and she saw the expression on Jeremy's face change. First puzzlement, then dawning recognition and disbelief, then a broad smile. He strode quickly across the grass, passing Mr. Brady, coming straight to her.

"Ruth!" Jeremy grasped both her hands. "It's really you. I couldn't believe my eyes."

Her heart seemed to stop beating as she looked into his eyes. "Jeremy," she breathed, hardly able to speak at all. Suddenly she became conscious of the Bradys. Blushing slightly, she drew her hands from Jeremy's and introduced him. "I work for Mr. Brady in New York," she explained.

Jeremy beamed. "Then I must ask you, sir. May I steal Ruth for dinner this evening?"

Brady needed only a glance at Ruth's shining eyes to tell what his answer should be. "Certainly, Lieutenant Valerian," he replied. He paused and a mischievous smile came over his face. "That is, if I can convince you to pose for me as I asked you a few minutes ago, there by the cannon."

I won't go, Ruth told herself as she sat in her room at the inn, trying to pin up a stray curl. He needn't think he can smile at me and I'll forget everything. But all the while she was doing her best to make herself as attractive as possible, knowing in her heart of hearts that she couldn't stay away from Jeremy Valerian.

"Good God, Ruth," he burst out when he met her at the foot of the stairs, "I never thought I'd find you again. I can hardly believe it's really you."

"You didn't look for me very hard," she murmured, her voice shaking despite her resolve to appear calm. He was here, he was close to her, and it was difficult to remember that anything else mattered. She forced herself to continue. "You knew where I lived."

A note of urgency came into Jeremy's voice. "You weren't there when I came, and your father gave me short shrift. To say nothing of your brothers."

Ruth smiled slightly.

"It wasn't funny. The three of them acted as though they'd just as soon kill me as look at me. And not a one of them would tell me where you were, no matter how hard I tried to explain."

"I was home all that night after your cousin found us in the library. You didn't come then."

"Ruth, I couldn't. Let me tell you . . ."

She looked away from him. "I don't care to hear," she said firmly.

"Ruth, please listen to me. Come, we'll go into the dining room." He offered her his arm, but she ignored it.

"You didn't say a word to Madame Valerian," she said fiercely. "You let her send me away. It's too late to listen to you now, Jeremy. Your talking should have been done then. If you cared for me, you'd have..."

Jeremy spun her around, forcing her to look at him. "Damn it, I'm in love with you!"

Ruth heard a giggle and glanced away, only to see a passing couple looking at them with amusement. She blushed.

"Did you hear me?" he demanded, lowering his voice.

"Yes, and so did everyone else." She put her hand on his arm and walked with him toward the dining room. "I'll listen, but that's all."

As soon as they were seated, he leaned forward, reaching for her hand across the table. "After she sent you to your room," he explained, "Cousin Adele told me you could keep your position if I left town on the next train. She sent Cousin Quincey with me to make certain I kept my word." He gave her a bitter smile. "I didn't doubt that she'd keep hers, but when I came back three weeks later, you were gone. She said you'd left without notice."

"She had me out of her house the same day you left." Ruth frowned down at the table.

Jeremy nodded grimly. "I should know Cousin Adele's ways by now. You never could trust her."

"I don't think I can trust you, either."

"But I've told you..."

"If you cared about me, you wouldn't have left me the moment your cousin found us together."

He sighed. "There were... problems. At home in Charleston. I couldn't have taken you there."

Ruth slowly drew her hand from his. "You're engaged to someone in Charleston," she said softly. "Rosalie Rhett."

He stared at her for a moment, coloring slightly.

"We're not engaged," he said abruptly. "Not exactly. It's difficult to explain."

"Don't bother on my account." Ruth pushed back her chair and stood up. "I find I'm not hungry after all. Goodbye, Jeremy." She turned away, feeling as though her heart was breaking, and head high, marched across the dining room. As soon as she was through the door, she raced up the stairs, fumbling in her bag for the key to her room, but she was blinded by the tears in her eyes. As she stood in front of her room still searching for the key, she felt a hand on her shoulder. "You!" she cried. "I never want to see you again!" Her hand closed on the key and she turned back to the door.

Jeremy paid no attention. Instead he calmly took the key and opened the door. She stalked in ahead of him, but he followed her, shutting the door firmly behind them.

"Get out of my room," she sputtered, her eyes blazing with anger.

"No. Not until I have my say." He took her by the shoulders and gave her a little shake. "You *will* listen to me."

She pulled away from him and folded her arms across her chest. "Very well. Talk."

"I have no intention of marrying Rosalie Rhett," Jeremy began, "despite what my parents and hers might think. Not since I met you." He hesitated. "But I can't marry you either, not as things stand." He touched his lieutenant's insignia. "Do you see this?"

"Yes. You're a lieutenant. So what?"

"I'm a lieutenant in the United States Army." His jaw tightened. "I came to West Point today to see an old friend graduate—and for another reason. To resign my commission. I don't belong to the United States, I belong to South Carolina. I'll fight only for my state."

"Fight?"

"Yes, Ruth. If South Carolina secedes, they may try to make us stay in the Union by force."

"They?"

"The government in Washington. Last month the Republicans nominated a man who hates the South, Abraham Lincoln. If he's elected president, there's certain to be a war."

Ruth, who paid little attention to politics, was bewildered. She'd heard talk of secession from Southerners at Madame Valerian's, but not of war. "Are you telling me the United States would go to war with South Carolina? With one of its own states?"

Jeremy scowled. "To keep us in bondage. We have a right not to belong to a Union we have nothing in common with. As Thomas Paine said, 'Tyranny, like hell, is not easily conquered.' If they want war, then war they'll have!" He touched her arm. "I can't offer you marriage until I see my future more clearly. If there *is* a war . . ."

Ruth shivered. "Don't speak of that." He was so near to her now, so tantalizingly near. When he pulled her into his arms, she tried to stiffen, but overwhelmed by her feelings, she clung to him instead.

"You're even lovelier than you were last winter," he murmured. "Will you wait for me?"

The words came out instantly, without any hesitation. "Oh yes, Jeremy. Yes, yes."

His lips met hers. Then, ever so gently, they traced a soft path down her throat, sending shivers along her spine. In a moment, his hands were caressing her breasts, searching, exploring, drawing her closer and closer. She felt the buttons of her bodice loosen, felt the silky folds of her dress slide to the floor. And all the while she was breathless, helpless, wanting only for him to go on and on, wanting his kisses to last forever.

With a smile, Jeremy lifted her in his arms and carried her to the bed. As she lay atop the coverlet, he tore at his uniform. An instant later he was next to her, gathering her against his chest, his bare flesh warm and exciting.

"Do you love me?" he murmured, sliding his hand along the curve of her hip.

Ruth reached up and stroked his cheek. "I'll never stop loving you," she answered, her eyes misting over. "I'll love you forever."

Jeremy sighed and lowered his head, brushing his lips over her breasts. Pulling him closer, Ruth arched her body to his, feeling his hardness against her, frightening and thrilling. Then he eased over her and suddenly the hardness was inside. There was a stab of pain, but at the same time a feeling that made the blood run molten in her veins. Slowly and deliberately Jeremy began to move within her in a rhythm that caught her up, a rhythm that grew faster and faster, more and more abandoned. With a cry, Ruth found herself at the crest of a strange and wonderful sensation. Jeremy shuddered and groaned above her, and then they both lay quiet, cradled in each other's arms.

"You're mine, Ruth, forever mine," Jeremy whispered. He lifted himself on one elbow and looked down at her. "We must never lose one another again."

She stared at him, eyes wide. Somehow, despite what he'd said, she'd believed they wouldn't have to part.

Jeremy gently brushed a lock of hair off her forehead. There was a great sadness in his eyes. "You're living in New York and I must go back to Charleston," he sighed. "My father is dying. I'm needed there." He leaned over and kissed her. "I can't promise when we'll meet again, but I'll come back and find you, wherever you are."

She gave him a loving smile. "I'll be waiting."

Jeremy nodded. "If the worst should happen and I don't get back right away—" There was a catch in his voice. "Ruth, promise me that if there's a war . . . that after the fighting's over, you'll meet me at the Willard Hotel in Washington, where I first fell in love with you."

Chapter 3

"That's the Lee mansion on Arlington Heights," Cornelius Woodward said, gesturing out a carriage window toward a columned home on the crest of a hill.

Vanessa Woodward nodded and tried to smile at her father, but a lump had come into her throat and it was hard to keep the tears back. They'd never been parted for any length of time since her mother had died six years before.

"And that's Long Bridge over the Potomac River. Surely you remember crossing the bridge?"

"Not very well." The words seemed to stick in Vanessa's throat. She'd been fourteen when her father had brought her to Washington the last time, four years ago. But that had been for a visit, not to live.

"We're almost there, Nessa." Her father put an arm around her shoulders. "You've been a good traveler."

They'd come all the way from New Market in the Shenandoah valley, from the home where Vanessa had been born. When would she see it again? Tears filled her eyes at the thought.

"Now, now, you promised me you wouldn't cry. Aunt Matilda will take good care of you, and . . ."

"Oh, Papa, I wish I could come with you." Vanessa sighed, then obediently wiped her eyes. If Papa could be brave, so could she.

*   *   *

Matilda Hardy, who was Vanessa's mother's sister, had been a widow for many years. Vanessa had happy memories of the comfortable brick house on I Street, and of her cheerful aunt as well. But even as she embraced her in the front hall, she was still sunk in gloom, knowing that her father's departure was now only moments away.

"I declare, Vanessa, you grow prettier every day," Aunt Matilda bubbled, ignoring her niece's long face.

"And you look no older, Mathilda," Cornelius announced gallantly. "You must have found a secret elixir."

Matilda dimpled up at him. "You surely will stay for dinner?"

Cornelius shook his head. "Much as I'd like to, I have appointments to keep before I head back to Virginia." He turned to Vanessa and put his arms around her. "Be my own sweet girl until I come back for you," he said, giving her a gentle hug.

At that, Vanessa began to sob, clinging to him as if she'd never let him go. "Oh, Papa, please be careful."

He kissed her cheek and put her firmly away from him. "Good-bye, Nessa." She caught a brief glimpse of tears in his eyes before he turned and strode out the front door.

As the rattle of his carriage faded down the street, Aunt Matilda put her arm through Vanessa's. "There, there, dear," she said, patting her hand. "Cry all you want to. I know it's hard to see your father leave."

Vanessa wiped her tears away. "I'm all right now," she replied a bit tremulously.

"Men!" Aunt Matilda shook her head. "Always worrying. Dear Mr. Hardy, God rest his soul, was the same as your father. Constantly predicting disaster of one kind or another. If it wasn't a flood, it was a drought."

"Papa thinks there may be a war," Vanessa explained. "He believes the Southern states will leave the Union over the slavery issue."

"*I* don't keep slaves," Matilda said virtuously, "but I do understand the need for them. These abolitionists drive me to distraction."

Vanessa knew her aunt's black servants were free, just as her father's at New Market were. "Papa says he'll support the Union if the worst comes to pass," she continued.

"It's getting to be a dreadful bore at parties," Matilda sighed. "The men all but coming to blows, choosing sides for a war that like as not we'll never live to see." She led Vanessa along the hall. "Wouldn't you like to rest in your room for the afternoon? I know the trip must have tired you."

After a short nap, Vanessa woke refreshed. Donning a gown that her aunt's maid, Doree, had put to rights, she came down the stairs.

"Miz Matilda be gone to a levee," Doree reported, scurrying out into the hall.

Vanessa merely nodded. "I think I'll go out myself."

"But she done took the carriage."

"Just for a walk. I don't need the carriage."

Doree looked dubious. "You best be coming back soon. Ain't safe for a lady to be walking alone after dark."

"I'm not going far." Vanessa smiled at Doree. "I'll be careful."

Vanessa put on her bonnet, but she left off her shawl. It was a lovely June day and the weather was very warm. It felt good to be out in the fresh air, so she walked on and on, up Delaware Avenue to Boundary Street. The houses gradually thinned out until finally there were only reeds and cattails along the side of the road. When the ground grew marshy, Vanessa turned to go back toward the city. She'd walked far enough, and the sun was low in the west. Her shadow stretched away from her, long and thin.

As she stood there in the road, a strange sound, almost a whimper, reached her ears. She listened and the sound came again, a piteous moaning, as though a puppy lay hurt somewhere nearby. Vanessa hurried to the edge of the road, pushing cattails aside with her hands, peering into the damp green gloom. She could dimly make out a small form huddled on the ground, half hidden in the reeds. Surely not a dog. Vanessa knelt, bent forward over her hooped skirt and reached in. What she touched was human flesh.

"Who are you?" she whispered, trying not to sound frightened. "What's the matter?"

The figure stirred and Vanessa saw a pointed brown face and dark eyes. "Please, miss, I be dying," a weak voice pleaded.

"Good heavens!" Vanessa edged closer and grasped an arm. "Come out. I can't help you if you don't."

With Vanessa's aid, the figure inched out of the reeds, groaning all the while. It was a black girl, and her brown dress was stained and damp. Vanessa thought the stains had been made by the swamp water until she glanced at her own hands and gasped. They were covered with blood.

"You're hurt!" Vanessa looked wildly about, but there was no one to help her.

"They gonna get me," the girl cried. "Gonna take me back. I'd rather die."

Vanessa wrung her hands and took a deep breath.

What would her father do? This girl must be a runaway slave, and it was against the law to help her. Vanessa straightened her shoulders and a determined look came over her face. Her father would help the girl anyway, she decided. He'd take her to safety and listen to her story before he did anything else.

Just then, a mule-drawn cart rattled from a path hidden by the reeds and turned onto the road. Vanessa stood and waved her hand. "You," she called, "you with the cart. Please come here."

The driver, a grizzled, roughly dressed man, stared down at Vanessa, ignoring the black girl who lay at her feet. "What you want with me, miss?"

Vanessa thought quickly. "I . . . we were walking, my maid and I, and she fell. I don't know what's wrong with her, but she doesn't seem able to walk. Would you take us back to my house on I Street. I'll pay you when we get there."

He touched his fingers to his cap. "I'll do that, miss." He got down from the cart and inspected the girl. "Looks like she's bleeding some."

Vanessa saw a pool of blood on the ground. "Oh my," she gasped. "It does look that way. Could you lift her up? I don't think she can make it by herself."

"Reckon so." The man spat a stream of tobacco juice onto the road, bent down and lifted the girl into his cart, settling her on a bundle of rags.

Vanessa hopped up and sat next to him on the driver's seat. He clucked to the mule and it moved forward slowly, ever so slowly. Gradually they made their way back to the city, turning off Boundary Street onto Delaware Avenue. As they did so, there was a clatter of hoofs behind them, and Vanessa glanced over her shoulder. Two men with pistols at their hips had ridden from the west along Boundary Street. They checked their horses when they saw the cart and swung onto Delaware Avenue.

"Hold up there, man," one called. "What've you got in the cart?"

As the driver stopped his mules, Vanessa turned to face the horseman. "Sir?" she said in her haughtiest tone.

The man pointed. "You got a nigger in that cart. Who is she?"

Vanessa raised her eyebrows as high as they'd go, praying he wouldn't notice the pulse beating rapidly in her throat. "I beg your pardon," she said frostily. "Are you presuming to question me?"

The man took off his hat. "I don't mean to give offense, miss, but we're looking for a runaway slave girl." He eyed the crumpled form in the cart.

Vanessa allowed her eyes to follow his, then did her best to look completely outraged. "Do you mean to imply that my Ancey, the girl I've owned since she was five years old, is some vagabond slave? Really!"

The man blinked. "Sorry, miss, but . . ."

"Why, I've never been so insulted! Is this what I can expect of Washington? My first day here and my maid takes a fit when we go for a stroll and then strangers come along and try to interfere. I do declare, I feel quite faint." Vanessa swayed in her seat.

"Here now, miss." The driver put a gnarled hand out to steady her. He looked sternly at the man on the horse. "You oughtn't to bother this lady no more. I come along just when the Nigra keeled over. I'm taking her back to the lady's home, like she asked me to."

"No offense meant, I'm sure, miss," the man stammered. In one quick movement, he and his companion wheeled their horses and turned back onto Boundary Street.

The driver said nothing else until they stopped in

front of the house. "Don't you worry about paying me," he told Vanessa, jumping down from his seat. "I don't favor them bounty hunters none." He lifted the black girl from the cart and carried her up the walk.

Vanessa watched as he laid the girl down on the foyer floor. "I *will* pay you," she insisted, "as soon as I can get help for . . ."

He waved his hand. "No need." With a grin and a wink, he slipped out of the house, closing the front door behind him.

He knew all along I was lying, Vanessa thought. But there was no time to brood about that. She looked at the girl and called loudly for Doree.

The servant came running, but she stopped when she saw the figure stretched out on the floor. "My good Lord, Miss Vanessa, what you doing with her?" She put her hands up to her face.

In for a penny, in for a pound, Vanessa told herself. "Oh, Doree," she cried, "the most awful thing happened. This is Ancey. She was my maid back in Virginia, and she came all this way because she couldn't bear to see me leave. Just look at her! Something terrible must have happened to her on the way, but she's so ill she can't tell me what it was. We must help her—what can we do, Doree?"

"Look like she need a bed."

Vanessa nodded. "Put a cot in my room." When she saw the frown on Doree's face, she reached out to touch her hand. "No, I insist. Ancey's been with me almost all her life. I want her in my room."

"You can't take care of her, miss." Doree sounded shocked.

"Please, do as I ask."

Doree shrugged and went off down the hall to the kitchen. "Horace," she called, "where you be, Horace? I need you."

* * *

Once the cot was set up, Doree insisted on bathing the girl herself. After she had put a clean white nightgown on her, she motioned to Vanessa and led her to the door. "She bleeding bad, miss," she said in a low tone.

"Her monthlies?"

Doree shook her head. "Worse." Her eyes slid away. "Like she gonna pass a begun-lately baby."

Vanessa's eyes widened. "Why, she's only a child!"

"She old enough, maybe fourteen."

"What can we do? Should I send for a doctor?"

Doree shook her head. "Doctor don't do no good. We just hope it happens quick, afore she don't have no more blood."

"Isn't there anything we can give her?"

Doree started to turn away, then hesitated. "Might be Tassie, who do the cooking, know of something. I'll see."

Vanessa hovered over the cot after Doree left. The girl's brown skin had turned a sickly gray. "Ancey," Vanessa whispered. Then she frowned. That was *her* name for the girl. She had no idea what the poor thing's real name was.

The girl's eyelids fluttered open. "I hear you give me that name," she said weakly. "Might be I keep it for luck."

Vanessa went down on her knees and took the girl's hand. She'd need all the luck in the world merely to stay alive. "I'll call you Ancey, then," Vanessa said gently. "Don't worry, we'll take care of you."

Aunt Matilda came into Vanessa's bedroom as she was helping Doree feed Ancey an evil-smelling brew that Tassie had concocted.

"Good heavens, Vanessa, what is all this?"

Vanessa straightened and turned slowly to face her aunt, realizing she must lie to her too.

"Don't you remember the slave girl Papa got in payment for a debt from Mr. Rogers?" she asked Matilda. "Ancey was only five at the time and Papa gave her to me. She's been with me ever since, and she must have thought I'd deserted her when I left her in New Market. She came after me, but I don't know yet what befell her on the way."

Aunt Matilda glanced at the cot. "But, dear, should she be in your room?"

"It's my fault she's sick. After all, I should have made certain she wouldn't follow me. So you see, I must have her here. I'm sorry if I'm causing any inconvenience."

Matilda fluttered her hands. "No, no, dear. Don't worry about that. Naturally, Doree will help you." She motioned for Doree to leave the room and followed her out.

When the door had clicked shut, Vanessa sat down on her bed and gave a deep sigh. She hated lies, and since she'd come to Washington it seemed she'd done nothing else but lie. Just then, Ancey moaned, and Vanessa hurried to her side.

Sweat beaded Ancey's face as she writhed on the cot. A great shudder rippled through her body and then she relaxed. "It be over," she whispered without opening her eyes. "Thank you, dear Lord."

Hesitantly, Vanessa pulled back the covers. A nasty red-purple mass of tissue lay on the cot, nothing that looked in the least like a baby. Vanessa bit her lip as she pushed the unspeakable thing into a chamber pot and hastily covered it. She found a cloth and wiped the fresh blood off Ancey's legs, then put a clean sheet beneath her. It was as she was helping Ancey to turn over that she saw her back, crisscrossed with welts that had barely healed. Vanessa had never seen a slave whipped, but she knew what the scars meant.

By the time Vanessa finished changing the linen, Ancey was asleep and the bleeding seemed to have stopped. Vanessa hurriedly washed herself and went down stairs to a dinner she had little appetite for.

"You'll be the belle of Washington," Aunt Matilda said gaily as Vanessa picked at the food on her plate. "So tall and willowy, and that lovely chestnut hair, so like poor, dear Henrietta's." Henrietta, Matilda's sister and Vanessa's mother, had been truly beautiful, petite and charming. But Vanessa had inherited her father's height.

"Your father told me he wanted you to go to all the parties and balls, to enjoy yourself. He doesn't want you to stay at home pining, and I intend to see that his wishes are carried out." Matilda's voice was firm.

Vanessa smiled. "At least I'll attend some of them," she answered. "I do like to dance."

"Perhaps it's just as well that miserable child came north to be with you," her aunt remarked off-hand. "When she recovers, you'll have need of her services. Doree is really quite busy doing for me."

Ancey was still asleep when Vanessa returned to her room. She gazed at herself in the pier glass next to the wardrobe. Willowy was a pleasant way of describing her figure—Aunt Matilda really was a dear—but she'd always thought of herself as thin. She did like her hair, thick and a dark reddish brown, but her face seemed plain to her and her gray eyes not at all unusual.

"You do be the prettiest lady in the world," a voice said. Vanessa turned to see that Ancey had raised herself on one elbow.

"Thank you, Ancey." Vanessa crossed to the cot. "How do you feel?"

"Like I ain't gonna die."

"I think you'll get better from now on. It . . . what happened . . ." Vanessa couldn't bring herself to say the words. "Anyway, that's done with."

"Be Massa Overning's baby that's gone, and I be glad." Ancey scowled. "He don't ask, he just take. Push me down in the hay and hurt me."

Vanessa put her hands to her mouth. She'd heard such things whispered about, but Ancey was hardly even a woman yet. "How old are you?" she asked.

"They tell me I be thirteen come this June."

"This is June."

Ancey nodded. "I run away 'cause I don't be spending no more Junes in that place. I'd rather die and be done. Miz Overning, she find out about him and she get me whipped, like as if I wanted what he done."

Vanessa swallowed, trying to conceal her shock. "Where were you heading?"

"To Canada. The others left me back 'cause I was bleeding so bad I couldn't run. The men, they be after us."

Vanessa looked down at her. "You're very brave, Ancey."

"Brave ain't much use, 'ceping you took me in."

"Yes, and I won't let them take you back. Never!"

"I surely hope not, miss. I surely do."

There was a knock at the door, and Doree poked her head into the room, her eyes wide with fear. "Miz Matilda say you come down. Some men be at the door about her." She gestured toward the cot.

Chapter 4

Vanessa stood still for a moment, trying to gather her wits together. Then she walked slowly to the door. As she started down the stairs, she straightened her back and raised her chin. After all, she thought, she wasn't a guilty child caught out in a lie. She was helping another, perhaps even saving a life. Whether she lied or not, God would be on her side.

Aunt Matilda's face was tight and cold as she stood in the foyer. "Gentlemen," she said, drawing Vanessa forward, "this is my niece, Miss Woodward." She didn't introduce the men.

Both visitors bowed slightly, but while the younger one stared rudely at Vanessa, it was the older, a man with a nearly bald head and a short gray beard, who spoke. His voice was rough and gravelly. "We have a report, Miss Woodward, that an escaped slave was smuggled into this house."

Vanessa's mind sifted rapidly through the possibilities. At first, she'd thought the men might be the bounty hunters who'd stopped the cart, but these men were well dressed. Perhaps they were some kind of magistrates. Had the cart driver reported her? One of Aunt Matilda's neighbors? Or perhaps the men on horseback hadn't been convinced by her story.

"I've no idea what you can be talking about," she

said, doing her best to appear bewildered. "I arrived only today from Virginia."

"I believe you were seen helping the slave into the house," the bald man continued. The younger man nodded, his eyes glinting.

"Helping an escaped slave? I really don't understand. What can you mean?" Vanessa allowed a touch of frost to creep into her voice. She glanced at her aunt, trying to decide how Matilda felt. Was she against her too?

With a wicked leer, the younger man spoke, stepping a pace forward in his eagerness. "What we mean, miss, is that you've been caught red-handed. That's what."

"I beg your pardon?"

"That will do!" Aunt Matilda moved to stand between Vanessa and the men. "I won't allow my niece to be bullied and insulted." She glared at the younger man, then spoke directly to the older. "You asked me to let you question her without interfering. I assumed you were a gentleman, or I wouldn't have agreed to such a thing. Perhaps *you* are a gentleman, but your colleague is no longer welcome in my home."

Vanessa turned to her aunt and Matilda put an arm about her.

"I'll ask you then, Mrs. Hardy," the bald man countered. "Do you have a slave in this house?"

"Yes." Matilda glazed at him with a calmness that astounded Vanessa.

The younger man took another step forward, but the bald one caught his arm. "Then why didn't you . . ." he sputtered.

"Oh!" Vanessa broke in, looking at her aunt. "Do you suppose someone saw Ancey in the cart after she was taken ill and thought she . . . thought I . . ."

"I'll thank you both not to waste any more of our

time," Aunt Matilda snapped, moving away from Vanessa. "You heard my niece. Yes, there is a slave in this house. Her name is Ancey, and she belongs to Miss Woodward. She has since she was five. I don't know where you acquire your information, but obviously someone told you stories just to embarrass me."

"We ain't seen this nigger yet," the young man protested. "It tells on the handbill about her back . . ."

"Shut up," the bald man muttered. Then he turned to Matilda. "You understand, ma'am, we have to follow up any report on contraband." He quickly retreated to the door, pulling the other man with him. "It's our duty," he mumbled.

"If your duty leads you into the homes of respectable citizens to harass and insult them, then I wonder that you're allowed to stay in such a position." Aunt Matilda's icy glare made it clear she now found both men beneath contempt.

Guilt mixed with triumph in Vanessa's emotions as she watched the door slam shut behind the two men. She regretted involving her aunt in her lie, even though it was the only way to save Ancey.

"Well," Aunt Matilda said, brushing her hands together, "good riddance. Such unpleasant men. Your father would be horrified if he knew you'd been subjected to . . ."

"Oh, please. Let's not talk about it," Vanessa murmured. "Although you were wonderful."

Aunt Matilda brightened. "Yes. It's just as well if we do forget it." She took Vanessa's arm and led her into the parlor. "Now, an invitation has come for a ball next week at the Thompsons. And there's a levee at the Mitchells the day after tomorrow. I can't wait to introduce you to Washington."

As the days passed, Ancey grew stronger, and

when her recovery seemed nearly at hand, her cot was taken to a small room off the kitchen. Even though they no longer slept in the same room, the girl followed Vanessa like a shadow and took great pleasure in helping her dress for the parties that seemed to fill Aunt Matilda's schedule.

"My, just look at you," Ancey said as she gazed in the mirror at Vanessa's reflection. "Pretty as a spring day, your eyes all sparkly like. With you to look at, ain't none of the gentlemen gonna recollect they's celebrating the Fourth of July."

Vanessa smiled. She couldn't help being amused by Ancey's extravagant praise, though she had no doubt that Ancey was sincere. Seeing the girl's reflection next to hers in the mirror, Vanessa noticed with a touch of surprise that Ancey's skin had regained its warm brown. She was actually quite pretty, and her heart-shaped face and trim figure made her look older than her years.

Aunt Matilda bemoaned Washington's inertia in the summer months, but it seemed to Vanessa that she'd been to more social gatherings in the past few weeks than she'd have gone to in six months at home in New Market. "Most of the really interesting men won't be back until late fall, when Congress is in session," Aunt Matilda had said apologetically. But as the summer stretched on, there was plenty to keep Vanessa busy.

In August, the corps of Chicago Zouaves came to Washington in their gaudy Algerian uniforms. Led by Colonel Elmer Ellsworth, they performed their drill on the White House lawn for President Buchanan. Vanessa, watching with her aunt, was at first entranced by the colorful spectacle, but soon she was sobered by the realization that her own father might already be leading a troop of his own, not of Zouaves but of soldiers in the United States Army. She'd gotten only two letters from him, and while the last one had told her that he was closing the house, it had also said he wasn't certain when he'd be visiting Washington. His appointment as a major had been confirmed.

In November, the social season began in earnest, but Aunt Matilda still wasn't pleased. "All the Southerners are forming their own clique," she complained. "I'll receive some invitations from them, of course, as well as from the Northerners." Then she sighed. "That means I'll have to watch my own guest lists. It would never do to invite Congressman and Mrs. Adams from Massachusetts if I had Southerners present, not with the way Mrs. Adams speaks her mind. I do wish people could be civil at social gatherings."

Despite the complexity of the season's politics, Aunt Matilda persevered, and it was at her first formal dinner, the "Northern" party, that Vanessa met Senator Zachariah Chandler of Michigan and his friend and associate, Robert Jamison.

"The Union will be better off for a little bloodletting," Zach Chandler exclaimed. He nodded across the table at Vanessa. "We'll show those state's righters!"

"We may have to at that, now that Lincoln's to be President," Senator Wilson agreed.

Their talk of war unsettled Vanessa. When her father had spoken of the possibility, it had seemed far in the future, vague. But these men ran the country, and they talked as though they wanted the war and wanted it immediately.

Robert Jamison, who sat to Vanessa's right, leaned toward her. "I can see you don't relish the conversation," he said gently.

Vanessa turned and gave him a sad smile. "My

father's a soldier," she replied. "I don't like to think of him fighting."

"And since you're from Virginia, I suspect your father is a loyal Southerner."

Vanessa paled. "Oh, no. He serves in the United States Army."

Robert Jamison smiled back at her. "A sensible man. In any case, he's certainly sired a beautiful daughter."

"Thank you." Vanessa had learned to accept compliments gracefully, whether she believed them or not. And it was certainly pleasant to hear such things from Mr. Jamison. He was most attractive, with dark hair and eyes. In his late thirties, she thought.

"Have you been shown around the Capitol as yet?" he asked.

Vanessa shook her head.

Jamison grinned. "Then I'd consider it an honor to take you through the building at any time you find convenient. The new Senate Chamber is quite splendid."

Her excursion to the Capitol with Mr. Jamison went very agreeably, so Vanessa consented to a drive with him a few days later. As he directed the buggy across one of the high iron bridges that spanned the old city canal, Vanessa wrinkled her nose at the unsavory smell.

"Yes, it's a disgrace. Ought to be filled in," Jamison remarked. "We wouldn't tolerate this in Michigan, you can be sure."

As he spoke, the red towers of the Smithsonian Institution rose above the greenery in the surrounding park. He pulled up the horse with a jerk and helped Vanessa down from the buggy, then offered her his arm.

"Will you be staying on for the entire session of Congress?" she asked politely as they strolled off through the park.

"Zach—that is, Senator Chandler—usually insists that I do."

"You are his assistant, then?"

"You might say so." He turned his penetrating gaze on her. "Are you interested in politics, Miss Woodward?"

"Lately, yes. It seems very much more to the point to be discussing elections rather than Tennyson's poetry."

"Or to be talking of Sir Walter Scott?" He laughed and quote a few lines. "Oh, what a tangled web we weave, when first we practice to deceive."

"Is that how you view politics, Mr. Jamison?"

He smiled and stopped walking for a moment. "Can't you find it in your heart to call me Robert?"

She looked into his brown eyes and found the intensity of his gaze distinctly unsettling. "Perhaps when we've known each other longer," she whispered, wondering if such a thing would be wise. Not that there was anything wrong with him. But he made her feel so strange, both attracted and wary.

When she mentioned him to her aunt later that day, she was rewarded with a knowing smile. "Robert Jamison has a reputation about Washington as a heartbreaker," Aunt Matilda warned. "He's respectable enough, but a trifle suspect. I trust you'll take heed."

Aunt Matilda's party for her Southern friends took place in December, after the senators from South Carolina had made it clear they had no intention of coming to the Capitol for the beginning of the new session of Congress. When Vanessa was asked about her father, she said he was serving in the army.

"A Virginian in the United States Army? Surely he plans to resign his commission soon," one of the other women commented.

"I don't think so," Vanessa replied. "He told me he believes in the union of the states."

A silence fell, and suddenly Vanessa realized that no one else in the room was in sympathy with her father's stand. It was not until the next afternoon at a levee that she met a Southerner who seemed at all interested in her news. Rose Greenhow was a full-figured fortyish woman who dimpled when she was introduced to Vanessa.

"I've heard your father has left you all alone in our wicked city," Mrs. Greenhow said mischievously.

"Not exactly. I'm staying with my aunt."

"Ah, yes. She's a widow, as I am," Mrs. Greenhow sighed. "How I miss dear Dr. Greenhow. But this is sad, dull conversation for a young lady, a girl who's yet to marry. Do you miss your father?"

"Very much."

"Ah, but a little bird tells me someone is taking his place."

Vanessa looked at her in surprise. How could anyone take her father's place?

"I was referring to our gallant Michigander. Forgive me, but he does seem almost old enough to be your father."

Vanessa could find nothing to say. She'd certainly not thought of Robert Jamison as fatherly! How dare the woman joke about such a thing!

But Mrs. Greenhow was relentless. "What news do you have from your father?"

Vanessa stiffened. She had absolutely no intention of telling his woman anything that might have been in her father's letters. "I'm sorry," she said brusquely, "I don't discuss private matters with strangers."

After that, Mrs. Greenhow quickly lost interest in the conversation.

On December twentieth, Vanessa went with her aunt to a wedding that was also attended by President Buchanan. When they arrived at the reception, all they heard were shouts and cheers, and throughout the room there was the hum of excited conversation. All around Vanessa, people asked each other what had happened. As she stood poised in the doorway, she saw President Buchanan, head bowed, hurrying out to his carriage.

"South Carolina has seceded from the Union!" a man shouted.

Vanessa looked at her aunt in dismay. Linking arms, they went out into the afternoon drizzle. From all sides, voices carried in the crowd.

"Do you suppose Virginia will be next?"

"When Maryland joins South Carolina, they'll make Washington the Southern capital."

"It's treason, plain and simple."

"This means war!"

It was in the new year of 1861 that Robert Jamison began to call Vanessa by her first name. She wasn't at all displeased. In fact, she noticed other women glancing at her with ill-concealed envy when Robert danced with her, and she couldn't help feeling that snaring him was quite a coup. At least it gave her something cheerful to think about as the bad news poured into Washington. One by one, the other Southern states seceded. Mississippi, Florida, Alabama, Georgia, and Louisiana were all in rebellion by the end of January.

"Oh, Robert, can nothing stop this?" Vanessa asked as they sat in his buggy on the way home from a dinner party.

"Not now." He put his arm around her shoulders, and somehow it comforted her. Actually, there was more than comfort in the gesture. There were also excitement and pleasure.

"What does Senator Chandler think?" she asked, trying to keep herself diverted from these unfamiliar feelings.

"He says never mind temporizing. Those rebel states are asking for war and that's what they'll get. The sooner the better."

"Surely President Buchanan won't agree?"

Robert shook his head. "Abe Lincoln will be President very soon. He's a different breed than Jim Buchanan." His arm tightened around her shoulders, drawing her closer. "You have nothing to worry about if war comes to Washington. I'll take care of you."

He smelled pleasantly of Havana cigars and bay rum, and Vanessa allowed herself to relax against him. Heartened, he leaned forward, tipped up her chin with his hand and kissed her. At the touch of his lips, a riot of emotions coursed through Vanessa's body. Suddenly, she felt as if Robert were drawing all of her being up to her lips, as if he were consuming her. It was a thrilling feeling, but it was also frightening. In confusion, she tried to ease away.

"You're as fresh and lovely as a magnolia bloom," he murmured, still holding her. His lips, warm and heavy, brushed against her throat, and something in her responded to his touch, desiring more. But at the same time, part of her was wary.

"I want you for my very own," he whispered.

Vanessa's heart beat faster. Marriage? No, he hadn't said that. But wasn't that what he meant?

"Robert," she begged, "please, you mustn't."

When they reached her aunt's house, he lifted her down from the buggy, holding her against him before he let her feet touch the ground. For a moment, he made her feel powerless, and she resented that, yet even as she did she felt an urge to surrender to him.

"Until Friday," he said softly, touching the back of her gloved hand to his lips. Staring into her eyes, he turned her hand and bent it gently back until her wrist was bared between the glove and the sleeve of her jacket. With a smile, he kissed the exposed flesh and then released her.

Blushing, Vanessa fled up the steps and into the house. When she reached her own room, Ancey was waiting there, ready to help her undress. But the girl was uncharacteristically quiet as she put Vanessa's clothes away.

"Do you feel all right, Ancey?" Vanessa asked vaguely. She was still thinking of Robert's kisses.

"I'se fine, miss." Her tone was sullen.

"You don't sound fine. Is something wrong? Are the other servants treating you badly?"

"No, they be real good to me. They's nice folks."

Vanessa sighed. "Then tell me why you look so cross."

Ancey hesitated, crushing Vanessa's gloves between her hands. "I don't like that man who take you out all the time. You gonna be mad 'cause I says it, but he just like that Massa Overning, the way he look at you." She nodded solemnly. "Just like him. Can't be trusted."

"Oh, Ancey, don't be silly," Vanessa laughed. "Go on to bed now. I don't need you any more tonight."

Ancey paused at the door and looked back. "I

knows what I knows," she muttered. Then the door
clicked shut behind her.

That night, Vanessa tossed and turned. Her wrist,
the spot where Robert had kissed it, felt hot, as if the
flesh were burning, and her body throbbed with a need
she didn't know how to fulfill. Poor Ancey, she
thought, with her fear of men. She wouldn't be like
Ancey, she wouldn't fear Robert.

When Vanessa awoke in the morning she was
glad to get out of bed. The night had been filled with
disturbing dreams, dreams she only vaguely remembered. She dressed quickly, and Ancey barely had time
to pull her hair into a bun before she went downstairs.

Aunt Matilda looked up as Vanessa walked into
the morning room. "I've been waiting for you," she
said, a stricken expression on her face. "These are unpleasant words to hear, but I felt you must be told as
soon as possible."

"Papa!" Vanessa cried, the blood draining from
her face.

Aunt Matilda looked puzzled. "No, no. Cornelius
is fine, as far as I know. I haven't heard from him."
Then she hesitated, giving Vanessa a long, sad stare.
"But I've news of Mr. Jamison from a friend who lives
in Michigan. It seems he's a married man."

Chapter 5

The woman in white tossed her head, sending her long blond hair tumbling down her back. "If I must die," she cried, "then let it be said I died unafraid!" She threw her arms toward the heavens, then slowly bowed her head. There was a moment of silence as the lights dimmed. With a muffled thud, the curtain came rippling down to the stage and a burst of applause swept across the theater. As it continued, the curtain rose, revealing all the members of the cast, five men and two women. Then the curtain was slowly lowered again and the clapping died away. The Southern Players had finished their last engagement in Grover's Theater. As a matter of fact, it was the troupe's final performance in any theater.

In the dressing room, Helena Swane changed from her white robe to a blue and green checked wool dress and a matching greatcoat with a broad velvet collar. She deftly swirled her blond hair into a chignon and pinned her dark green hat above it.

The other woman, tall and dark, sat watching her. "What do you expect to do in Washington, Helena?" she asked at last.

Helena shrugged. "Something will turn up."

"Someone, more likely. Some man."

Helena's green eyes flashed. "You never did like me, Nell, and I know why. You're jealous. You never attracted a man in your life except poor old Charlie, and all these years you've had to make do with him. But let me tell you something—even Charlie'd rather have me." As Nell glared at her, speechless, Helena picked up her carpetbag and swished out of the dressing room, the hoop under her gown neatly compressing to clear the narrow doorway.

The Southern Players were disbanding so the men could enlist in the armies of the Confederacy. Since Nell was married to one of the actors, Charlie Mann, she'd be going with him. That left only Helena, with no plan in mind. At first, she'd considered returning to Georgia, but the more she thought about the idea, the less she liked it. Her father was still overseer at Blankenship's plantation, still lived in the small frame house on the grounds. And that sort of life wasn't for her. Of course, the Blankenship sons would be eager to bring her to their beds, but none of them would marry her, that was for damn sure. They were country louts, despite their father's wealth, and they'd still try to lord it over her. In Georgia, she'd always be Helen, the overseer's daughter, not Helena, the actress.

As she walked toward her hotel, having told herself it was foolish to spend her remaining money on a hired hack, a contingent of cavalry clattered past, and when she entered Willard's she found the lobby crowded with army officers. Helena paused to survey the noisy scene. She set her bag on the floor, took a deep breath and said in a clear voice, trained to carry to the back rows of a theater, "Gentlemen, I cannot get through."

Those who were nearest turned her way and she smiled sweetly, waiting. Then a captain stepped up and shouted, "Clear a path for the lady." Bowing, he offered her his arm and escorted her through the crowd.

Helena glanced from side to side as she walked

among the officers. "I'll certainly sleep well tonight," she called out, "knowing you're all here to guard me." She smiled as she looked at their eager faces. Something *had* turned up. The army. And tomorrow she'd begin her campaign.

Colonel Patrick Armitage, Ohio-born and -bred, eyed the attractive blonde woman walking toward him on the brick sidewalk. By God, she was a pretty thing. Perhaps not quite a lady, but it would take a keen eye to tell. He was tempted to tip his hat, but before he'd even raised his hand a ragged figure darted from an alley and rushed past the woman, knocking her down. An instant later he was gone.

Pat Armitage hurried forward. "Are you all right, miss?" he asked, going down on one knee beside her.

"I . . . I don't know." Her look of fear and bewilderment summoned up all his gallant instincts. He gently put his hand behind her shoulders

"Let me help you up," he urged.

Passersby stopped, staring, but the colonel merely frowned at them. "Go along," he ordered, "don't distress the lady any further." Then he turned back and pulled her to her feet. She swayed, leaning against his arm for support. "Colonel Armitage, at your service," he announced, still keeping a firm hold on her.

"Oh, thank you. I . . . I don't know what . . ." Her words trailed off as she looked wildly about. "My bag," she wailed. "My bag! It's gone!"

Alarmed by her ashen face, the colonel hailed a passing hack and all but lifted her inside. He climbed in after her and ordered the driver to circle the area to the north, though he knew such a hunt was futile. The thief would be long gone by now.

"My money." The woman had begun to cry. "He's taken all my money. What will I do?"

Her perfume filled the cab with the scent of roses. She was lovely, even in distress. Particularly in distress. Her soft full breasts brushed his arm as she leaned against him, sobbing.

"Never mind, my dear," Colonel Armitage crooned, drawing her closer. "I'll take care of you."

Helena nestled against him and wiped away her tears, careful not to let her elation show. She'd schemed for two days to set up this meeting with Colonel Armitage. Thank heaven she'd discovered that her actor friend Louis hadn't left town yet. The ruse had been perfect.

She gave the colonel a brave little smile. "I'm Helena Swane," she whispered. "I owe my life to you."

Helena's new brocade gown fit to perfection. The hoop was as wide as any she'd seen in Washington, and the gold in the fabric brought out a hint of amber in her green eyes. Patrick was so generous. He'd bought all the clothes she could possibly want and had installed her in his own suite of rooms at the Willard Hotel. He'd even included her in his invitations to parties and balls, despite the scandal such boldness might cause him.

When she accompanied him to such gatherings, Helena was not surprised to discover that her popularity was entirely limited to the men. So she was instantly on her guard when a smiling dark-haired woman approached to compliment her on her gown.

"I've heard so much about you, my dear," the woman said, holding out her hand. "I'm Rose Greenhow and I've always wanted to meet an actress. You're certainly a very lovely one."

Helena touched her hand briefly. "Thank you." She warily looked the woman up and down.

"I understand you're from Georgia," Mrs. Greenhow continued, unperturbed.

"Yes."

"Don't you long to go back home now that this dreadful crisis is upon us?"

"No, not particularly. I like Washington."

"But we may be at war any day." Mrs. Greenhow eyed her very carefully.

She wants something from me, Helena told herself. I wonder what.

"Naturally, your sympathies lie with Georgia," Rose Greenhow ventured.

Helena blinked. She hadn't thought much about the impending war, despite the frantic atmosphere that had descended upon the capital. If war came, it came. And her sympathies? She'd be smart to cast them with her colonel, with the North, yet somehow she didn't really feel at home among Northerners. She never wanted to live in her father's house again, but it was true that she missed the Georgia countryside. A wave of nostalgia swept over her, a longing for the familiar surroundings of her childhood. "I'll always be a Southerner," she said quietly.

"Ah, I thought so. I knew when I set eyes on you that we could be friends." Rose Greenhow smiled and took Helena's arm, leading her to a secluded corner of the room. "I believe you're a polished and accomplished actress," Mrs. Greenhow declared when she was sure they could no longer be overheard.

Here it comes, Helena thought, tensing. "I've been told so," she answered cautiously.

"It's certain you're very pretty. An attractive woman can accomplish a great deal." Rose Greenhow modestly cast her eyes down and smoothed her dark hair.

Helena waited.

"An attractive woman who's also a professional actress would be able to do even more, or so I believe," the woman went on.

"Do more of what?"

Rose Greenhow gave her a knowing smile. "Why . . . intrigue," she replied. Then suddenly she became very serious. "What would you do if you knew a man who held the future of the South in his hands? Imagine that this man could destroy Georgia. Now think of yourself. You know this man, he's interested in you. Without too much difficulty, you might be able to find out how he intends to go about the destruction of your home. Would you try?"

Helen stared at the woman beside her. "Would I try to discover his plans? Yes, I think I would."

"And once you'd found out, then what?"

"Why, I'd see that someone in Georgia heard about the plans."

Rose nodded. "Exactly. I felt you'd help us."

Helena frowned. "Us?"

"The Confederate States."

"I'm not sure I can."

Rose waved her hand. "Don't worry. All that's needed is information. The war will begin sooner than you think, and we must know all we can about troop strengths and invasion plans. You should have no trouble at all finding out these things."

Helena looked at Rose Greenhow for a moment. After all, she thought with a smile, she *had* been becoming just the tiniest bit bored with her generous colonel. Then her smile faded. "You're asking me to be a spy, a Confederate spy. Am I right?"

Rose Greenhow nodded ever so slightly and slid her arm through Helena's. In a moment, the two women had moved back into the crowd.

Chapter 6

"This is Lieutenant Jordan, dear." Rose Greenhow turned to Helena. "He's wanted very much to meet you."

A bright-eyed young man raised her hand to his lips.

"Helena is our new friend," Rose continued, "as you know."

The three were alone in Rose's rear parlor, where a soft April breeze teased the curtains at the windows. Helena stared with interest at the soldier, who gazed back just as frankly. At last he turned his attention to Rose.

"Fort Sumter will be in our hands within hours," he reported. "The shore batteries began firing from around Charleston harbor early this morning. But the real fighting will come soon in Virginia, so I'll need everything you can bring me." He glanced at Helena. "The plans for troop movements that you gave Rose were very useful. Now try to find out about the supplies, if you can."

Helena nodded, a coil of excitement tightening inside her.

The lieutenant took Rose's hand and kissed it. "I won't be here much longer. I'm resigning my commission when Virginia secedes, which will be any day now.

I'll look forward to your dispatches until then." With a final bow, he turned and strode from the room.

Helena stayed only a few minutes longer than the young officer. When she left Rose's house, she rode through streets that were filled with soldiers. Finally, as she reached Pennsylvania Avenue, she found that she couldn't go any farther. Up ahead, a troop of cavalry blocked the road, a carriage in its midst. Helena craned her neck to see who they were escorting and caught a glimpse of a tophatted man in black with strong features and a short black beard. It could only have been President Lincoln.

She'd had just a glimpse, but certainly the President didn't look as ugly as the cartoonists in the illustrated weeklies had pictured him. In fact, he looked rather interesting. She wondered if she'd meet him someday. Think what a triumph it would be if she managed to charm information from Abraham Lincoln! Helena smiled at her imaginings. She found that spying was very thrilling indeed.

On May twenty-fourth, Colonel Ellsworth of the Zouaves was shot to death by an innkeeper in Alexandria, Virginia, when he lowered a rebel flag. Washington was shocked, and Helena even heard that President Lincoln had cried when the news was reported. But Rose Greenhow's reaction was considerably more brusque.

"Now maybe these Yankees will understand we're not to be trifled with," she snorted.

In the weeks that followed, the tension in the capital of the embattled Union continued to rise. Then, in early July, the lumbering armies began to move. One morning, Helena was with Rose when she summoned a quiet dark-haired girl named Betty Duvall into her back parlor. As Betty fastened a small packet of papers inside her chignon, Rose turned to Helena with a triumphant smile. "Your news confirmed what I heard from my own sources," she announced. "General McDowell is ready to start for Richmond, and Betty's taking the word to General Beauregard."

Helena was silent until Betty had left the room. "I would have liked to carry the message myself," she remarked with more than a touch of regret.

Rose shook her head. "You're too noticeable. People forget they've seen Betty, but no man would forget you."

"What about a disguise?" Helen argued. "I've played old women on the stage, you know, and I looked every inch the part."

Rose's impatience with Helen's complaint was quite plain. "You're one of my best sources of information," she replied briskly. "I don't want to risk you as a courier. And if you were caught . . ." She didn't need to say any more.

Helena sighed. Deep inside, she knew that Rose was right. She could do more good for the South by providing information than by carrying it. But that didn't prevent her from thinking of Betty slipping out of the city dressed in a rough, drab frock, then mounting a horse and speeding off to Fairfax Court House, where General Beauregard had an advance post. Helena's eyes sparkled as she pictured the scene. She could see herself standing before the general, pulling out her tucking comb to let her hair fall. He'd be fascinated by the sight of her golden hair spilling down over her jacket, but when she handed him the message he'd give all his attention to that for the next few minutes. Then, remembering her, he'd. . . .

Helena shook her head and brought her thoughts back to the present. But as she prepared to leave, Rose gave her another jolt. "I'd think about taking a trip away from Washington after the fighting starts," she said firmly. "I'll keep you posted."

"A trip?" Helena stammered. "Go south, you mean?"

"No. North. New York is my choice."

"But I don't understand."

Rose laughed. "Why, my dear, haven't you thought? Beauregard may very well push McDowell back across the Potomac, and then Washington will become a battleground."

Helena stared at her in surprise. Did Rose know more than she'd told her? After all, she was a woman who liked secrets. "I'll keep your advice in mind," Helena murmured. But on the way back to the hotel, she decided she'd stay right where she was. Somehow, the idea of watching a battle was very exciting.

Vanessa Woodward tilted her white hat to a more becoming angle and pinned it to her hair. But as she compressed her hoop to pass through her bedroom doorway, she was again struck by doubts. What would her father think if he knew she was jaunting off to watch a battle? A battle he might be fighting in, for all she knew. Still, would Robert have invited her on this outing if he thought there was any danger? A picnic on the hills overlooking Centreville, scarcely twenty miles from the city, shouldn't be hazardous.

Aunt Matilda was waiting in the morning room despite the early hour. It was clear that she too was pondering the wisdom of Robert's plans. "So you still intend to go?" she asked hesitantly.

Vanessa nodded.

"Well, I can't forbid you," Aunt Matilda sighed. "The good Lord knows, enough of my friends are planning to do the same. And on a Sunday!"

Vanessa took her parasol from its silk case.

Though it was not yet seven o'clock, the muggy July heat lay heavy over the city. She wore her lightest muslin dress, white with yellow embroidery, and planned to take no shawl.

As Vanessa moved toward the door, Aunt Matilda rose and caught her hand. "Do be careful. I couldn't bear to have anything happen to you. I'm beginning to feel as if you're my very own daughter."

Vanessa smiled and kissed the older woman's cheek. "Robert wouldn't expose me to danger. I'm certain he'll see me safely home before evening."

Aunt Matilda's mouth tightened. "You know how I feel about Robert Jamison."

"But he explained it all to you," Vanessa cried. "He told us both about his circumstances."

Aunt Matilda shook her head. "I feel sorry for him, I can't deny that. It must be difficult to be tied to a woman the doctors say is hopelessly demented, who has to be cared for by nurses as though she were an infant. But the fact remains, Vanessa, he *is* a married man. It does your reputation no good to . . ."

"He's an honorable man," Vanessa snapped. "Should he be denied the companionship of all women because of his tragic circumstances?"

"I hardly think your father would agree with you."

Vanessa looked down at her gloved hands. She knew that what her aunt said was true. People whispered about her, she was sure, and her father would be most upset if he knew. On the other hand, her sympathy for Robert kept her from refusing to see him. Or was it just sympathy? Be honest, she admonished herself. You need to see Robert. There's something about him that's exciting, something that keeps drawing you back to him. With a shiver of anticipation, she hurried from the room.

* * *

Robert drove the hired gig himself, explaining that the driver didn't care to go to war. "I tried to tell him we'd only watch from a distance," he laughed, "but he wouldn't reconsider."

It soon became apparent that very few other drivers had felt the same way, and as they turned toward Long Bridge, the large number of carriages, buggies and wagons heading in the same direction made the going slow.

"We're an army ourselves," Vanessa remarked, "a picnic army."

The Potomac looked silver in the morning light as they crossed to Virginia, and all seemed peaceful and quiet. But as they drove through the wooded hills, they passed farms where no workers toiled, houses that had been deserted. If the fearful owners had abandoned their homes, Vanessa wondered, was she being wise to continue?

"Robert," she ventured, "there's no one about except a few Negroes. Maybe we should turn back."

"What, and miss the sport?" He patted her hand. "Don't be afraid." With a flourish, he slapped the reins and set the horse off at an even faster pace.

After they passed through the village of Fairfax Court House, the road grew rougher, dug up by the passing of heavy wagons, and dust hung in a cloud over the turnpike. Vanessa tried to imagine the caissons lumbering south, the wagons loaded with supplies, the soldiers marching row on row. Then she heard a muffled pounding, a sound like distant thunder. With a start, she realized that it must be cannon fire.

"We're almost to Centreville," Robert announced. "We'll cut off the pike here and picnic on one of the hills above Cub Run. Is that all right? We could go closer, but so many already have that we'd be in a crowd of picnickers."

Vanessa hesitated, thinking they might be better off in a crowd. And yet she didn't want to go any farther. "All right," she said quietly, but Robert was too busy driving to notice the tremble in her voice.

When they'd climbed to the top of the rise, Vanessa saw what Robert had meant. The hills to the south were covered with people and carriages. Beyond them, even farther south, smoke and dust rose over the woods and fields. The thump of the cannon sounded more clearly now.

Robert stared at the scene through a telescope, then offered the glass to Vanessa. She took it, and refocusing, saw trees, a meadow, birds . . . crows. Carrion crows, tearing at a dead animal. Hastily, she shifted the glass until she could see puffs of white smoke, wagons and blue-coated soldiers. What if one of them is my father? she thought suddenly. I wouldn't recognize him this far away. What if I saw him fall? She hastily shoved the telescope back at Robert.

"The stream below us is Cub Run," he said, consulting his map, "so the one beyond it must be Bull Run. Looks like that's where the battle is, just past Bull Run." He looked through the glass again. "I can't make much sense of it, though. There's too much smoke to tell who's winning, but it's bound to be the Union forces. We have more men, more artillery, more everything."

"Please," Vanessa whispered, "I'd rather not stay here."

Robert lowered the telescope and peered at the girl's stricken face. He gently put his arm around her shoulders. "What's the matter, Vanessa?"

"I keep thinking of my father." She looked down at her lap, struggling to keep the tears from her eyes.

Instantly, Robert pulled her to her feet. "I'm a fool for not remembering," he confessed. "Of course you don't enjoy the battle. I'm sorry."

Vanessa took a few steps back down the hill. "Please," she pleaded. "I want to go back to Washington."

As Robert and Vanessa made their way back to the capital, they passed other men and women, in carriages and on horseback, still headed toward the fighting.

"I didn't mean to spoil your outing," Vanessa said shyly as the gig clattered over Long Bridge.

Robert smiled and patted her hand. "We can still have our picnic."

"Where? All the parks and malls are filled with militia encampments."

"Ah, I have my secrets," he laughed. And with that he headed the horse down I Street and pulled up before Zach Chandler's house.

When she still seemed puzzled, he winked and gave her a conspiratorial grin. "Zach is at the battle, but we can use his garden for our picnic bower."

Vanessa stared back in astonishment. Robert often stayed in the mansion when he wasn't living at the Willard, and he was certainly one of the senator's most trusted confidantes, yet somehow it seemed wrong to picnic on Chandler's grounds when he wasn't at home.

"Please, Vanessa," Robert pleaded. "I've looked forward to being with you today, more than you can possibly know. I'll try to make up for my insensitivity if only you'll let me."

It was an appeal that she couldn't resist.

At the rear of the house, a hedge provided privacy and a magnolia cast a welcome shadow over a stone bench. Glad to be out of the sun, Vanessa sat down and watched as Robert opened the hamper and took out a bottle of wine. In a moment, two goblets were filled and raised, ready for a toast.

"To victory at Bull Run," Robert proposed, touching his glass to hers.

Vanessa smiled up at him and took a sip. The cool liquid tasted wonderful, especially after the dust and heat of the road, and she realized that she was very thirsty. She took another swallow and then another, almost emptying her glass. "Do have something to eat," she said hurriedly as Robert sat down beside her. "I'm not hungry, but you shouldn't let that stop you."

"Who needs food?" he teased. "When I'm with you, nothing else is important." He reached for the wine bottle and refilled their glasses.

Vanessa sipped the second glass more slowly, trying not to be aware of how close he was sitting. She must remember that Robert wasn't for her. They could be good friends, but . . .

As if in answer to her thought, Robert took the glass from her hand, set it down on the grass and pulled her into his arms. When his lips sought hers, they were demanding, forcing a response she couldn't help as her body molded itself to his. His hand touched her breast, and suddenly she tingled with electricity. She knew it was wrong and tried to draw back, but he held her firmly until she relaxed against him.

"We'll go inside," he murmured.

"Oh, no." Vanessa felt weak now, short of breath. And Robert seemed so strong.

"Yes, my pretty girl, my own Vanessa," he whispered. "I want you and I'll have you. You were made for love, for me to make love to." Before she could protest, he stood up and lifted her into his arms.

"No," she cried, somehow shocked back to her senses. "Put me down! Robert!"

He laughed and kissed her instead, moving all the while toward a door that was almost hidden by honeysuckle vines. His mouth, his hands, the heavy sweetness of the honeysuckle all combined with the wine to make her head spin. She wanted him to take her inside, to his bed, to make love to her, but at the same time she knew she mustn't allow it. She began to struggle more fiercely. He wasn't being fair, he was pushing her too fast down a road she knew she shouldn't travel. Not now, not with him.

The hot sun beat down on her face, and yet she heard the rumble of distant thunder. No, not thunder. The guns of war. With a convulsive twist, she freed herself. In an instant, she was racing around the house and past the gig, fleeing not so much from Robert as from the sound of the guns.

Chapter 7

Just after dawn on Sunday, July twenty-first, two wagons shrouded with black cloth jounced in the dusty ruts of the road that stretched south from Centreville. The bitter smell of chemicals rose up from them, an acrid scent that made the soldiers who passed them grimace.

"What the hell is it?" a red-haired private called out to the nearest wagon. "Hey, mister, what kind of rig you driving there?"

Mathew Brady, straw hat squarely on his head, turned to smile at the young man. "I'm thinking of naming it the What-is-it-wagon. You're not the first who's asked. I'm Brady, the photographer."

"You mean you're going to take pictures of us fighting?"

"I plan to try."

"Well, I'll be jiggered." The private shook his head, grinning. "If you get one of me, I'd sure like to have it for my ma back in New Jersey."

Ruth, perched on the wagon box with her employer, glanced around again at the soldier, whose sparse beard was as red as his hair. I'll bet he's Irish, she thought, with that freckled face and those sky-blue eyes. So like her own brother George, who had also joined up. In fact, George might even be marching somewhere in this mass of men. Thank God Michael was too young. She closed her eyes and crossed herself, sending up a quick prayer. "Keep him safe, dear Jesus."

Just ahead, Ned Hause, the darkroom assistant, drove the other wagon, just like the other one she and Brady rode in. Both were stocked with chemicals in containers nailed to shelves, along with all the supplies for processing the plates. They were traveling dark rooms, enlarged and improved over the simple wagon Brady had taken to West Point. The cameras were tied securely on shelves near the wagon box, but as the rig bounced and swayed along the road, Ruth feared for the safety of the fragile glass plates.

It wasn't long, though, before her thoughts returned to the one thing that she couldn't seem to banish from her mind. Jeremy, she cried to herself, oh, Jeremy. Where are you? She hadn't seen him since that night at West Point, and now that she'd been transferred to Brady's Washington gallery, perhaps a letter wouldn't reach her. Was Jeremy with General Beauregard, whose army would surely be routed by Union troops today? Or was he to the west, where she'd heard General McClellan had annihilated two Rebel armies? How could she ever find out where he was? If he were dead or alive? She blinked back a sudden rush of tears.

A booming rumble made her start. The cannon! Unconsciously, she edged closer to Mr. Brady.

Brady gave her a reassuring smile. "Just some artillery fire to scare the Rebs," he explained, reining in his horse as the wagon ahead came to a halt.

A confused shouting rose from the soldiers in back of them, and Ruth craned her neck to see what was happening up ahead. Off to the side of the road, the red-haired soldier and some of his companions were picking the ripe blackberries that grew in profusion at the edge of the fields, and now officers on horseback were trying to round them up, at the same time shouting orders to the men who were still in the ranks. For a while, the soldiers milled about in confusion, raising clouds of dust, but finally they fell into two lines and marched off across a field to the right of the road, sunlight glinting off the brass of their guns.

Yesterday, Mr. Brady had taken shots of abandoned Confederate fortifications at Fairfax Court House and of Union troops at their ease, cooking, eating, resting. But she knew that his great desire was to record the actual fighting. "There never was such a chance," he proclaimed. "Think of it! A war shown in pictures from beginning to end. The truth, for all to see. Six months from now, when the war is over, I'll have a complete record, a priceless view of history as it happened."

Ruth, catching his enthusiasm, had looked forward to the beginning of the fighting, and now that they were actually in the midst of a marching army, her excitement mounted. As they moved forward, they passed fields of ripening corn, then crossed a narrow bridge over a muddy creek. To the left were hills, but to the right and ahead the country rolled away, green and brown. A strange popping sound rose over the creaking of harnesses and the rattle of wheels.

"Rifles," Brady said eagerly. "It's beginning." His eyes gleamed with anticipation. "I've got to get closer."

With a vigorous slap of the reins, he urged the horse to a faster pace, drawing near a cabin where a woman stood in the doorway. The woman caught Ruth's eye and called out to her. "You better stay here with me, Miss Yank. There's enough Rebs across Bull Run to whip the lot of you. My man can kill ten to any Yank's one. You'd best get off that wagon unless you want to meet your Maker."

Ruth swallowed and looked away, but the sound of the woman's laughter followed them along the road.

Now she could also hear shells being fired from nearby cannon, exploding in loud bursts somewhere ahead. Surely the Rebels must have artillery too, and would soon start shooting back.

"Mr. Brady, we must be getting quite near the fighting," she cautioned, raising her voice to make sure he heard.

"Not near enough; there's nothing here worth a picture."

"But the plates and the equipment. If a shell burst close to us . . ."

He looked at her assessingly. "I won't take you any farther," he said after a moment's consideration. Then he scanned the area and motioned toward a barn set back among the trees. "You and the wagon can stay over there, and I'll go on with Ned."

It wasn't until he had tethered the horse and lifted out the camera that Ruth realized how determined he was to move to the very thick of the fighting. "But you might be shot!" she burst out.

Brady merely shook his head and lifted up the camera.

"No," he said calmly. "I won't be. And when I have some processed plates, I'll bring them back for you to take into town." He smiled at her, tipped his straw hat and walked off toward the rising smoke.

Ruth climbed down from the wagon, but the trees were between her and the battleground, blocking her view. She cautiously eyed the barn. Perhaps if she climbed into the loft and looked out the hay-loading window she could see something of what was going on.

As she entered the barn, kittens, nursing from their mother, scattered in every direction, and the mother cat crouched and hissed as Ruth headed for the ladder. Up above, she picked her way through the

straw-strewn floor of the loft until she came to the
open window. Shielding her eyes until they adjusted to
the sun, she peered out over the treetops. Below her,
she could see the supply wagons, grouped near a stone
bridge. There were soldiers in blue on the near side, in
gray on the far, facing each other across the stream.
Muskets cracked, white puffs of smoke rose and men
fell on both sides. The acrid reek of powder drifted
back on the breeze.

Suddenly, a shell exploded behind the Rebel soldiers in a great blast of smoke and flame. Ruth gripped
the rough wooden window sill with both hands and fell
to her knees. Then another shell burst between the
barn and the bridge. The Confederates had begun firing back.

As she watched in horror, more men fell. Others
ran forward to take their places, straddling fallen
bodies, and on the other side of the stream, riders
galloped back and forth, plunging madly through the
smoke. She saw the gaudy red pants of Zouaves, then
realized they were on the wrong side of the stream.
Confederate Zouaves? Or were Union troops crossing
the bridge?

Ruth looked for Brady's rig, but all she could see
were ammunition wagons, trundling off the road and
across the field, heading upstream. It seemed as if the
cannon rumbled continuously now, and she could also
hear the rapid pop of musket fire, like strings of fire-
crackers. Atop a hill, a line of tiny figures advanced,
then wavered. A shell blossomed into flame in their
midst, and when the smoke cleared, the men were gone.
Confederates? Union? She didn't know.

As she looked down, a flurry of movement on her
side of the bridge caught her eye. She saw soldiers,
some carrying wounded comrades on their crossed
muskets and others supporting men who limped and

swayed. As one wounded soldier sagged, his red-haired companion eased him to the ground, knelt beside him for a moment, then rose and looked around for help. Ruth wondered if he was the red-haired soldier she'd seen earlier.

She watched riveted as he tried to lift the man from the ground and failed. Finally, he dragged him to a grassy bank off the road, hovered over him for a moment, then walked back. In a daze, he looked toward the fighting, then turned to stare at the soldiers hobbling to the rear, poised uncertainly in the center of the road. At last he headed back to the battle.

He'd gone no more than a few paces when he paused again and staggered forward. Ruth gasped as he caught himself, then slowly crumpled to the ground and lay still. She didn't fully understand what had happened until she saw a pool of blood spread in the dirt beside him. She clenched her hands. "No," she begged, "no, no."

Somewhere out there, Mr. Brady was trying to take pictures of killing. Of men dying. Who'd want to see what she'd just seen? Men wounded, a man shot down, his blood soaking into the dust of the road? Hurriedly, Ruth climbed down from the loft and ran back to the wagon.

She didn't know how long she sat before she became aware of shouts nearby, of horses neighing over the noise of the guns. She peered through the trees and saw wagons and soldiers heading back toward Centreville. She frowned, trying to understand what it meant. Was the battle over? No, the cannon roared as loudly as ever, and she could still hear the lighter crackle of rifles.

Then she made out the U. S. Army stencil on the wagons' canvas sides. These were Union troops heading north. Retreating? Ruth's eyes opened wide. How could they lose the battle when everyone had said they'd win? But if they were retreating, wouldn't the Rebels be in pursuit? Ruth turned and stared apprehensively back toward the stream, but the trees blocked her view of the stone bridge. Mathew Brady! Where was he?

Ruth jumped down from the wagon, only to stand indecisively by the horse, which was now stamping uneasily. What should she do? Should she leave without Mr. Brady? But what if he and Ned Hause couldn't get the other wagon back here? She took a deep breath and reached up to untie the horse. At least she'd turn the wagon and get closer to the road.

As Ruth watched, the trickle of soldiers grew to a torrent. Plainly nervous, her horse flicked his ears forward and whickered, tossing his head, but she couldn't summon up the will to try to soothe him. She was simply afraid to leave the wagon box. She slowly edged the rig toward the road.

"You'd best get out of there, miss," a drover shouted. "The Rebs have routed us."

Ruth knew then that she could wait no longer. She frantically slapped the horse with the reins, and Brady's wagon jounced forward. But by now the road was crowded with men and wagons, and Ruth had difficulty wedging her way in. As she was jostling for position, a shell whined shrilly overhead and exploded close to the road, sending a shower of dirt over the canvas. She fought desperately to control the horse.

Another shell struck behind them and smoke drifted over the road, partially hiding the surging mob. Ruth knew there was a bridge ahead, the narrow one over Cub Run, the one she and Brady had crossed that morning. Would she ever get over it? There seemed no way to move forward, and now she saw that the road was clogged not only with men and army wagons, but with carriages filled with fashionably dressed men and women.

A shell screamed so close overhead that she ducked. There was an explosion up ahead, a burst of flame, shouts. The line halted in a melee of wounded horses and splintering wood. Then as the roar of the guns increased, Ruth's horse plunged and reared, his eyes ringed with white. Ruth felt the wagon tip and yanked up her skirts, jumping free as it went over, horse and all. She tumbled onto the verge of the road and stumbled to her feet.

As she watched, a soldier ran up and slashed at the harness, but the horse, his foreleg shattered, was beyond saving. Quickly, the soldier put a pistol to the horse's head and pulled the trigger. The shot was scarcely audible in the uproar.

Terrified and sickened, Ruth was now only partly aware of what she did. Stumbling through the wreckage, she made her way back to the wagon, snatching up three unbroken plates and wrapping them in a torn black curtain. For a moment, she stood in the dust-covered grass beside the road, gazing helplessly around her. From all sides, soldiers called to one another.

"Damn wagon's blocking the bridge."

"They'll be after us, those bastards in the black horse cavalry."

"What's he saying?"

"The black horse cavalry's coming."

"The Rebs are after us! The black horse cavalry!"

As the cry went up, men fanned to either side of the bridge, splashing into the water. Soldiers dropped their gear and drivers abandoned their wagons to rush toward Cub Run. Somewhere a woman screamed, on and on.

When Ruth turned to locate the sound, she saw a carriage just ahead. Inside, a disheveled woman, her head flung back, her eyes blank, thrashed in the hands of a portly man who was dripping with sweat.

"For God's sake, help me!" he cried, spotting Ruth's face at the door.

Ruth knew she must help shock the woman back to sanity. She climbed up at once, reached in and slapped her as hard as she could across the face. Once, twice. The screams stopped abruptly, and the woman collapsed, sobbing quietly.

The man grasped Ruth's arm. "Stay with her. My driver ran off. I've got to take the reins."

Ruth nodded numbly and sat down next to the crying woman. Images shot through her mind, images of Mathew Brady in his duster and straw hat, the smashed What-is-it-wagon, the dying horse, the dead soldier in his pool of blood, the red-haired man. Was he the same freckled-faced Irish boy, blackberry smears about his mouth, who wanted a picture for his mother? She saw the cat in the barn, nursing her kittens in the middle of war.

"We'll all die," the woman sobbed.

Ruth looked down at her lap and saw what she carried, knotted into the black cloth. She took a deep breath and turned to the woman. "No," she said grimly. "No, we won't die. Because I have to get these plates back to Washington. Because the pictures will show everyone."

The woman wiped her eyes, staring at Ruth.

"Eating blackberries," Ruth mumbled. "The soldier ate blackberries and died in the road. Shot, like the horse. They'll see Mathew Brady's pictures and stop the war from going on."

Chapter 8

Captain Jeremy Valerian, tightening the cinch of his saddle in the early dawn light, heard the first cannon shell explode below him, near the stone bridge over shallow stream called Bull Run. Another shell burst immediately afterward.

"Saddle your mounts!" Jeremy shouted to his men, vaulting onto his own big chestnut.

The noise of the heavy Union cannonade from across the stream startled the birds, making them fly up from the trees. A rabbit burst from its burrow near the feet of the chestnut and dashed wildly into the bushes. Jeremy controlled his horse's involuntary shying and wheeled him away from the other riders.

A ground fog hid the stream from view, but white puffs rose above the mist and the air reeked of powder. Jeremy felt his muscles tense with anticipation. This was it! His first battle and the first for his men as well. He rode up the hill to get his orders from Colonel Evans.

As he reached the crest, gunners were setting up their field pieces and foot soldiers milled about, trying to get their gear together. Mounted officers rode through the throng, shouting orders. Below, the mist was thinning as the sun rose. The day would be clear and hot.

"I received a message from one of the lookouts,"

Evans told Jeremy. "He says the Yankees are moving up on our left. They'll ford the stream and attack our flank."

They both stared down the hill at the stone bridge, now clearly visible, as were the lines of blue-clad soldiers advancing along the road beyond it. Jeremy glanced at the colonel.

"What you see is just a feint, meant to keep us here." Evans explained. "I want you to take your squad north and scout along this side of Bull Run. I'll leave four companies here and lead the rest of my men north. Report to me what you find, and don't engage the enemy unless you're forced to."

Moments later, Jeremy's squad was trotting north in a single file. As they rode away, Jeremy could hear the Centreville church bells ringing. For the first time, he remembered that it was Sunday.

Across the stream, there was a flash of light, the glint of the sun on brass muskets. Jeremy cautiously led his men closer, behind the cover of a grove of small oaks. He sucked in his breath at the sight of what lay in wait on the opposite side of Bull Run: row on row of blue-clad infantrymen, at least four regiments. He watched them move off along the stream, sending one of his men back with a report. Then he and his men withdrew from the grove and rode on to the north, taking care to keep out of sight.

Cutting through the fields and woods, Jeremy's squad finally came to a stand of trees at the bottom of a rise. Above them, a small frame farmhouse looked down on the run. Leaving his men below, Jeremy tethered the chestnut and climbed the hill on foot. He peered down through a screen of brush at the blue coats of the enemy. From where he stood, he could see that the Union's advance column was already splashing across Bull Run at Sudley Springs Ford, farther to the north.

Now that the lookout's word had been proven out, Jeremy knew it was time to hurry back to the main body of the army. Almost tumbling down the hill, he raced back to his men, leading them south at a gallop. But before they had gone very far, they found Colonel Evans, already on the march with two companies and a cannon apiece to support them.

"We'll take a stand on that crest," Colonel Evans ordered, pointing to a red brick farmhouse at the top of a hill. "The Yanks are aiming to surprise us, but we'll turn the tables on them."

At the top of the hill, Jeremy's men dismounted and moved into position to the rear of the foot soldiers, who formed a line behind the stone walls and weathered sheds of the farm. As they waited for the enemy to advance, the sun climbed higher and higher and the day grew hotter. Shells exploded to the southeast along Bull Run, and there was the ragged pop of musket fire. Jeremy wiped the sweat from his face and stared off to the north.

Colonel Evans, hidden behind a tree near the crest of the hill, suddenly raised his sword. In an instant, soldiers had aimed their loaded muskets, eyes darting from the colonel to the slope of the hill and back again. Then Jeremy heard shouts, the creak of leather, the thump of boots hitting the ground, and the first blue-coated soldiers appeared at the crest of the hill. The colonel's sword dropped with a flash of sunlight on the blade, and a volley of fire cut down almost every Yankee in sight. After the snick and thud of reloading, another volley tore at the bluecoats who followed.

Stunned, the Yankee line faltered, then turned

and retreated down the hill. There, hidden behind trees and bushes, they returned the fire, too far away for their bullets to be effective. But the big guns of the Union artillery were far more devastating. As soon as they found the range, their shells began to shatter the stone walls and demolish the sheds that harbored the Rebels, leaving them sprawled, mangled and bleeding, along the hilltop.

Jeremy turned his head away and took a deep breath. When he looked back, the Yankee foot soldiers had begun to advance again. The hills and fields below seemed to teem with their blue coats.

"We can't hold here without help," Evans shouted. "Valerian, ride to headquarters for reinforcements."

Jeremy spurred his chestnut south over the fields, crossing the pike that angled off to the west. He checked his horse when he saw a Rebel brigade marching toward him. At the head of the column was General Bee.

"Go to the rear and notify General Johnston," Bee ordered when he heard Jeremy's report. "I'll back up Evans."

As Jeremy continued to the south, he passed another rise and on it he saw more Confederate troops, taking up positions around a white farmhouse. Then, as he neared headquarters, he heard the comforting roar of Confederate cannon answering the Union artillery.

General Johnston hardly let Jeremy finish before he turned to General Beauregard and snapped, "To the left, damn it. The battle's over there—and that's where I'm going." He flung himself out the door and onto his horse.

General Beauregard stared after him for a moment, then shouted at his aides to start the troops moving to the left. As he ran to his own horse, he motioned Jeremy to follow.

"Sir," Jeremy shouted, "I request permission to join my unit."

Beauregard glanced at him and nodded. "Granted." Then he turned and raced after General Johnston.

Jeremy was riding back, still south of the pike, when four of his own men came galloping toward him. "Captain, we've fallen back," Sergeant Yancey cried out. He pointed at the tall white house Jeremy had passed on his way to headquarters. "Our new line's just in front of that hill."

"Why are you here?"

"Colonel Evans ordered the cavalry to remount and fall back as skirmishers, sir."

Jeremy stared at the four men. "But where's the rest of the squad?"

"Dead, sir."

Jeremy's eyes widened.

"It was hell up there," the sergeant cursed. Then he drew his horse closer to Jeremy. "What are your orders, sir?"

Jeremy looked quickly around and pointed to the hill. "We'll back them up." Wheeling around, he directed his men through the woods to the south slope of the hill, deploying them well to the rear of the infantry positions. Then he rode up toward the house to see who was in command.

As he reached the crest, a shell exploded directly over the building, and chimney bricks flew in every direction. Before the dust from the first blast had died away, another shell made a direct hit, sending splintered wood and shards of glass sailing into the trees.

Soldiers in gray spilled out of the house and sprinted toward him. "There's an old lady inside in her bed," one screeched. "The Yankee cannon done killed her."

Undaunted, Jeremy picked through the rubble and worked his way around the house until he came to a black-bearded man who sat quietly on his horse, hands folded on the pommel of his saddle. "General Jackson," Jeremy shouted, raising his voice to be heard over the boom of the cannon.

The general turned his head, acknowledging his presence with a nod.

"I've four horsemen in the woods to the rear," Jeremy cried. "All that are left of my squad, sir."

"Keep 'em there," Jackson barked. "I'll use 'em if I need to." He pointed down the hill to a stand of trees. "We'll need every man we can get if that line breaks."

Through the smoke, Jeremy caught a glimpse of General Bee. The Union cannon were firing grapeshot at pointblank range, fifty lead balls spewing out with each blast. In the woods below, the trees were splintered and smashed, toppling over. But they seemed to fall soundlessly, muffled by the explosion of the shells. As the bombardment continued, Rebels dashed in disorder from the woods, scattering to both sides of the hill.

Finally, General Bee rode straight up the hill toward Jackson, shells bursting all around him. "General," he shouted, "they're beating us back."

"Sir, we'll give 'em the bayonet," Jackson called back.

Bee stared up at him. "By God, we will," he cried. "I'll rally the men." And with that he plunged back into the smoke.

Impulsively, Jeremy followed, spurred on by Bee's courage. When he reached the bottom of the hill, he looked frantically about and spotted Bee rounding up a group of retreating soldiers. Spurring his horse, Jeremy dashed to head off another knot of stragglers.

"To Bee!" he ordered. "Follow your general!"

As Jeremy led the men forward, he saw Bee rise in his saddle, partially obscured by the drifting smoke. Bee lifted his sword and waved it at the hill behind them. "Look!" he shouted. "There's Jackson standing like a stone wall! Rally behind the Virginians!"

But as he swung forward, Bee doubled over, sliding from his horse. Jeremy raced to his side, but he was too late. In a moment, a lieutenant who kneeling by the stricken man leaped up and swung back into his saddle. "You heard your general," he screamed. "Follow me! We'll rally behind Stonewall Jackson!"

Mathew Brady stopped at the What-is-it-wagon and watched as General Sherman's men forded Bull Run to the north of the stone bridge. He'd sent Hause back to find Ruth and the other wagon, but he'd not ventured this close to the battlefield alone. He turned and winked at his two companions.

"Close enough for you?" he asked Alfred Waud, a sketch artist for *Harper's Weekly* who'd been riding with Hause.

Waud shook his head but Jake McCormick, a newspaperman and a friend of Brady's disagreed. "Too damn close," he muttered. "And the horse agrees with me."

Brady glanced at the trembling animal, then across the run at the clouds of white smoke drifting over the trees. "I guess I'd better head back to the pike," he agreed, clucking to the horse. As they moved off across the field, the wagon jounced and swayed. Brady wiped at the sweat on his face, but the gesture just made him filthier. Dust covered them all. He'd never seen so much dust in his life.

If only there were some way to take a photograph of motion, Brady mused, some way to capture the image of soldiers advancing to attack, the flare of an exploding shell, the drama of an officer on horseback waving his sword. He was excited to be a part of this, and he had used the camera as much as possible, but he missed so much because of the three to five seconds he needed for an exposure, even in the best light.

Brady headed south toward the stone bridge, but when he neared it he realized he shouldn't have come that way. Shells were dropping all around, and he was afraid the skittish horse might panic. Instead of going on, he turned the wagon parallel to the road and stopped in a grove of trees, pulling the big camera from its shelf.

"Come on, Mat, you're not going to set that damn thing up here," McCormick pleaded.

But Brady was adamant. "I want a shot of the bridge," he insisted.

McCormick moaned. "The damn Rebs are still lobbing shells from the other side of it."

To their right, supply wagons trundled off the pike and across the field. Brady jerked his head toward them. "They'll be shooting at those, not me."

Almost before he'd finished speaking, a shell scored a direct hit on a supply wagon. Brady ducked back, the noise deafening him, his eyes blinded by the flare.

"You damned fool, we've got to get out of here," McCormick yelled, grabbing the camera. Brady scrambled aboard as Waud urged the horse toward the pike. The edge of the field was littered with the shards of the supply wagon, stained with the blood of the horses that had pulled it. One of them was alive and

screaming, but all that was left of the drover was
an arm.

Brady made no objection as Waud headed the
photography wagon back toward Centreville, coming
onto the road and stopping well past the range of the
shells. They looked back, but all they could see were
the clouds of smoke that hung over the hills and fields
to the west. The thump of cannon and the popping of
muskets came clearly to them through the hot, dusty
air.

Waud handed the reins to Brady and climbed
down. "Going to make a sketch," he shouted.

McCormick shook his head. "Picture takers and
picture makers. God preserve me from them."

By the time Waud was satisfied with his efforts, a
few Union soldiers had begun to trickle past.

"Notice that they're not wounded," McCormick
said. He raised his voice and called out to them.
"What's happening? Is it all over? Have you won?"

A grimy soldier paused to give him a scathing
glare. "We're pulling back to Centreville. That's all I
know."

Soon more soldiers came onto the road from the
field to the north, walking briskly, not running but not
losing any time either. Waud climbed back into the
wagon and headed the horse for Centreville. When
they neared the narrow bridge over Cub Run, they
were astounded to find sightseers' carriages and buggies
clogging the road ahead of them. And all the while,
more soldiers, accompanied now by caissons and supply wagons, piled up behind them.

"A retreat," McCormick wondered aloud, "or a
rout?"

As he spoke, a shell burst to their rear, and
women screamed in the carriages. Another shell ex-

ploded overhead. In a frenzy, men whipped their horses, shouting at the slower drivers to get out of the way. Finally, a shell arched overhead and smashed into a wagon in the middle of the bridge.

As the smoke billowed, the mass of men and wagons was plunged into chaos. Frightened horses reared and kicked, teamsters swore, men shouted, women screamed. In the turmoil, both Waud and McCormick jumped down from the stalled wagon, calling back to Brady that they'd find a way to get across Cub Run and come back for him. More intrigued than frightened, Brady watched the melee for a while, then managed to extricate himself from the tangle.

Climbing from the seat, Brady led his wild-eyed horse between a buggy and a supply wagon and down into a shallow ditch. From there, he drove the wagon across a field and entered a stand of trees that ran beside the stream. The confusion at the bridge was hidden from him now, but he could still hear the shouts and cries. And the horse could still hear the roar of the shells. As Brady bent to tie the animal in the shade, it bolted, rearing up and smashing him against a tree. Stunned, he slumped to the ground.

When Mathew Brady came to, it was pitch dark. He blinked his eyes, listening for the sound that had roused him. A hand touched his foot, closed on it. Sprawled on the ground, Brady heard the slither of a sword being drawn from a scabbard.

Chapter 9

There was no way to get a decent picture with the dust and smoke drifting over the hills and fields, obscuring the fighting. The shouts and oaths of the soldiers—God only knew whether they were Union or Confederate—came through clearly, but you couldn't photograph sound. Langston Cook cursed softly and began to pack up his camera and equipment. "What's happening?" he shouted in frustration as a soldier in gray came riding by.

"Them Yankees are just marching up and being shot to hell," the soldier called, slowing down for only a moment as he passed.

Cook nodded. He'd been lucky to get some good shots earlier. Now maybe he'd get some behind the lines. He hoisted the canvas satchel onto his back and started toward the far side of the hill, heading back to the tent that served as his makeshift darkroom.

Luck seemed to be on Cook's side lately, ever since the spring, when General Beauregard had stopped by his gallery in Richmond to have a portrait made. Pierre Gustave Toutant Beauregard, a small and graceful man in a faultlessly tailored uniform, had been easy to photograph. And it was obvious that Beauregard had been pleased with the results.

"Sir, if I could help you in any other way, if I could use my camera to assist our cause—I'd like to

try." Langston Cook had spoken with tense eagerness.
"I planned to enlist as a private, but it seems to me
that photographs of soldiers, of the fighting, might let
the people at home realize what was really happening,
might spur them on."

Beauregard had studied him, pursing his mouth.
"I've seen the photographs taken at Sebastopol during
the Crimean War," he'd said thoughtfully. "I like what
you say. I'll attach you to my staff and we'll try it."

Cook had been with Beauregard ever since, but
today was the first time he'd been in battle, the first
time he'd caught death with his camera, seen men and
horses strewn on the ground like so many toy soldiers.
As he hurried toward the rear, he passed a bedraggled
crowd of Union prisoners.

"I've caught me a real live Yankee congressman!"
a Rebel soldier shouted.

Cook paused. "Where?"

When the soldier pointed to a man dressed in a
suit of summer linen, Cook fell into step alongside him.
"Is this true?" he asked the man.

"I'm Alfred Ely of New York, if that's what you
mean," the prisoner snapped.

"A congressman?"

Ely nodded curtly.

Cook followed along until the troops reached the
barn where the prisoners were to spend the night, but
when he set up his camera Ely turned his back and refused to pose. Cook didn't think it proper to have the
soldiers hold him, as several offered to do, so he gave
up and began to pack away his equipment once again.

Cook noticed that one of the prisoners was watching him intently. "My sister works for a man who does
that," the young man remarked.

"Your sister works for a congressman?"

"No, for a man who takes pictures. His name's Mathew Brady."

Cook glanced again at the red-haired Yankee soldier. He'd heard of Brady. What photographer hadn't?

"She told me he was thinking of hiring a regular crew of men to go out and photograph the war," the young man continued. "You can take my portrait if you want. I'd like for me old da to have it, and maybe sis too."

Cook shook his head and started away, but then he hesitated as an idea struck him. He slowly walked back to the prisoner. "I'll take a photograph of you," he said, looking the Yankee up and down, "and if you'll tell me your name and where you live, I'll see your father gets a picture. Your sister too, if you like. What did you say her name was?"

"Ruth. Ruth O'Neill. I'm George. Me da lives in Washington, and Ruth's there now, with her photographer, Mathew Brady."

Langston Cook managed to see General Beauregard the next day. By then he'd had a chance to think about his scheme, and the more he thought, the more exciting the prospects became. When he'd heard Cook out, the general was quick to give him permission to travel north through the Confederate lines.

"Take care, young man," Beauregard smiled, giving him a clap on the back. "After all, I'll want to have you photograph me again after our final victory."

"It looks like that'll be soon, sir."

Beauregard frowned and shook his head. "I don't underestimate my enemies. I was at West Point with General McDowell, you know. He's no fool. And a battle won isn't a war won, not by a long shot."

The sullen sky drizzled rain when Cook set off on

horseback the next day. He took none of his photographic equipment, carrying only prints of pictures he'd taken near Bull Run, including several of George O'Neill, who looked jauntier than he'd have expected of a prisoner of war.

As he rode through the battleground, Cook passed Confederate troops piling captured Union arms and gear onto wagons. Other soldiers were beginning to haul away the dead, while men in civilian clothes walked among the bodies.

"Who are they?" Cook asked a passing private.

The soldier spat and squinted up at him. "Relatives come to look for their kin."

"Rebs?"

The private shrugged. "Both sides, I reckon. Orders was to let 'em through."

Cook took another look, longing for his camera, and then rode on, his horse picking its way through the rutted mud to the turnpike. Scattered canteens and haversacks littered both sides of the road, and farther along he passed hogs from a nearby farm rooting in a smashed picnic hamper. Below the bridge at Cub Run, a dead horse fouled the stream. No soldiers were on guard here. In fact, he seemed to be all alone.

As the morning wore on, the rain increased. On the far side of Centreville, Cook overtook a line of Yankee wagons inching back toward Washington. Boldness was his best recourse, he decided, so he rode up to the rear wagon, a boxlike affair with an open back, and peered in, only to be greeted by moans and cries of pain. He hastily wheeled away from the ambulance and rode on the verge of the road, passing wagon after wagon. It was not long before he realized that the pitiful cavalcade must stretch the entire twenty miles back into Washington.

An occasional driver shouted as he hurried by,

not to question him but to damn him for riding past while the wagons could barely move. He was also hailed by groups of mud-bespattered Union soldiers who straggled in the fields along both sides of the road.

"How about a ride, mister?" one called out. "That nag can hold me and you both."

Cook didn't reply. Urging the horse on faster, he did his best to ignore the man. Back to Washington with your tail between your legs, he thought exultantly.

Cook was amazed that no one questioned his right to be where he was, not even when he finally crossed Long Bridge into the city, his horse wedged between a sutler's van and a canvas-covered supply wagon. By now there was a driving rain, and soldiers huddled around smoldering fires in the middle of the streets, begging passersby for money and food. Cook eased his horse through the crowds, making for Pennsylvania Avenue, but once he was there he found the wide street so mobbed with people that he had to dismount and lead his horse. As he worked his way along, voices rose through the hiss of the rain.

"Every man jack of them wore a mask, the whole damn regiment," a soldier with his arm in a sling told gaping listeners. "And all the horses were black. They swooped down on us and we was cut to pieces."

"The black horse cavalry," another soldier added. "I heard of them Reb devils."

Cook raised his eyebrows. He'd never seen Rebel cavalry like that, and he doubted if it existed anywhere except in the imaginations of the defeated Yanks. Devils hadn't won the battle. Southern soldiers had, fighting for their rights.

Cook almost missed the sign lettered on a storefront: National Gallery, Mathew B. Brady, Photographer. He tethered his horse and tried the door. There was no one in the gallery, but he heard voices from the next room.

"All right, Ruth, I'm ready."

The connecting door was ajar, so Cook pushed it open and looked in. Before him, in profile, stood a small bearded man in a wrinkled and soiled linen duster. A woman, her head under the camera cloth, was taking his picture.

Cook waited until he saw her straighten. "I don't mean to intrude," he said, stepping into the room. "I'm Langston Cook, and I'm looking for Mathew Brady."

The man turned to face him. "I'm Brady," he replied, "but I'm afraid we can't take any more portraits today." Brady looked as though he was about to drop with fatigue.

Cook shook his head. "No, no. I'm a photographer," he explained. "I've brought some pictures to show *you*."

Brady's face brightened. "I have time to look at photographs. Yes, always time to do that. Where are they?"

"In my knapsack." As Cook came forward, the young woman gave him a searching look and took the plate into a back room.

Brady squinted at the prints. "I'll be damned," he muttered, "you were at Bull Run too." He looked up at Cook. "Good shots. Rebs, though."

"That's because I live in Richmond," Cook answered. "A photographer doesn't have to be a Reb or a Yank, does he?"

Brady gave him a wide grin and clapped him on the back. "No sir, you don't. Come into the gallery. I want to show you the photographs I took at Bull Run." He sighed. "I lost one wagon and not all the plates I had in the other survived the bouncing around. But I saved a few."

The young woman standing in the connecting doorway shook her head and scolded him. "You were lucky to come back at all. I thought you were dead."

Brady smiled at her, then turned to Cook. "I couldn't get across Cub Run, so I took the wagon into the woods and somehow knocked my head. In the middle of the night, I was accosted by a Zouave and nearly scared to death." With a flourish, Brady yanked a sword from under his duster and waved it in the air. "The Zouave gave me this sword when he found out who I was. Told me to watch out for scavenging Rebs. But I just got back into the mob and headed home. I've only been in Washington a few hours."

Cook looked from Brady to the girl. "I'm sorry to burst in on you," he said apologetically. "You must be exhausted. Look, I'll come back later and . . ."

"No, no," Brady burst in. "I want to talk to you. Wait here a bit while I look at my negatives." Brady hurried into the other room. "Sing him a song, Ruth," he laughed as he passed by the girl.

Her face flushed. "You don't really want to hear a song," she said softly. "I'm Ruth O'Neill, Mr. Brady's assistant."

Cook took her hand and raised it to his lips. "Charmed," he replied. "But why does he want you to sing to me?"

"I sometimes do, to make people relax for their portraits. It was Mr. Brady's idea. He's just having his little joke."

Although Ruth was attractively turned out in a peach cotton gown and her curls were brushed to a shining gloss, Cook saw that she looked pale, with shadows under her eyes.

"You weren't at the battle too, were you?" he asked, half in jest.

"Yes."

He stared at her in disbelief.

"Mr. Brady is trying to hire other photographers to work with him, but none were available this last weekend, so I went along."

"It was no place for a woman."

"Or anyone else."

Cook was surprised by the ferocity with which she said those words. Then he recovered himself. "Excuse me, I'm terribly sorry. I completely forgot." He went to his knapsack and pulled out two more pictures. "I have news of your brother George."

Suddenly, all her sternness left her and she seemed like a frightened child. "Is he all right? He wasn't hurt, was he?"

"See for yourself." He handed her the pictures of George.

She looked at them, then back at Cook. "How . . . ?"

"He's a prisoner, Miss O'Neill. A prisioner of the Confederates."

"Oh, no!" Her face had gone even paler.

"But he's not hurt, as you can tell. He says you mustn't worry about him."

Ruth took a step backwards. "You said you weren't a Rebel."

"I'm not."

"But you talked to George after he was taken prisoner. You'd have to be pretty friendly with the Rebel army to do that."

Cook smiled his most disarming smile. "I live in Richmond, as I told you. I simply asked General Beauregard's permission to go with the army, and he gave it."

She frowned at him and held her silence.

"Your brother told me about Mathew Brady, and I came here to ask him to hire me."

Ruth shook her head. "Mr. Brady won't want a Reb."

"I won't want a Reb to do what?" At that moment, Mathew Brady bustled back into the room, carrying a pile of prints.

Cook gave Ruth another smile and looked back at Brady.

"Your very charming assistant believes I'm a Confederate because I was able to take pictures of prisoners held by the Rebel army. But I'm here to ask you for work." Cook allowed a faintly pleading note to creep into his voice. "While you're photographing the war from the Union side, I'll do the same from the Reb. They trust me. I'm a Virginian." He took a deep breath and then continued. "After all, what good is a one-sided picture record? We need to show both sides, Rebel *and* Union."

Brady beamed. "A capital idea. I never hoped to find a man who could go into Rebel territory. And I like your pictures. You're a fine photographer—and you're hired!"

"But Mr. Brady—you don't know anything about him," Ruth protested.

Brady shook his head. "I know what he tells me." He reached over and chucked her under the chin. "Ruth, Ruth. You're growing more distrustful every day."

"And you believe everyone!" she retorted.

"But I'm right just as often as you are, Ruth. Come now, smile at Mr. Cook. Langston, is it?"

Cook nodded and grinned at Ruth.

She gazed at him for a long moment and finally gave him a tiny suggestion of a smile.

"Now, you must look at my pictures," Brady urged and hurried Cook out of the room.

* * *

Finally, Ruth managed to persuade Brady that he had to get some rest. "You go home," she ordered. "Think how worried your wife must be."

Brady gave her an absentminded stare. "Oh, Julia. Yes, she'll be upset. I must get home."

"I'll close up," Ruth added, firmly guiding him out the door.

But even with Brady gone, there was still Langston Cook to deal with. "Did you just arrive in Washington?" she asked as they stood awkwardly in the empty gallery.

"I came directly here."

"There won't be a room at any hotel tonight." She looked about. "I suppose you could sleep here in the gallery."

"Thank you."

Ruth sighed. "It's what Mr. Brady would want. He's too tired to think about such things or he'd have offered."

Cook stuck his hands in his pockets and gave her a long look. "But you'd rather I turned around and headed across Long Bridge to Virginia. Right?"

Ruth colored slightly. "I don't want him hurt. He's a very trusting man and people sometimes take advantage of him. He can't seem to see meanness or ill will, and it has nothing to do with his glasses."

Cook reached out and took her hand. "I swear, I've no notion of harming a hair on Mr. Brady's head." And that was certainly true, he reflected wryly. Brady wouldn't be hurt at all if his plans went properly. Then he had a flash of inspiration. "I'd be happy to take blankets and food to George when I cross back into Virginia."

She hesitated. "Oh, could you do that?"

"I think so. I'll certainly try."

Ruth's voice became gentler now. "Oh, Mr. Cook,

I don't mean to be so cross-grained. It's just that yesterday was so . . ." Her words trailed off and her lips began to quiver. Tears filled her eyes. "The fighting was terrible!" she whispered. "Horrible!"

Without thinking, Cook put an arm about her, and she buried her head against his chest, shaking with sobs. "There, there," he soothed, "there, now. I know how bad it was."

He did feel sorry for her, a woman exposed to all the terrors of battle, but he was surprised to feel something else as well. Abruptly, Ruth stepped back, and he knew by her wide eyes, still wet with tears, and her uneven breathing that she was aware of his strong surge of desire. She was so close to him, so very lovely. Aware that he shouldn't, but under a compulsion he couldn't resist, he brought his lips to hers.

Ruth felt herself enveloped in warmth. Langston Cook's lips pressed to hers, his arms close about her, holding her in a cocoon of safety where there was no fighting, no cannon fire. The only pounding was her heart, the only fire was inside her, driving out the fears and terrors.

Ruth opened her eyes and looked into Cook's face. Suddenly she gave an inarticulate little cry and pulled away.

"Ruth, it's all right," he murmured.

"No, no." She stared up at him, bewildered by what had happened. He was a stranger. She didn't love him. In fact, she wasn't sure she even liked him. How could she have let him kiss her, have felt a spark of desire?

Chapter 10

"She's living here in Washington with an aunt." Calhoun Preston handed the report to the army officer who stood before him.

Captain Thornton gave Preston a speculative look. He'd worked with the man before, when Thornton had been a lieutenant on the frontier fighting Indians and Preston a scout. Yet now Preston was here in Washington, in civilian clothes but with a major's rank. And now he was the one giving the orders. Top secret orders to boot.

"What is it you want me to do in regard to Vanessa Woodward?" Thornton asked.

"Pinkerton's been keeping an eye on her for us," Preston explained. "We know she isn't seeing Jamison these days." He smiled, a mocking smile. "She's being escorted by a number of young officers. You can be one of them."

"I don't know what my wife will think of that!"

"I promise not to send word back to Missouri," Preston laughed. "Otherwise . . . well, you know why you were chosen."

Thornton grinned wryly. "Because of my looks."

"Exactly. You're the indispensable man."

Thornton frowned. "I still don't understand why you don't make Miss Woodward's acquaintance instead of me."

Preston laughed. "In the first place, she's attracted to officers and I'm not in uniform. In the second place, I don't care for spoiled young ladies and I'd be certain to show it. And, finally, if everything goes according to plan, I'll have to be with her later, and I don't care to complicate matters."

Thornton sighed and riffled through the pages of the report. "I won't argue, but you're single and I'm not. Betsy will never understand if she should get wind of this."

"And I'll never understand why men marry when they don't have to."

"For love, Cal, for love."

Preston shrugged. "Love? I've been lucky enough to avoid that particular affliction."

Vanessa stared at the man who was waiting in Aunt Matilda's parlor. All she could see was his back. Then she caught a glimpse of his profile.

"Papa!" she cried, dashing into the room.

The man turned to face her, and she stopped so quickly she stumbled.

"I . . . I'm so sorry," she murmured. "I beg your pardon. I thought you were . . ." Her words trailed off as her face flamed red. How could she have believed this man was her father? He was much younger, and blond besides.

"You thought I was your father?" He sounded amused.

"It was a trick of the light," she explained, struggling to recover her poise. "Aunt Matilda's maid just said there was a soldier calling. She doesn't bother with names. You're much the same height, and there *is* a slight resemblance."

The soldier smiled and took her hand. "I'm Captain Thornton," he said, bowing. "I apologize if I've caused you any distress. I'm here as your escort in place of Captain Freimuth. His regiment left the city unexpectedly, and he was most concerned because he didn't have time to let you know. I promised to deliver his regrets as well as stand in for him. That is, if you'll have me in his place."

The more Vanessa looked at Captain Thornton, the less he reminded her of her father. "That's kind of you," she replied.

He shook his head. "Not at all. It's a pleasure to have the chance to take the beautiful Miss Woodward to the Fall Festival Ball."

Vanessa felt a smile creep across her face. It would be nice to meet someone new. She'd enjoyed the company of most of the officers she'd met these past few months, but none of them had stirred her emotions the way Robert Jamison had. He'd left Washington in August, when Congress adjourned, but before he'd departed he'd come to see her. Somehow, she'd managed to sound cool and detached when she said good-bye.

"Until November," Robert had said. "Don't think I'll be put off forever, Vanessa. I know you feel as I do. I'll be back in November."

Already she was counting the days, even though she'd vowed never to go anywhere alone with him. Her eyes darted back up to the man who stood before her. He had asked her a question, and now he was having to repeat it.

"I take it your father is an officer?"

Vanessa bit her lip. "Yes. Yes, he is."

"You seemed distressed. Is something wrong?"

"I haven't heard from him for months and months." She looked away. "I don't know where he is or if he's all right. I think about him all the time."

"What's his regiment?"

"That's the trouble . . . I don't know. He didn't

tell me—just that he planned to join a loyal Virginia regiment. Some of the other officers I've met have tried to trace him, but so far they've failed." Vanessa sighed. "I'm not even certain of his rank. He was a major when he brought me here, but I suppose he could have been promoted."

Thornton tried to sound reassuring. "I'll certainly do my best to find out whatever I can."

Vanessa acknowledged his offer with a wan smile. "I'd welcome any help you could give me," she replied quietly. "Sometimes I think the war will never be over. At first, everybody said one battle would do it, but even though General McClellan has replaced General Scott as commander of the Army of the Potomac, the Union defeats seem to go on and on. I was told he said this war was different from any we'd ever fought, that there'd be no treaty with the Rebels, that the South must be crushed completely." She paused, wondering whether to continue, then plunged ahead. "I read in a Richmond newspaper that the Rebel army is God's instrument for punishing the wicked North. There's so much hatred, Captain Thornton. Where will it all end?"

"I hope and pray that in time it will end in peace, and we'll be a united nation again."

"But will the hate be gone, even then?"

Thornton was beginning to look a bit uncomfortable. "General McClellan will see us through," he said gruffly. "The soldiers love him. They'd follow him to hell and back."

She noticed that he hadn't answered her question.

In November, Robert Jamison came to call on Vanessa.

"Well," he said, keeping hold of her hand as they

stood in her aunt's parlor, "I hear you're the belle of Washington."

"That's not difficult in the summer and fall," she replied airily. "So few women stay here the year round." She blushed ever so slightly. Could he tell how his touch affected her?

"I also understand you've not become engaged to any of the young officers you seem to be seeing so much of."

"I've made promises to no man."

Robert smiled. "I said you belonged to me."

Blushing more deeply now, Vanessa took her hand from his. "No."

"We'll see."

She took a deep breath. "And how does Senator Chandler view the war? I understand he called on General McClellan the day after he returned from Michigan."

Robert shrugged as if to say the war was of less importance than the feeling that lay between them. "Zach wants action, an advance into Virginia. McClellan assures him that now that General Scott has retired, there'll be a raring good fight."

"There was a battle up the Potomac at Ball's Bluff just last month." Vanessa shuddered. "Afterward we had a heavy rain, and the bodies of dead soldiers floated down the river past the city."

"Yes. I heard Senator Baker was killed heading the battalion that tried to break the Rebel blockade of the river. A sad loss."

At this, Vanessa could no longer keep her own sadness to herself. "I've not heard from my father for ever so long," she cried.

Robert came a step closer. "Vanessa, I'll try again to locate him." He took her hand and kissed it, letting his lips linger for a long moment before he took his

leave. It was all she could do to keep herself from running after him.

Now that the war had begun in earnest, the press
of work kept Robert busy night and day. It was over a
month before Vanessa saw him again. One morning
just before the New Year, he appeared again in Aunt
Matilda's parlor, looking pale and grim.

"I've word of your father," he announced, striding
quickly into the room.

Vanessa grabbed his sleeve and stared into his
face. "Tell me where he is, how he is," she demanded.

Robert put an arm around her shoulders. There
was no way he could tell her gently. "He's in a Rebel
prison in Richmond."

She buried her face in his chest for a moment,
then pulled away. "Is he . . . well?"

"I was told he has malaria."

"How . . . how did you find this out?"

"A captured Union officer who was set free on
parole brought a message to Zach Chandler about
Congressman Ely of New York. You recall, the man
who was captured at Bull Run. Well Ely's in Libby
Prison, where this paroled officer was, and your father's there too. We're making arrangements now to
get Ely freed."

"And my father? Can he be paroled too?"

Robert sighed. "There's a roster of the officers in
the prison who are eligible for parole. But your father's
name isn't on the list."

Vanessa drew back a pace, panic-stricken. "You
say he has malaria. Why would the Rebels want to
keep him?"

"Vanessa, I don't know."

"They'd have to use medicine, quinine and such,
that could be used for the own soldiers. You'd

think they'd want to rid themselves of sick prisoners. Wouldn't you think so, Robert?" Her voice was trembling now.

When he didn't answer, a stab of fear shot through her. "Are you keeping something back?" she whispered.

Robert found that he was unable to look her in the eyes. "Quinine's in short supply in the South," he explained quietly. "I'm afraid your father isn't being treated. The parolee who brought the news about Ely begged the government to smuggle quinine and morphine into Libby for the Union soldiers who're imprisoned there."

She stared at him. "And is the government doing that?"

Robert hesitated. "There are problems. We'll try."

"Try?" Her voice rose. "If you can't, then someone must. I'll take medicine to my father myself if I have to."

"Now Vanessa," he urged, "don't be hasty. You couldn't even get across Long Bridge without a pass, and traveling in Virginia is dangerous. The Rebs wouldn't let you anywhere near Richmond."

But Vanessa was adamant. It was the only shred of hope she had, and she clung to it. "I won't have my father lying ill and untreated in a Confederate prison," she cried, "not if I can do anything to help. At the worst, I'll be turned back."

"You don't understand, Vanessa. Ladies aren't necessarily respected by soldiers. You might suffer . . . unspeakable things."

Vanessa shook her head. "I don't believe Rebel soldiers are any different from Union ones. I grew up in Virginia, Robert. Men there are gallant."

"War changes everything." He tried to take her hand, but she moved away from him. "Trust Zach and me to make arrangements for the medicine," he urged. "Promise me you won't go dashing off to Richmond."

She gave him a grim smile. "I told you before. I make promises to no man."

After Robert left, Vanessa sat in a straight chair by the parlor door and stared at the wall. It was all very well to talk bravely, but how would she go about arranging to leave for Richmond? After all, there were two armies blocking her way.

When Ancey came to fetch her, she was still in the chair. "You gonna change to go riding, Miss Vanessa?" Ancey asked hesitantly. "That soldier be here any time."

Soldier? Vanessa looked up, puzzled. Oh yes, Captain Thornton. William. He'd insisted she go riding this afternoon, but now she didn't feel like riding. She didn't even feel like talking. She'd have Ancey tell him she had a headache.

Vanessa was about to do just that when a glimmer of a plan shot through her mind. Wait. Maybe William could help her. At least, he might be able to arrange for a pass across Long Bridge and through the Union lines.

"I'm not going riding, Ancey," she said firmly. "I'll see the captain in here."

Ancey frowned. "That Mr. Jamison, he bring you bad news. I can tell."

"It's about my father. He's a prisoner of the Rebs."

Ancey knelt down beside her. "That do be a shame, Miss Vanessa. That be truly bad news."

"I should be glad he's alive but—oh, Ancey, he's sick and alone in a prison." Tears filled Vanessa's eyes.

Ancey put out her arms and Vanessa leaned against her, sobbing until she could cry no more.

* * *

William Thornton had been most sympathetic and had promised to see what he could do. When he returned a week later, he brought a man with him, a civilian, not a soldier. Vanessa eyed the stranger with suspicion. He was tall and dark, and there was something about him that made her uneasy. Why had William brought him?

"This is Calhoun Preston," William explained. "He's going to take you to Richmond and try to get you into Libby Prison to see your father."

Vanessa gave him a crisp little nod. "How do you do, Mr. Preston?"

"Tolerably well, Miss Woodward." He eyed her appraisingly, then shook his head. When Vanessa gave him a puzzled look, he cracked a faint smile. "Not that your gown isn't becoming," he drawled, "but we can't have hoops."

"I beg your pardon?"

"No hoops on the journey. Wear a riding habit. I can't be bothered with any more foolishness than is absolutely necessary."

Vanessa stiffened. "I won't wear hoops," she said icily, "and I assure you I shan't be foolish."

Preston looked at her skeptically.

"I want to reach my father as quickly as possible." Vanessa looked straight back at him, trying to hold in her anger.

Preston merely nodded. "The captain said you wanted to bring medicine. I can get you the quinine and morphine at a good price."

Vanessa, taken aback, looked from one man to the other.

"Mr. Preston is a sutler," William hastily put in.

"Looks like you didn't tell the lady," Calhoun Preston remarked, raising an eyebrow.

"I haven't had a chance," William replied somewhat stiffly.

"Never mind, I'll do it myself since I'm here." Preston turned back to Vanessa. "I'm willing to take you to Richmond, Miss Woodward, but I'll need to be paid for the trip. Three hundred dollars. In gold. And a hundred more if I can get you inside Libby."

He was certainly an unlikable man. In fact, Vanessa was repelled by him. She glanced questioningly at William.

"I'd have offered to pay myself," William said, "but on my military . . ."

"I wouldn't hear of it!" Vanessa interrupted. "Naturally, I'll pay you the money, Mr. Preston."

"Before we start."

She looked him in the eye. "How do I know you'll see that I get there once you have the money?"

He sketched a bow. "You'll have to take me on trust." He smiled one-sidedly.

On trust? She wouldn't trust this man out of her sight. He looked every inch a scoundrel.

"If anyone can get you to Richmond, Preston can," William assured her.

"I'll take only three hundred now," Calhoun Preston offered. "The extra hundred you can pay me when we get back. You see, I trust *you*."

How could she stand to travel in such company? Vanessa asked herself. Yet what choice did she have? She could set out alone, but how far would she get? And William surely wouldn't have brought this man here if he thought she'd come to any harm while she was with him.

"Very well," she said, still a bit reluctant. "I'll give you the money. When do we start?"

Preston glanced quickly at Thornton. "Not for a month or two. It'll take some time to set things up."

There was a slight pause. "One more thing, Miss Woodward."

"Yes?"

"If you mention a word of this to anyone the trip is off."

By the light of a single lamp, Vanessa glanced at her reflection in the pier glass as she put her bonnet on. Dark green riding habit, riding boots, gloves—all very proper, except for the bonnet. The costume cried out for a rakish riding hat with jaunty plumes, but Mr. Preston had insisted that she wear a bonnet. "The less attention we attract, the better," he'd warned.

Well, she thought grimly, she'd do as he told. Within reason. At least they were finally setting off. As the weeks had gone by, she'd sometimes thought they'd never be able to leave. Imagine, here it was past the middle of March!

Her lips tightened. It had taken almost all the gold papa had given her to pay for the medicines and the journey. Papa was worth more than any amount of gold, but she wasn't so sure of Mr. Preston's worth, despite what William told her. "Some of these sutlers have contacts on both sides," William had explained. "They travel with either army to sell to the soldiers. Calhoun is the best at this business, at least the best I know of. He drives a hard bargain, but he's honest, Vanessa." She'd soon find out about that.

Vanessa sighed and took one last look in the mirror. What was most difficult was leaving without telling Aunt Matilda or Ancey. She'd left a note for her aunt, but Ancey couldn't read, so Matilda would just have to tell her.

Ever so quietly, Vanessa picked up the tarpaulin bag that held her belongings and slipped out of her bedroom. Then she was down the stairs and out the door, a silent, swiftly moving shadow. At the end of the street, she saw the outline of a canvas-covered wagon. Preston had told her they'd pretend to be photographers, traveling in a dark-shrouded twin of Brady's What-is-it-wagon.

She hurried her pace, eager to start on her way, but as she did so she heard the sound of running feet behind her. Glancing over her shoulder, she slowed down, anxious not to be noticed now, of all times. Out of the darkness, a small figure rushed at her, clutching at her arm.

"You ain't going nowhere without me," Ancey whispered.

PART II

SPRING 1862-
SUMMER 1862

Chapter 11

All quiet along the Potomac tonight.
No sound save the rush of the river.
While soft falls the dew on the face
    of the dead—
The picket's off duty forever.

Helena Swane spread her arms as she spoke the last line, gazing out at the audience. After a moment, the room filled with applause.

"She's quite good, isn't she?" one woman said to another.

"My dear, you should hear her do Sir Walter Scott. It gives me chills."

Helena smiled as the audience crowded around her. She must arrange to do more of these readings before the weather became too warm. She must be seen everywhere, become a familiar figure, a trusted member of Washington society. She was determined not to be caught out like Rose Greenhow, who'd been a prisoner in her own house for all these months. Rose had been too outspoken, her intrigues too obvious. But Helena Swane wouldn't make that mistake.

There were rumors that Rose would be transferred to the Old Capitol Prison any day now to await trial for treason. Some of her couriers had been arrested too, and the men were now imprisoned at Fort

Lafayette in New York. It was all Allan Pinkerton's doing, thought Helena bitterly. Luckily he and his military intelligence agents didn't seem to associate Helena with Rose, or even suspect her of spying. Helena knew she'd rather die than be thrown into prison, but even so, she couldn't give up the dangerous game she was playing. The thrill of it was simply too appealing.

Helena made her way through the throng, nodding and smiling, and sent the maid for her greatcoat. There was plenty of time for a stop at Brady's Gallery on the way back to the hotel. She'd been there only once before, when her colonel had had his portrait taken.

Mr. Brady wasn't in, and neither was the man Helena wanted to see, Langston Cook.

"I've heard Mr. Cook does portraits," Helena explained to the curly-haired young woman at the desk. Rather a pretty girl, but she lacked elegance.

"Yes."

"Do you make appointments?"

"I can't at the moment. Mr. Cook hasn't let me know when he'll be available."

"Isn't he in the city?"

"Yes and no. You see, Mr. Brady takes pictures of the war, and Mr. Cook helps him. I'm never certain exactly when they'll be in the studio."

Helena raised her eyebrows. "That doesn't sound like a very good way to run a business."

"We have staff photographers available. Do you . . . ?"

"How can they take photographs of a war?" Helena cut in. "Do you mean the battles?"

"As much as possible. As you know, movement makes a blur on the picture."

"But battle must be all movement—guns shooting, soldiers charging, horses dashing about."

"The aftermath is quiet."

It took Helena a moment to realize that the girl was referring to the dead. Not sure quite how to respond, she looked more carefully at the figure before her. Actually, the girl seemed rather pale. "Are you all right, Miss . . . ?"

The girl nodded a bit tremulously and took a deep breath. "My name is Ruth O'Neill, and I'm fine. It's just that my father told me today that my brother Michael has joined the army. He's only seventeen." She made a visible effort to pull herself together. "Another of Mr. Brady's photography staff can do a portrait of you . . . if you wish."

Helena paused for a moment, as if she were considering what to do. "No," she answered at last, "Mr. Cook was recommended to me, and I'll wait until he's available. You can send a message to my hotel when he's in town." As Helena pulled on her gloves, she gestured around the gallery. "I didn't see any war scenes when I passed through."

"Mr. Brady keeps them on a separate table. They're not framed. I can show you . . ."

Helena shook her head. "No, no. Another time, perhaps. Just be certain that Mr. Cook knows I called. My name is Helena Swane, and I live at the Willard."

Ruth stared after Miss Swane as she left the gallery. Was this golden-haired, high and mighty woman one of Langston Cook's conquests? Ruth was used to customers insisting that they'd sit for no one but Mathew Brady, but this was the first time anyone had requested Langston Cook. Langston wasn't well known in Washington, and he was usually off with the army.

Ruth frowned. Maybe Miss Swane had heard of

Langston from a portrait he'd made in Richmond. Or maybe she'd met him at a party and wanted to further the acquaintance. She certainly looked bold enough to do such a thing. Or maybe they were already very friendly. Lovers, perhaps. He *was* an attractive man . . .

Stop it, she warned herself. Langston means nothing to you. After all, what was between them? Just a kiss or two. Though she had to admit it wasn't Langston's fault there wasn't more. He'd invited her several times to see his rooms on Eleventh Street, and she'd gone so far as to walk past the brick building once or twice. She even knew what his room number was. But despite all this, she'd never gone inside.

Ruth stood up and walked to the window. The day was cloudy, but the rain had held off, thank heaven. The streets had been a mess all winter, and even this morning her father had been muddy to his knees when he'd come to tell her about Michael. And Jeremy.

"Funny how I heard about that old friend of yours, Ruthie," he'd said, giving her a sly grin. "Happened to meet up with the old bitch herself, right here on the avenue, and I says, 'Good morning to ye, Mrs. Valerian. So you're still hereabouts? Thought ye'd be off south to live with those who suit ye better.' And she gives me one of those nasty looks. I don't figure she'll answer me, but she ups and says, 'Mr. O'Neill, I believe?'

" 'That's me.' I tell her. 'And how is your daughter?' she asks. 'Working for Brady the photographer, a fine position,' I says. 'And how's your cousin?' I ask. 'I suppose he's a Johnny Reb.' 'An officer with General Lee's army,' she says, as though that's the same as sitting on the right hand of God Himself. 'Twas a good day's work when ye rid yourself of that lad, Ruthie."

But I never have, she thought, staring out into the

gray afternoon. Langston attracts me, and I might even come to love him if it weren't for Jeremy. But even if I wanted Langston to make love to me, I couldn't let him. Simply because he's not Jeremy.

It was March before the message came asking Helena to meet Langston Cook at Brady's Gallery. When she arrived, Ruth went into the operating room with her to explain about the head clamp and the need to be perfectly still, but Helena cut her short.

"I've posed many times before," she said with a dismissive wave of the hand. "I know all about such things." Then she smiled, directing her gaze at Langston. "Really, Miss O'Neill, I know what I'm doing."

Langston had hardly taken his eyes off Helena from the moment she'd walked into the room. "I don't think I'll need assistance, thank you," he said very firmly, fixing Ruth with a meaningful glance.

Helena laughed as Ruth stalked out, pulling the door shut with a sharp crack. "Why, Mr. Cook," she purred, "for all you know I might be terrified of being alone with a strange man."

"Somehow I doubt that," he grinned, moving out from behind the camera. "No beautiful woman is truly afraid of men."

Helena tilted her head and gave him an appraising stare. She'd avoided any entanglements with couriers. Until now such a dalliance had seemed too risky, but perhaps Langston Cook might be worth it. He was one of the best-looking men she'd ever seen. His wavy brown hair glinted with gold, and his beard was even more golden than his hair. What she liked best, though, were his hazel eyes, which were set at a slight angle, giving him a feral look.

"You said you've often posed for portraits?" he asked, nonchalantly meeting her stare.

"I'm an actress."

"Helena Swane? I must apologize for not recognizing the name. I've not been in Washington very long."

"Oh, I'm not on the stage at the moment. My troupe disbanded. Perhaps after the war . . ." She waved a hand vaguely.

"I'm flattered you chose me to photograph you."

She shrugged. "One hears things."

"All the way from Richmond? It can't be from anyone in Washington. I've done only two portraits since I've been here, and both were of children."

Helena fixed her eyes on his and lowered her voice. "Yes," she said, "all the way from Richmond."

His face tightened and the smile disappeared.

"But I'm here to pose, not to discuss mutual acquaintances," Helena continued, glancing casually about the room. "Shall you want me standing or seated?"

Langston glided back to the camera, his mind racing. But the next move would have to be hers. "Standing," he replied quietly. "We'll try several different shots. I fancy one of you looking back over your shoulder."

Helena assumed the position, gazing at Langston with half-lowered lids, teasing him. When she saw him draw in his breath, a pleasurable glow began to warm her body. She found that enticement was often more exciting than what came afterward. And she'd yet to decide if there would be an afterward as far as Langston Cook was concerned.

Helena Swane was expecting a packet of information about ship movements from a clerk in the War Department, a packet that must go south as soon as possible. Langston was here and available, and her source in Richmond had said he was reliable. She glanced at him again as he handed the plates to the darkroom assistant.

"I'll see you to your buggy," he offered, helping her into her coat.

"That's very kind of you," she murmured. How could she get the packet to Langston when it came? She pondered. She hesitated to draw attention to the gallery by coming again. On the other hand, the colonel was leaving town tomorrow, and he'd be gone for at least a month. No, she reminded herself, she'd made it a rule never to have a courier come to the Willard, and it wasn't a good time to make exceptions.

As she and Cook walked between the rows of framed portraits, Helena paused before a picture of Vice President Hannibal Hamlin. "If looks made a man President," she remarked, "he'd be in the White House instead of Abraham Lincoln." She gestured at the next portrait, one of Lincoln seated by a table. "I swear his hair isn't properly brushed, and his boots certainly aren't polished."

As Helena spoke, she slid her eyes right and left. No one was in the gallery except the Irish girl, and she was too far away to overhear. Helena inclined her head as though she were listening to Langston. "Meet me at the Smithsonian Park," she whispered. "I'll send a message with the night and the time. Come prepared to travel south."

The chosen night was cool and clear with a waxing crescent moon. Helena bundled herself in a sable-trimmed coat with a matching bonnet that hid her blond hair and set out alone, driving a hired rig. She found Langston waiting at the southwest corner of the park. As she slowed down, he climbed into the rig beside her and took the reins.

"I left my horse close to the bridge," he murmured. "We'll drive there instead of staying here in the park. A stopped vehicle is more noticeable than a moving one."

"But I don't want to be seen with you," Helena protested.

"No one will see me," he hissed. "The horse is tethered in deep shadow, and I'll drop from the rig next to him. You won't have to stop at all." He peered at her intently. "Don't worry, I'm a careful man. I've got a lot more to lose than you do."

"I wouldn't say that!"

Langston gave a grim chuckle. "I don't think you'd hang. I would." As he was speaking, he guided the horse around a corner. Just ahead, Helena could see the traffic passing on Maryland Avenue.

"Don't turn onto Maryland," she ordered.

He glanced at her. "I told you. I'm a careful man."

Frantically, Helena reached for the reins, and Langston was forced to halt the rig, pulling up under the overhanging branches of a tree. A stone's throw away, wagons rumbled toward the bridge. The clatter of men on horseback rang through the chill night air.

"Give it to me," he said brusquely.

Helena pulled out the packet of papers, but before she could hand them over, Langston cursed and jerked on the reins, bringing the horse's head up. Helena almost fell over backwards as the startled animal, reacting to Langston's whip, yanked the rig abruptly forward.

"What are you doing?" Helena cried. Langston had turned onto Maryland Avenue, forcing his horse and rig in front of a dray.

As the dray's driver shouted curses, Langston whipped his horse alongside a wagon covered with dark tarpaulin. Helena watched in astonishment, as he threw the reins to her and leaped across to the box of the other wagon. Quickly, Helena eased the horse to a walk, falling into place behind the covered wagon. Whatever Langston Cook was up to, she wasn't going to be involved.

"What in hell are you doing with this wagon?" she heard him demand. "Where did you steal it?"

Oh my God, she thought. He'll have the sentries off the bridge and over here in no time, what with all the commotion he's making. I'll have to pull off on the next street. All she could think of now was to get safely back to town. Langston Cook simply wasn't dependable. She'd have to find another courier, try again another night.

Suddenly, the wagon ahead turned off the road. "Get down, all three of you, and make it fast." Langston's voice came back to Helena, sharp and clear.

Hurriedly, Helena reined in her horse as three figures climbed from the wagon—a man, a woman and a black girl. She saw the woman's face for an instant in the glow of the lantern and drew in her breath. It was a face she'd seen many times at the city's finest parties and balls. But what in God's name was Vanessa Woodward doing in a stolen wagon heading toward Long Bridge in the dark of night?

Helena sat back on the seat of the rig, determined that no one would catch a glimpse of her. Vanessa was going south, and in secret, and Helena could think of only one reason for that. Vanessa was a spy. Not a Confederate spy, for Helena would have known about that, but a Union spy, heading south to work for the Yankees. Hadn't she heard the girl was from Virginia? She sank further back into the shadows as she watched Vanessa hurry away from the wagon. I'll have to send her name and description to General Johnston, she told herself. His men can pick her up before she does any harm.

By now Helena had forgotten all about returning to the city. What did Langston plan to do? she wondered. Did he have information about Vanessa?

"Keep your damned wagon." A strange male voice rang out. "I told you I bought it fair and square. I'm no thief! And point that blasted gun somewhere else, if you don't mind. As far as I'm concerned, you're little better than a highwayman yourself, taking my wagon at the point of a gun and frightening my wife."

Aha, whoever he is, he's lying, Helena thought. Vanessa Woodward isn't married.

There was a sudden scuffle, and Langston swore. Then she heard the sound of running feet. In a few moments, Langston sauntered round to the rig.

He cursed again as he climbed back up beside her. "He got away. Shoved past me and ran. I didn't dare risk the noise of a shot."

"Hs was lying," she said quietly.

"I know he was lying," Langston snorted. "That's one of Brady's wagons. Didn't you see his name on the side? That's why I went after it. Brady has no plans to send a wagon south."

"You mean you risked discovery just to retrieve a photography wagon?"

"It must be the one we lost last year near Ball's Bluff," he continued, paying no attention to her. "Looks a bit battered."

"Did you hear what I said?"

He stared at her. "I wasn't going to let some thief drive it away. The man tried to tell me he worked for Brady, and that was his big mistake. I know everyone on the staff."

Helena slouched back on the seat. "You're a fool," she said bitterly.

Langston grabbed her by the shoulders. "Don't call me names," he snarled.

"You put a cheap photography wagon ahead of the Confederate cause," she insisted. "Only a fool would do something that stupid."

Langston's grip tightened. "It's not cheap, not by any means. And I didn't put any one thing ahead of another. I'm a photographer, damn it. And a Confederate too. Are you compromised because I went after the wagon? Is the cause?"

"Take your hands off me!"

"Answer me first."

"I don't choose to." Helena tried to wrench away from him. "Let me go!"

Instead, Langston bent his head and crushed his lips against hers, hard and demanding. Although she continued to struggle, her lips parted under the relentless pressure of his, and, almost against her will, Helena felt a swift stab of desire. Here was a man who'd try to dominate her, one she might not be able to control. It was clear now that she'd vastly underestimated Langston Cook.

She clung to him for a brief moment, savoring his kiss, then went limp in his arms. As he shifted to regain his balance, she bit his lip and at the same time kicked him savagely in the shin. With an oath, he let her go, reaching down to clutch at his leg.

Helena smiled sweetly across at him. "When you're quite recovered, Mr. Cook," she drawled. "I'll give you the packet."

Chapter 12

"What do we do now?" Vanessa demanded. She stood beside Ancey, staring at Calhoun Preston, though in the dark she couldn't see his face. "You've managed to lose the wagon, and we're still in Washington. Did you steal it like the man said?"

Preston ignored her question. "He had a woman with him. Did you see her by any chance?"

Vanessa blinked. "I didn't see any woman."

"In the rig."

"I only saw the man, the one who claimed to be a photographer. A *real* photographer. Why did you put Brady's name on the wagon?"

Preston's voice came back harsh and low. "Everyone knows who Brady is. We'd have had no trouble in Union territory. I planned to paint over the name once we got to Reb country." He shifted impatiently. "This is wasting time. I'll need to get us some horses. Three, since you've seen fit to bring your maid."

Vanessa clenched her hands into fists. "She doesn't have anyone except me. I told you that."

"Miss Vanessa, she save me." Ancey stepped up. It was the first time she'd opened her mouth since they'd met Calhoun Preston. "I run away, and she help me. I be staying with her, wherever."

There was a tense silence.

"Well then, Ancey. I hope you can ride," Preston

said finally. "Now you'll both have to come with me while I locate the horses. This isn't the safest place for women to be at night."

"I wonder if we shouldn't just go back to the house," Vanessa whispered to Ancey as they trailed after him. "I'm not sure he'll even be able to get us out of Washington."

"You start, you best go on," Ancey replied. She hesitated a moment, then murmured, "He don't be a bad man."

No, Vanessa thought, maybe not. But selfish and inept. That was for sure.

"Ssh." Up ahead, Calhoun Preston had come to a halt. He turned back to the women, gesturing for them to keep silent. "I'm going ahead," he murmured. "You two hide in the shadows by the fence."

"Why must we hide?" Vanessa argued. "What are you going to do?" She peered at the tall picket fence that blocked their way. "Where are we?"

From inside the fence came the whicker of a horse. Vanessa wrinkled up her nose as she caught the smell of manure on the night air.

"Don't talk," Preston whispered. "It upsets them." He moved away so quietly that she couldn't hear him, and after a few moments she couldn't see him either.

Was it a stable? She didn't recall that there were any in this part of town. Anyway, this was far to big to be a . . . Wait. The army had a temporary corral near Long Bridge. Could this be where they were? Vanessa put a hand to her lips. Mr. Preston wouldn't dare try to steal army horses!

The wait seemed endless. The two women crouched in the shadows, listening to the sounds that came from the other side of the fence. They could hear the movement of horses, soft whickers, the creak of

leather. The night was cold, and soon Vanessa and Ancey were huddled together for warmth. Would Preston
never come back?

Suddenly, there was another creak of leather, but
this time it was closer. Then a hoof clattered on a
stone. Vanessa stiffened, staring into the darkness.
Gradually, she made out the dim shape of a mounted
man.

"Come on out," Preston called in a low tone. "I
got three, but I'm afraid they only had regular saddles.
You'll have to make do as best you can."

As they rode back to Maryland Avenue, Vanessa
urged her mount alongside Preston's. "Are these army
horses?" she demanded. "Did you steal them? And
how are we going to get past the sentries at Long
Bridge?"

Preston shifted uneasily in his saddle. "Yes, sort
of, and I'll manage," he replied curtly. "And those are
the last questions I'm answering tonight. Now don't
speak unless I tell you to, not until we're safe in Virginia. And then, for God's sake, don't chatter on about
stealing army horses."

Vanessa let her horse drop back. She was acutely
aware of sitting astride instead of sidesaddle, and although her skirt was voluminous enough to cover her
legs, the position embarrassed her.

"Are you all right, Ancey?" she asked nervously.
"I know it's a strange way to ride."

There was a soft chuckle from beside her. "I
never rode no other way," Ancey responded.

No, of course slaves didn't ride sidesaddle. In fact,
they often didn't use a saddle at all. Vanessa blushed.
The thing was, she didn't think of Ancey as a slave.

"I asked you not to talk," Preston hissed. With a
sharp dig of his heels, he wheeled his horse onto Mary-

herself. His men can pick her up before she does any harm.

By now Helena had forgotten all about returning to the city. What did Langston plan to do? she wondered. Did he have information about Vanessa?

"Keep your damned wagon." A strange male voice rang out. "I told you I bought it fair and square. I'm no thief! And point that blasted gun somewhere else, if you don't mind. As far as I'm concerned, you're little better than a highwayman yourself, taking my wagon at the point of a gun and frightening my wife."

Aha, whoever he is, he's lying, Helena thought. Vanessa Woodward isn't married.

There was a sudden scuffle, and Langston swore. Then she heard the sound of running feet. In a few moments, Langston sauntered round to the rig.

He cursed again as he climbed back up beside her. "He got away. Shoved past me and ran. I didn't dare risk the noise of a shot."

"Hs was lying," she said quietly.

"I know he was lying," Langston snorted. "That's one of Brady's wagons. Didn't you see his name on the side? That's why I went after it. Brady has no plans to send a wagon south."

"You mean you risked discovery just to retrieve a photography wagon?"

"It must be the one we lost last year near Ball's Bluff," he continued, paying no attention to her. "Looks a bit battered."

"Did you hear what I said?"

He stared at her. "I wasn't going to let some thief drive it away. The man tried to tell me he worked for Brady, and that was his big mistake. I know everyone on the staff."

Helena slouched back on the seat. "You're a fool," she said bitterly.

land Avenue. Ahead, by the bridge, loomed the sentry huts.

Before Vanessa knew what was happening, they'd drawn abreast of the guards. As she watched, Preston maneuvered so that he was closest to the sentry, then leaned down to hand the soldier a paper. Vanessa held her breath as the sentry squinted at the pass in the yellow light of the lanterns.

An instant later, the soldier was waving his hand. Vanessa's breath rushed out in a sigh as she urged her horse onto the bridge. Then the questions began to race through her mind. Where had Mr. Preston gotten a pass that was good for the three of them when he'd only expected two? And they'd started out posing as photographers. How could he switch their cover so quickly? Vanessa sighed again. There was no use asking him. After all, he'd told her he wouldn't answer any more questions. How arrogant he was! Now that she thought about it, she was glad that Ancey was along. With the antagonism that was already growing between Vanessa and her guide, she'd need someone to be a buffer.

The horses' hoofs rang hollowly on the planks of the bridge. It seemed to take forever to cross. Halfway over, a cloud passed over the crescent moon and Vanessa glanced up, praying that it wasn't a sign of rain. Then at last they were off the bridge and onto Virginia soil. Well, thought Vanessa, Virginia mud would be more like it. The Warrenton Turnpike was in the same state as the streets of Washington. It would be slow going for any travelers.

By dawn, the three riders were nearing Centreville. They had been challenged only once, by a Union sentry who had looked at the pass and then quickly let them go on. Nevertheless, their progress along the road was very slow, and the rhythmic cadency of the horses' hoofs was mesmerizing. Vanessa dozed in the saddle. At the sound of a voice she started, looking about in a daze.

Calhoun Preston was riding by her side. "We'll stop to eat and rest soon," he repeated.

She nodded, staring in amazement at the country-side around her. In the early dawn light, she saw shat-tered trees and the blackened ruins of houses. Off in the distance were trampled wheat fields, muddy and bleak.

Preston caught her look. "War interrupts every-one's lives," he muttered. Then, as if embarrassed by this small show of feeling, he guided his horse off the road and jumped to the ground.

In a scrawny stand of trees, he brewed tea over a small fire and handed Vanessa a ham sandwich. "We'll sleep for a few hours," he explained. "We're near the Rebel lines, and though I've heard they're pulling back, I want to wait until it's near dusk to pass through."

"Will we ride all the way to Richmond?"

Preston shook his head. "No. I'm making for the railroad station below Manassas Junction. If the trains are running, we'll ride in style to Richmond." He glanced at her, then away. "I think it's best that I say you're my wife . . . for safety and convenience."

Vanessa was amused by his discomfort. "I sup-pose you must," she said solemnly. "We don't look very much like brother and sister."

He cast her a suspicious look.

"What if the trains aren't running?" she ventured.

"Then I'll come up with another plan."

"Like stealing horses from the army?"

Preston scowled. "Look, do you want to get to Richmond or not?"

She bit her lip. "You know I do."

"Then stop questioning my methods. You paid me to get you there and get you there I will. How I do it is my business."

After they'd eaten, Vanessa and Ancey rolled themselves up in Vanessa's blankets and tried to get some rest. Vanessa was so tired that she expected to sleep as soon as he stretched out, but to her surprise she remained awake, staring up at the treetops. Calhoun Preston lay a yard away, his head propped on a deadfall, snoring slightly. Vanessa watched him through half-closed eyes. Was it because he was so near? Was that why she couldn't fall asleep? She sighed and rolled over. That was a silly notion. Mr. Preston could be trusted, at least as far as her virtue was concerned. William Thornton would hardly have recommended him if he couldn't. In any case, Ancey was lying right next to her.

"Miss Vanessa?" Ancey whispered.

Vanessa opened her eyes.

"I hear him say we go on the train."

"That's right, Ancey."

"We gonna stay on the train? Not stop and get off afore we gets to Richmond?"

"I hope not. Why?"

" 'Cause I belongs to Massa Overning, there in Rappahannock Station. His place be by the railroad track, and I sure don't want to see him no more."

Vanessa gave her a faint but reassuring smile. "With the war and all, he's probably given up on finding you. Besides, maybe he's off fighting for the Rebs."

Ancey's face took on a sullen cast. "You don't know what he like. He be looking, all right."

"Well, he can look all he wants. I won't let him take you." Vanessa spoke positively, certain that Ancey was imagining dangers that no longer existed. After all, Ancey didn't look like the same scrawny waif she'd been a year ago. It was possible that Mr. Overning might not even recognize her—except for the scars on Ancey's back. Vanessa shook her head. Even if they did meet up with him, he'd never see Ancey's back.

Ancey watched Vanessa close her eyes. "He be a mean one," she insisted. "He never give up."

When Vanessa finally fell asleep, she dreamed strange and troubling dreams. She was at a masked ball, and the dancers' gold and silver costumes glittered as they circled in a vast room. But Vanessa wasn't dancing. One by one, men approached her and dropped to one knee while she gazed at their masked faces. She shook her head, rejecting them, whereupon each found another partner and joined the dance. Then a man approached who wasn't dressed in the costly finery of the others. Instead he wore buckskins like a frontiersman. This new man didn't kneel to her or show his face. Without a word, he swept her into his arms and off to the waltz.

"No," she cried, struggling against him. "No, I didn't choose you. Let me go." She tore off his mask and stared into his face. Into Calhoun Preston's face. . . .

With a start, Vanessa opened her eyes and found herself looking at her guide.

"Time to go on," he said, turning away.

She sat up and gazed around her, still confused by her dream. A few paces off, Ancey was busy rolling up her blanket.

"Mr. Preston," Vanessa began, "I think I ought to tell you more about Ancey."

Preston flashed a wry smile. "Shall we make a pact for the rest of the journey?" he asked. "I'll be Cal and you'll be Vanessa. Only for convenience on the trip. After all, if you're to be my wife I can hardly call you Miss Woodward."

Vanessa hesitated, then shrugged. "I don't mind. But about Ancey." She took the black girl's hand and drew her close. "She escaped from her owner last year and nearly died in Washington. I found her." She paused for a moment, then hurried on. "I've told everyone she's my slave, but she's not. Her owner mistreated her terribly . . . and her back is scarred from the whip. Other things happened, too." She looked back at Ancey. "The man who did all that lives in Virginia, near Rappahannock Station. A man named Overning. We must make sure Ancey doesn't fall into his hands while we're on the way to Richmond."

Cal Preston regarded both women, hands tucked into his belt. "I told you to leave Ancey in Washington," he said brusquely. "She was safe enough there. And I can't guarantee her safety here."

Ancey turned her dark eyes to Vanessa, and Vanessa squeezed her hand. Ancey'd been so determined to come, and selfishly, Vanessa had wanted her along. Now she wished she'd forced the girl to go back to Aunt Matilda's.

"I'll watch out for you," Vanessa assured her, glaring at Preston. "Everyone will believe you're my maid, just like they did in Washington."

Preston shrugged as if it wasn't any concern of his and squinted off at the sun, now beginning to lower in the west. "We'll say we're heading to Richmond to see your sister," he explained to Vanessa. "She's been ill and needs care. I'm traveling with you, planning to join the Rebel army when we get there. We've just come from the West, from Nevada, where I've been mining silver."

"I don't know a thing about Nevada," she protested.

Preston laughed. "That's all right. Not many other people do either. But if someone asks, tell them you lived in Virginia City. Say it was nothing like the real Virginia, just dry and barren, with the wind always blowing."

"I'll try to do as you say."

Preston nodded, then frowned as something else occurred to him. "Do you have another name? Vanessa is unusual, and someone might remember that Major Woodward has a daughter named Vanessa. I don't want you to be connected with him in anybody's mind."

"My father used to call me Nessa," she offered.

Preston considered this for a moment. "Nessa it is," he pronounced. "Your maiden name was Anderson, and your sister's name is Olive."

"I think I can remember all that." Vanessa felt a shiver of excitement.

"Now about Ancey's name . . ."

"Oh, I gave her that name. I don't know what it was before." Vanessa looked inquiringly at Ancey.

"They use to call me Etta," she mumbled, her head down.

Preston grinned. "Then Ancey's as good as anything. It's best to keep names you know so you won't forget to answer to them."

"You sound like you've done this before," Vanessa remarked.

Preston avoided her gaze. "A sutler gets to know a lot of tricks. He has to if he expects to make a profit." He turned and began to saddle the horses. "We'll try to avoid the Confederate sentries by using the woods. I have a pass that I think will get us through to the railroad, but I'd rather not test it if I don't have to. Once we're on the train, we're as good as in Richmond."

* * *

They left the main road, riding through the fields and woods. The fading light cast eerie shadows, and Vanessa found herself looking nervously from side to side. Suddenly there was a scream behind her. Vanessa looked back and watched in horror as Ancey's horse reared up and threw her, bolting off into the trees.

"Cal!" Vanessa shouted. She checked her own mount and slid to the ground. She ran back to Ancey, dropping onto her knees beside her.

"What's wrong? Tell me what's wrong!" Vanessa cried.

Ancey rolled her eyes and clung to her, shuddering so violently she couldn't speak.

Before Vanessa could get anything out of her, Preston came riding up. "Couldn't catch the damn horse," he cursed. "What's the matter?"

"I don't know. Ancey can't seem to tell me."

Preston dismounted and plucked Ancey away from Vanessa. "You must tell me," he urged, his voice surprisingly gentle. "What frightened you?"

Ancey pointed to the left, keeping her face averted, and both Preston and Vanessa turned to look.

"Oh!" Vanessa drew in her breath. Among the green undergrowth, scattered bones gleamed white in the dim light. It was a skull, staring at her with empty eyes.

"Skeleton bones," Ancey quavered. "Grinning at me, gonna grab me."

"Get back on your horse." Preston jerked Vanessa to her feet.

She obeyed blindly. "But the bones . . . ?" Her voice was husky and faint.

He lifted her into the saddle and thrust Ancey up behind her. "It's a soldier from the battle of Bull Run, I'd say. The bones have been picked clean."

Ancey clutched Vanessa tightly about the waist. "Dead men can't harm anyone," Vanessa told her tremblingly.

They followed behind Preston, riding out of the woods into a long clearing. But they had gone no more than a few yards when a call rang out.

"Halloo! You there! What's all the commotion?"

Lanterns bobbed as three riders came toward them from the right. Vanessa glanced back at Preston.

"Don't run," he ordered. "They're too close. We'll have to bluff it out."

None of the three was in uniform. The leader, a heavy-set bull of a man, swung a lantern in their faces.

"Traveling late, ain't you?" he growled.

Preston nodded. "We're looking for a place to spend the night."

"Ain't much comfort for a lady in them woods." A leer spread across the man's face as he caught sight of Vanessa.

Preston shifted slightly in his saddle. "Why did you ask us to stop?" he demanded.

" 'Twas too dark to make out what color you was." The man's guffaw was echoed by his companions. "Only the one of you is nigger. I see that now." He gestured toward Ancey. "I heard the gal screaming. That's how come I rode to take a look at you." He paused, staring at the girl. "You can always tell when it's a nigger yelling."

He reached for Ancey's arm, and she shrank away. "Ain't gonna hurt you none," he cackled. "Just want to get a better look at that face."

"Don't you touch her!" Vanessa cried, turning the horse away. Clinging behind her, Ancey buried her face in Vanessa's back.

Before she could move any farther, Preston grabbed her horse's halter. "Shut up," he hissed.

The lantern light flickered on the evil smile of the man before them. "Think I'll have me a look at the nigger's back," he muttered.

"We found her," Cal said hurriedly in a loud voice. "We can split the fee. It's not fair for you to take all the money."

"Damn it, I knowed the gal was contraband." The man's grin widened.

"No!" Vanessa cried. But Preston still held her horse. With his free hand he reached over and slapped her, hard.

"We're gonna be rolling in money," the man called gleefully to his companions. "Four contrabands."

Preston yanked again at the halter of Vanessa's horse. "I want my cut." His voice was steady and cold.

Vanessa stared in disbelief from Preston to the three bounty hunters. For the first time she saw that the two men flanking the leader had pistols in their hands.

"I'm gonna be real nice to you and the lady," the man sneered, "seeing as how you didn't try to fool me. You take her and ride back the way you came like a gentleman and no one gets hurt. That's your reward." He laughed again and leaned forward, grabbing at Ancey, who screamed and clung even tighter to Vanessa.

With a jerk, Preston brought Vanessa's horse closer and pried Ancey's hands loose. Before Vanessa could think of what to do, the bounty hunter had hauled Ancey onto his horse and sat her in front of him.

Waving his hat in a salute, Preston kicked his horse into a trot, pulling Vanessa's horse back into the forest along with him. "If you say one word," he muttered to her as they jogged away, "they'll be after us. They'd as soon kill us as not—after they have their fun with you, that is."

"How could you?" she gasped, tears in her eyes.

Preston released her halter and straightened in his saddle. "To stay alive I can do almost anything."

Chapter 13

Vanessa rode alongside Cal Preston in icy silence. He seemed no more interested in speaking than she was, and so they continued for almost an hour, wordlessly making their way through the forest. Then, suddenly, the stillness gave way as Preston hurriedly reined in his horse.

"Pull up," he whispered, jumping to the ground. "There are lights ahead. Get off your horse and hold his head so he won't make any noise."

As Vanessa swung down from the saddle, she could hear the rattle of wheels and the clink of metal on metal.

"Reb soldiers," Preston muttered. "We'd better lie low until they're gone." Swiftly and silently, he tethered the horses and tossed down the blanket rolls.

Vanessa had just begun to wrap herself in her blanket when Cal spun around and pushed her to the ground. "Keep still. Someone's coming."

A few paces off, a light bobbed through the trees. As Vanessa peered out from the shadows, she heard the creak of a saddle, the jingle of metal. Then she made out the silhouette of a rider. She held her breath, squinting against the glare of the lantern he held in his hand. For a long moment, he sat there, poised and listening; then he wheeled his horse and disappeared. Gradually the thud of hoofs grew fainter and fainter.

"The Rebs have got scouts out." Preston's lips were close to her ear. "We'll stay here until I'm certain they're well past."

Although he wasn't touching her, his nearness made Vanessa nervous. Each pore of her skin seemed to be aware of him as they lay side by side in the shadows. Abruptly, she sat up and edged away.

As if he too were uneasy, Cal Preston rolled over and began fumbling with his pack. "I've been saving this for a special occasion," he whispered, "but right now will have to do."

She had no idea what he was talking about.

"Sorry I don't have glasses." There was the pop of a cork, and he handed her a bottle. "A toast to the cause."

Vanessa put the bottle to her lips and drank, choking a bit as she tasted the dry wine. But despite its bitterness, the wine was warming. Reluctantly, she took another sip before she handed the bottle back.

"What cause?" she remarked acidly, watching in disgust as he took a long swallow. "I wouldn't think a sutler who sold to both sides cared who won the war."

Preston shrugged. "To your cause, then. May you be reunited with your father."

"If I ever get to Richmond," she sighed. Then her voice hardened. "Perhaps you'll trade *me* for your safety next time."

"Would you have preferred being raped by those three louts? Before they killed you?" Preston gave a bitter laugh. "They'd still have Ancey, one way or the other."

Vanessa, shocked by his bluntness, cast about for something to say.

"Have another drink." Awkwardly he thrust the bottle into her hand.

She had a brief longing to break it over his head,

but before she could even consider such a thing, she heard a shout, far away, the words too faint to be intelligible. Vanessa eased her grip on the bottle. If they were captured by Rebel troops because of any noise she made, she might never get to Richmond. But at the same time, she knew she no longer believed anything Preston said. After all, hadn't he bragged about having a pass that would get them through the Confederate lines? She took another swallow of wine, but it failed to soothe her.

As she passed him the bottle, she thought again of Ancey. By now she realized that Preston was right, that only his quick thinking had saved her from sharing Ancey's fate. But still she detested what he'd done. And he'd made no effort to follow the bounty hunters to rescue the girl. He was so cold, so ruthless. Shivering, more from fear of him than from the cold, she pulled the blanket close about her and stretched out on the ground. In a moment, she had fallen into a troubled sleep. Tossing and turning, she dreamed that strong fingers held her in their grasp. Warm fingers, closing about her neck.

"No!" Vanessa jerked her head away. In her terror, she had shouted out the word.

Preston grasped her shoulder and spun her onto her back. "Shut up!" he muttered through his teeth. "You'll get us both captured. Is that what you want?"

"I hate you," she whispered, still half lost in the terror of her dream. "You're the most abominable person I've ever met."

He wasn't touching her, but he was there, close. As she began to come awake, her breathing quickened and the pulse in her throat pounded. Without thinking, she flung herself from him, rolling onto her hands and knees. Pushing herself from the ground, she thrust forward blindly, her hands groping to part the underbrush, not heeding the noise she made, not thinking of the direction in which she fled.

With a dull thud, she struck her shoulder against a tree trunk, then shoved herself to one side and ran on. She knew he was behind her, pursuing her through the darkness. She could hear the snap of twigs beneath his feet, and the sound drew closer with each step. Frantically, she tried to run faster. Branches flayed her face, caught in her loosened hair and stung the backs of her hands.

Gasping for breath, she staggered and fell as her foot struck a rock. Stumbling to her feet again, she stopped, poised and listening, but no sound came from behind her. Did Cal stand waiting too, waiting for her to reveal herself? She shifted slightly and a stone slid from beneath her foot, clattering against another rock. She held her breath.

There was a rustle behind her, and before she could move Preston had her in his arms, pulling her back until they fell together onto the damp leaves of the forest floor. Vanessa struggled beneath him, but it was no use. He rolled over, easily pinning her, his hands grasping her wrists, his knees straddling her body as he knelt over her.

His face was just inches from hers. "You damn little fool," he cursed. "You may hate me, but I'm the only one who can keep you alive. I won't be so forgiving next time you pull a stunt like this."

"Let me go," she gasped.

"Not until you promise to come back to the horses and stay there."

"I won't unless you promise not to touch me."

"I've absolutely no desire to."

She didn't quite believe him, but she knew she had no choice. "All right," she muttered. "I'll come back quietly. Let me go."

*   *   *

Vanessa shivered in the grey light of early dawn, rose and looked about. Cal Preston was slumped against a tree asleep, his back to her. The horses were tethered by his side.

I must get away, she told herself as she stared at him. She shivered again as she remembered what had taken place the night before. He'd threatened her, flaunted his power over her, and now the thought of what else he might be capable of doing was terrifying, more terrifying than facing the Rebels on her own.

There was no chance of reaching the horses without waking him, so she eased off in the direction they'd come from, setting her feet down carefully to make sure she made no noise. In a few minutes, she could no longer see him when she looked back through the trees, and as she got farther away she quickened her pace.

The light was strengthening, but Vanessa could see that the day would be overcast. She paused a moment and sniffed. Was that smoke she smelled on the breeze? As she moved forward, the trees suddenly thinned out and Vanessa found herself at the edge of a field of tents. She put her hand to her mouth and ducked back out of sight behind a splintered bole. Carefully, body close to the ground, she raised her head and looked again. Here and there among the tents, men in gray tended tiny fires, and now she could smell the aroma of frying bacon. She'd found the Confederate encampment.

Vanessa crawled back on her hands and knees until she was certain she was well hidden by the trees, then got to her feet and retraced her path. But she'd gone no more than ten yards when two Rebel soldiers came crashing through the bushes in front of her. They stopped and stared at her, eyes widening.

Vanessa licked her lips, took a deep breath, and blurted out the first thing she could think of. "Did you see him?" she gasped. "Did he run past you?"

"Uh, no, miss, we didn't see nobody," the taller soldier replied, eying her up and down.

"I meant my horse," Vanessa snapped imperiously. "Can't you see I've been thrown?"

"We didn't see a horse either," the shorter one added. He turned to his companion and lowered his voice, but Vanessa still heard what he said. "We best take her to camp. You know what the captain told us."

The tall soldier nodded. "You come with us, miss," he ordered. "The captain can help you."

Vanessa narrowed her eyes. She didn't like the feel of this, but she had little choice. "I certainly hope your captain can find my horse," she said scornfully. "I don't know how I'm going to get back to my cousin's without him." She brushed at her wrinkled riding costume, touched her hair, then realized for the first time that she'd forgotten her bonnet. "I suppose it's too much to expect you've found my hat?"

The captain's tent was larger than the others, large enough for two chairs and a small table. Vanessa ignored the chair that was offered to her.

"Well?" she demanded, fixing the captain with a haughty stare.

"I'm Captain Thompson," he said, sketching a bow. "May I ask your name?"

"Miss Anderson." She gestured back through the flap of the tent. "I told your men there that my horse had thrown me. But instead of helping me find him they marched me into camp. I trust you intend to do something about it."

Thompson frowned. "Miss Anderson, I'm afraid I

must ask you a few questions. Are you sure you won't have a seat?"

"No, thank you," Vanessa bristled. "I suffered some bruises in my fall, and I prefer to stand. Anyway, I don't understand why I should have to answer your questions. Back home . . . in . . ." she tried to think of a town near New Market, "in Strasburg a gentleman wouldn't think of inconveniencing a lady. As you can see, my riding habit is filthy, I've lost my hat as well as my horse, and I confess to some pain from the fall. One would think a *gentleman* might try to be accommodating." Her tone made it obvious that in her opinion Thompson didn't fit into that category.

"I beg your pardon." The captain appeared somewhat embarrassed, but his eyes remained cold. "You say your name is Miss Anderson?"

"I don't say so, that *is* my name. And I demand that you either find my horse or lend me one so I can return to my cousin's home."

Thompson clasped his hands behind his back and gave her a speculative look. "Strasburg's a long way from here," he drawled. "Over the mountains."

"I didn't say my cousin lived in Strasburg . . . I live there," Vanessa replied tartly. "If it's any of your business, and I fail to see that it is, I'm staying near Thorofare with my cousins, the Prestons. I took an early morning ride on an unfamiliar horse and he threw me. If this is all the help one receives from a Confederate officer, I swear I might better have come across a Yankee."

Captain Thompson's face flushed. "I don't mean to be discourteous," he explained. "It's just that I've received an order to stop and question any woman who seems suspicious."

Vanessa stared at him indignantly, saying nothing.

"You must admit," he continued, "it's unusual to

spine. How did a story like that get started? Then another thought flashed through her mind. If she was considered a spy, then Captain Thompson would surely think Cal was a spy as well. She bit her lip. Female spies were thrown into prison, but they hanged men who were spies. And much as she disliked Cal Preston, she knew she didn't want to see him die.

Chapter 14

"Thank God I've found you!" Cal Preston rushed toward Vanessa, brushing past the captain as though he weren't there.

Vanessa took a deep breath. "Cousin Cal," she called out, quickly and distinctly, "Thank God you're here. Captain Thompson suspects me of being a Yankee spy. I'm most upset."

Preston glared at the captain, frowned, then looked back at Vanessa. "One of the field hands discovered Achilles limping home," he said, shooting her a questioning glance. "I set out immediately to find you." He took her hands in his. "Are you hurt?"

"Not seriously. But I do declare I've been insulted."

Preston swung back to face the captain. He dropped Vanessa's hands and straightened. "Sir," he demanded, "explain yourself."

Captain Thompson's eyes were still cool, though his face was flushed. "I've been instructed to make inquiries of suspicious women," he replied stiffly.

Cal's eyes blazed. "You find my cousin a suspicious woman? If we weren't united against the damned Yankees, I swear I'd call you out."

By now Thompson was having second thoughts. "I apologize, Mr. Preston," he answered, carefully measuring his words. "I was merely carrying out orders."

"It's Major Preston. I'm on leave at the moment. Come, dear coz, I'll take you home." Preston put his arm about Vanessa and began leading her from the tent. She held her breath as they passed through the flap, but the captain did nothing to stop them.

"I rode Pericles over, so we'll have to double up going back. Really, coz, you shouldn't have chosen Achilles. He's not a woman's horse." Cal continued to scold her as they walked away from the tent.

"The stable boy did say something about that," she managed to reply, "but I didn't believe him." She gave a very convincing sigh. "You can be sure I shan't tackle Achilles again, at least not so early in the morning and alone. It's been a dreadful experience."

Vanessa had an impulse to walk faster and faster, but Preston's arm held her to a slow, steady pace. At the edge of the encampment, his horse stood waiting, tethered to a post. Vanessa started to speak, but Preston shook his head.

"Up you go, coz." Cal lifted her into the saddle, swung up behind her and urged the horse into the woods.

With their combined weight, the animal moved slowly, and Vanessa was jittery with impatience. "Will they come after us?" she whispered.

"Who knows? Don't talk just yet."

Preston directed the horse in a circuitous route among the trees, then drew to a halt. Before them, in a narrow recess between two large boulders, Vanessa saw her own horse.

At this, she could keep her silence no longer. "How did you know what to do?" she asked as Preston helped her down.

He flashed a surprisingly forgiving smile. "I followed you. In fact, I'd just about caught up when the Rebs nabbed you. I heard your tale of woe, and after that I hesitated to show up with your horse." He backed her mount out of the recess and helped her up, then swung into his own saddle. He sat there for a moment, gazing at her reflectively. "I must say, you do think fast."

"So do you." Now, in the relative safety of the forest, she was beginning to realize how foolish she'd been.

Preston shook his head and gave an exasperated sigh. "I didn't think fast enough to keep you from sneaking away this morning. Why did you?"

Vanessa hesitated. Although she still disliked him, she was now willing to grant Cal Preston a grudging measure of respect. "Well," she said slowly, "there's Ancey."

"She's a sacrifice we had to make."

Vanessa glared at him, her resolve stiffening. "No. We must get her back. I can't go on until we at least try to rescue her from the bounty hunters."

"Not even for your father?"

Vanessa bit her lip. "Not even for him," she murmured. "I couldn't live with myself otherwise."

"And that's the only reason you left?"

She glanced down. "No. But the most important."

Preston frowned. "If you're going to be running off every time I fall asleep, we may as well part company."

A few minutes ago, she'd been grateful for his help, but now she was reminded of his tyranny. On the other hand, she had to admit that she hadn't gotten very far without him. "I'll call a truce until we reach Richmond," she said softly.

He smiled one-sidedly. "An armed truce, I presume."

"But I want to find Ancey. I insist that we try."

Preston sighed. The hardness seemed to have left him, at least for the moment. "All right," he replied, "we can make a stab at it. I have to admit I'd enjoy seeing those louts get what they deserve." He began to urge his horse back through the trees, then paused. "I don't suppose you know why you were mistaken for a spy?"

Vanessa went very pale. Silently, she shook her head and kicked her horse forward.

Vanessa's stomach cramped with hunger. They had made a wide detour around the Confederate camp, but the smell of the cook fires reached them all the same. Nevertheless, pride kept her from asking Preston for something to eat. After all, it was her own fault she'd had no breakfast.

"I reckon those bounty hunters will be making for the railroad," he remarked when they were safely away from the Rebel troops. "You said Ancey's owner lived near Rappahannock Station, didn't you? By now they'll have gotten all that out of her."

"Her mistress was the one who beat her," Vanessa murmured.

Preston looked at her appraisingly. "Ah well," he said softly, "Some women are like that."

Preston avoided the main road, keeping to the woods and fields as much as possible. Vanessa was thankful he'd recovered her bonnet, for the wind was damp and cold, even though the rain held off. As the day wore on, they passed cabins where black faces peered from the cracks of partly opened doors, but they managed to avoid white folk until late afternoon, when they left a stand of pine and found an old farmer with a mule team ploughing a stubbled field. On the far side of the field, smoke rose from a log house.

The farmer stopped his mules and stood staring at them as they came across the field.

"Have you seen three men with a small group of slaves?" Preston called out.

"Might have," the old man drawled. "Might not."

"They're looking for me," Preston continued. "One of the slaves is mine. Come, tell me if you can."

The farmer gave Preston a sly look. "They get all that reward money." He spat on the ground. "Never did like them bounty hunters."

Preston shrugged and started to turn away.

"Wait a bit, there," the farmer shouted. "If you was to throw some of that money my way, I might recollect where they went."

Scowling, Cal pulled a coin from his pocket and spun it toward the farmer, who grabbed it deftly and grinned, showing the wide gaps between his yellow teeth. He pointed a dirty finger toward what looked to be a faint trail paralleling the woods at the far edge of the field. "Goes clear into Manassas," he remarked, then turned abruptly back to his plowing.

They hadn't gone very far along the trail when Preston reined in his horse and held up his hand for silence. In the quiet, Vanessa heard a faint clink of metal on metal. She frowned, puzzled, then recalled that runaway slaves were often marched back to their owners in chains. What she was hearing was the rattle of a line of slaves, all chained together.

"We won't go on," Preston said softly. "They'll have to stop soon now—they can't make Manassas before dark. There's probably a decent place for us to camp in the woods alongside the trail." He turned his horse and jumped down.

Was Ancey chained? Vanessa shook her head, trying not to imagine what such a thing must feel like. She swayed as she got off her horse, her knees weak, her head spinning. She hadn't eaten since the day before, and her legs ached from riding astraddle. She hastily dropped to the ground and leaned up against a rock.

Preston busied himself with the horses, then tossed his haversack alongside her. "I don't dare risk a fire," he explained. "We've only beef jerky left, and water to wash it down. I'd expected to be able to buy supplies by now."

The dried meat was hard to chew, but ravenous as she was, Vanessa found the taste delicious. She quickly finished her share, then rose to get her blanket, wincing as her sore muscles protested.

Eyes narrowed, Preston watched her as she stumbled back from the horses. "Too much riding for you?"

"I usually ride properly," she said coolly, "on a sidesaddle."

He gave a soft chuckle. "I always thought that was a crazy kind of contraption. I tried one once when I was a half-grown boy in Missouri, but I couldn't stay on the damned thing. My sister laughed at me for weeks. She had no trouble at all with it."

It gave Vanessa a shock to think of Cal Preston as a boy, growing up with a mother and father and a sister, just like anyone else. She could see him only as the man he was now. Wrapping the blanket around her, she sat down again, but warmth eluded her.

"I can see you're shivering," he said quietly. "If I didn't think it'd make you light out of here, I'd offer to share the blankets—we'd both be the warmer for it."

"N . . . no, thank you," she shot back, teeth chattering.

He shrugged.

A whippoorwill called, his eerie cry startling them both. Then another bird, far off in the woods, answered.

Why did n't he give her his blanket? Vanessa thought crossly. A gentleman would, even if he'd be left in the cold. Share indeed! She watched as Preston wrapped himself in his blanket and turned his back to her. A rush of tears came to her eyes, and she couldn't hold them back. She was so miserable here in this damp place, with the sun going down, night coming on. Vanessa tried unsuccessfully to stifle a sob.

"Damn it!" Preston exploded. "Don't be such a little prig. Here, we'll be sensible about this." He jerked her up, pulled her blanket off and spread it on the ground. Then he pulled her down with him and yanked the other blanket over them both. "Turn onto your side," he ordered.

Numbly, Vanessa obeyed, putting her back to him. His arms went around her as he fitted himself against her, spoon fashion. Vanessa was surprised that he felt so warm. She snuggled up against him. He was right. There was nothing wrong with being sensible, with being warm at last. Her eyes closed and she drowsed.

When she woke, dusk had settled over the woods, and for a moment she couldn't recall where she was. Then her eyes opened wider and she found herself face to face with Cal Preston, his arms holding her next to him, still fast asleep. She looked curiously at his bearded face, feeling a strange tenderness. No, no, she told herself. It wasn't possible to be attracted to a man like Cal Preston. She pulled away, but his arms tightened around her and he woke.

They stared at each other for a long moment. Then, ever so gently, his lips met hers, asking nothing, spreading a strange warmth inside her. She closed her eyes and felt the pressure of his mouth increase, felt the increasing response within her. Her arms went around his neck and she held him closer.

As they lay there, his kisses gradually grew demanding. At first, his hands pressed her to him, but then they glided over her body, brushing her breasts, caressing her thighs, gently loosening her clothing. She trembled, but not with cold, for her body was aflame. She wanted him to go on forever, kissing her, caressing her.

But then his hands were gone, and as he raised himself over her, everything changed. Suddenly, he was hurting her, and she writhed beneath him, trying to get away. But he didn't seem to understand. In an instant, he was inside her, hurting, piercing.

"No!" she cried, beating on his back with her fists. "Don't!"

He paid no heed, and suddenly the pain lessened and a delicious throbbing began. Vanessa's fists unclenched, and her hands pressed him closer as she arched her body to meet his. Now she had no sense of who she was, who he was, or where they were. Instead, she rose to a crest of sensation, higher and higher, until she could hardly breathe. She gasped for air just as Cal gave a cry, and they clung together as if they were one.

In the stillness that followed, Vanessa gradually became aware of her disheveled clothes, of Cal lying next to her, of the blanket underneath her—of all that had happened. All that she'd let happen. She covered her face with her hands, and when she look them away, Cal was gone.

When Vanessa finished rearranging her clothes, she found that there was blood on her hands. So he *had* hurt her! She took a deep breath and began pacing back and forth. She wouldn't allow herself to remember the rest, refused to recall her own part in it, her own abandon. Of all the men in the world, why had it happened with this one? It was as though a part of her was drawn to darkness, to men who were somehow dangerous. She might have come to this with Robert Jamison. Would it have been the same if she had?

When she heard Cal's footsteps, she turned her back, unsure of what to do, what to say. It had grown so dark that she could scarcely see the outline of the horses, but she didn't have to see him to know that Cal was standing close behind her. Suddenly, that strange tender feeling rose inside her again. She wanted to kiss him gently, to hold his head against her breast, to forget everything but the two of them. Holding her breath, she waited for him to speak, waited for him to tell her he felt the same way.

But when he finally spoke, his voice was filled with anger. How could she know that he was really angry with himself?

"Like the rest of Washington," he said brusquely, "I thought you were that blasted Michigander's mistress. It would have saved us both time and trouble if you'd told me you were still untouched."

Chapter 15

Vanessa sat wrapped in her blanket, listening to the sounds of the night woods. Rustlings in the underbrush, the distant bark of a fox. She had nothing to say to Cal Preston. She might never have anything to say to him.

"I'm off to reconnoiter," he announced.

She started to get up.

"No, you stay here. You can't move quietly enough."

"What if they capture you?" she snapped.

"Not a chance. I know how many of them there are, so they can't surprise me."

"It's still three against one," she insisted.

Preston gave her a sour smile. "This is your idea. Remember?"

Vanessa frowned and looked down at the ground. "That's why I want to help."

But Cal was not to be convinced. "I told you," he repeated, "I'm scouting, not attacking. I'll be back when I've learned the lay of the land."

She tried to follow his progress through the brush, holding her breath to listen, but she couldn't hear him. Far away a hound howled, was still, then howled again.

So far, she'd managed not to think of what he'd said to her about Robert, but now that she was alone, his words kept echoing through her mind. Everyone in

Washington had thought she was Robert's mistress. She closed her eyes in anguish. Aunt Matilda had warned her that she risked her reputation. How could she ever face everyone when she returned?

If she returned. She opened her eyes and smiled a grim smile. Would she go back to Washington at all? The city seemed very far away just now. As far away as the Richmond prison where her father lay ill. She nervously peered out into the forest. What was Cal doing? Had he found the camp? She knew not much time had passed, even though it seemed like hours.

She watched and waited, but still he didn't return. Finally, she rose, wrapping the blanket around her, and began to edge out into the dark. What was happening? There'd been no shots, no sounds of commotion. But where was Cal?

With a jerk, she was caught from behind. A hand grasped her arm, another was clapped over her mouth, muffling her shriek.

"It's me. I'm back," Cal whispered, letting her go.

"You almost scared me to death!" Vanessa was still trembling.

Cal's teeth flashed white in the moonlight as he grinned at her. "I was trying to show you the advantages of moving quietly. You were stamping around like a buffalo pawing up the prairie."

"Indeed!"

Cal's tone was more serious now. "Nessa," he urged, "we can't afford that much noise when you follow me back to their camp. I need you there to help while I create a diversion."

"Is Ancey all right?"

He nodded. "She's in leg irons, chained to three men, the other contrabands." He paused and looked at her very steadily. "We've got to get the keys to those irons. They're probably in one of the bounty hunters' pockets."

"How can you, without . . . without killing someone?" she ventured.

"I can't."

Vanessa swallowed. She hadn't thought about the possibility of having to kill to get Ancey back.

Cal ignored her silence. "We'll creep to the camp," he instructed, handing her a knife, "and I'll leave you near their horses. When you see a flare of light and hear an explosion, cut the horses loose and make certain they run off. If the noise hasn't frightened them enough, use a stick to get them started."

"I can do that. But the explosion . . . ?"

"A device I fashioned with gunpowder," he answered. "Once the horses stampede, be sure to hide, and fast. I want them chasing those horses, thinking they tore loose because of the scare, so try not to leave any cut ropes lying around. And whatever you do, don't show yourself until I tell you to come out."

Vanessa tried to move quietly as she followed Cal through the dark woods. He moved at a snail's pace, without a sound. It seemed as if they'd been walking for hours, but finally Vanessa smelled smoke. Then off among the trees, she caught the flicker of a fire. Cal stopped, took her hand and led her to a hollow behind a thick mat of bushes.

"Hide here afterwards," he whispered. Before she could answer, he had glided away into the forest.

Vanessa looked around and saw that the bounty hunters' horses were tethered only yards away. She held the knife in her hand, tense with nervous excitement. Beyond the horses, the small campfire flamed yellow. The men were gathered around the glow, and she could smell their coffee brewing. Then, somewhere in the shadows past the fire, she heard the clink of chains. Ancey!

"You reckon there's gonna be enough whiskey in Richmond to fill us up?" A gruff voice floated to her on the damp night air.

"I ain't gonna spend my share on rotgut," came the answer. "I know a pretty little redhaired gal who'll be whooping and hollering with joy when she sees me."

"When she sees your gold, maybe." There was a cackling laugh.

"Watch out, you bastards," called a third voice, "you're spilling the damn coffee."

Hurry up, Vanessa pleaded. Hurry up, Cal. She knew the horses were aware of her presence. She could see their ears pricked toward her, their heads turned. The nearest one shifted uneasily.

Suddenly a blast came from her left, a blinding flare of light. Debris rattled down into the trees as Vanessa lunged with her knife, darting about to avoid the rearing horses as she severed the ropes. The panicked animals galloped off through the woods and she flung herself to one side to avoid them, then scrambled to the hiding place in the hollow. She could hear shouts and curses as she thrust herself into the damp recess and pressed against the ground.

There was a muffled thud of feet hurrying past. "Shoot the goddamned bastard!" someone shouted.

On the far side of the clearing, a gun cracked. But whose? Vanessa caught her breath and listened, but there was no second shot. Something crashed through the brush nearby; then the sound grew fainter and disappeared. For a moment, she thought she heard chains clink together. Then there was nothing.

Vanessa waited and listened, but there were no footsteps, no shouts. Her calf muscles cramped, but she clenched her teeth to keep from crying out, and finally the cramp eased. If only, she thought to herself, she could will her thoughts away like that. What if Cal didn't come to her? she wondered. What if he couldn't come? What if he lay dead? She closed her eyes tightly to shut out the vision. Surely if the bounty hunters had captured him she'd have heard them coming back by now. But she didn't hear anything. Were the chained slaves lying as silent as she, listening, wondering what was happening?

Finally, Vanessa could stand it no longer. Cautiously, she inched her way out of the hollow. Slowly, carefully, she parted the bushes and looked out, but darkness was all she saw. Little by little, she eased through the brush until she was free of it, then stood and listened. Still there was nothing.

Beyond the trees in front of her, the dying campfire flickered. There was no one within its light. Had the slaves fled, chains and all? Where was Cal? And the bounty hunters? Vanessa felt for her knife, but it was gone, lost when she had rolled away from the horses.

Glancing about with every step, she crept toward the camp, determined to skirt the fire and try to find Ancey. Dodging from tree to tree, she was almost to the spot where she'd heard the rattle of chains when a deep hoarse voice rumbled from the shadows. "Look out, miss."

There was a blur of movement and an arm snaked about her neck, strangling her scream.

"Gotcha!" With a shudder, Vanessa recognized the voice. It was the leader of the bounty hunters.

Desperately, Vanessa struggled and writhed, but her captor only increased the pressure on her neck until her ears roared and she went limp. Dimly, she felt him dragging her back to the campfire. From somewhere off to the side she thought she heard Ancey cry out, call her name.

"You want her alive, you show yourself," the man holding her shouted loudly. "You got ten seconds afore she's a goner." He began to count.

Chains rattled in the brush, and Vanessa caught a glimpse of eyes gleaming in the darkness beyond the fire. The slaves. Ancey.

"Seven," the man counted, "eight, nine."

Vanessa could see the pistol in her captor's free hand. Don't come, she wanted to shout. He'll kill you. But the pressure on her throat barely allowed her to breathe.

"Ten."

"I'm here." It was Cal's voice, from the other side of the clearing.

The bounty hunter laughed. "I knew I'd flush you out. Come nearer the fire."

"So you can shoot me?" Cal sneered.

Vanessa could feel the man's muscles tighten. "I know you done for my pals," he called back, "garrotted them, you son of a bitch. I'm gonna carve up your woman real pretty 'less you come out where I can see you." He paused. "You can listen to her scream. Listen good, now."

He dropped his hand, and when Vanessa could see it again the pistol had been replaced by a knife. Her eyes went wide with fear.

Again there was the sound of rattling, and the bounty hunter chuckled. "You ain't getting free, none of you nigger bastards. I picked good stout trees to chain you to."

"Miss Vanessa!" That was Ancey's voice now, clear and high and full of fear.

"That your name, honey?" the man inquired mockingly. "Vanessa. A real lady's name." He gave a low laugh. "But you ain't gonna look like one when I get through." He raised his voice and shouted back across the clearing. "I start with her face, you hear me?"

Helpless, Vanessa watched the knife come closer and closer until the point pricked her cheek.

Ancey called again, her voice raising to a shriek. "Jonah!" she screamed. "Jonah!"

There was a tense silence, and a moment later a figure moved on the other side of the fire.

"Hold it, I'll meet your terms."

"Just show yourself, that's all I ask," the bounty hunter cried, his knife leaving Vanessa's face as he reached for the pistol. Vanessa felt a trickle of blood run down her neck.

Off to the side, there was a clank of chains, then a snapping sound. As her captor leveled his gun, Vanessa saw a movement beyond the glowing embers of the fire. She tried to jerk her body against him, but he choked her into limpness.

Suddenly, a flurry of motion erupted and shouts rang out. In an instant, Vanessa was grasped and flung aside. There was a metallic rattle, then a sound like a watermelon smashing on the ground. She could hear Cal's voice repeating her name, Ancey screaming. Hands pulled at her, lifted her, and she struck out weakly.

"No, Nessa, it's Cal. You're safe."

She sank into his arms, clinging to him as if she'd never let go.

"You get them other two like he say?" a deep voice asked.

Vanessa turned her head and saw a gigantic black man standing beside the fire.

"They're all dead," Cal answered.

The man nodded and threw a branch onto the

fire. When it flared up, Vanessa could see that he wore an iron band on his right ankle. A short length of chain trailed behind him.

There was silence for a moment, and then a whimper came out of the darkness. The black man turned and limped toward the sound. "Don't you be going on like that, Ancey," he soothed. "She be fine. Truly."

At the sound of Ancey's name, Vanessa let go of Cal, but as she looked around, she caught sight of her captor, lying next to her on the ground. With a gasp, she averted her face, gagging. His head was a bloody pulp. A bloody length of chain was still draped over one shoulder of the corpse.

"The Negro broke his chain. God knows how," Cal explained. "He saved our lives."

"I want to see Ancey." Vanessa took a few hesitant steps, then darted around the campfire.

On the other side, off in the shadows, the black giant was kneeling beside Ancey, unlocking her leg iron, murmuring to her. "Hush, you all right. Everybody fine. Old Jonah done took care of that man."

Vanessa threw her arms around Ancey. "Thank God," she cried. "Oh, thank God you're safe."

Ancey's small figure trembled against her as she hugged Vanessa with all her strength.

"They didn't hurt you, did they?" Vanessa demanded. You *are* all right?"

Ancey tried to smile. "Boss man say I be too scrawny for his taste. He say if I was a fish he'd of throwed me back. The others don't bother me much 'cause he make fun of them when they try."

Vanessa looked up as Jonah returned from unlocking the leg irons of two other men, who'd been chained to a nearby tree. With a satisfied smile, he sat down and began to take off his own shackles.

"Jonah break his chain," Ancey said proudly. "I tell him don't let nothing bad happen to Miss Vanessa, and he take the chain in his hands and he break it open and he go for . . ."

"Yes," Vanessa interrupted, "yes, I know. Jonah's a very strong man. And brave."

Ancey beamed.

Just then, Cal came up behind her. "You men are free to go anywhere you wish," he said, looking from Jonah to the other two. "We're heading south, so you won't want to travel with us."

At that, two of the men stood up and melted into the trees without another word. But Jonah made no move to join them. Instead, he looked at Ancey.

"He be going with us," Ancey said softly.

"Oh, come on, Ancey," Cal groaned. "If you and Jonah want to stay together that's your business, but you should both get out of Virginia as quick as you can. You've got to head north."

Ancey fixed him with a defiant glare. "I be staying with Miss Vanessa. And Jonah, he come with me."

Cal turned to Jonah.

"I go where she go," Jonah said firmly.

Cal stared from one to the other in frustration. Finally, he shrugged and threw up his hands in defeat. "Well, I guess we have no choice," he sighed. "I suppose we can use you to make us look more like Confederates, but you'll be in danger. You know that, don't you?"

Jonah nodded, and that was that.

"I knowed you'd come back for me," Ancey whispered to Vanessa.

While Cal and Jonah buried the chains and the bodies, the two women rummaged through the bounty hunters' belongings. They discovered enough beans and

coffee to make a meal, and as they set about preparing
it, Jonah went off in search of the runaway horses.
Half an hour later, he came limping back, leading a
single scrawny mare. It was clear that neither Cal's
horse nor Vanessa's would be able to manage Jonah's
weight, and the mare looked barely able to carry
Ancey.

Vanessa handed Jonah a plate of beans. She
looked down at his leg, then back up at his huge
scarred face. "Does your leg bother you, Jonah?" she
asked gently.

Jonah shook his head. "No, miss. It be broke a
long time ago."

"Oh, Miss Vanessa," Ancey broke in, "you got a
scratch on your cheek."

Vanessa remembered the knife and took a deep
breath. "It's nothing," she murmured, and leaned back
out of the firelight.

Beside her, Cal sat sipping a mug of coffee, staring into the flames. "I've been thinking," he said at
last. "We can't avoid the Rebs at Manassas Junction,
so what we have to do is convince them we need to get
on that train." He paused and looked steadily at the
others. "I've got some white linen in my pack that'll
make a convincing head bandage, and maybe there's
enough for a sling for my arm too."

"You'll be a wounded soldier?" Vanessa asked
nervously. "I suppose that means you plan to wear that
gray uniform we found in one of the packs."

Cal nodded. "One of the bounty hunters must
have been using it as a disguise so he could reconnoiter
around the fringes of the army—and I don't see why I
can't use it to get past the same damned army." He
took another sip of coffee, then looked back up at
Vanessa. "You'll pose as my wife," he instructed, "and
you're helping me home to Richmond to convalesce.

Jonah's my body servant. I took him with me when I joined the army. And Ancey's your maid."

Cal fixed his gaze on Ancey. "You must call your mistress 'Miss Nessa.' Can you remember that? Don't use the name Vanessa. She's Nessa Anderson Preston. Mrs. Preston."

Ancey nodded. "I can do that. I sure will do that."

"Good. He stood up and tossed the rest of the coffee into the fire. "I'll get out the linen and you, Nessa, my dear wife, can do the honors."

The four travelers had barely gotten back onto the road when they came upon a cavalry unit. As the troops cantered toward them, Cal held up his hand and called to their commander.

"I'm Cal Preston," he shouted. "I'm trying to get on a train for home. If you're going that way, I'd be grateful for an escort."

Hours later, surrounded by a mass of Confederate troops, they arrived at the railroad station. As they drew near the platform, Jonah reached up to help Cal off his horse. "Careful," Cal ordered. "Easy now." He winced as Jonah set him on his feet and offered him a makeshift crutch.

Vanessa was next, with her riding habit sponged off and her hair tied in a neat chignon. She graciously allowed Jonah to help her off her horse, then hurried to fuss over Cal. Ancey trailed after her, carrying the packs and blankets.

"I hope the regiment makes good use of the horses," Cal called out to the captain who'd ridden with them to the station. "It's the least I can offer for all your kindness."

The captain smiled and saluted. "It's our duty to help one another. It's been my pleasure."

Before there was time for any further conversation, the locomotive on the tracks ahead shot out a cloud of steam. Hurriedly Jonah helped Cal into the car, and Vanessa scurried up behind him. The passenger coach was crowded, but they were able to find seats, leaving Jonah and Ancey to crouch on the floor in the rear of the car, as slaves were expected to do.

The coach jerked forward, and the engine slowly built up steam, tooting a warning when it left the station. As the sound died away, Cal eased back in his seat and closed his eyes. "We're off to Richmond," he whispered.

Vanessa turned and smiled at him. When he reached for her hand, she let him take it. Suddenly she felt comfortable, protected. And as she relaxed, she began to realize how very tired she was. Surely it must be safe to sleep now. What could go wrong? She looked over and saw that Cal was already dozing next to her. Reassured she closed her eyes, and almost instantly she was asleep, lulled by the sway of the coach.

Vanessa came awake with a start as she was thrown violently forward. All around her, she heard roaring, the rattle of stones raining on wood. The air was filled with smoke. Where was she? Someone called her name, but she couldn't move. There seemed to be a heavy weight pressing her down. The voice kept on calling, closer now. And with a jerk the pressure eased. She felt hands lifting her.

The air cleared, and suddenly Vanessa was staring up into Ancey's frightened face, Jonah's vast bulk looming beside her. She blinked and tried to raise her head, but everything spun around.

"Rest easy a bit," Ancey urged.

The train? What had happened? Vanessa struggled to sit up. She looked around and saw that she was on the ground, surrounded by splintered wood and rubble.

"It just blew up, Miss Nessa," Ancey exclaimed. "The train."

"Cal," Vanessa murmured vaguely. "Where's Cal?"

Jonah shook his head. "Look like he dead."

Chapter 16

Vanessa knelt beside Cal's still form. Blood stained the unraveling bandage on his head and matted his hair. His face was pale and waxy, and his eyes were closed.

"Cal!" she cried, frantically shaking his arm.

He didn't move. In fact, he was so still she couldn't tell if he was even breathing. Stifling a sob, she laid her head on his chest, trying to hear a heartbeat, trying to shut out the sounds of weeping, the crackle of flames that filled the air. But it was no use. She wasn't sure if she heard a faint throb or not.

In desperation, she stood up and looked around, searching for help. Jonah had carried Cal away from the tracks to the edge of a strip of pine woods, but they were still very close to the wreck. The locomotive lay on its side, the cars splayed out behind it, smashed into kindling. The iron rails of the track were twisted askew, and everywhere fires flared in the debris.

"Yankees done blow up the train," Jonah muttered. "Kill Massa Cal."

Vanessa stared blankly down at the figure beside her. Blood seeped from a cut on Cal's head and trickled down his face. Did the dead keep bleeding? "Please," she whispered, "please," unsure whether she prayed to God or to Cal, pleading with him to live. She knelt back down and unbuttoned his coat, exposing his chest. Then she pressed her ear on his cool bare flesh, her entire being concentrated on that on point. For a moment, she couldn't hear anything. Then faintly, like a drum beating far away, there came a muffled sound.

Vanessa raised her head. "Jonah, Ancey, his heart's still beating!" But her smile of joy and relief quickly faded. How could she find a doctor? How far were they from help? Up and down the tracks was nothing but pine woods, not a single house in sight.

Vanessa hastily rebuttoned Cal's shirt, looking anxiously at his ashen face. "We have to keep him warm," she murmured. "He's so cold. We need blankets." She looked about wildly. "Watch over him, Jonah. Try to keep the bleeding from his head. Ancey and I will go find help."

Closer to the wreck, all was chaos. Men rushed back and forth beside the broken rails, cries came from under the splintered wood, and mangled bodies sprawled amidst the wreckage. A pall of dark smoke from the fires hung over everything.

"Is anyone here a doctor?" Vanessa demanded, racing from one cluster of survivors to the next. If she got an answer at all, it was the shake of a head. At last, confused and frightened, she sagged against the ruins of one of the cars.

Ancey pulled on her arm. "They's a coat on the ground over that way," she urged. "We could use it for Massa Cal."

Vanessa stumbled forward and lifted the coat, only to see the ravaged face of a dead man. Flinching, she let it go and started to turn away, then hesitated and looked about. With a grimace, she bent and snatched up the coat again, keeping her face averted from the corpse. "Take it to Jonah," she ordered, hurling it at Ancey. "Tell him to put it on Cal."

By now Vanessa realized the futility of trying to get help from any of her fellow survivors. She'd have to find food and blankets herself. She'd have to find a way to transport Cal to a doctor. But how?

She looked down and saw a briar pipe lying on the ground. She had no use for it, but the canteen a few feet beyond would come in handy. Vanessa straightened her back and hardened her heart to the task ahead. She must be a vulture, scavenging among the dead. When at last she hurried back toward Cal, she carried the canteen, a wool shawl, and a sack with half a loaf of bread and a crumbling cheese.

"I dress him in the coat like you say," Jonah told her. "He be hurt inside, 'cause he moan when I move his arms. Look like it be in the rib bones. I 'spect they broke."

As Vanessa stood staring down at Cal, a thin drizzle began to fall. "We can't stay here," she decided, glancing up at the leaden sky.

Vanessa carefully considered their situation, Ancey was dressed warmly enough, but Jonah was not so lucky. Though he'd scrounged some ill-fitting clothes from the dead bounty hunters, he had no shoes for his huge feet. Cal had the greatcoat now, but he could ill afford to be soaked by the rain. As for herself, she was all right, with only bruises and a headache. Obviously, the first thing to do was to get them all out of the rain.

"Jonah," she directed, "you carry Cal into the woods, and Ancey and I will bring everything else. We'll have to try to build a shelter."

A short time later, Jonah had managed to throw together a lean-to of pine branches. At the entrance, Ancey hovered over Cal while Jonah hunted for dry wood to start a fire. Vanessa was about to join him when she heard the sound of barking, far off in the distance.

"A dog," she cried. "And a dog means a farm." She eased past Ancey. "I'm going to find that dog."

*   *   *

When Vanessa finally got past the snarling animal, she spotted the farmer, slopping his pigs. He was as fat as they were, and his eyes squinted at her over his puffy cheeks.

"Do you have a horse and buggy? A wagon? Anything that I can hire?" she asked desperately. "I was in the train wreck. Surely you heard the noise. I need to take an injured man to a doctor."

The farmer leaned casually against the fence. "I heard it all right. Thought it was soldiers fighting. Heard the Yankees was coming."

"The train was blown off the tracks."

He clucked his tongue. "Imagine that."

Vanessa tried to curb her impatience. "That's why I need to hire transportation from you," she pleaded. "Do you have anything, anything at all, that I can use? Or buy, if you prefer."

He gaped at her.

"A buggy?" she prompted.

The farmer shook his head and gave her a stubborn glare. "I only got one mule left on account of the Army wanted the horse. Ain't gonna sell you my mule. I need him to plow."

"But I must have a way to take . . ."

"Got an old cart, though," the farmer went on. "I'll sell you that, but I don't know where you'll get an animal to pull it. Ain't nobody got horses since the army took 'em. Don't know a man hereabouts got a horse anymore."

Vanessa sighed in disappointment, absently watching the pigs root in the trough. Certainly a pig couldn't pull a cart. "You're sure you won't sell the mule?"

"Can't. It'd be like cutting my throat. Couldn't

find another mule round here for any money 'cause
they ain't none."

Vanessa frowned. Jonah was strong, she thought.
Perhaps he could pull the cart until they found a doctor. She looked back up at the farmer. "Let me see the
cart."

The farmer demanded both her gold coins, her
last two, for a rickety cart with a mended shaft. And at
the last minute he agreed to fill the cart with straw.
Vanessa managed a curt thank you before she set off,
though she felt far from grateful, knowing he'd taken
advantage of her need.

In the drizzling rain, she trudged back over the
muddy fields and into the woods, dragging the cart until she thought she'd drop from exhaustion. Finally, she
left it among the trees and went on to the shelter,
guided by the faint flicker of flames from Ancey's small
fire.

Inside the lean-to, the air was already warmer,
pleasantly scented with the fragrance of the pine. Cal's
skin didn't feel quite so cold, but he didn't open his
eyes or respond to her voice.

"Jonah," she said, sinking slowly down by the
fire, "I've brought a cart. Do you think you can pull
Cal to a doctor?"

Jonah gave her a solemn nod. "Yes, miss. Be no
trouble. Looks like I owes him."

Vanessa gazed out at the night and listened to the
rain. "Do you know the country around here?"

He shook his head. "I be from Carolina, miss.
Use to be, that is."

"Ancey?"

"No, Miss Nessa. Massa Overning, he never let
me go off the place."

Vanessa's head had begun to throb. As she

looked again at Cal, she reached out and touched his cheek. "We'll have to wait until morning," she told him, forgetting that he couldn't hear her.

Vanessa woke at dawn, but Ancey was already up. When she looked around, Jonah was nowhere to be seen.

"He be fetching the cart," Ancey explained.

Vanessa sighed. How cold the ground must be on his bare feet. She turned back to Cal, trying to trickle some water between his lips. When she was finished, Jonah had come back.

Bustling about the camp, Ancey doused the fire and gathered their meager supplies together. Then both she and Vanessa followed Jonah as he carried the unconscious man as gently as a mother holding her newborn babe, threading through the trees to the clearing where the cart lay in wait. He carefully laid Cal inside, covering all but his face with straw to keep him warm.

As they moved off, the sky was already showing patches of pale blue. Vanessa shivered in the chill morning air, but she was grateful that the weather seemed to be clearing. At first she worried about the jolting of the cart, but after a time they found a narrow, rutted road. Following it, they came to a small cluster of houses.

Vanessa stood in the road, trying to decide which one to approach. Finally, she headed for a two-story brick house set back under a pair of tall sycamores. The mistress of the house, a handsome gray-haired woman, was kindly, but there was little she could do to help.

"My son's fighting with General Johnston," she explained, "and I know how it is." She thought for a moment. "The nearest doctor is at Warrenton. I can direct you there and give you some food to carry along, but I don't have a horse to spare. I'm sorry."

*   *   *

By the time they got to Warrenton, Vanessa was
so tired she could barely stand. And her headache had
come back, throbbing hard. She was amazed that
Jonah, pulling Cal in the cart, seemed less exhausted
than she did.

Some of the other wounded from the wreck had
been brought to Warrenton, but Vanessa was almost
glad for the wait before they could see the doctor. She
was frightened now, reluctant to hear just how serious
Cal's condition might be. Perhaps she had a premoni-
tion, for when the examination was finally over, the
news that the doctor gave her wasn't good.

"He's got a skull fracture," Dr. Yancey told her.
"I don't think the bone is depressed onto the brain, but
he has a bad concussion. That means the brain is
bruised." He hesitated, then went on. "It's not a good
sign that he hasn't come around in all this time. I'm
sorry to have to tell you this, but he may never wake
up. He may just sink deeper into the coma and die.
There's not a thing anyone can do." Vanessa had begun to protest, but he put up a hand to silence her.
"He has a couple of broken ribs too. He's not moving,
so I won't bind up his chest. The ribs'll heal. The
head's another matter." He gave her a fatherly pat on
the shoulder. "Take him home and nurse him the best
you can, ma'am. That's all I can tell you."

There was a moment of silence, then he narrowed
his eyes and peered at her more closely. "Looks like
you've been hurt too," he scolded. "You've got a bad
bruise near your right temple. Does your head ache?"

"Yes." Vanessa put her hand to her forehead and
winced.

The doctor sighed. "I'd tell you to put on cold
cloths, but I know you're traveling. Just get home as
quick as you can."

Vanessa nodded, then looked up at him, a faint flush spreading across her cheeks. "I . . . I'm afraid I can't pay you," she said softly. "Our money is gone."

"I wouldn't have charged you anyway," the doctor replied gruffly. "Terrible accident. Damn the Yankees. Damn the war."

Jonah lifted Cal back into the cart. Then he and Ancey sat down by the side of the road, looking expectantly at Vanessa.

Oh dear God, she thought, what am I to do? Home. The doctor had no advice except to go home. She touched Cal's forehead. Should they go on to Richmond? But she knew no one there. Back to Washington? But could she pass through the Confederate lines with Cal, then safely cross the Union ones? She shook her head. Home had always been New Market. She knew everyone in town, and they knew her. She'd open the house. She and Ancey and Jonah could care for Cal. And the neighbors would help, she knew they would.

With a grim smile, she waved the two blacks back to the wagon. "We've got a long way to travel," she called, "but I'm taking Cal home. To my home, in the Shenandoah valley." How far was it? Sixty miles? Seventy-five miles?

"The road takes us over the Blue Ridge Mountains," she told Jonah. There was an unspoken question behind her words.

But Jonah merely shrugged and moved back between the traces of the cart. "Don't make no matter. I ain't worn down yet."

The journey was at least as bad as Vanessa had feared. The only encouraging sign was that Cal opened his eyes the first day out of Warrenton. He didn't seem to know any of them, but he took water and bits of food. Vanessa tried to tell herself he'd be better when they could let him rest in a proper bed, but it wrung her heart when he looked into her face and there was no sign of recognition.

Steadily they made their way west, bouncing along the rutted roads, fighting against the mud, shivering in the chilly spring air. And as they headed up into the mountains, the weather got even cooler. It took three days to get through Manassas Gap and down into the Shenandoah valley.

"You best look out for them Yankees," Vanessa was told by a Rebel soldier they met on the way. "They're thick to the north of here, around Winchester."

Vanessa thanked the man but continued on her way. "We're heading south, up the valley," she explained. "We'll be all right."

The weather grew milder as they descended into the valley. It was spring, and the trees showed the pale green of new leaves. Coming from Manassas Gap, Vanessa cut through the woods to avoid Front Royal. That night they made camp to the west, near Strasburg.

As Jonah lifted Cal from the cart and propped him against a tree trunk, Vanessa frowned with worry. Cal had been restless all day, and she feared he was feverish. He'd been calling out from time to time, and his skin was hot and flushed.

He took no notice of her when she knelt by his side. "I found the Indians," he murmured. "Lieutenant Thornton, there's an ambush ahead."

Vanessa stroked his brow. "Cal," she soothed, "Cal, you're safe with me."

He didn't look at her. Instead he gazed up at the

treetops, cursing under his breath. Suddenly, he tried to pull himself to his feet. "Don't give the order to ride," he shouted. "Those Comanches will massacre the troop."

Vanessa put her hands on his shoulders. "Cal," she said firmly, "you're in Virginia."

He glanced about, confused. "Indians," he muttered. "There's a sign."

"No," she answered. "There's no sign. Just rest, Cal." Even through his clothes she could feel the heat of his body.

Vanessa sat for a moment, brooding. Finally she unpicked a seam of her petticoat and took out a dose of the morphine she'd carried from Washington for her father. Gently, she coaxed Cal to swallow it, hoping she wasn't giving him too much. Within a few minutes, he'd fallen into a deep sleep.

In the morning, Cal seemed groggy as Jonah loaded him into the cart. They traveled for more than an hour before Vanessa decided it was safe to risk the road. But as soon as they did, their luck changed. They'd gone less than half a mile when Jonah said, "I hear soldiers."

Vanessa paused, making out the thud of many hoofs. She darted back to the cart and took a look at Cal, who was asleep, his face turned to one side. Jonah had piled straw all over the rest of him to keep him warm. Hurriedly, Vanessa laid a handerchief over his face and piled straw atop the cloth to cover his head.

"Yankees?" Jonah called.

"I don't know," Vanessa replied, "but I daren't take a chance with him in that grey uniform. It's too late to try to hide. Just keep moving."

They rounded a curve and saw a cavalry unit trotting toward them. Even at a distance, their blue uniforms were easy to make out.

A few moments later, Ancey dropped back from Jonah's side to walk with Vanessa. "Jonah say take this," she whispered, handing Vanessa a knife.

Vanessa thrust the weapon beneath her jacket. Surely she wouldn't need it, she told herself. She took a deep breath. If only there were a way to ask the Yankee soldiers for help. But who'd believe her story? Cal didn't seem to know where he was or what was going on around him. There was no way he could corroborate what she said, and besides, he was wearing Confederate grey. The Union soldiers might very well take him prisoner. And if they did, would they bother trying to treat his illness? Before she could decide what to do, the troop was upon them.

"Halloo the cart," an officer cried. She could see he was a lieutenant. "Where are you headed?" he demanded.

"To New Market," Vanessa answered, never slackening her pace as he drew alongside her. "I live there," she added, somewhat lamely.

"What's in your cart?"

"Straw. I ride in it when I'm tired."

The lieutenant looked from Vanessa to the cart. "Some horse you've got there," he laughed.

By now the rest of the horsemen had clattered up, eight besides the lieutenant. For a moment, they peered at her, but the lieutenant soon spurred his horse and they moved off, heading east, toward Front Royal. A scouting party, Vanessa thought. Thank God, they hadn't bothered to stop and inspect the cart.

Perhaps half an hour passed before Vanessa heard a horse behind them. When she looked over her shoulder, she saw the Union lieutenant, riding back alone. With a leering smile, he pulled up next to her and slowed the horse to a walk, keeping pace.

"I could give you a ride you'd never forget," he said in a low voice.

She glanced up at him, not understanding at first, but one look in his eyes made his meaning quite clear. She gave him a frosty glare.

He slid off his horse to walk next to her, leading the animal. "Don't be like that, honey," he pleaded. "You're a right pretty woman, the kind a man likes."

When she didn't answer, he grasped her arm. "Hey, I'm talking to you," he snapped.

She wrenched away. "I don't care for your conversation *or* your company," she replied coldly. "Please leave me alone."

Jonah kept glancing over his shoulder as he pulled the cart, and Ancey, next to him, walked sideways to watch what was going on.

"You tell your niggers to mind their own business." The lieutenant let his hand slide to the pistol in the holster at his side.

Vanessa nodded. "I can handle this," she called out, fearful now that the soldier might use his gun. Then she lowered her voice. "I understood that officers were gentlemen," she hissed.

"When we're treating with ladies, that's true," he retorted, putting his arm about her waist. "But I don't see a lady hereabouts."

"Indians."

With horror, Vanessa heard the mumbled word and realized that Cal was waking up. At any moment, he might try to sit, and the lieutenant would see him.

"What did you say?" the soldier asked. "Sounded like 'Indians.' That's a funny damn thing to say."

"I meant that Indians do things differently," she ventured, desperately summoning up a smile. She took his arm from her waist and held his hand. "Come into the woods, and I'll show you what I mean." She tugged him toward the trees, but unaccountably he hung back.

Vanessa tilted her head and lowered her lashes. "Are you afraid?" she teased. "I've heard you Yankees were bold, but I must have heard wrong."

The lieutenant colored slightly. "Hell, honey, I'm willing. I told you that."

"Then come with me. I'll show you something you'll never forget."

Leading his horse, he followed her under the trees. But when they were out of sight of the road he halted, pulling her against him. "This is far enough for what I got in mind," he announced, bringing his mouth down on hers.

Clumsily, his hands clutched at her hips, and he pushed her onto the ground, pulling up her skirts. As he shoved them above her thighs, he groped at her legs, yanking on her pantalettes. Vanessa, taken off guard by the swiftness of his attack, saw with horror that he'd already opened his trousers. She'd meant to get a jump on him and frighten him off with the knife.

With a low moan, he dropped on top of her before she could reach for it. Frantically, she grasped the sheath at her side with one hand and managed to work the knife loose as she struggled beneath his weight.

"Lie still, damn you," he cursed, trying to spread her legs.

Vanessa knew she'd have to stab him. But I can't, she cried to herself in anguish. Then suddenly he thrust at her. She tried to recoil, her throat raw with bile, but she couldn't move. Sucking in her breath, Vanessa tightened her grip on the knife, raised it, and plunged the blade into his side.

Chapter 17

The lieutenant grunted as Vanessa pulled the knife free. Then he rolled away from her, leaving a smear of blood on her hand. Pulling down her skirts, she scrambled to her feet, watching in horror as he groped for his pistol.

The roar of a cannon startled them both. Then came another cannon blast and the rattle of musket fire. While the soldier stared about, blinking, Vanessa fled into the woods, dodging among the trees, expecting at every turn to feel a bullet in her back. But the shot never came.

Gasping for breath, Vanessa paused to look over her shoulder and found that she could no longer see the lieutenant. Moving cautiously, she angled back toward the road, but the increasing roar of the artillery hid any noise she made. As she reached the fringe of the trees, she heard a clatter of hoofs, and peering through the brush, saw the troop of cavalry galloping west toward Strasburg. She couldn't tell if the lieutenant was among them. He certainly hadn't acted as if he were mortally wounded. She closed her eyes and shuddered, reliving the horrible moment when the knife had sliced into his flesh.

The cannon blasts seemed uncomfortably close now. But where were Ancey and Jonah? She had to find the cart and get them all to safety. "Ancey," she called. "Jonah." But no one answered.

In desperation, Vanessa left the shelter of the woods and walked along the road, calling first one name, then the other. Acrid smoke drifted through the trees, and each explosion seemed to come nearer and nearer.

"Miss Nessa, Miss Nessa!" Suddenly Ancey darted from the trees along the opposite side of the road. "Thank the Lord you is safe."

Then Jonah appeared, pulling the cart. In the straw, Cal's arms were flailing wildly as he shouted hoarse, unintelligible orders.

"He be fighting a battle all by his ownself," Ancey cried. "He all riled up since the guns start."

Vanessa hurried to the cart. "Cal," she soothed, trying to touch his brow. But he knocked her hand away.

"Horse," he demanded through cracked, dry lips. "Got to . . ." His words trailed off into incoherent ramblings.

Hastily, Vanessa ripped at the petticoat seam that held the morphine. "Bring the canteen, Jonah," she shouted. "Help me get this down him."

As soon as Cal had settled into an uneasy sleep, Vanessa handed Jonah Cal's knife and waved him back onto the road. "It's dangerous to be so close to the fighting," she told him, "but we can't get the cart through the woods very fast. We'll have to stick to the road and hope to find a side road before we get killed." She was surprised at the calmness of her voice.

"Seem like if we was behind the Rebs we don't have to worry none about Massa Cal," Jonah added. "We best get moving."

Vanessa nodded. "The Union forces were sup-

posed to be to the north, around Winchester," she said.
"So the Rebs must have come from the south—we'll
look for a side road heading that way." As she spoke,
she thought how strange it was that safety lay in turning away from the side she was committed to, the side
that was in the right. For the moment, though, the
Union was her enemy.

A shell burst in the air to the north, and the
smoke drifted along the road, choking them. By now,
Jonah was moving so fast, despite his limp and the
burden of the cart, that Vanessa and Ancey had to trot
to keep pace.

Vanessa tried to control her increasing panic by
reasoning with herself. The artillery must be Union, firing on attacking Rebs. If the Rebs pushed hard, the
battle would shift farther north, away from them. But
her logic had another side. After all, the battle could
just as easily go the other way. Still, New Market was
south, and south they'd head.

As the smoke cleared, Vanessa saw a church
steeple above the trees. They were nearing Strasburg.
On the outskirts of the town, a road swung off to the
south, and Jonah pulled the cart onto it, laboring up a
steep rise. At the top of the hill, as he paused to rest,
Vanessa looked back. The sounds of fighting still
echoed on the morning breeze.

Off to the northeast, she could plainly see the
battle lines, though the distance was too great to make
out blue from grey. Artillery shells burst with flashes of
flame, shaking the ground with their thunder. Between
explosions, the pop of musket fire erupted beneath
clouds of white smoke. Men and horses moved forward, then back, but at this distance they seemed un-
real, like toy men, toy animals.

"They's getting shoved back," Jonah said quietly.

Vanessa saw that what he said was true. Both

lines seemed to be moving southward. "The Rebs are
losing," she whispered.

Jonah stood up and moved back to the cart.
"Reckon we best get off this perch."

As they jolted down the other side of the rise,
Vanessa counted the days since they'd left Washington.
It was now the twenty-third of March. Would she ever
get to her father in Richmond? She certainly couldn't
leave Cal helpless, and she had to consider Ancey and
Jonah as well. She hung onto the side of the cart and
looked at Cal curled in the straw, sleeping despite the
bumpy ride. It was the morphine, no doubt. When she
touched his forehead, his skin felt like fire.

They were passing farms now, but there was no
one in the fields. Vanessa tried to ignore her hunger.
Even if they did stop to look for food, she asked herself, would the farmers open their doors with the battle
so near?

Farther along, the narrow road took a right-angle
turn, then joined a wider, macadamized road. "This is
the Valley Pike," Vanessa cried, "the road that goes
to New Market!"

She'd been down the Shenandoah valley several
times with her father, and she was sure that soon she'd
begin to recognize the countryside. Despite all her
fears, Vanessa couldn't help feeling excited. After all,
she was heading home.

Late in the afternoon, they came to a tiny community Vanessa remembered as Woodstock. By now
either they'd outdistanced the noise of the cannon or
the guns had fallen silent. Vanessa wondered if the
Rebels were in retreat, whether they'd soon be streaming up the Valley Pike. She frowned and looked down
at her dusty skirts. If she were dressed as a man, no

one, soldier or otherwise, would spare her a glance. After this morning's adventure, she knew all too well that a woman traveling on foot with two blacks drew far too much attention.

While Jonah set up camp, Vanessa and Ancey walked to the nearest farmhouse and begged the owner for food. They were almost ready to return when Vanessa turned back to the woman who'd met them at the door. "And if you'd happen to have some breeches ready for the rag bag," she added, "I could use them for the sick man in the cart. He's my husband," she explained, "wounded fighting the Yankees." Vanessa had seen enough to know that this usually melted the hardest heart.

Vanessa and Ancey returned to camp with a jar of skimmed milk, biscuits and a chunk of bacon. Vanessa also carried two threadbare pairs of trousers.

"Them be too small for Massa Cal," Ancey pointed out.

Vanessa laughed. "I'm going to wear one pair and you the other," she told her. "I'll be Cal's younger brother, bringing him home to get well—so don't call me miss. My name will be Nathan."

"Massa Nate," Ancey said tentatively.

Vanessa nodded. "And I'll call you Ance."

"Reckon there won't be no more soldiers making eyes at you," Ancey smiled.

After they'd eaten, the two women left Jonah with Cal and went off into the trees to prepare their disguises. With his knife, they riped their bodices loose from their skirts so they could be used as shirts, then left them hanging loose over their breeches. Then there was the problem of what to do with Vanessa's hair. Ancey could go bareheaded, but it was clear that Vanessa would need a cap. Hurriedly, she trimmed away most of the material on her bonnet, leaving enough to cover the knot she made of her hair, with a small brim at the front. It made an odd-looking piece of clothing, but it would just have to do.

Ancey giggled, hand over her mouth, as she stared at Vanessa. And when they both came back in sight of Jonah, he laughed a deep, rumbling laugh, rolling his eyes and shaking his head.

During the night Vanessa woke several times, but all she heard was the croaking of frogs. Then, near dawn, there came the unmistakable sounds of an army on the march. All of them but Cal had been roused by the din, and they listened without speaking as the wagons and horses clattered down the nearby road. For hours they lay there, afraid to show themselves. The sun was high above the trees by the time the last of the army had rumbled south. When Jonah had finally gotten the cart back on the road, the ragged band set off again. Very soon they came upon a farmer riding on a mule, heading north.

"You're on the heels of old Stonewall Jackson and his men," the farmer told Vanessa. "I don't doubt he'll be back to take on them Yanks again once he rests up."

As they continued south, they met very few people, and no one bothered them. Encouraged, they trudged bravely on, and by the late afternoon they'd reached the outskirts of New Market.

"We're almost there!" cried Vanessa excitedly. "Another mile and we'll be able to see the house."

Now they were passing all the old familiar landmarks: the abandoned barn, the pond, the orchard that grew the juiciest apples in the valley. Next she'd be able to see the chimneys of the brick house where she'd been born. Vanessa hurried forward, then stopped short. Where were the chimneys? She couldn't be mistaken, couldn't have forgotten. Panic-stricken, she broke into a run. Her cap fell off and her hair came undone, flying in the wind as she raced toward the spot where her home had been. Where her home should be. But it wasn't there.

Vanessa stood in the road, gasping for breath, staring at the blackened ruin of the house. "It's gone," she whispered. "Gone."

Ancey came up to stand beside her. "Look like the house burn down," she said softly.

Vanessa nodded, tears in her eyes.

Just then, a grey-haired man came out of the house across the road. Vanessa recognized her neighbor, Hamar Jones.

"You looking for something?" he called.

Vanessa faced him. She'd known Hamar Jones all her life. "Don't you recognize me?" she asked.

"I know you," he replied evenly. "And if you're looking to stay around here you can just move on."

"But I'm Vanessa Woodward!" she cried.

Jones fixed her with an icy stare. "I said I knew you, and my advice is the same. We don't want you here."

Vanessa couldn't believe what she was hearing. "What happened to my house?" she cried, turning back toward the ruins.

"We burned it. Then tore down what didn't burn." Jones spat on the ground. "Got no place in New Market for traitors. No place for their spawn, either."

"But I . . . I don't understand . . ."

"You understand, all right," Jones snarled. "Your father ran to the Yankees instead of joining up with the Confederate army. He took you with him, and you ought to have stayed where he left you. Get away now, or I'll set my dogs on you."

Jonah picked up the cart shaft and looked at Vanessa.

"Wait," Vanessa begged. "You don't understand what I . . ." Her voice faded out as he stamped back into his house, slamming the door behind him.

"We best be gone from this place," Jonah said quietly. "They done closed their hearts to you."

Ancey tugged at Vanessa's hand, and in a daze, eyes blurred with tears, she reluctantly trailed after Jonah and the cart. She was silent for a few minutes, brooding, but when she finally spoke up her voice was hopeful. "They can't all feel that way," she ventured, looking toward the large house set off the road. "You wait here and I'll . . ."

She gasped as a man stepped out from behind a huge oak by the gate. It was Mr. Koenig's overseer, a man she'd never liked, and he was carrying a musket.

"You ain't welcome here," he called out. "We got word from Hamar Jones that you was coming this way, and the mistress said you wasn't to be let through the gate."

Vanessa turned back to the road, but now her sadness had been replaced by fury. They had no right! No right to condemn her father for doing what he felt he must. Once again Ancey tugged at her hand, and she set off with the cart, fuming at the treachery of her former neighbors.

"We best make a night camp somewheres," Jonah advised. "I might try to get me some rabbits, 'cause it sure looks like you ain't gonna be lucky with food hereabouts."

"Yes," Vanessa answered absently. "All right." She followed Jonah as he turned away from the houses and headed for the forest. Morton's Woods, Vanessa said to herself absently.

As she tagged along, she tried to think of what to

do next. Jonah would lift Cal from the cart, and she'd have to look at him and see that he wasn't better—and now there was nothing she could do for him. But there *had* to be something. Vanessa clenched her fists, and once again the tears rushed into her eyes. Old Fedalia would have known just what to give Cal for the fever, just how to ease his tortured mind, but Fedalia had died three years ago. Vanessa had cried for the old black servant who'd raised her, just as she was crying now.

Angrily, Vanessa wiped her eyes. Tears solved nothing, she told herself. Fedalia was dead, but there were other free blacks like Fedalia who lived in the abandoned slave cabins in Morton's Woods, not far from where they were now. Would they hate her too?

A woman stood outside the first of the cabins, arms akimbo. Vanessa's heart sank as she recognized Tilla, the sharp-tongued wife of Gideon, the black man who'd worked for a while as her father's groom. Tilla was always cross. Nothing ever suited her.

"Miss Vanessa," Tilla said stiffly, "what you want here?"

Vanessa flushed and gave Tilla a pleading look. "May we stay for the night?"

Tilla took a few steps toward her. "What you want to bother us for?"

Vanessa bit her lip. "I've got a sick man in the cart," she said earnestly. "He needs doctoring, but I don't know how. I remembered Fedalia's concoctions and . . ."

Tilla gave Jonah a sidelong look and peered down at Cal, thrashing restlessly in the straw. She shook her head. "He don't look good."

"This is Ancey and this is Jonah," Vanessa explained. "They're . . ." She paused, unwilling to betray them as runaways. "They're my friends," she said finally, realizing that she spoke the simple truth.

Tilla looked from Jonah to Ancey, then back to Vanessa. "Reckon you can camp in the woods tonight," she said grudgingly. "But you can't stay come sunup. We don't want no trouble."

Touching Cal's hot face, Vanessa drew in her breath. "Do you know of anything I can give him?" she asked desperately.

Tilla frowned. "Old Meg might cure him, was she here. But she ain't. I don't mess with potions."

Vanessa could feel her eyes filling with tears. "Send for Meg," she begged. "Please send for her."

Tilla scowled. Without giving Vanessa an answer, she stamped back into her cabin.

By the time it grew dark, Jonah had managed to erect a simple shelter in a cleared space past the cabins, using old boards for siding and pine boughs for a roof. Inside it, Vanessa lay on straw from the cart. She smiled grimly to herself. And tonight she'd expected to sleep on her own feather bed! She didn't know where she could find the strength to face whatever lay ahead. They'd rest here tonight, but what about tomorrow? And what about Cal?

Vanessa sat up in the dark and bowed her head. "Dear God," she whispered, "he's a good man. He killed only to save others. To save Ancey, who's suffered enough. To save me and Jonah and the other two men. Don't let him die. Please, God, let Cal live."

She lay down again, but before she could even begin to doze the sound of harsh voices came echoing through the woods. As she got to her feet and peered from the shelter, Tilla came hurrying toward her, outlined by lanterns that bobbed behind her.

"You got to get," Tilla shouted. "Right now, this

minute. They's come for you. We don't want no trouble with white folks. Get our cabins burned and worse."

Then there was a man's voice, from out of the shadows. "We know you're in there with the niggers," he called. Vanessa knew it was the overseer.

With a frightened screech, Tilla ran behind the shelter, disappearing into the darkness as the men approached. There were six of them, some carrying lanterns, all carrying guns.

"We warned you," the overseer cried, closer now, so she could see his gloating smile. "Now you got to take what's coming to you."

Chapter 18

Helena Swane slipped from the officer's grasp and playfully shook her finger at him. "Absolutely not," she smiled, leaning forward and kissing him on the tip of his nose. "You've really been very naughty already. I never permit a man to spend the night here."

She pulled her robe closer, knowing full well that the emerald green silk would accent all the curves of her body. But as the major reached for her again, she quickly backed away. "My 'no' means just that," she purred. "You won't often hear it, but when you do . . ." She waved her hand in a dismissive motion, then gave him a sidelong glance. "There's always tomorrow," she added wickedly.

The major's expression darkened slightly. "You know I'm off to join General McClellan in the morning."

"All the more reason you can't spend the night here," Helena countered. "Besides, I expect you'll be back from Richmond in a few weeks, with the war won. Think how we'll celebrate!" She glided toward the door and let her hand rest on the knob. "As for now—*au revoir*."

The major took a long look at her. "Ah, you're cruel, Helena," he sighed.

She smiled again, allowing him one more kiss before she closed the door behind him. But as soon as the lock clicked into place, her smile faded. Shoulders slumped, she stood there for a moment, leaning against the door. How tiresome men could be. And the major was so disappointing as a lover. The very thought of him made her laugh.

Still, Helena reminded herself, the major had other attributes. After all, he was an aide to General George McClellan and he loved to talk, especially about the Union commander's campaign plans. And he'd given her valuable information that Langston Cook would have to take to the Rebels as soon as possible. She knew that General Johnston would also be pleased to hear that McDowell's corps of thirty-five thousand men would not be joining McClellan in the attack on Richmond. They'd been held back at the last minute, left behind to protect Washington on the orders of President Lincoln.

Reviewing all this in her mind, Helena slipped into a dark blue gown and tucked her hair up into a bonnet. There was no time to lose, and she set off almost immediately for Brady's gallery, a seven-block walk from the Willard. Langston had promised to stay there each night this week so she could bring him any news.

It was already dusk, but as Helena approached the gallery, she caught sight of Ruth O'Neill. She turned her face so the girl wouldn't notice who she was, then watched as Ruth disappeared into the twilight. What was Ruth doing at the gallery so late? Helena half smiled as she answered her own question. No doubt the poor thing was infatuated with Langston.

The door was locked, so Helena gave the prearranged signal: three rapid knocks, a pause, then two slower knocks. After a moment, she heard the key turn from the inside and the door swung open.

"I have information," she whispered, stepping quickly into the dimly lighted room. "There's no time to lose."

Langston Cook nodded, then bent to relock the door. "I told Brady I'd join O'Sullivan in the Shenandoah valley," he mentioned. "So that means I leave any time." A lock of hair trailed over his forehead, and Helena had to curb the impulse to brush it back.

Langston chuckled. "Brady wanted me to sail with him to Fort Monroe on the Virginia Peninsula. I had a devil of a time persuading him to take Woodbury and Gibson instead." Impatiently, he pushed his hair back, but it fell forward again. "I told him I'd reach Richmond ahead of him—by following General Banks down the valley."

Helena frowned. O'Sullivan, Gibson, Woodbury. Why was he bothering to tell her about his fellow photographers? Sometimes she thought Langston was too wrapped up in taking pictures. "Then you can go tonight?" she urged.

He gave her a broad smile. "Later tonight."

Damn, but he was a handsome man. And the session with McClellan's major had left Helena keyed up, restless. "I saw your pretty little receptionist leaving as I came up the street," she said coyly. "Shame on you for keeping her so late. Was it on gallery business? Or your business?"

"Do you care?"

Helena shrugged. Did he always have to be so direct?

"Who did this latest information come from?" Langston countered with a mischievous grin. "That aide of McClellan's? The one with the toothbrush mustache?"

Despite herself, Helena laughed. "The major is very proud of that mustache." With a toss of her head, she moved past Langston, gliding into the shadows of the gallery.

An instant later, she felt his hand on her shoulder, gasped as he turned her to face him.

"I hate to think of you with those cardboard soldiers," he grumbled.

Helena brushed his hand aside. "We may be seen."

"Then come into the camera room. There aren't any windows there."

She tilted her head. "Do you want me to pose again?"

Langston's voice was husky now. "Shall I tell you what I want?" He opened the inner door and ushered her through. Inside, a low-burning lamp filled the room with shadows.

"All men want the same thing," Helena replied, fixing him with a challenging stare.

Langston stared back for a moment, then swept her up into his arms and carried her to a dark corner of the room. When he laid her down, she found that she was nestling against something soft and warm.

"A buffalo rug," he whispered, kneeling down beside her.

"Should I be impressed?"

"Why don't you wait and see?" As he pulled her into his arms, his tongue flicked along her lips and slipped into her mouth. His kiss was hard, urgent with desire, and as she responded to it his hand slid down to cup her breast. Helena sighed and relaxed beneath him. She had meant to stop him after the first kiss, but now she wanted him to go on, yearned for him to assuage the hunger that was growing within her. He was an experienced lover, that was obvious, and who would ever know?

She gave a soft moan as he bent to unbutton her

bodice, baring her to the waist. In the half-light, he pushed her gently back against the fur of the buffalo robe, slowly sliding each of her garments off onto the floor, slowly caressing every inch of her as she was revealed. Finally, when she lay naked before him, he rose to his feet, his eyes on hers, and stripped away his own clothes.

Helena lowered her gaze to take in the ripple of his muscular arms, the breadth of his shoulders, his taut stomach. As she lowered it still further, her breath came faster and faster. She closed her eyes, feeling him sink down beside her, feeling him lift her over him. As he eased her down onto him, he brought her breasts to his mouth, his tongue circling each erect nipple. She quivered with anticipation, feeling his hardness inside her, not moving, only promising.

Pulling her tightly against his chest, he turned on his side, bringing her with him, then pushed her gently onto her back and drew slightly away. Before she could reach out for him, he had brought his lips to her breasts again, then let his tongue trail down her body, lower and lower until she clutched his shoulders and cried out, begging him to enter her again. When he did, she was ready and eager, moving with him as he thrust into her.

"Now. Oh, please now," she gasped.

Suddenly, he stopped moving. In a frenzy, she pummeled his back with her fists. "Damn you, damn you," she cried, thrusting her hips up against him. She heard an exultant laugh, and then he plunged deeper inside her, launching into a rapid rhythm that sent her to a shrieking climax, her fingernails digging into the warm flesh of his back.

Ruth shivered as she stood inside the alcove of a storefront directly across from the gallery. She shifted uneasily from one foot to the other, peering out into the gloom. She wasn't certain how much time had passed since she'd passed Helena Swane in the street, but she was sure it was well over an hour. Why would Langston choose to meet that woman at the gallery? she brooded. One thing was certain. It was not to take photographs. After all, Washington gossip had it that the blonde actress entertained many officers in her suite of rooms at the Willard. But why didn't Langston visit her there? It would certainly seem better suited for an affair than Mathew Brady's gallery.

Just then, a flutter of movement across the street made Ruth shrink back into the alcove. Yes, there was Helena, slipping out the door. Did she truly believe that all she had to do was conceal her face in order to go unrecognized? As she hurried down the street, her sinuous walk was every bit as distinctive as her lovely face.

Ruth waited until Helena was out of sight before she crossed the street and tried the gallery door. It was locked, as she'd expected.

Using her own key, Ruth opened the door and stepped into the room. As her eyes adjusted to the light, she smothered a shriek. There, before her, was Langston, bare to the waist, a pistol in his hand.

With an exasperated sigh, he lowered the gun. "I thought you were a thief," he growled. "What're you doing here?"

"I came to talk to you."

Langston grinned and came a bit closer. "Just to talk?"

She flushed. "I came back because I have to tell you about her . . . what I've heard about her."

"About who?"

Ruth shot him a pleading look. "Please don't play dumb. About Helena Swane. I know she was here tonight. And I know you've met her at least one other time because . . . because I followed you."

Langston scowled. "Who in hell gave you the right to follow me?"

"I took the right," Ruth retorted. "Do you know what they say about her? That she's a courtesan, that's what." She took a deep breath, then plunged on. "So why do you meet her here and in a carriage by Rock Creek when you could see her in her room as the other men do? I think she's trying to use you, Langston."

"I haven't the slightest notion what you're talking about."

"You're from Richmond. She . . . she wants to use you as a spy for the Confederates." The suspicion had been in the back of her mind, but she hadn't believed she'd be brave enough to say the words.

Langston gave a weary shake of his head. "Ruth, you practically accused *me* of being a spy when I came to work for Brady. You see spies lurking everywhere."

"But I'm almost certain Miss Swane *is* a spy. She entertains the same officials who used to see Rose Greenhow. And all those army officers . . ."

Langston smiled. "Next you'll tell me I am."

"No, no. You're like Mr. Brady," Ruth replied, coloring slightly. "I know that now. All you want to do is take photographs. You haven't got time to be a spy." She looked up at him in desperation. "But she could inveigle you into it. If you wanted to please her . . ."

Langston's smile broadened as he put his hands on her shoulders and looked down into her face. Ruth felt the warmth his nearness always gave her, but she told herself she wouldn't be swayed by it. She'd decided long ago that Langston Cook was a man any woman would be drawn to, that her feelings about him had nothing whatever to do with love.

"My dear Ruth," he murmured, "I know what your problem is. You're jealous of Helena. Admit it, you are."

"I can't deny that she's a beautiful woman," Ruth said stiffly.

"Ah, Ruth, you're just as beautiful in your own way." Langston's lips were very close to her, and the scent of his bare skin was in her nostrils.

I'll run away, she told herself, right now. But she stood as if mesmerized while his lips touched hers. And when his arms closed about her, she found herself pressing against him. No, no! a voice cried within her. This wasn't why she'd come back to the gallery.

Ruth awkwardly pulled away, but Langston followed, backing her up against the wall, his arms on either side of her. Eyes wide, she stared up at him, her breath coming in short gasps as she tried to compose herself.

"I'm flattered that you'd follow me," Langston whispered, his voice soft and caressing. "You're very appealing, Ruth, very desirable."

His hazel eyes, sometimes brown, sometimes green, glowed now with an amber light. He made her feel helpless, as though she might do anything he asked. Her lips parted and she waited like a frightened animal. He slowly brought one hand away from the wall and ran it across her breast. She shivered as a thought flashed through her mind. He's made love to Helena Swane tonight, she told herself, and now he'll make love to me. His hand on her breast seemed to burn through her clothes. As she looked down, he began to unbutton her bodice.

"No," she whimpered. "No, don't."

"You want me, Ruth," he said softly, his breath tickling her ear.

Yes, she did want him. She longed to press her

bared breasts against his naked chest, longed to feel his lips, his body. But what she wanted was a sin. Without love it *was* a sin, no priest had to tell her that. And she didn't love Langston Cook.

With a quick twist of her body she freed herself, and with one hand on her half-opened bodice, fled to the door. She clutched at the knob with her other hand.

"Don't be a goose," Langston called. "Come back."

Ruth shook her head. "I don't think you should trust Helena Swane. She's up to no good." And with that she darted out into the street.

Ruth ran the four blocks to her rooming house, her mind in a turmoil. How much of what she believed about Helena was true, how much the product of envy and jealousy? Though she'd managed not to surrender to Langston, still her heart twisted when she pictured him making love to Helena Swane.

If she went to Allan Pinkerton and told him she suspected Helena Swane was a Confederate spy, would he laugh at her? Call her a goose? Ruth thought of her brother George, now held at Libby Prison in Richmond, and then of little Michael, who'd soon be off with McClellan's Army of the Potomac, fighting his way to Richmond. What if something happened to Michael because of information sent south by Rebel spies? What if one of those spies was Helena Swane?

I'm not a goose to think of women spies, Ruth told herself. In the Old Capitol Prison there was a whole crowd of them: Mrs. Greenhow, Mrs. Phillips and her sister Miss Levy, Miss Poole, Mrs. Baxley—all accused of spying for the Rebels. Should Miss Swane be added to the roster? Ruth took a deep breath and made up her mind. I'll make an appointment to see

Mr. Pinkerton as soon as I can, she decided. Even if he laughs me out of his office.

Allan Pinkerton was a stocky, bearded man. He was about as tall as Mathew Brady, but nothing else about him reminded Ruth of her employer.

"I understand you came here with information," Pinkerton began, leaning across his desk to frown at her as though she were the spy.

Ruth blinked, then raised her chin. "I have no proof," she replied, "but I suspect that a woman by the name of Helena Swane is a Confederate spy." However, as she went on to tell him why, Ruth began to think her reasons were as flimsy as Langston had said they were.

Allan Pinkerton listened carefully as she talked, frowning all the while. When she had finished, he nodded politely and rose to his feet. "Thank you for coming in, Miss O'Neill," he said with a slight bow. Before she knew it, Ruth was out of his office, feeling distinctly foolish. She had the impression she'd been subtly advised to mind her own business.

In the days that followed, Ruth stopped tailing Langston. Even if she'd wanted to, it would have been impossible to manage. He was in and out of Washington and there was no way she could keep an eye on him. Besides, she was unusually busy at the gallery. The man who assisted in the darkroom had left to join the army, and Mr. Gardner, who managed the gallery in Mr. Brady's absence, had to call on Ruth until he could find a replacement. Thus, in addition to her other duties, Ruth now spent hours working on the plates Mr. Brady sent back from Virginia. The fighting on the Peninsula had begun, and every day there seemed to be a new selection of pictures to be printed.

*   *   *

"I'm going out for a bite to eat," Mr. Gardner called to Ruth. He stood in the doorway for a moment, a look of concern on his face. "When I come back, you can go home," he said gently. "You've been doing the work of two or three men these past few weeks. I want you to get some rest."

Ruth smiled wanly and nodded. She *was* tired, and tomorrow would be busy, with four sittings scheduled. She watched him leave, then went off to check the chemicals in the darkroom, a messy process she'd been putting off for too long. She pinned up her hair and looked around for the protective snood, then remembered it had been torn and discarded. With a shrug she picked up her hat and pinned it in place over her hair. That would just have to do, she told herself wearily.

Locking the gallery door, Ruth went into the operating room and fastened a long rubber apron over her gown. Then she walked into the darkroom, leaving the door ajar to let the smell of the chemicals escape.

As she worked, she lost herself in thought. How she wished Mr. Brady would return. In the past month, she'd overheard Mr. Gardner speak to others as though he meant to leave and open his own gallery. But how could he desert Mr. Brady? It would be a blow, she knew, for Mathew Brady considered Gardner one of his best photographers. In fact, Brady was almost as attached to Mr. Gardner as he was to Langston Cook.

Ruth raised her head as the sound of voices drifted into the room. Was it Mr. Gardner? But why would he have returned so soon? And wasn't that a woman's voice too? With a jolt, Ruth realized whose voice it was. She stood very still and listened, eyes wide.

"Are you sure she's gone?" Helena Swane demanded.

Ruth tiptoed to the door and put her eye to the crack. To her surprise, she saw that Helena wore a black wig. But who was she talking to?

As if to answer her, Langston Cook stepped into view. "Her hat's nowhere in sight, so she's not here," he replied coolly. "The gallery door was locked—we're safe enough."

"Whoever could have betrayed me to that awful little man?" Helena was pacing about the room now, her heels clicking on the parquet floor. "I'd die if they were to send me to prison."

"What exactly did Pinkerton say?"

"What difference does it make? I tell you, he knows what I've been doing." Helena's voice became shriller. "I'm not going to stay in Washington while he tries to prove it."

"Calm down," Langston ordered. "All I want to know is whether he thinks I've got anything to do with you."

Helena's laugh was short and bitter. "He didn't ask about you. Why should he? I took pains not to involve you."

There was a brief silence as Langston glanced toward the darkroom. Ruth held her breath.

"Hurry, Langston. Let's go." Helena took him by the arm, and as he looked back at her Ruth tiptoed away from the crack.

A moment later, the door pushed farther open. Behind it, Ruth was rigid with terror, afraid even to breathe.

"What's the matter?" Helena demanded.

Langston pulled the door shut. Slowly Ruth let her breath out and closed her eyes in relief.

Langston's voice came faintly through the wood. "The door was ajar. I checked inside—no one's there."

"For God's sake, come on. Are you sure we'll get past the sentries all right?"

Ruth could hear Langston's laugh, loud and clear. "In a Brady What-is-it-wagon I can get you past the entire Union army. You'll be in Richmond before Pinkerton even realizes you're gone."

Chapter 19

In the chill of the March night, Vanessa stood before the lean-to, watching in terror as the crowd of men made their way through Morton's Woods. For the first time, she knew how a runaway slave must feel. Hoping the dim light of the lanterns wouldn't show how much she was trembling, she stepped back and gestured toward the crude shelter behind her.

"I can't stop you," she cried, "but you'll have to carry my husband. He can't walk."

The men hesitated before the opening. Vanessa quickly stepped inside, but the overseer pushed in after her.

"You can't get away," he snarled.

Ignoring him, Vanessa bent and threw off the coat that covered Cal's body. "This is Major Preston," she said, glaring up at the overseer.

In the yellow light, Cal's face looked like a dead man's. He stirred as she spoke but didn't rouse.

Behind Vanessa, the other men were crowding into the small hut. There was a tense silence as they stared down at the helpless figure before them.

"He's wearing grey," someone muttered.

The overseer scowled. "Don't pay attention to that. It's a trick."

Vanessa straightened up and looked him fiercely in the eyes. "Think what you will of me, but don't

malign my husband!" she snapped. "His regiment was
in Tennessee, and he . . . he was wounded there. He
hasn't been right since. His mind . . ." She covered
her face with her hands and began to sob.

Behind her, the other men moved about uneasily.

In the stillness, the wounded man groaned and
rolled over on his side. "Lieutenant," he mumbled.
"the attack . . ."

There was a shuffling of feet, a few covert
glances. Finally, one of the men spoke up. "Look here,"
he said slowly. "We'll stop bothering you. Our quarrel
ain't with you. It's with your father."

The overseer started to protest, but another man
took his arm and pulled him out of the lean-to. The
others followed silently.

The last man paused in the entrance. He held his
hat awkwardly in his hands, looking from it to
Vanessa. "I hope the major gets well, ma'am," he said
hoarsely, glancing back at Cal. "He looks mightly
poorly."

In the days that followed, Tilla grumbled, but she
didn't insist that Vanessa leave Morton's Woods. And
when jars of milk and baskets of eggs and meat began
appearing outside the lean-to, Vanessa knew that her
white neighbors had also decided to let her live among
them in peace.

Old Meg arrived the next week. When she came
in to peer at Cal, she shook her head and disappeared,
not even stopping to talk to Vanessa. A few hours
later, she returned with a strange-smelling concoction.
Every day for a week, she dosed Cal with her brew,
and almost miraculously, in the first week in April his
fever broke. He no longer raved, no longer lost himself
in delirium shouting of Indians and ambushes. But in
place of his fever there was something almost as

frightening—amnesia. It seemed that Cal no longer remembered his past, any of it.

Cal grew stronger with every day, and by May he was able to get around without Jonah's aid. When he no longer needed her nursing, Vanessa moved out of the shelter and into another with Ancey. Now there was nothing to do but wait, and every morning when Vanessa greeted Cal she looked hopefully into his face, praying she'd see the sardonic smile she'd once thought she hated. But every morning she saw the same curiously blank stare. Even his eyes looked different. It was as though she'd nursed a stranger back to health, and Calhoun Preston had died somewhere on the road to New Market.

He called her Vanessa simply because that was what she'd told him her name was. She'd never heard him ask for Nessa. And how could he, without knowing what they'd shared? The new Cal made no attempt to touch her or caress her. Instead he was unfailingly courteous, disturbingly remote.

As Cal's strength returned, he took to spending much of the day alone, off in the woods. This troubled Vanessa, and one morning she decided to follow him. It was a lovely spring day and the air was warm. The trees were fully leafed now that May was well along, and the nearby orchards showed tiny nubbins of apples forming where the blossoms had been. In the fields beyond, the breeze rippled the newly sown corn, oats and wheat.

Vanessa heard Cal's voice before she saw him. She slowed, moving quietly under the oaks and hickories, recalling that he was the one who'd taught her to go silently through a forest.

"Calhoun Preston, Calhoun Preston." He was saying the name over and over, like a chant.

Finally, she saw him, standing beside a giant oak, striking the trunk with his closed fist as he droned out the words. She gasped as she saw blood on his hand.

"Don't, Cal, please," she cried, dashing out from her hiding place.

He turned a despairing face toward her. "What use am I to anyone? To you, to myself?"

"Give yourself time . . ."

"I've had time. All I know is what you've told me. I was taking you to Richmond, we rescued Ancey and Jonah, there was a train wreck, I was injured, you brought me here. You say I'm a sutler, loyal to the Union, masquerading as a Confederate. You say your father is a Union officer, ill in Libby Prison, and I was to help you get to him."

"Yes," she said urgently. "Yes, I've told you over and over."

His eyes blazed. "But how do I know it's true?" He grasped her shoulders. "How do I know my name is Calhoun Preston? How do I know I'm any of the things you say I am?"

His face was alive with anger and desperation. As she stared up at him, she felt the familiar breathlessness, felt the thrill of being near him. All at once, she threw her arms around his neck, brought his head down and kissed him.

After a moment's hesitation, his arms came around her. For one long moment, he returned her kiss. Then, with a violent shudder, he released her, stepping back as if in panic. "Don't you see?" he moaned. "How can I even give way to passion when I may be betraying someone? A wife, perhaps."

Vanessa swallowed. "I . . . I don't think you're married," she said softly. She'd never told him of their lovemaking; she didn't intend to tell him.

Cal's eyes were angry again. "But you don't

know," he insisted. "And if your father actually is in a Confederate prison, how do you think it makes me feel, knowing you stay with me because of a sense of duty when you long to go to him?" He leaned back against the oak. "Jonah says I raved on about Indians—Comanches—when I had the fever. But I don't remember raving, or Comanches either."

"You talked as though you'd lived in Virginia City, in Nevada," Vanessa said eagerly. "I forgot that until now. You must have been west." She gazed at him with a hope that gradually faded. The blank look in his eyes remained unchanged. Finally, she could bear it no more. Awkwardly, she turned away, blinking back her tears.

Cal's face softened. "I'm sorry I shouted at you," he said gently, reaching out to touch her arm. "I don't believe you lied to me, not really. It's just that I can't stand facing a wall I can't find a way to climb over or go around." His hand dropped from her arm. "You've cared for me, brought me back to life. I know that." He raised his face to the green canopy of leaves that shut out the sun. "Why can't I remember?"

Ancey woke Vanessa near dawn. "I hear soldiers," she said urgently. "They be marching again."

Vanessa scrambled into her patched and threadbare gown and hurried from the shelter. Off under the trees, Tilla, Gideon and some of the other blacks stood in front of their cabins, talking in low tones.

"Miss Vanessa," Tilla called when she saw her, "you best see what's going on down to the pike."

Vanessa glanced at Jonah and Cal's lean-to.

"No use looking for them—they be gone," Tilla shouted.

Vanessa gasped. Without waiting for Ancey, she took off down the path through the woods. At the end, where the trail crossed the Valley Pike, a farmer's wagon had been pulled off the road. From beyond it came the snort of horses, the tramp of hundreds of feet, the rattle of wheels. In the gray dawn a Rebel army was marching steadily down the valley toward Strasburg.

Jonah and Cal stood on the ground below the wagon, talking to the man who sat up on the box. When Vanessa reached them, she hurled herself at Cal, taking a fierce hold on his arm with both hands.

"What is it?" she cried.

Cal jerked his head toward the wagon. "This fellow's a farmer from up the valley. He says Stonewall Jackson and his men are going north to whip the Yanks."

As Cal spoke, a passing horseman, a major, glanced down at them. His gaze suddenly became intent and he wheeled off the pike to circle back. Vanessa caught her breath as his eyes fastened on Cal, who still wore the same tattered gray uniform he'd found outside Manassas.

"Soldier!" the major exclaimed.

Cal came to attention. "Yes, sir," he said briskly. Without thinking, he brought his hand up in a salute.

"You belong to this brigade?"

"No, sir."

"Where's your insignia?"

"Lost, sir. I was wounded."

The major gazed steadily at Cal. "You look pretty fit to me."

"I've recovered, sir."

"Where do you belong?"

"Missouri Eighth Cavalry." Again, the words came out without any hesitation.

The major flicked his eyes to Vanessa. "She your wife?"

There was a moment's pause. "Yes, sir."

The major scowled for a moment, then brought his horse closer to Cal. "We need every man we can get, soldier. Especially a cavalryman. Consider yourself temporarily assigned to this outfit. I'll find you a horse and a gun." He reached down and Cal took his hand. An instant later, he had sprung up onto the horse behind the major, and the two had whirled off toward the rear of the army.

Vanessa was frozen in her tracks. "No!" she cried, but by the time she started to run after them it was too late.

Jonah caught her only a few paces down the road. "Ain't no use," Miss Nessa," he said sadly, pulling her off under the trees. "Massa Cal's gone for a soldier."

Chapter 20

The feel of the horse underneath him, the heft of the gun, jolted through Cal, and he knew this was as familiar as breathing, that he'd been on a horse and handled a gun many times before. But where? Vanessa, beautiful Vanessa, whose face was a stranger's, said he was a sutler. Jonah told him he'd raved about Comanches. He recalled nothing of either.

A gaunt-faced man with a black beard rode along the side of the road, heading toward the rear, his piercing blue eyes raking over the soldiers. Cal saw the stars on the officer's collar and stiffened in his saddle. Old Stonewall himself, informally reviewing his men. The general shot a sharp glance at Cal but went on past. Had he ever seen General Jackson before? He had no idea. And why had he said Missouri Eighth Cavalry when the major asked for his regiment? The words had come to him from nowhere.

As the day wore on, Cal's cavalry troop made its way down the Valley Pike toward Strasburg, but to his surprise the greater part of the army, the foot soldiers, veered east, heading for the mountains. And General Jackson went with them.

Back on the pike, the officer who'd impressed Cal into Jackson's forces, Major Cunningham, rode beside the troop, joking with the men. "We're the foxes again," he called out, "and Banks' Yanks are the hounds." He wheeled in his saddle and flashed a dashing smile. "Don't forget our motto! He who fights and runs away, lives to fight another day!"

Cal frowned and Cunningham caught the look. "Preston, here, isn't used to being a fox," he laughed. He trotted a bit closer and lowered his voice. "We're the screen, Preston," he explained. "We make ourselves seem to be ten troops rather than one—give them a sortie from one side, ride like hell and come on them again from another quarter, then still a third. We're the foxes, leading the hounds, forcing them to concentrate on us so the wolves on foot can surprise General Banks and his army from the rear. Understand?"

"Yes, sir."

"Banks will be waiting for us at Strasburg," Major Cunningham added. Then he kicked his horse and darted forward again. "Look lively, boys," he shouted, spurring to the head of the column.

Something in Cal responded strongly to the notion of being in this advance patrol. When the man next to him motioned him to follow, he grinned his thanks and dismissed everything else from his mind. He was a cavalryman and he'd obey orders.

When Major Cunningham split the unit, Cal rode off with a squad of seven others, leaving the pike for the shelter of the woods. They were to tease the Yankees from the left while Cunningham took his group straight down the pike before dashing off to the right.

Cal threaded his horse between the trees, frowning at the crash and clatter of the cavalrymen. He should be doing this alone, should leave the horse behind and creep silently toward the camp. His eyes widened. Where had he done that?

"I hope to hell Stonewall catches the Yankees bareassed and scatters them to kingdom come," a man called out from beside him. "We damn sure need supplies, and they damn sure got a pile in Winchester."

Cal noted that the man looked as shabby as he did. His beard was ragged, his uniform dirty and torn. And the other men were no better. Cal rode a bit closer. "Winchester?" he repeated.

"That's where their main encampment's been for half a year now." The man glanced hard at Cal. "You must not have fought around these parts before."

"I didn't," Cal replied. "I was in the West."

The other rider nodded. "Well, we been up and down this valley all year. Seems like I know every tree." He raised slightly in his saddle and squinted into the distance. "We're getting close to Strasburg. Ought to hear them Union boys taking a few cracks at Cunningham."

I *was* in the West, Cal told himself excitedly. I didn't plan to say that. It came from somewhere behind the wall. But before he could pursue the thought any further, the crash of a musket rang out ahead. Then two other shots cracked in quick succession.

"There, I told you." The man beside him spurred his horse. "Come on, we'll give 'em a lick."

Cal followed the others, breaking free of the woods and mounting a rise. Twenty-five yards ahead and to their right, they spotted a troop of blue-clad horsemen. With a whoop, the men galloped forward, guns waving.

Cal's blood froze in his veins as earsplitting yells exploded all around him. Comanches! He'd ridden into an ambush! He grabbed his gun, whirling in his saddle, only to stare blankly as his companions swept past him, yelling as they rode.

Rebel yells. Not Indians. He wasn't in Texas, he was in Virginia. With Jackson's army. Fighting Yanks. Cal spurred his horse and rode after the others. What the hell was he doing? He wasn't a Reb. He was a . . . The memory faded as his horse raced unchecked toward the leveled guns of the Yankee cavalry.

"Shoot and skedaddle," one of the Rebs shouted as Cal passed him.

Giving him a quick nod, Cal pointed the muzzle of his gun into the air and fired, then wheeled his horse and raced for the woods. The others were ahead of him now, and from behind came the sound of pounding hoofs. Something whirred over his head, and he recognized the zing of a bullet. I've been shot at before, he told himself, urging the horse on. But the animal lunged ahead only for an instant. Staggering, it went down on its forelegs and collapsed.

Cal jumped free of the wounded horse, aware as he did so that he'd also had horses shot out from under him before. Somehow, the memory was more immediate than the Yanks behind him. He landed in a crouch, watching as the last of his squad disappeared into the woods. There was a sharp whine, and something hit his left arm. Cal flung himself behind the dying horse, bullets kicking up the dirt beside him.

Then a voice called out from the advancing line. "Throw down your gun, Reb, and save your life."

Cal saw that he was still clutching his musket. With a jerk, he flung it over the body of the horse.

"Stand up, hands out in front of you."

Cal slowly rose. When he saw blood dripping from his left hand, he realized numbly that he'd been wounded.

Three Yanks cautiously advanced. "Winged him, by God," one shouted.

A young lieutenant motioned for Cal to approach, and as Cal stared at his beardless face, he imagined a mustache altering the boyish features. In his mind, the face changed, the hair grew lighter . . .

"Thornton!" Cal cried. "Lieutenant Thornton!"

The officer frowned and backed off a pace. "What the hell's the matter with you, Reb? You're our prisoner. March! You're going to headquarters for questioning."

Cal blinked. No, this wasn't Lieutenant Thornton. But that's who he should be reporting to. "Take me to Lieutenant Thornton," he insisted, staring back at the officer.

"Shut your mouth! You can do your talking to General Banks. March, I said!"

Cal's mind whirled. Comanches. They were waiting, they'd attack from the rear of the column. No, not Indians. He was wrong. It wasn't Indians. He staggered, dizzy, trying to recollect what came next. The Indians would attack from the rear, falling on the troop with lances and knives and the new rifles they'd stolen from the ambushed supply train.

"He's bleeding a lot," a voice said, from very far away.

Cal saw dead men left with blood for hair, their scalps gone. "Thornton," he cried, "for God's sake, Thornton." Then blackness rushed in from all sides and overwhelmed him.

Cal opened his eyes. It was night and the lamps cast a dim yellow light against the canvas walls of the tent. A man looked down at him, a young man with a shaggy mustache. Cal saw gold braid on the shoulders of the blue coat and struggled to sit up. He had to salute the general. He fell back with a gasp, hampered by the sling that strapped one arm to his chest.

"No need to salute me, soldier," the general said gruffly.

I know his name, Cal told himself. It'll come to me. "Major Preston, at your service, sir," he offered.

The general blinked. "Major? You're not wearing any insignia."

General Banks, that was it. Cal had met him once. "Major Preston, formerly of the Missouri Eighth Cavalry," he explained. All of a sudden, the words were spilling out of him. "At present assigned to Washington with Colonel Campbell's Special Forces. Sir, I request you notify Captain Thornton in Washington that I'm here with you."

As General Banks stared at him, Cal managed to ease himself onto his right elbow. "It's urgent, sir."

"If you're who you say you are, what in hell were you doing with Jackson's cavalry?"

Memories flooded Cal's mind in such a torrent that for a moment he couldn't speak. The bounty hunters, Vanessa, Jonah, himself astride the Rebel horse, Jackson's piercing blue eyes.

"Jackson," Cal gasped. "He's tricked you. His main column isn't coming down the pike. He's circling behind you, between you and Winchester. He intends to cut you off, sir."

Banks' face darkened. "Damn the man!" he exclaimed. Then he looked at Cal very thoughtfully. "You may be lying, but I can't take the chance." He abruptly turned away and snapped out an order to someone Cal couldn't see. "Warn Colonel Kenly at Front Royal. Tell him Stonewall's wolves are about to fall on him."

"Right away, sir," a voice replied.

"Now, Major." The general returned his attention

back to Cal, but before he could speak, shouts sounded
outside the tent. Frowning, he turned his head back
toward the entrance.

Cal twisted his body so he could see past the general and watched as a captain hurried in, a disheveled
soldier at his side.

"Sir, he's from Colonel Kenly. Tell General Banks
what happened, Private."

The man gave a quick salute, then fixed a mourn-
ful gaze on the general. "Stonewall got us, sir," he said
hoarsely. "He captured the colonel and almost got all
the rest of us too. I was at the outpost nearest Strasburg or I wouldn't have escaped. He's coming on, sir."

The muscles stood out in Banks' face as he
clenched his jaw. He stood silently for a moment, gazing at the soldier, then shifted his eyes to the captain.
"Goddamn it, Jackson's forcing me to retreat. He's not
coming for us; his real target is all those supplies. Give
the order for a forced march to Winchester. We'll
evacuate immediately. If we beat him there, we can
hold our line."

Cal swung his legs over the edge of the cot and
tried to stand. His head spun, but somehow he staggered to his feet. General Banks flung him an impatient
glance. "Well, Preston, your friend in Washington will
just have to wait while we fight off Stonewall Jackson."

Early the next morning, Cal, still in his ragged
grey uniform, rode with General Banks' aides at the
head of the column hurrying up the pike to Winchester. As they jogged along, he tried to sort out everything he could remember, fearful lest there be blanks
he wasn't aware of. What did Thornton think, not
hearing from him all this time? The way he figured it,
he'd been gone over two months. And he'd expected to
have Vanessa in Richmond within two weeks at the

find a lady in the woods by the camp claiming to have lost her horse. And so early in the morning, too."

Vanessa drew herself up to her full height. "I intend to write to President Davis about the conduct of his officers," she snapped, but inwardly she'd begun to tremble. She knew that Captain Thompson didn't quite believe her story.

Thompson gave her a gently mocking smile. "Miss Anderson, I do apologize for upsetting you—if you're who and what you say you are. But I've information that a Union spy was sent into Virginia just two days ago. A woman named Vanessa Woodward. She fits your description quite closely."

Vanessa hoped the shock didn't show in her face. Her mouth went dry, and she swallowed, praying that her voice would stay calm. "I certainly never expected to be taken for a spy," she retorted. She wished now that she'd accepted a seat. Her knees felt ready to give way.

There was an awkward pause. Finally, Thompson gave a slight cough. "You understand why I'll have to ask you to stay here until inquiries can be made about your cousins," he continued. "Did you say their name was Preston?"

Before Vanessa could answer, there was a flurry of movement outside the tent. Then a voice called out. "Captain, Captain Thompson, sir. There's a man here who wants to see you, name of Preston."

Vanessa closed her eyes as the captain strode to the flap. Cal had come after her. Now he'd be brought into this and they'd both be caught. He wouldn't know her story, he might say anything. He might say that she was Vanessa Woodward. Or he might say that she was his wife. Whatever he said would prove her a liar, and then the captain would be sure she was a spy.

A spy! The word alone sent a shiver down her

most. What had happened to the plan? Had they gone ahead without him? That would mean they'd gone ahead without Vanessa, and he doubted if they could have managed such a thing.

Cal shook his head as he thought of Vanessa, alone in New Market. He couldn't leave her there, whatever the plan for Richmond might be by now. What a hell of a welcome she'd had in her home town. At least Ancey was with her. And Jonah. Between the three of them, they'd saved his life. He sighed, hoping somehow that another plan had been substituted for the one that was to have involved Vanessa.

Suddenly, a shriek split the air, then another. A volley of yells rang out, making the hair rise on the back of Cal's neck. He knew now that they were Rebels, not Comanches, but he still felt the danger. He had no weapons and his left arm hung useless at his side. He looked nervously back along the road. Banks' column was strung between Strasburg and Winchester, slowed by supply wagons and artillery. They'd have one hell of a time forming for defense.

"Pass the word," Banks ordered, wheeling his horse out of line. "Fight but keep moving. We can make it. We're fresher than Jackson is."

By now, the scattered shots had increased to a steady fire. In the distance, Cal heard shouts and curses as the Union troops tried to face an enemy who struck and ran, then struck again. The road echoed with cries of pain, the screams of wounded horses, the rattle of the guns.

In the confusion, Cal's horse was pushed off the road into a nearby thicket. Beside him was a captain from the general's staff. The two men tried desperately to still their horses as bullets flew past like swarms of bees.

Then a voice came out of the brush, terrifyingly

near. "I got me a couple trapped in here," it drawled.
The captain swung his pistol toward the sound.

"Don't be a fool," Cal whispered. "You shoot,
and we're both dead. Get off your horse and under that
bush."

"What the hell for?"

Cal motioned his companion to silence. "You
want to come out of this alive and not a prisoner?"

"Who doesn't?"

"Then get off the damn horse."

As soon as the captain was on the ground, Cal
kicked the officer's horse as hard as he could. The animal snorted and reared, then burst out of the brush.
Guns blazed, but Cal could hear the horse galloping
on.

"Don't shoot me," he shouted. "I'm coming out."
He paused, then raised his voice and bellowed again.
"Goddamned Yanks took me prisoner. I'm a Reb.
Don't shoot." He slid off his horse and leaned down to
the captain. "Tell Thornton I'll see him in Richmond,"
he whispered.

An instant later, Cal stepped out of the bushes,
leading his horse. "Where's Major Cunningham?" he
called. "I'm attached to his unit. Don't shoot. I'm a
Reb."

Out of the trees, four men on horses loomed over
him, their riders staring down in amazement.

"Looks like you can't do much good one-
handed," one of them remarked as Cal came closer.

Cal gave him a mocking grin. "A one-handed
Reb's better than two Yanks," he snorted. And with
that he climbed awkwardly into the saddle. "I got me a
Union horse out of it, anyway."

The four men laughed and trotted off after him,
back to the Rebel lines.

*   *   *

Cal saw that the fight was progressing just about as General Banks had predicted. The Union force was losing men, but it was still moving, making good the retreat into Winchester. Jackson's soldiers, tired after so much marching, didn't seem able to thrust forward with the verve they had shown the day before.

That night, Cal camped with the Rebs outside Winchester, managing to sleep despite the throbbing of his wounded arm and the occasional barrage of gunshots. But by morning he was shaking with fever, obviously unfit for battle. His horse was confiscated and he was sent to the rear with the other wounded. He was there when Jackson struck hard at Banks' troops in Winchester, and he was there when the news came in that the Union army was retreating to the northeast.

"Back to Washington," beamed a young private sitting beside him. "Old Stonewall will follow 'em to Abe's doorstep if he has to." He shifted his bandaged leg. "Wish I was going."

Soon the word came to move into Winchester, wounded and all. It was then that Cal knew that Banks had given up the fight.

Cal and the wounded private arrived in the town of Winchester to find the cavalry awash in captured supplies. Cal picked ham and brandy and dates from the mass of foodstuffs, and he and the private, who by now had identified himself as Tom, feasted until they could eat no more. As they sat by the side of the road, Cal carefully watched the Rebel forces, gradually realizing that most of Jackson's army wasn't in town, had probably gone off after Banks. And the soldiers who were left in Winchester seemed to be preoccupied with enjoying their booty.

"You're not going to fight any till that leg of yours heals," Cal told Tom as they finished the last of the brandy. "So we both might as well head back up the valley."

The young man nodded. "Ain't a bad idea," he remarked placidly. "You find a way and I'll go. I live in Staunton, and I'd like to get home to mend."

After a bit of searching, Cal came up with an abandoned wagon, then spotted a mule in a shed. Between them, he and Tom managed to hitch the mule to the wagon and set out before anyone thought to ask them any questions.

As they bounced out of town, Cal flicked the reins and headed the mule back up the pike toward Strasburg. Toward New Market. Toward Vanessa.

I can't go through with the Richmond plan, he thought desperately as he sat huddled on the wagon box, once more beginning to shiver with fever. I won't do it. But he knew he had no choice.

Chapter 21

Ruth heard the door to the operating room open and close. Langston and Helena had left. They were on their way south. Slowly, she came out of the darkroom, then eased into the gallery. It was empty.

She stood there for a moment, hesitating. She must hurry and try to catch them. No, she'd let them go, but inform Pinkerton of their plans. No, she'd let them go and not tell anyone. What should she do?

Helena Swane had admitted to being a spy. She belongs in prison, Ruth told herself. But what about Langston? Did they hang men who spied for the enemy? And was she so certain that Langston was a spy? Maybe the truth was as she'd feared—that Helena had enticed him to help her. And if that was the case, should he hang for what he'd done? She grimaced as she imagined the black hood covering Langston's handsome face.

What would Mr. Brady do if Langston was put in prison? Mr. Gardner had spoken of leaving, and where would Mr. Brady find two new photographers? Besides, he admired Langston. They had the same ideas about photography. And beyond all that, Langston was his friend.

"He's my eyes when we travel with the army," Mathew Brady had told Ruth, "just as you're my eyes in the gallery. What would I do without you both?"

She knew Mr. Brady's vision was getting worse. The blue-tinted lenses of his spectacles were thicker than they'd been before, but he still had trouble seeing. For Brady's sake, and Langston's, perhaps she should keep silent. But if she didn't give the alarm, Helena would escape unpunished.

Would Langston stay in Richmond with Helena? Ruth slowly shook her head. He was taking a Brady wagon. He'd bring the wagon back, she knew he would. And when he did, would he use it to spy for the Rebs? Not Langston. No, she couldn't believe it of him. Not Langston, who joked with Mr. Brady, who held her in his arms. No, she couldn't believe it.

I'll watch him, Ruth vowed. If I think that's what he's doing, I'll report him. But I'll give him a chance. I have to.

Langston returned to Washington with the wagon the following week, brandishing negative plates of Confederate troops. He'd taken portraits of some of their officers, including one of General Jeb Stuart, the Rebels' most daring cavalryman. Ruth kept her eye on Langston as the days passed, but she discovered no evidence of spying. He did go south twice more, but both times he returned with pictures.

Had he also acted as a courier? She couldn't be sure, and the uneasiness made her jumpy. When at last she dared to approach the subject, Langston was maddeningly noncommittal.

"I haven't seen Miss Swane in town lately," Ruth ventured. "The rumor is she fled to Richmond, that she was a Rebel spy."

Langston merely shrugged. "Talk," he replied vaguely. "She did leave, though." He eyed her narrowly, and suddenly Ruth wondered if he suspected she was the one who'd warnéd Pinkerton about Helena.

As the days passed, Ruth's doubts were buried under a deluge of work. Spring gradually gave way to summer, the worst season in Washington, a season of enervating heat and plagues of mosquitoes. From the swamps around the city, they brought the dreaded fevers that scourged the populace. Malaria was the specter that loomed over the capital.

That summer's gossip had it that Mary Lincoln was headed for insanity, unhinged by the death of her young son, Willie, in February. The President had reportedly pointed out the asylum on the hill and told her she'd end up there if she didn't get hold of herself. And Mr. Lincoln's personal tragedy was not the only trouble to be talked of in the city. At first, there had been invigorating news of Union victories as McClellan's Army of the Potomac took Yorktown and Norfolk, advancing toward Richmond. But this was followed by word of the slow retreat of McClellan's troops to Harrison's Landing on the James River. In a fury, the President reacted by splitting the army command, making Major General John Pope the head of a new force, the Army of Virginia. Then, on July eleventh, Lincoln named Major General Henry Halleck chief of all the armies of the United States.

Soon thereafter, Mathew Brady returned to Washington. He printed his plates of the Peninsula fighting in Virginia and mounted them on cards for the stereoscopic viewer. These were an immediate success, and crowds poured into the gallery to buy them. Brady was jubilant, but he was also eager to get back to the fighting. In the West, the Union armies were faring better. They had already driven the Rebels from Missouri, western Tennessee, northern Alabama and Mississippi, and they had occupied New Orleans and Memphis.

Anxious to cover all the action, Brady increased his staff until by August he had thirty-five bases of operation with the armies in the field.

"You're spending almost every cent you take in," Ruth warned him.

Brady waved his hand dismissively. "The war views we bring back will show a profit, I'm convinced of it."

Ruth gave him a weary smile. "And *I'm* convinced you'd find a way to take the pictures whether anyone bought them or not."

Brady chuckled. "Quite a difference from our two little wagons at Bull Run, eh Ruth? Now every soldier recognizes my What-is-it-wagons. Why, they even crowd around, asking to have their pictures taken!"

Ruth had a guilty vision of Langston Cook taking Helena Swane through the lines, hidden in a Brady wagon. She'd told no one, and she couldn't bring herself to tell Mr. Brady now. "We've done nothing but lose battles in Virginia since August began," she replied, changing the subject. "Yet you never seem to care."

Brady frowned slightly and shook his head. "It's the recording of what happens that really matters," he said solemnly. "I don't fight battles, I take photographs."

"But the death." Ruth shuddered to think of what he must have seen.

Brady nodded and took her arm. "The dead are ghastly sights, my dear. But my pictures will show the horror of war to everyone. I make people face the reality of war. And that's a very important job."

PART III

FALL 1862

Chapter 22

"Thank you, sir." Jeremy Valerian saluted smartly, then turned on his heel and strode from General Lee's headquarters, blinking as he came out into the light of the crisp September day. Major Valerian. He savored the sound of the words. From lieutenant to major in eighteen months. And he'd earned it, too. Not that he'd fought for the rank. No, he was proud of the promotions, but he'd fought for the Confederate cause first, last and always.

Jeremy hadn't really expected the war to go on so long, but now that they were winning, pushing the Yankees north again, it might be over soon. He knew that Rosalie waited in Charleston for his return. Both his family and hers looked forward to their marriage, and somehow, he'd never had the heart to tell her he wouldn't marry her.

Would Ruth meet him at the Willard in Washington after the South's victory? Jeremy sighed and shook his head. How could he expect a pretty girl like Ruth to wait so long? Surely she must have forgotten him. And even if she hadn't, wouldn't she hate him now that the war had become such a long, bitter struggle? Despite all that, he couldn't get her out of his mind. And Rosalie, with all her charm, seemed faded and artificial beside her. He'd never forget his night with Ruth at West Point. Did she still think of him?

Remember him? But marriage to Ruth couldn't work. His family, Rosalie . . .

Jeremy swung into the saddle and guided his horse toward his troop's encampment. The men would cheer his promotion, and that would ease his troubled mind at least for the moment. He believed he loved every one of them, all these brave and loyal soldiers he led into battle. Each man who was killed left an ache in his heart, and just days ago, he'd lost ten men at the second battle of Bull Run.

Yet they'd won the battle. That was what counted. They'd finished up August with a great victory over the Yankee General Pope, a poor excuse for a commander, not a worthy opponent for a man like Robert E. Lee. With Lee heading the Army of Northern Virginia, they were bound to win the war. And soon.

Jeremy had scarcely dismounted before his men crowded around him.

"Hell, they've sent us some strange major from headquarters," one shouted. There was a chorus of laughter.

"Three cheers and a tiger for the new major." The cry went up and was swiftly carried throughout the camp.

When the uproar died down a bit, Sergeant Yancey, who'd been with Jeremy since the beginning, motioned for silence. "I hear we're moving in a day or two," he shouted. "Heading north into Maryland."

Jeremy nodded. "I know we're moving out," he said, looking at the expectant faces around him. "I'll be briefed on where in the morning."

That night around the campfires, the men started

up a tune that Jeremy knew but hadn't heard them sing before.

> The tyrant's heel is on thy shore
> Maryland, my Maryland . . .

The citizens of Maryland would surely welcome Lee's forces with open arms, Jeremy told himself. He was certain they'd be headed there. He'd heard the rumors too, and Yancey's hunches were never wrong. Lee would send Jackson to capture Harper's Ferry while the rest of the army marched through Maryland to Pennsylvania, cutting the North off from the West. Then they'd be on to Washington!

The morning's briefing proved the rumor correct. Lee's Army of Northern Virginia moved out, and on September fourth they crossed the Potomac River into Maryland, looking forward to cheering crowds, new recruits and much-needed supplies.

Jeremy rode at the head of his troops, seeing the silent watchers, the hostile eyes as the Confederates passed through the little country towns. Not all Tarheels, it seemed, were Rebs. To the rear of his cavalry marched soldiers who were ragged, some even barefoot. All were in desperate need of decent food, but it was beginning to look as if they wouldn't find it on the far side of the Potomac.

By the time they reached the town of Frederick, there wasn't one Rebel soldier who didn't realize that Marylanders wished them any place on earth but in their state. What had happened to all the loyal secessionists who were supposed to live here? After Frederick, the army bands stopped playing "Maryland, My Maryland." Instead, they struck up "Dixie" as they headed west toward South Mountain. Over the ridge, they'd be out of sight, and then the Yankees would have to guess where they were going.

Unbeknownst to Jeremy or even to Lee himself, on September thirteenth, as the Union army slowly and cautiously followed the Rebels, a Yankee private named John Bloss casually picked up a discarded envelope from the grass beside the road. Inside was a paper wrapped around two cigars. When Private Bloss unrolled it, he stared thunderstruck at the message he found written there. In his hands he held a copy of Lee's Order Number 191, containing the general's plans for his army during the next four days.

Private Bloss ran shouting to his commander, and within the hour McClellan knew exactly where the Confederates were headed. Generals Robert E. Lee and James Longstreet were near Hagerstown with nine brigades. General A. P. Hill had five more brigades at Boonsboro, twelve miles south. The rest of Lee's army, in three separate columns, was marching on Harper's Ferry under Jackson.

"If I don't crush Bobby Lee now," McClellan exulted, "I may just as well go home."

The next day, McClellan's Army of the Potomac advanced on the South Mountain passes. Thanks to the reconnoitering of Jeb Stuart's cavalry, the Confederates now knew that their cover had been blown.

"They'll cut off Jackson," General Lee told his assembled commanders. "We'll have to make a stand at the passes."

Longstreet's hand left his curly black beard and tapped at the map. "Forget South Mountain. We can't hold it. If we fall back to Sharpsburg, we have a chance."

Lee shook his head. "We'll hold the mountain."

*   *   *

Jeremy, who'd accompanied Longstreet to the meeting, was sent with his cavalry to Turner's Gap. As they rode to scout the terrain, he and his men spotted the Confederate infantry, already in place. Trotting to the edge of the forest, they pulled up behind a row of sharpshooters who lay on their stomachs behind a low rock shelf, guns ready. Suddenly there was a flash of movement. Flushed from its hole by the horses, a rabbit jumped on the back of the first man and ran down the entire row from back to back before disappearing into a thicket. It came and went so quickly that none of the men even had time to turn.

"Call yourselves marksmen," one of the cavalry called. "Ten to one, and you let the rabbit outsmart you."

Their laughter was cut short by an explosion a few hundred feet short of their position. The first shells had begun to whistle in from the Union artillery below.

The big guns continued for nearly an hour, and when they finally fell silent, the first wave of Yankees came swarming up the hillside. Muskets cracked and bluecoats fell, but the advance never faltered. In moments, a Yankee cavalry unit had swept up the hill.

Jeremy dashed out from among the trees, waving his men forward, spurring his horse as his troops galloped down the slope. In an instant, the horsemen had closed, a blur of firing pistols and slashing sabers. Jeremy ducked away from a wild swing, then thrust forward and gutted his opponent. As he wheeled about, he caught a glimpse of the first wave of the Union infantry. They were coming up very quickly, and it would be suicide to be trapped between them and the Rebel lines.

Jeremy dug his spurs into his horse and shouted above the din. "Back, men," he called. "Follow me."

* * *

Once they were safely among the trees, Jeremy ordered his men to dismount. They left behind one soldier for every four horses; the rest quickly loaded their muskets and ran to reinforce the infantry. As Jeremy's men hurried back to the lines, a horde of Rebel infantrymen slammed into the enemy, firing as they rushed down the hill. Within minutes, the Union artillery had begun shelling again, the boom of the cannon like a drumbeat accenting the lighter musket fire. All across the hillside, smoke rose and dispersed in the brisk September breeze.

Jeremy held the maple grove for an hour, but it was clear that the enemy was simply too strong. As the Union lines advanced, Jeremy and his men were forced to remount and fall back to avoid being cut off. Higher up the hill, they were preparing to make another stand when a rider raced up with orders from General Longstreet. Jeremy was to take his men six miles south to Crampton's Gap to plug a hole in Rebel lines.

"Three men down," Sergeant Yancey shouted as they rode off. "Magruder, Knowles and Richardson. Magruder wasn't killed."

Jeremy noticed a patch of crusted blood on Yancey's upper arm. He jerked his head toward the wound.

"That?" Yancey laughed. "Don't worry, I did for him. He won't scratch another Rebel mother's son."

At dusk the fighting slowed, gradually trickling off to an occasional burst of musket fire. Then, as night closed in, the word went down the Rebel lines. "Don't make camp. Stand by for orders."

When Jeremy returned from Lee's headquarters, his face was grim. "The army's taking up a new position at Sharpsburg," he told Yancey. "We march tonight." Wearily he swung back up into his saddle. "Have the men ready to move," he ordered. "We're to advance."

The morning was shrouded in mist, but as the sun rose higher the fog thinned. Ahead of him, Jeremy saw that the road crossed a stream. "Antietam Creek," he muttered to himself, remembering from the maps that the stream ran west of Sharpsburg. Along the hills on the opposite side, he could see Lee's army forming a battle line.

Just then, the last of his scouts came clattering up the road. "The Yanks are behind us," the man cried. "A long ways back. Sure are a lot of them, though."

After Jeremy had hurried his cavalry across the bridge, he went off alone to report to General Longstreet, who was directing the placement of his artillery. But Jeremy was not the only one looking for Longstreet. As Jeremy spotted him, he saw General Lee approaching.

"Put them all in," Lee shouted. "Every gun you have, long and short range."

As he waited for the generals to finish making their plans, Jeremy tried to calculate just how many men were spread across the hills. Maybe eighteen thousand, allowing for yesterday's casualties. How many men did General McClellan have? Somewhere over fifty thousand; and Jeremy hated to think about how many more could easily be brought from Washington.

Soon the first of the Union army could be seen on the heights to the east of Antietam Creek, and not much later, artillery shells began to explode on the hillside below. The artillery would try to do as much damage as possible, and then the troops would advance. Jeremy gripped the reins tightly and waited.

Afternoon faded into evening, and the attack never came. All day the shells had burst around the Rebel positions, but as night closed in the Union cannons fell silent. What would happen next, Jeremy wondered. Would they fight tomorrow or would they pull back and cross the Potomac into Virginia? What would he do if he were Lee? He was as brave as the next man, but it was obvious that the Confederates were fearfully outnumbered.

As Jeremy rode to Longstreet's tent, he heard a shout.

"He's done it! Old Stonewall's done it again!"

Jeremy's heart leaped and he hurried up to hear the news.

"Jackson took the whole damn garrison at Harper's Ferry," a colonel was bellowing. "At least ten thousand prisoners plus all the garrison's arms. Artillery and rifles, he's got, and he's marching to join us!"

It was more than ten miles from Harper's Ferry to Sharpsburg. Would Jackson make it in time? His men were known as the fastest marchers in the army, but they'd just fought a battle and they were sure to be exhausted. There was still a very good chance that the Yankees would attack before Jackson could bring up the extra men and supplies.

In the morning, a thick fog blanketed the valley along the creek, stretching all the way up to the hills. The heavy mist also hid the Union troops. Alert and tense, Jeremy waited for the first shots, but not a single cannon fired. Finally, around noon, the fog thinned, but by then Jackson's men had begun to file into the encampment.

Stonewall Jackson himself rode up later in the afternoon, just as the Union artillery began to boom. We must have close to thirty thousand men now, Jeremy exulted. Better odds, much better. And Hill's division was still to come from Harper's Ferry.

Near sundown, Jeremy heard sporadic rifle fire to the north, but it died away almost as quickly as it had begun. Why hadn't McClellan attacked in force? He'd wasted a day and a half. The Union general was known to be a slow, methodical man, but this time his caution had cost him dearly.

As the bivouac fires blossomed among the tents, a steady drizzle began to fall. Jeremy heard none of the usual joking as the men heated and ate their rations. No banjos were plucked, and the songs that echoed around the campfires were the slow laments of men who knew they faced a battle.

> Many are the hearts that are weary tonight
> Wishing for the war to cease;
> Many are the hearts looking for the right,
> To see the dawn of peace.
> Tenting tonight, tenting tonight,
> Tenting on the old camp ground.

Jeremy couldn't sleep. He tossed and turned, brooding about what tomorrow might hold in store. Now that Jackson's men had brought him back to strength, Lee would go after the Yanks. But would Lee win? Even with Jackson on the field, the Yanks were still stronger. Jeremy shook his head. The Rebels had been outnumbered before and beaten the Yankees back. They could do it again.

He closed his eyes, but sleep continued to elude him. A melody threaded through his mind, one the men often sang.

> Dearest one, do you remember
> When we last did meet?

Ruth's face came before him, her tumbling black curls, her shy smile, the wonder in her eyes when he first kissed her.

> When you told me how you loved me,
> Kneeling at my feet.

Ruth was the one he remembered, the only woman he'd ever loved.

> Weeping sad and lonely.
> Sighs and tears, how vain.
> When this cruel war is over,
> Praying then to meet again.

Jeremy was up before dawn, rousing his men in the misty drizzle. As he readied his cavalry, he heard the heavy boom of the artillery. A brigade commander, Colonel Gordon, came riding up.

"You're with General Hill today?" he shouted.

Jeremy nodded.

"You're to be the back-up, then. He wants you held in reserve."

Muskets began to pop to the north as Jeremy watched Gordon's men march off. Just then, the sun broke through, and in minutes the mist had vanished. Impatiently, Jeremy paced back and forth, waiting for the order to move up. He could hear the crash of shells, the continuous rattle of musket fire, but neither was close enough to put his men in any danger. From his sheltered position behind a small rise, the battle was invisible.

"Waiting's worse than fighting any day," Yancey grumbled.

Frowning, Jeremy glanced up at the sun to see how much time had passed, then stood gaping at the sky, unable to believe what he saw.

Yancey followed his gaze. "A goddamned pink balloon," he gasped. "I see it, but I don't believe it."

"It's no observation balloon, that's for sure."

They stared up at the gaily striped pink and white balloon, which looked more suited to a country fair than a battlefield. Yancey raised his musket, took aim, then lowered the gun.

"Too high," he remarked, vainly trying to suppress a smile. "Anyway, it's just too damn pretty to shoot at."

The balloon, pushed by a brisk wind, passed overhead and grew smaller. Finally it was only a speck on the horizon.

Jeremy was so intent on following the balloon's progress that he didn't notice the courier until he was almost upon them. It was a young corporal, his face grimy with powder. "Colonel Gordon needs you," he cried. "He wants your cavalry dismounted to fight. Follow me."

Jeremy swung into the saddle and gave the order to advance, his men following on foot. As soon as they'd crested the hill, he saw the smoke of the muskets ahead, giant clouds hanging over the skirmishing. Following the corporal, he hurried his men along a lane, past cornfields that had been slashed to stubble.

Moving even faster now, the corporal skirted a few columns of Confederates who were marching toward a white building that looked like a church. As musket fire rattled from all sides, he led Jeremy and his men across the Hagerstown Turnpike, down a nar-

row road past two cannon, then through a smashed
fence.

The corporal frantically waved them forward.

"Down in there."

At first, all Jeremy could see were distant lines of
bluecoat soldiers. They were advancing, flags flying,
directly toward him. Then he saw a sunken road down
below. In it, the Confederate troops waited, guns aimed
and ready, while the Yanks came on with fixed bayonets.

Jeremy had his men take cover as best they could,
a short distance behind the road. When he turned
back, the Yanks were still coming. Why they didn't
fire? he asked himself. Why were they trying to
dislodge Gordon's men with bayonets instead of bullets?

Gordon waited until the first rank was only rods
away, then called out the order to fire. As the rattle of
shots broke out, the line of bluecoats went down, every
last man, and their commander's horse was shot out
from under him. Behind them, the other Union lines
fell back, reformed, then came on again. Jeremy
watched in disbelief as the Yankee commander led another bayonet charge, this time on foot. Were they out
of ammunition? Again, the line fell under the withering
Rebel fire.

Jeremy checked his men and saw some of them
glancing apprehensively to their right. Beyond them, he
could see a column of Yankees marching to flank the
Confederate position. He looked back at the blue line
beyond the ditch and saw, with amazement, the begin-
nings of yet another Union bayonet charge. There was
no time to lose.

"Face the right flank, men," Jeremy shouted.
"We'll stop those damn Yankees."

Sword held high, he spurred his horse, his men

racing after him. The din of the battlefield swept over them, the sound of muskets in front, Rebel yells from behind. Suddenly Jeremy's horse screamed and reared up. It toppled to the ground so quickly that Jeremy barely managed to avoid being pinned underneath. He leaped to his feet, sword gone, and looked up to see a Yankee officer bearing down on him, pistol in hand. Jeremy desperately flung himself sideways, rolling toward the sunken road. He felt himself falling, heard the roar of a musket, then slammed into someone.

"You damn near spoiled my aim." A Rebel soldier gave Jeremy a wry smile as they untangled themselves. He peered out of the ditch. "Got the bastard, though."

All along the road, Gordon's men were firing, and the whir of bullets overhead told Jeremy that the Yankees had finally gone for their guns. Just beside him, a dead soldier lay slouched against the ditch. Crouching, Jeremy picked up the dead man's gun and took his ammunition. As he was loading up, a corporal hurried toward him.

"Colonel Gordon's been evacuated to the rear," he shouted. "He's hurt bad. Looks like you're the ranking officer, sir."

Jeremy glanced back over the ditch. The Yanks were coming on again, a seemingly endless wave of them. He dashed up and down his own line. All along the road, Rebel soldiers lay dead and wounded. It was obvious that those who could still fire simply couldn't hold out much longer. Just then, a deadly hail of bullets rained down from along the ditch rather than from above. The Yankee troops were coming at them from the side.

Jeremy raced along the ditch. "Retreat," he shouted, pulling up those who could still stand. "We haven't a chance down here. There's a farm to our rear. Make for it."

Jeremy was the last man out. As he clawed his way over the top, he felt something slam into his right leg. Rolling out onto the bank, he tried to stand, but it was no use. The bullet had broken the bone. He crawled doggedly away, gritting his teeth against the pain, but after a few yards, his head began to spin, and his entire body felt strangely light. Bullets kicked up the dirt beside him.

Then a voice came out of the din, a familiar voice.

"Goddamn, Major, I been looking all over hell for you." Yancey's face swam hazily before him. "I'll have you out of here in two shakes."

With the sergeant's strong arm helping him, Jeremy managed to hop on his good leg until they were out of range of the enemy rifle fire. Only then would Yancey let him sit down to rest.

"You saved my life, Yancey," Jeremy gasped, tears in his eyes.

Yancey shrugged. "You'd do the same for me."

Before Jeremy could reply, a hideous whine split the air. He and Yancey froze as a shell crashed to the ground beside them, unexploded. For an instant they watched in horror as it spun crazily in the dirt, hissing like a copperhead.

"Move!" Jeremy screamed. "Run, Yancey!"

But the sergeant reached down to help him up. A moment later, a vast roaring explosion filled Jeremy's ears. He felt himself thrown through the air, felt the heat searing his eyes, his brain. And then he felt nothing more.

Chapter 23

Mathew Brady stood in a Maryland field beside a young man who wore a Union officer's uniform. Both gazed curiously at the mass of ropes and fabric in front of them. They watched in awe as the limp cloth on the ground slowly began to rise, to take on shape.

"Marvelous!" the young man remarked. He spoke with a faint German accent. "Pardon, that I address you when you do not know me," he added, bowing slightly to Brady. "I am Ferdinand von Zeppelin."

Count von Zeppelin, Brady had been told. He liked the young man for not mentioning his title. "I'm Mathew Brady, the photographer," he replied.

"Ah, I have heard of Mathew Brady. Even in Germany we know of your magnificent daguerreotypes."

"I do mostly paper prints now, from wet plate negatives."

"Of the war, yes. I was told." Von Zeppelin nodded at the rising mass before them. "What do you think of this balloon?"

Brady smiled. "I'd like to go up in it. I've seen them used as observation posts in Virginia, tethered to the ground by ropes." Brady looked past the filling balloon into the sky. "What scenes I could photograph!"

"This, I believe, is not what you call the observation balloon," von Zeppelin said dryly.

By now, the gaudy pink and white stripes showed clearly on the varnished silk material. Brady smiled and shook his head.

"I spoke to Professor Lowe, who is a creator of balloons," von Zeppelin continued. "He explained the principle very simply. The silk is a thin envelope to hold the hydrogen gas. And hydrogen, being lighter than air, causes the envelope to lift from the ground."

The striped balloon, now more than half-filled with hydrogen, continued to rise, gradually revealing the passenger basket that lay on the ground beneath it.

"I met Professor Lowe in Virginia. Is he here?" Brady glanced about.

"No, no. This one is not his."

They were silent for a time, watching while the balloon expanded until it was almost full.

Suddenly, a voice shouted from near the gasometer, and the men who'd been tugging at the ropes stood very still.

"Enough," the voice cried again. "Stop. You'll put in too much." A tall thin man rose from his crouch by the gas line. "Hold those ropes," he shouted. "Don't a single one of you let loose."

Von Zeppelin stepped forward. "Pardon, you are Professor Robertson?"

The man nodded.

"My friend and I, we would like to go up in your balloon with you. General McClellan thinks I might observe something of use."

Robertson glanced around, expecting to see another soldier.

"He is Mathew Brady, the photographer," von Zeppelin explained. "No doubt he will take a picture of your marvelous balloon in exchange for the privilege." Von Zeppelin winked at Brady.

Brady blinked, then gave Robertson a sheepish

grin. "Would it be possible to take a camera up with us?" he asked. "I understand you plan to float over the armies fighting near Sharpsburg."

Professor Robertson eyed the two men. "I can take you both, yes, but the camera is another matter. Would you be prepared to toss it over the side of the basket, Mr. Brady, if circumstances required?"

"Throw out my camera when we're up in the air?" Brady was astonished at the mere thought. "No, of course not."

Robertson frowned and shook his head. "You see," he explained, "weight is all-important. Camera equipment is very heavy, isn't it? I could rise with it, but once we're aloft, all weight is ballast and subject to being jettisoned."

"Including Mr. Brady and myself?" von Zeppelin asked with a wry smile.

Robertson laughed. "I've never yet thrown out a passenger."

"In that case," von Zeppelin replied, "I take a chance on becoming an aeronaut, even if we are shot down by the Rebels."

Robertson clapped him on the back. "We'll be safe enough," he declared. "Come aboard, if you wish." At that, Robertson climbed into the basket, quickly followed by Brady and von Zeppelin.

"I'm removing ballast," Robertson called to the ground crew. "Let me know when she tugs to get away." He loosened the sand bags that were attached to the rigging and began to toss them to the ground one at a time.

"I feel her wanting to go," a man called.

"Let's try her for lift, then. Ease me up."

As the eight men holding the ropes let the balloon slowly rise, Robertson threw off three more sandbags. "She feels right," he shouted. "Drop to a two-man hold. Good. Easy now! You last two let go to the count of three. Ready? One. Two. Three!"

The men released the ropes and the balloon went soaring up, carrying the basket with it. Astonished, Brady stared down at the ground and shook his head to clear his vision. Perhaps it was his glasses, he thought. The ground seemed to be leaving him rather than he leaving the ground. He waved at Gibson, standing beside the What-is-it-wagon, gaping up at him.

Robertson threw off the unattached ropes and began letting down a rope that was toggled onto a hoop above the basket. "The trail rope," he explained. "We use it as ballast when we come down close enough for it to trail on the ground. It helps us to control our landing, to slow us."

"Why not fill the balloon full of hydrogen?" von Zeppelin asked. "I overheard you tell them to stop before it had filled."

"Gas expands in the lighter air as we go higher." Robertson pointed up toward the open neck of the giant balloon above them. "See, it's like a safety valve. It's left open so the expanding gas can escape without bursting the envelope."

Brady nodded, then looked back down at the ground below. The balloon was drifting over the fields, yet he had the sensation that the fields were moving while he stood still. There was no rush of wind, as he'd expected. We're drifting with the wind, he told himself, at the same speed as the wind, so we don't feel it. We'd never feel it, even in a storm.

As they passed over a farmhouse, a dog rushed out and began to bark. Chickens in the yard scattered, and Brady could hear their excited clucking. An instant later, the farmhouse had disappeared, and the balloon was soaring higher and higher. They drifted on and on.

Now silence surrounded them, broken only by the creak of the lines against the basket.

"How high are we?" Brady asked nervously. The ground seemed very far below.

Robertson consulted an instrument attached to the inside of the basket. "Five thousand feet," he replied proudly.

Almost a mile high! Brady peered over the side, noting with amazement that the fields were laid out in neat checkerboards. And at this distance, the stands of trees between them looked like tiny green bouquets. What he wouldn't give to photograph them!

Suddenly, a light gauzy vapor swept around the balloon and a chill crept into the air, but almost before Brady noticed what had happened, they floated back into the sunlight. To his surprise, he saw, about thirty yards away, another balloon exactly like theirs, haloed by a rainbow of color.

"We have a twin," von Zeppelin exclaimed.

Robertson laughed. "That's our own image. It happens among the clouds sometimes. It has to do with water vapor." He turned from his two companions and tugged gently on a rope. "I'm taking us down a bit," he explained. "This rope controls the gas valve at the top of the balloon. I'm letting out some of the hydrogen because the sun's warmth makes the gas expand."

As the balloon descended, Brady heard a series of faint booms, like an echo of rolling thunder. It took him a few seconds to realize that the sound had nothing to do with the balloon. Looking down, he saw silver ribbons snaking through the green and brown of the countryside. Rivers, he told himself. Then, to his left, he saw tiny white clouds that hung over the ground. He heard a noise like popcorn popping and identified it as musket fire, the white clouds as puffs of smoke. The faint booms would be the sound of the cannon.

"Can you take us lower?" he asked Robertson.

"Certainly." Robertson tugged on the valve rope. "If it seems dangerous, I'll throw out a sandbag to take us up again."

There was no sensation of dropping, but Brady noticed that details on the ground grew larger, clearer. Now he saw a cluster of houses like a child's toy village, the steeple of a church, the dome of a courthouse. Tiny tents showed white among the trees, and he made out a horse and wagon beside them. Brady was amazed at how much he could see, even with his poor vision.

"The tactics, they are wrong," von Zeppelin cried. "See, the Union soldiers fight against massive odds to cross the bridge when they might better discover a ford." He pointed from the bridge to a spot where lines of men faced one another under a haze of white smoke. "There, you see? Union men are needed there to sweep the Rebels from the field. And where are they? Held back at the bridge." He shook his head. "Napoleon wouldn't have made this mistake."

Near a clump of woods to his left, Brady saw dead horses and men and the wreckage of cannon. A stream's silver stripe threaded among the armies. The stone walls, the zigzag fences, the yellow burst of shells, the horsemen galloping across the fields—everything was in miniature, toy horses, toy cannon. He couldn't follow the battle as von Zeppelin had.

"That's Antietam Creek down there," Robertson called out, a map in his hand. "The town was Sharpsburg. I'll try to set us down in the fields past the fighting, behind Union lines, before we get to the high country."

As Brady stared down, he saw a tent with men in blue lying all around it. A hospital, he told himself.

But before he could look again, the balloon passed on to the east, leaving the battlefield behind. How he longed to have a camera in his hands.

"If only one could maneuver a balloon, send it where one wished," von Zeppelin sighed, "instead of having to trust to the winds."

"Some aeronauts have tried," Robertson replied. "Any day one will succeed." He reached up and opened a red bag that was attached to the hoop above the basket. Inside it was a red rope. Holding this in his hand, Robertson pulled on the valve rope, letting more and more gas out of the balloon until the basket barely skimmed the treetops. Brady saw the ground flying past him faster and faster. Then, suddenly, Robertson yanked on the red rope. An instant later, a ripping sound came from the silk envelope above them, and the balloon caved in on itself.

"Grab the lines and climb up on the basket rim," Robertson shouted, hurling out a grappling hook.

The ground was rushing up at them now, and the basket bounced roughly beneath them as it dragged along. With a mighty jerk, it stopped abruptly when the hook caught somewhere behind them. Shuddering, the mass of silk collapsed.

Von Zeppelin was out first. He turned to help Brady crawl from beneath the balloon, then gave Robertson a hand. "A first class trip, I do thank you," he beamed. "However, I much preferred departing to arriving."

Robertson laughed. "I used the rip cord," he explained. "It pulls away a piece of the cloth inside the envelope and lets all the gas out quickly. I didn't want to be caught in the mountains." He knelt beside the deflated balloon. "I'd appreciate your help in packing this up. I'm heading for New York to give a lecture. 'Battle From a Balloon,' I think I'll call it."

*   *   *

With their help, Robertson soon had the silk envelope folded into a smaller package than Brady would have dreamed possible. As they worked, the sound of cannon and musketry could clearly be heard. It seemed they weren't far from the fighting.

"Will you be reporting to General McClellan?" Brady asked von Zeppelin.

"Yes." The German hesitated, frowning. "This type of fighting you do in America is not, how shall I say . . . romantic? Not done in the European way I am used to. Oh, the men are brave enough, valor abounds on both sides. But to skulk about in swamps as we did on the Virginia Peninsula, that is not for me." He waved his hand in the direction of the shooting. "Even now it is not masterful. Still, your President Lincoln has given me a commission and I will fight. Ferdinand von Zeppelin is no coward!"

"I don't think I'll join you," Professor Robertson remarked dryly. "I've seen the battle at close enough range to suit me. I'll look for a farmer with a wagon I can borrow." He flashed them both a smile. "Goodbye. I've enjoyed your company, and I hope to see you again."

"While you're in New York, drop by my gallery at Broadway and Tenth," Brady offered. "Tell whoever's there that I want your balloon photographed." From his pocket, he pulled an orange throwaway sheet printed with an advertisement for his galleries. He scribbled a note on the back, signed his name and handed the paper to Robertson.

"Thank you, I'll do that." Robertson tipped his hat, and towing the packaged balloon in the basket, set off across the fields, heading east. Von Zeppelin and Brady watched him go, then started walking west, toward the roar of the artillery.

Woodbury would be somewhere near Antietam Creek, but Brady knew he'd have no trouble locating him. The What-is-it-wagons were so distinctive that the soldiers always knew where they were. In all the excitement, he hadn't thought to try to spot the wagon from the balloon.

"I think I could design an engine to move a hydrogen-filled balloon," von Zeppelin remarked as they strolled off through the fields. "First, I believe one would have to make the gas envelope from some rigid material." He looked at Brady. "Is it not a fascinating notion, the idea of controlling a machine that is lighter than air? One could cross oceans, travel anywhere. And as for war—what an advantage the side with such a machine would have!"

"I thought more about taking pictures from the balloon," Brady confessed.

Von Zeppelin nodded a little impatiently. "Napoleon's tactics would win this battle for the Union," he declared, "but from what I saw . . ." He shrugged. "Still, Napoleon also said numbers will tell in the end, and so the Union has the advantage. Is that not true?"

Brady gave a weary sigh. "I suppose you're right."

Von Zeppelin left Brady when they came to General McClellan's headquarters, a two-story yellow frame house on a rise overlooking the battlefield. Brady stood there alone for a few moments, looking down at the fighting. The din set his teeth on edge— the continuous roar of the cannon, the shells bursting, the rattle of musket fire, the shouts and screams. He knew it was Langston Cook's dream to be able to record the sounds as well as the sights of war, but at the present he couldn't bear such a thought. He squinted out at the battlefield, trying to block out the noise.

Through the smoke, it seemed to Brady as if the Union troops had advanced toward a line of Rebel troops, then somehow passed over them, neither paying any attention to the other. He took off his glasses and rubbed his eyes. Near him, a captain peering through a telescope offered him a look.

When Brady adjusted it, he found that the Rebels were in a sunken lane. They were in a line, but it was a line of dead men. No, not all of them, he thought with a chill. Here and there a hand waved feebly, as if for help. But the Union soldiers never stopped. Instead, they stepped over the piles of bloody grey bodies and surged on, in search of live Confederates concealed in the woods beyond. Union artillery boomed out on either side of Brady, and explosions blossomed as shells bombarded the Rebel lines. He had no notion which side was winning.

Brady gave the telescope back and moved off to his left, toward the big tent of the field hospital. The sentry at McClellan's headquarters had told him he'd find one of his wagons there. That bloody lane, he thought. As soon as we can get to it, I'll photograph those dead Rebels, the dead horses by the woods, the windrows of fallen men in the field next to it. I can see it now, the next series of war views—the battle at Antietam Creek.

Woodbury was at the wagon. "I saw the balloon go over," he cried. "Did you get a picture of it?"

Brady laughed. "Believe it or not, what I got was a ride."

"I'll be damned. Over the fighting?"

Brady nodded. "No pictures, though. The aeronaut said the camera was too heavy. In any case, we moved too rapidly. Did you get anything interesting here?"

Woodbury shrugged. "The usual. McClellan's headquarters, a good shot of the signal station, one of Knap's Battery. I thought I'd take another of the battery, if I can, when the fighting's over, maybe with one of the dead horses in the scene."

Brady nodded.

"You must have seen everything from the balloon," Woodbury remarked. "How's the battle going? Are we winning?"

Brady shook his head. "I couldn't tell. There seemed to be as many grey uniforms as blue. Count von Zeppelin was in the balloon with me, and he thought the Rebs had the edge."

Before he could say any more, a shell whistled over, exploding to their left. As the smoke cleared, litter bearers ran past, carrying a soldier whose chest was a mass of blood. They deposited him next to the hospital tent, then hurried off again.

"Don't let me die," the soldier begged. He gasped as the words choked in his throat. "God, don't let me die."

Woodbury turned his face away. "I never get used to it," he whispered. "Never."

"It's not something one *should* get used to," Brady replied. "If we can't make the stay-at-homes hear the pleas of the wounded and the cries of the dying, at least we can make pictures so they can see what it's like to be here. So they can see how ugly war really is."

Chapter 24

Ruth O'Neill stood beside the iron bedstead, a pistol in her hand, gazing down at her father. He lay on his back snoring, the reek of cheap whiskey almost a tangible cloud about him. And why shouldn't he be drunk? she thought grimly. If she were the kind it would help she'd be drunk too, but the taste of the stuff made her gag. Da would be dead to the world for hours, till noon or later. He wouldn't know what she planned to do, even if he did notice that his pistol was gone.

Ruth had watched, a wide-eyed young girl, when Da had shown George how to load and fire the gun. She'd watched again, almost fully grown, when he showed Michael. Girls didn't use firearms, so Da had never taught her, but she thought she knew. She could remember well enough, for she'd longed to be able to shoot that pistol when she was younger. And now she would.

The morning was fair, with a cool September breeze promising relief from the stifling heat of the last few days. Ruth lifted her black skirt above her petticoats to avoid the mud of Swampoodle as she made her way up the path toward the road, carrying the pistol in a canvas bag. She'd hired no hack. Instead, she'd walk, as she used to when she hadn't the money to pay for a rig.

As she strode along, her thoughts were tugged back to her childhood, to memories of those peaceful days. She, George and Michael had had happy times up north, when Ma was still alive. Back then, September had been the month for the final harvest, for putting up the last vegetables, for picking apples and storing them for the winter. Everyone dug in and helped and Ma made a game of it, with contests to see who could strip a tree of apples the fastest, who could bind up the fanciest corn shock. And she gave prizes, little squares of maple sugar saved from the winter before. They all loved maple sugar.

I haven't had maple sugar in years, Ruth thought sadly. Maybe the last time I had any was when I won a square for my corn leprechaun. In her mind's eye, Ruth could see Michael, still a bit smaller than she, for he hadn't shot past her yet, his chin quivering as he tried not to cry. He was too big a boy to shed tears over losing, but he couldn't keep his blue eyes off the square of maple sugar in her hand. She'd looked at the square, at Michael, then back at the square. Finally, she'd broken it and given him the lion's share. How he'd smiled. Michael could melt your heart with his smile.

Tears blurred Ruth's eyes and she stumbled over a root in the path. She shook her head angrily, dashing away the tears. She hadn't time to cry. She was heading to do what she should have done months ago. What she should have done when she'd stood in the darkroom and listened to Helena Swane admit she was a Rebel spy.

Up North Capitol Ruth marched, turning off before she came to the railroad station, onto E Street, past City Hospital, past the Post Office, past the new Ford's

Theater. Then there was a turn onto Eleventh Street and she was there.

The pictures Mr. Brady and Mr. Woodbury had brought back from Maryland forced their way into her mind again. Those ghastly photographs of swollen bodies, arms and legs in the air as though grotesquely alive, row on row of decaying bodies still lying indecently atop the ground, eyes staring at a pitiless heaven. What had *Humphrey's Journal* said? "The public is indebted to Brady of Broadway for his excellent views of grim-visaged war." Ruth stopped and closed her eyes. Dear God, she prayed, forgive me.

She opened her eyes and went into the four-story brick building. She'd known what she must do ever since she'd seen Brady's Antietam Creek war views. Known before her father heard, before he'd come weeping into the gallery to tell her the news. She'd seen what the pictures didn't show in their sepia tones for the stereoscopic viewer. She knew that one of the soldiers who stared so blankly at nothing had bright blue eyes. And as she looked at the photograph, the hand he held so stiffly in the air was aimed at her, pointing out what she must do.

Ruth climbed a flight of stairs and made her way along a corridor. It was still very early, and no one was about. She halted in front of a door and tried the knob. As she'd suspected, it was locked. She lifted her hand to rap on the door, then paused. Smiling grimly, she tapped three times, waited, then tapped twice more.

There were a few moments of silence. Then at last, Langston Cook, hair tousled, eyes still sleepy, opened the door. He had a blanket wrapped about him.

"May I come in?" she asked.

Langston was speechless for a moment, staring at

her. Then he stepped back, clutching at the blanket. She could tell he was naked underneath.

Ruth strode into the room. "I can wait," she said curtly. "Please get dressed."

Langston shot her a puzzled glance. Then he nodded and shut himself into the small bedroom, leaving her alone in his sitting room. She glanced about. He'd left no mark on the room, she saw, as though he didn't live here. Of course, he didn't really live here, she told herself angrily. He was a Southerner first, last and always. She'd been foolish to think photography meant more to him, to believe that he shared Mathew Brady's vision. He was nothing but a sneaking Rebel spy. Ruth took the pistol from the canvas bag and held the gun in a fold of her black gown.

A moment later, Langston opened the bedroom door, fully dressed, his hair brushed. "Ruth," he murmured, advancing toward her, "I want to tell you how sorry I am about . . ."

"Don't lie to me. I'm through with your lies." Her voice cut through his words like a knife. "And don't come any closer. I'd vomit if you touched me."

Langston stopped. "Ruth, I know you're upset . . ."

She lifted her right arm and aimed the pistol at his chest.

"My God, Ruth."

"I'm going to kill you," she whispered. "Do you know why?"

Langston took another step forward. "Listen, let's talk about this. You have no reason . . ."

Ruth waved him off. "I have *every* reason," she hissed. "Did you see the photographs of Antietam? Did you see Michael, my baby brother Michael, lying by the rail fence, dead and bloated? Did you see his arm out, pointing? It points at you, Langston Cook. You killed Michael with your spying, with the information you carried south." She took a deep breath and tightened her finger on the trigger. "But you'll never take them another report because I'm going to kill you."

She tried valiantly to steady her aim, but before she could squeeze the trigger, Longston was lunging at her. The pistol went off just as he knocked it from her hand, his body slamming into her, sending her sprawling. They fell together, Langston on top of her. As his body pressed against her, she gasped for air, struggling to break free.

Suddenly, she felt his weight ease off, but by the time she'd scrambled to her feet, he stood before her, her pistol in his hand. There was no blood, no sign of a wound. Ruth closed her eyes in anguish. She'd failed.

Haltingly, she stepped back from him and raised her head to look him in the eye. "I'll go directly from here to Mr. Pinkerton and tell him everything," she threatened. "I'll tell him how you were a courier for that Swane woman, how you still carry information south, how you seek to destroy the Union by your spying." She glared at him. "I pray they hang you."

Langston gave her a sad little smile. "I have your gun, Ruth," he said softly.

She blinked, then stood taller. "Shoot me, then," she cried. "Finish your dirty work. Kill me!"

Langston looked down at the pistol in his hand, then back at Ruth. She waited for the bullet, consigning her soul to God.

"Ruth," he said gently, "I haven't reloaded the pistol." Shaking his head, he tucked it in his pocket, then strode past her and locked the door, removing the key. She watched in astonishment as he disappeared into the bedroom, returning a moment later with a knapsack. As she hurried toward him, he shoved her backward into the room, tossing the pistol after her.

"Goodbye, Ruth," he called, slamming the door behind him.

She heard the key grate in the lock.

Ruth flung herself against the door, but she knew she was too late. Desperately, she banged on the wood with the butt of the pistol, calling to someone, anyone, to let her out. "Stop him, stop him!" she cried. "He's a spy, a Rebel spy!"

Helena Swane smiled at Jefferson Davis. The president of the Confederacy was too bloodless for her taste, not lusty enough to show desire for her. Or perhaps he wasn't well. He certainly looked haggard. Yet she respected his position, his power.

"I'll do anything I can for the Confederacy, sir. You know that," she said sweetly. "Your praise has meant more to me than any gift I've ever received."

His answering smile was rueful. "I'm afraid at the moment I place gold above praise," he replied wryly. "Miss Swane, we need everything, but gold will buy much of it. For the rest, we also need men, soldiers. If you can persuade the English to send us both, or either, the Confederacy will be forever grateful."

"I'll do my best, Mr. President. I . . . have a certain talent for persuasion."

"I can well believe that." For just a second, something gleamed in Davis' eyes, making Helena wonder if she'd misjudged the man.

"I've arranged for an aide to take you to Wilmington, in North Carolina," he continued. "With luck, the *Shakespeare* will have you in London in two weeks."

Helena clapped her hands in delight. "What a wonderful name for a ship! I look forward to being aboard a vessel named for the great bard."

Davis frowned slightly. "Our ships successfully

run the Union blockades every day," he cautioned, "but there *is* a risk, Miss Swane. I can't deny that. Not every blockade runner makes it. You'll be in danger."

Helena smiled. "I thrive on danger, sir."

Davis sighed. "Well, it certainly seems to agree with you. All the same, you may want to think over my words for a time before you sail."

"And miss crossing the Atlantic on the *Shakespeare*? Never! No, I'll sail as arranged."

England, she thought gleefully. London. Royalty. With a *lettre de créance* from President Davis, all doors would be open to her, to Helen Swane, the daughter of a Georgia overseer.

Impulsively, she got up from her chair and crossed the room to where Jefferson Davis sat behind his desk. He half rose, but she pressed her hands on his shoulders, pushing him back down. Before he knew what was happening, Helena had bent and kissed him quickly but firmly on the lips.

"You're a wonderful man," she said softly as she drew away. "Like all other Southern women, I can only worship you."

His face flushed as he got to his feet and took her hand. "My dear Miss Swane," he replied with a bashful grin, "you make me wish that I too were sailing on the *Shakespeare*."

Once he was past all possible pursuit, Langston Cook eased up his horse. He knew he was finished as far as Washington was concerned, finished as a spy anywhere in Union territory, for that matter. Pinkerton would have his description widely circulated, and his men would be sure to take a good look at all the photographers they came across.

Who would ever have thought that little Ruth would turn on him like that? If his reflexes had been slower, he'd be a dead man for sure. She'd pulled the trigger without a flicker of remorse. Langston grimaced as he thought of Ruth's blazing eyes.

What the hell, he was sorry her brother was killed at Antietam. It was a goddamned shame that Brady had unwittingly photographed his body. But to say that he, Langston Cook, was responsible for some Rebel soldier putting a minie ball into Michael O'Neill—well, that was plain craziness. True, he'd fetched information south, secret plans from General McClellan, secret instructions from Secretary of War Stanton, but to translate that into a death on the battlefield . . . Yet it wasn't beyond the realm of possibility.

Brady's photographs had been excellent. The swollen, putrid bodies took on a horrid fascination as you gazed at them, safe in your protected home, your haven far from the battle. How must Ruth have felt when she realized one of these ghastly corpses was her brother? Langston clenched his teeth. Jesus, what an awful shock it must have been! And when she'd seen the prints, she'd never let on, never said a word to him or even to Brady. She must have planned right then and there to shoot him.

He could hardly blame her, but he was damned if he'd think of himself as a murderer. Men died in wars. Only one side could win; the other had to lose. The Confederacy was his choice, and he'd go on helping her. Not by spying. No, his usefulness there was over. He'd photograph the battles if General Lee would permit it, carry a gun if he must.

It would be too bad if he had to stop taking pictures of the war. After all, Brady's notion of recording history for everyone to see was too good to be left half-finished. His cameras and equipment were stored in Richmond, and he could make himself a What-is-it wagon just like Brady's. That was it. He'd go to Richmond and get his gear together.

Richmond, he thought suddenly. Helena was in Richmond. He hadn't seen her since he'd brought her through the Union lines in Brady's wagon. He'd sent messages to her, telling her where he'd be in Virginia and when, but she hadn't ventured out of Richmond to see him. Beautiful, elusive Helena, so easy to embrace, yet so hard to hold. He'd been surprised to discover that he loved her as he'd never loved any woman, never expected to love any woman.

Would she ever love him? He tried to tell himself he didn't care, that seeing her, having her in his arms would be enough. She was in Richmond, and he'd be there too. They'd be together, live together, now that they'd left the enemy's country. They'd even marry, if only she'd agree.

"Miss Swane checked out yesterday." The clerk at the Spotswood Hotel looked up from the register. "Said she didn't know when she'd be back. And I sure don't know where she went."

Langston dashed about Richmond like a madman, tracking down everyone he knew. But no one could tell him anything about Helena Swane. As the hours passed, he grew frantic. He must find Helena, had to find her. Nothing else counted. At last, he ran into an old friend, a major, recently released from the hospital, his left arm gone below the elbow, the stump still bandaged.

"Lost it at Slaughter Mountain, when we licked the Yanks," the major explained proudly. "Lived to fight again. Lucky it was my left arm."

"Do you know Helena Swane?" Langston demanded.

The major thought a moment, then smiled. "Why, yes. Pretty little gal. Did some play-acting for us at the hospital. Gave us all the will to get well, let me tell you."

Langston seized his friend's good arm. "She's left Richmond. Do you know where she is?"

The major shook his head. "No, but I can find out if it's important to you. I'm on my way to the War Department. Someone there's sure to know. They're supposed to be up on everything that goes on."

Langston waited in the square, pacing across the grass for over an hour, staring at the windows of the capitol with its columned front, the statue of Washington beneath the dome. An ugly building. The one in Washington would be much more graceful, once it was completed. But buildings were really the furthest things from his mind. He looked up expectantly as the major approached.

"The story is that Miss Swane's gone to Wilmington," he told him. "Sailing for England on the *Shakespeare*. Going to charm gold from the limeys. Something Jeff Davis thought up, I hear."

"Thank you. I can't thank you enough." Langston clapped his friend on the back and dashed across the square.

"Where are you off to?" the major shouted. "Wait and we'll have a drink."

"Some other time," Langston called back, not slowing a bit. "I have to catch a train." He trotted back to where he'd left his horse and swung into the saddle. He had to get to Wilmington without delay. Damn it, he'd sail to England, too. Anything to be with Helena.

* * *

Langston reached Wilmington two days later at dusk. There was no sign of a ship named *Shakespeare* at the docks.

"The *Shakespeare*?" a grizzled old sailor repeated. He shook his head.

"I was supposed to sail on her," Langston insisted. "To London."

Slowly, a look of recognition spread across the old man's face. "Well, in that case, you got a long swim ahead of you," he drawled. "She pulled outa here maybe an hour ago. There ain't no way you can catch her less'n you be a fish."

Chapter 25

The Confederate private brought a weak and feverish Cal back to New Market. Vanessa, after listening to his story, asked the soldier if Jonah could take him to his home in Staunton and then return to New Market with the mule and wagon.

"I know my husband will want to see to it in person that they're given back to the army," she explained, reflecting that she was becoming more accomplished at lying every day. Where would it end?

Since the private had no objection, Vanessa found herself with transport to Richmond. The difficulty was that Cal was once again too sick to make the trip. As she nursed him, the summer passed, the hot fruitful summer of the valley. Grain, vegetables and fruits flourished, ripening in the warm sun. And the people prospered as well. Tilla's daughter, Kezia, delivered a baby boy. Only Cal languished, thin and grim-faced in this season of growth, not even sharing Vanessa's joy at the return of his memory.

Ancey was fascinated with Kezia's infant, and she carried him about crooning to him as often as his mother would allow. "Look now," she'd say to whoever was near—even Cal—"see how he smiles at me. Look how he holds my finger." Everything the baby did was a marvel to her.

"You're going to have him spoiled with all this attention," Cal told her. "Too much coddling's not good for a boy."

"Can't be too much loving for a baby, be he boy or girl," Ancey countered. "Little folks needs loving."

Vanessa, unseen, watched Cal reach his hands out for the infant, saw a smile brighten his gaunt face as he gently jiggled the baby, supporting him on his knee. "Ancey," he said softly as he disentangled the baby's fingers from his beard, "all folks need loving. It's a human condition."

Vanessa felt her heart contract. She loved Cal, she'd do anything for him. So why did he hold himself apart from her?

Near the end of September, Ancey and Jonah announced their plans to marry.

"Be it all right with you, Miss Nessa," Ancey added shyly.

Beaming, Vanessa gave the girl a delighted hug. "I think it's wonderful! But in any case, Ancey, I have no right to tell you yes or no. I don't own you. And if President Lincoln has his way, I don't doubt you can stop worrying about anyone owning you."

"When do President Lincoln say we be free?" Jonah asked.

"When we win the war," Vanessa replied firmly. "He made the law to free you, but he can't force the South to obey that law until then."

Vanessa swallowed her pride and went to the white community to ask for donations of clothes or yardage. She was determined that Ancey would have the most beautiful wedding gown she could give her.

"And is your husband recovered from his terrible wound?" asked Mrs. Higgins from Applegate Farm. "I understand he fought with General Jackson at Winchester. What we'd do without our Stonewall, I just don't know."

Mrs. Higgins gave Vanessa an old pink silk ball gown, a yard of plaid taffeta and half a peck of corn.

At the next farm, Mrs. Hoefferle donated four outgrown muslin dresses. "I'm getting so plump my husband says he won't be able to afford to keep me dressed." She laughed coyly, then gave Vanessa a kindly smile. "Take some milk for your husband, dear. Nothing like milk to give strength." she sighed. "Meat's better, of course, but I can't spare any. We have little enough for ourselves."

Everyone she spoke to gave Vanessa something: a ribbon or two, four pairs of old satin slippers, petticoats, an apple-green bonnet, odds and ends of yardage, and heaps of fruits and vegetables. Once everything was collected, Tilla sent a message to a black preacher from up the valley.

Ancey's face glowed with happiness as she stood in her gown of pink silk, its skirts thrust out by stiffened petticoats. White satin ribbons decorated the scoop-necked bodice, and ruffles of white gauze circled the lower edge of the skirt. The dress fit her diminutive figure perfectly.

Beside her, Jonah smiled down at his bride, his face filled with love and tenderness. He looked magnificent in the blue muslin shirt Ancey had made for him. Vanessa had once told her the meaning of his name, that it was from the Bible and symbolized peace. Now she saw that Ancey had embroidered a white dove onto the back of the shirt.

The bride and groom held hands, standing before the minister under the trees of Morton's Woods, for there was no church for blacks within miles. As she heard the familiar words of the marriage ceremony, tears came to Vanessa's eyes. Of all the weddings she'd ever attended, this one had the most meaning. Some had been more fashionable, but no bride had ever been more beautiful than Ancey in her made-over finery, no groom prouder than Jonah.

I want to be standing like Ancey someday, with Cal by my side, Vanessa thought to herself. I want to be Cal's wife. She glanced sideways at him, catching a glimpse of his anguished face before he turned away from her. What was the matter? What she'd seen hadn't been a look of physical pain. Were there terrible memories he hadn't shared with her? It was almost as though he couldn't bear the sight of her.

She glanced down at her own dress. She'd used the blue and green plaid taffeta alternating with blue muslin for the panels of her skirt. The bodice had a square neck and was of solid muslin, the only trim a dark green ribbon threaded about the neckline. She looked better than she had in months. Surely it couldn't be what she wore that upset him.

Cal took Vanessa aside after the wedding feast. "We're overdue in Richmond," he said gruffly. "It's high time we were on our way."

Vanessa stared at him in indignation. She'd been waiting for *him*. Did he think she didn't care about her father?

"I don't like what I have to do, and that's a fact," he went on, staring down at the ground.

Vanessa thrust up her chin. "If you don't want to go to Richmond, I'll go alone."

Cal looked back up at her. His eyes searched hers. "Don't be foolish. We'll go together, as we planned—how long ago? Six months, at least. Yes, together. You need my help and I . . ." He stopped and sighed. "You paid me to go with you." She had the notion he'd started to say something else entirely.

"We won't take Ancey and Jonah with us," he added. "They're safer here. Everyone in New Market believes they belong to us. We'll leave them passes saying we're in Richmond and they're to stay here on their own until our return."

"But Ancey . . ."

"Don't tell me how Ancey feels. She'll stay here with her new husband willingly enough if you tell her she must. We'll leave in the morning."

Vanessa reached out and touched his arm. "Will we ever come back?"

Cal closed his eyes for a moment, then gave her a look that was filled with sadness. "One or the other of us, yes. Ancey and Jonah have less to worry about than you or I."

For the journey, Cal put on his shabby, patched Confederate uniform instead of the simple shirt and trousers he'd been wearing while he convalesced. His wounded arm had healed into an angry puckered scar, but he was still much too thin and the grey uniform hung loose about his slender frame. Vanessa's old riding habit was too ragged to be of further use, so she wore the gown she'd made for Ancey's wedding. At the last moment, she donned the apple-green bonnet. Though she disliked the color, she somehow felt it was best to look as ladylike as possible.

Cal gave her a one-sided grin when he saw the bonnet. "You look every inch the country girl," he remarked.

"That's because I am," she snapped, annoyed at his teasing. She'd worked hard on her gown, making something from very little, and she was proud of her efforts, simple as the dress might be. She couldn't help the bonnet.

"I meant it as a compliment," he said softly. "The less attention we attract, the better. The bonnet hides your hair and shades your face from view."

She stared straight ahead.

"Ah, Nessa, you know you're beautiful," he whispered, touching her shoulder lightly. She tingled where his fingers brushed her. "But beauty attracts trouble," he added. "That's why I'm for the bonnet, strange as the color might be. Please, let's not quarrel before we must."

What a strange thing to say. She glanced at him and saw the same unhappy look he'd worn the day before. Impulsively, she put a hand on his arm. "Cal, what is it that bothers you, that pains you so?"

He gazed into her eyes, and she held her breath as his head bent, his lips neared hers.

"Oh, Miss Nessa, I can't hardly bear to let you go." An anguished cry split the air as Ancey came running toward them, tears streaming down her face.

Cal straightened, and the moment was over.

The entire black settlement turned out to see them off, and Jonah and Ancey followed the wagon all the way out of the woods and down to the pike. Before the wagon rolled around a bend in the road, Vanessa caught one last glimpse of their tiny figures. Even at a distance, Jonah seemed so much taller.

Vanessa turned back, blinking away her tears. She couldn't speak for the lump in her throat. Somehow, she felt she was leaving her home for the last time. Not a house—after all, the house had been burned—but a home, a place where she'd had ease of spirit no matter how hard she'd worked, a place where she'd been accepted for what she was, for herself, not for her looks or her social graces.

"It won't ever be the same," she murmured.

"The war has changed us all," Cal said gently.

She didn't answer. As they bounced along, she forced herself to relax, enjoying the warmth of the late September sun. By noon it would be hot, but now the day was pleasant, just right. She began to think ahead to Richmond. Her father had taken her there several times before her mother had gotten too ill to travel. She had a dim memory of stately brick houses under flowering magnolias, streets that looked down onto the James River. On the outskirts of town, she recalled pine woods with trees so huge and lofty the branches met overhead. A lovely city, gracious and friendly.

If only she could think of someone she might have met while they'd been there. They hadn't stayed in a private home but at a hotel with elegant carriages coming and going in front. She remembered her mother hushing her father's swearing when their carriage sunk hub deep in the sandy roads. It was all such a long time ago.

"You must know Richmond well," she said to Cal.

He shook his head.

"But William . . . I thought Captain Thornton said . . ."

"I have people I can contact there who might help me—help us. I've never been in the city."

It seemed such a long time since she'd met Cal in Washington. She could hardly believe she'd taken such an instant dislike to him. He wasn't what she'd thought him to be—ignorant, uncouth, ill-mannered—though it almost seemed he'd gone out of his way to make her think so.

"You've certainly earned the money I paid you a

thousand times over," she sighed. "Forced to fight as a Reb and . . ."

He turned toward her so abruptly that she stopped in surprise. "Forget the money," he snapped.

"But you mentioned it yourself only yesterday."

"I left the money in Washington. You'll get it back when we return." Cal gave her a fiery look. "I couldn't take money from you. My God, Vanessa, you saved my life more than once. You nursed me after I treated you like a . . . well, like anything but the woman you are. The lady you are. I owe you far more than money could repay. You owe me nothing."

He shifted his gaze back to the Valley Pike.

They rode in silence for a while before Vanessa ventured another question. "What will you do after you take me to my father in Richmond?" she asked.

He didn't reply for so long a time that she thought he didn't intend to. Finally, he looked over at her.

"I can't give you the answer to that," he said hoarsely. "I just don't know,"

They turned off the pike as the sun set, pulling into the shelter of the trees.

"You sleep in the wagon," Cal ordered. "I'll bed down on the ground."

Vanessa didn't protest, but after they'd eaten she came and sat beside him under a tree. "I remember when we slept in a woods once before, without a shelter," she said softly. As she leaned against him, he turned to her, taking her into his arms. Their lips met, and she drew him close. She ached with the need for him, yet there was tenderness intermixed with that need, a tenderness she'd never felt with any man. She touched his face, stroked his hair, sighed as his lips moved downward, his tongue tracing circles in the hollow of her throat.

But an instant later, her sigh turned to a gasp.

Suddenly, Cal stiffened and thrust her away from him. Shaking, he leaped to his feet. When she looked up, she saw him leaning against the wagon, his head on his arm. The toe of his boot kicked the ground, sending dirt scattering into the underbrush.

Vanessa rose and took a step toward him. "What's wrong?" she asked huskily.

"I can't," he murmured, not turning. "Damn it, I can't."

"Once you . . . wanted me," she said, her voice trembling.

With a deep sigh, he swung about and strode back to her. Vanessa caught her breath as he stood before her, but he didn't touch her.

"The time's wrong, Nessa. Because of what's happened. And what will happen."

"That's talking in riddles. Why is the time wrong?"

"Stop asking me questions." His voice rose. "One damned question after another. Leave me alone. Just leave me alone."

After that, Vanessa slept in the wagon each night. Rage at her stupidity in offering herself to him, and her humiliated anger at his rejection, made her withdraw into silence. Cal rarely spoke either, and as the days passed she thought there'd never been such a lonely and interminable journey. Yet at the same time, Vanessa dreaded its end, for then she'd be that much closer to never seeing Cal again.

On the morning of the last day, the day they'd arrive in Richmond, Cal grew more talkative. "Tell me about your childhood," he said, seemingly out of nowhere. When he noticed her surprised glance, he added, "I'm curious because you so rarely speak of your mother. It's mostly your father you seem to remember."

A weight lifted from Vanessa's heart at Cal's attempt to be friendly. She'd hated the bitterness between them. "My mother died when I was twelve," she replied. "I don't have many memories of her because she was an invalid for years before she died."

"Then you were close to your father?"

Vanessa smiled. "We had no one else, he and I. He took me almost everywhere he went, taught me to ride—even how to play cards, I'm afraid."

"And he discussed his feelings with you, his philosophy of life?"

"No, not really. He was—he is—a private sort of man where his feelings are concerned. I know he missed my mother, although he never said so. He . . . well, he does have convictions. After all, he joined the Union army."

"Did that surprise you?"

Vanessa hesitated. "Not exactly. Before Fort Sumter was fired on, before President Lincoln was nominated by the Republicans, Papa spoke of our country's greatness. He called Virginia the home of Presidents, a land with a proud heritage, the state that made the Union possible."

"Did he approve of President Lincoln?"

"I don't know. He didn't say. All I know is that I love my father, and I respect him for his sacrifices."

"Sacrifices?"

"I often felt he didn't marry again because of me, in order to pay more attention to me. And then there was the way he went against the current by becoming a Union officer. You saw how New Market reacted. No wonder he took me to Aunt Matilda."

Cal nodded. She thought he looked as gloomy as she'd ever seen him. "Is your father alive?" she asked.

He gave a short laugh. "Oh yes. Back in Missouri. He feels I'm the prodigal son." He shifted on the wagon box, then pointed ahead. "I can see church steeples. We're getting close."

The bridge across the James River was jammed with carts, wagons and carriages. It seemed as if the entire population of the city was going in or out of Richmond. On the other side, Cal drove along a narrow street near the river, reading the lettering on windows and on the plaques near shop entrances along the way. In among the ship chandlers, rooming houses and warehouses, Vanessa saw private residences, dilapidated survivors of an earlier era.

"Ah." Cal stopped the mule and jumped down. Hurriedly, he helped Vanessa from the wagon, then climbed the steps of a brick house, leaving her to trail behind.

The curtainless windows on each side of the door stared blankly at them. The panes were covered with a gray film and one was cracked. Vanessa watched as Cal knelt on the stoop, pried loose a brick and reached into the recess to bring forth a key. Replacing the brick, he unlocked and pushed open the door. Inside, the house smelled of emptiness and decay.

After locking the door behind them, Cal immediately headed for the stairs. He seemed very sure of himself, Vanessa thought as she followed him, as though he'd been in this house and climbed these stairs many times before. Yet he'd told her he'd never been to Richmond.

At the landing, Cal strode a few steps down a corridor and pushed open a door. Nodding to himself, he stood surveying the interior. She looked past him to see a dark box of a room with a brass bedstead, a patchwork quilt folded on the bare mattress. Beyond the bed were a writing desk, chairs, and a porcelain pitcher and bowl on a commode. The single curtainless window faced a brick wall.

"You stay here," Cal ordered, "while I find out what's what and how best to go about getting you into Libby Prison."

Vanessa stared at him, puzzled. "How did you know about this house?"

"I was told." He shrugged. "It makes little difference."

Vanessa looked around again and took a deep breath. "I want to go and see the prison. See Libby Prison, where my father is. Now."

He sighed. "You can't see him until I make arrangements."

"I don't care. I must see where he is. I refuse to stay shut up in this room until I do." She laid her hand on his arm, the first time she'd touched him since that night in the woods. "Don't you understand, Cal? I have to be able to picture him somewhere, now that we're so close. Please take me there."

Cal led Vanessa down the narrow streets, turning corners and cutting through alleys until she was thoroughly lost. All she knew was that they were near the James River, for she sometimes caught a glimpse of the water between the buildings. Finally, Cal stopped and pointed. Ahead, she saw a solid four-story brick building.

"Libby," he announced. Then he lowered his voice. "It used to be a tobacco warehouse."

"I want to go closer."

Cal shrugged. They continued along the street until they were almost across from the prison. Then suddenly Cal halted, pulling Vanessa back into the shadows.

"That man, the one taking photographs of Libby," he hissed. "Have you ever seen him before?"

She frowned, staring at the man who was setting up his camera and tripod at the side of the road. Just then, he turned his head slightly and Vanessa gasped. "He's the man who accused you of stealing Brady's wagon back in Washington!"

Chapter 26

"Don't run," Cal cautioned Vanessa as they turned away from Libby Prison. "He didn't see us. If we don't attract his attention we're safe."

Vanessa slowed her pace, fighting the impulse to flee as fast as she could. If the man worked for Mathew Brady, what was he doing in Richmond? Who was he?

When they arrived at the shabby brick house and Cal let her into the little room, Vanessa made no complaint when he told her he must leave.

"Lock yourself in," he warned, nodding his head at the key in the door. "I'll be back as soon as I can."

After he'd gone, she stared for a moment at the paneled wood. She could trust Cal, couldn't she? Had he known the photographer was in Richmond? Was that why he wanted her to stay hidden? No, that was impossible. But it seemed a strange and menacing coincidence that the same man who'd stopped them from leaving Washington in the wagon was now here in Richmond. To stop her from getting into Libby? No, that was too far-fetched a notion. He didn't know her. He couldn't dream she wanted to help her father. Perhaps he was there to take pictures of everyone who went inside. But why? She could hardly believe he might simply want a photograph of the prison.

Vanessa walked to the window, but there was

nothing to see except the brick wall of the next building. Tugging at the catch, she finally managed to get it
open. As she leaned out, she managed a glimpse
along the narrow alleyway to the street in front of the
house. A wagon trundled past, followed by a Confederate soldier, riding at a fast trot. Did her father have a
window in his cell, she wondered. What was it like inside that tobacco warehouse? She began to pace about
the bedroom, feeling as though she too were imprisoned.

The door. She'd forgotten to lock it. Vanessa hurried over and opened the door a crack, peering out into
the corridor. The house was quiet and empty. Was she
the only one in this decaying old place? She closed the
door and turned the key, leaving it in the lock.

For a few moments she stood by the door, still listening, then went to sit in one of the two straight-
backed chairs. She sighed and stared at the bed. Her
thoughts, she realized, were as much a patchwork as
the quilt. The patches formed a design on the quilt, but
could she as readily find a pattern in all that had happened to her?

The photographer. Was he the key? She didn't see
how he belonged in her pattern at all. And what was
Cal doing? She thought about how Cal had changed
since she'd first set eyes on him. Back in the woods
he'd said the time was wrong. He'd said he couldn't
touch her because of what had happened. Did that
mean he regretted making love to her? He said he
couldn't because of what was going to happen.

Vanessa frowned. That might mean he didn't
want to marry her, didn't want to become involved
with her any more than he already was. When his
memory had returned had he recalled something that
made it impossible for them to marry? A wife?

*   *   *

A long time passed before Vanessa heard Cal's footsteps on the stairs. When she let him in, he gave her a quick, searching glance, then hurried to the table, laying out bread, cheese, and a pail of milk.

"Your father is still quite ill," he said, his back toward her. "He needs our help."

"Did you see him?"

"No, but the man I talked to has. From what he says, we'll have to get your father out of Libby in a hurry, before it's too late."

Vanessa sat down at the table and stared at him. All the medicines she'd brought from Washington had been used up during Cal's last illness. "What can we do?" she whispered.

"We have some problems." Cal gestured at the food "Have something to eat and then I'll tell you my plan."

Vanessa forced herself to drink some milk, to nibble at the bread and cheese. She'd learned over the past few months that it was wise to eat when you had food, lest there be none again for a long time.

When she'd finished, Cal crossed to the desk. Frowning, he pulled open the drawer and took out paper, ink, and a steel-pointed pen. Then he turned back to Vanessa. "I want you to write a letter to your father."

She started toward him, reaching eagerly for the pen, but he waved her away.

"I've been told your father has turned down an offer to be sent north in exchange for a captured Rebel officer. He insisted that men who were sicker than he be traded first."

"But you told me *he* was very ill."

"He is now. And if he hears you're in Richmond, he may be less stubborn about asking for his own exchange. There's a chance we could arrange it." Cal gazed steadily at her. "What I want you to say in your note to him is that he should trust the bearer—put my name there—and say that I brought you to Richmond, that you're in good health, and he's to do as I say."

Vanessa sat by the desk, thinking a moment before she began. She wrote quickly, waved the paper to dry the ink, then handed the note to Cal.

" 'Dear Papa,' " he read aloud. " 'I'm in Richmond with Mr. Calhoun Preston, who brings this letter to you. Please trust Mr. Preston and do everything he says. I'm in good health, but I miss you and want so much to see you. With all my love, Nessa.' " Cal hesitated a moment. "Yes, I suppose that'll do."

She frowned at him. "I wrote exactly what you said."

"Not exactly, but I don't think it matters."

There was something in his manner that made Vanessa very nervous. "I hate this room," she burst out. "I feel as if I'm in a prison cell. Must I stay here?"

Cal's face darkened. "Do you think I'm enjoying myself outside the house?" he demanded. "This is a risky, nasty business. It's bad enough I have to worry about being discovered, being challenged whenever I'm in the streets, having to deal with the enemy. I don't like any part of it, but it'd be ten times worse with you to worry about."

Vanessa looked down at her hands. "I realize you're doing this for me," she acknowledged. "I don't mean to be ungrateful." She clenched her fists. "But how I hate this war. How I wish all this fighting were over."

"So do I," Cal answered grimly. "At first I thought the South couldn't survive six months. They have no industry, hardly any railroads—and yet they've proved to be tenacious and dangerous fighters. Who can say when the war will end? Will it ever end?" Cal's voice took on a hard, bitter edge. "We get used to the killing, the maiming, the lies, the deceptions. You, I, your father, all of us will bear their marks long after the fighting's done."

She looked up at him, astonished by this burst of emotion.

Cal took a deep breath, then carefully folded the message to her father and put it in his pocket. "Wait for me," he ordered, "and no matter what happens, stay in this room. You're safer here than anywhere else."

"I will. Cal . . ." she hesitated, then went on. "I'm eager to have my father free. I want you to hurry to help him, but at the same time I . . . I wish you could stay with me." Color rose in her face as she said the words.

He studied her from the doorway, his forehead creased. "Damn the war," he muttered. In one long stride, he came back across the room and caught her to him in a savage kiss. Then he was out the door and gone.

It was after dark when Cal returned, and he seemed preoccupied. "Yes," he told Vanessa when she looked at him questioningly, "I delivered the message, but I can't tell you any more. I have to go out again."

"How was my father? Did he . . ."

"I had to pass him the paper in secret. I couldn't speak to him. He doesn't seem as ill as I'd been told." Cal turned back to the door.

"I didn't hear anyone in the house," she pleaded. "Must I stay in this one room? I promise not to go out in the street."

Cal shook his head. "The house is used by others, and you mustn't be seen." He paused. "Don't be alarmed if you hear them, though. They won't disturb you if you keep your door locked. My room is next door, and I'll be coming back there later tonight. I won't see you until morning."

"But . . ."

"I've no time to talk." Without looking back, he slid out into the hall, closing the door in her face.

Slowly Vanessa turned the key, then spread the quilt and lay on the mattress, trying to sleep. But sleep was impossible. Instead, she listened for footsteps, any sounds in the house. She lay there for what seemed an eternity, until finally a church bell tolled twelve times. Midnight. Had something happened to Cal? She twisted and turned.

Somewhere a door opened and closed, then footsteps sounded downstairs. Vanessa slipped from the bed and opened the door a crack. There was a flicker of candlelight in the lower hall, and she saw shadows loom up the wall. Two people? Then a door closed, and once again the hall was dark. Vanessa tiptoed back to bed, alert for any slight sound, but for the rest of the night the house was silent.

When Vanessa opened her eyes, the room was light. She ate some more of the cheese and bread and drank a sip of milk, noting that it was starting to turn sour. As she sat huddled over the table, Cal tapped on her door.

"I've come to take you outside for a few minutes," he explained. His face was drawn, and one look at his bloodshot eyes told her he hadn't slept all night.

"My father?"

"Nothing new. It's too soon to hear."

Cal led her downstairs, along a lower corridor, then out a back door into a weed-choked yard strewn with debris. A high board fence shut off any view of the street. She glanced wryly around her.

"It's the best I can offer." He leaned closer and spoke softly, almost whispering. "Everything I do is for the Union, you must understand that."

When Cal returned her to the room, Vanessa saw that someone had brought fresh water. Whoever it was had also provided a pillow. She hadn't slept on a pillow for months. She turned to ask Cal who had been so thoughtful, but he'd already slipped away.

As the day wore on, Vanessa heard comings and goings on the floor below, footsteps, doors opening and closing. The hours passed, and still Cal didn't come back. Restlessly, she paced about the small room, then lay on the bed staring at the ceiling. Finally, she got up and opened the window to peer along the alley at the wedge of street. With a sigh, she went back to bed, leaving the window partly open for a bit of breeze.

Night came, but still there was no sign of Cal. The next morning, he paid her a hurried visit, bringing food, and led her out into the dismal yard for a few minutes. But soon she was back in her room again, and he was gone. The day stretched out before her.

It was dark, and Vanessa lay on the bed, dozing. Then her eyes blinked open. What had that been? A cry? She sat up, swung from the bed and padded to the window. From the back of the house there came the faint shuffle of steps, the grunts of men struggling with something, a door opening. A curse cut through the night air, and Vanessa caught her breath. The voice sounded just like William Thornton's. But what would William be doing in Richmond? She must be mistaken.

Vanessa crossed to the door and felt for the key. But it wasn't there. And when she turned the knob, she found that the door was still locked. Frowning, she fumbled to light the candle by her bed. She held the flickering light close to the door, but her key was nowhere in sight. What on earth could have happened to it? She knelt and looked into the keyhole. The light glinted on the tip of a key in the other side of the door.

Vanessa got to her feet, bewildered, and hurried to the window. Below, a strip of light appeared on the brick of the building next door, as though from a window, then vanished. What was happening? Who'd locked her in and why? I won't be kept here like a prisoner! Vanessa vowed. She blew out the candle and crept back to the window. Carefully, she pushed it open to its fullest, then tucked up her skirts and climbed to the sill. Looking down into the darkness, she couldn't see the ground, but she knew she was only one story up. How far could that be? Taking a deep breath, she slid off the sill and jumped out. An instant later, her feet hit something hard, and she tumbled to her knees, unhurt.

After she'd caught her breath, Vanessa rose, looking up and down the alleyway. She flinched as something scuttled past her and was gone. A rat. Vanessa shook her head. She'd grown used to wild creatures when she'd lived in Morton's Woods. No rat could terrify her now.

As her eyes began to adjust to the darkness, Vanessa inched her way along the alley. In the house she'd just left, a slit of light showed at the side of a recessed basement window. She knelt cautiously, leaning forward, and looked through a tear in the curtain. Inside the room she saw a man with a lamp in one hand. Even though he stood with his back to her, she knew that it was Cal. Suddenly, Cal walked out of her line of vision, revealing a man sitting in a chair, bound and gagged. Vanessa froze, her mind reeling as she peered in the window. The man tied to the chair was her father.

Chapter 27

As Vanessa leaned against the window, staring in at her father, she heard the murmur of voices. She struggled to make sense of what she saw and, although she couldn't make out what was said, she thought there was a third man in the room, one she hadn't seen. Could it be William Thornton?

Her father had been freed from Libby Prison, but why was Cal holding him captive? It made no sense.

Vanessa stood up and hurried to the front of the house. She had to get inside, had to find out why . . . But wait. Would she do her father any good by rushing in and confronting Cal?

She ran up the front steps and found that the door was locked. She knelt on the steps, as she'd watched Cal do when they arrived. Which brick had he removed? Their rough edges cut at her fingers as she tested them. Finally, one shifted in her hand, and she pulled it loose, feeling inside the cavity, her fingers closing on a key. She quickly unlocked the door and held it open while she replaced the key behind the brick.

Once inside, Vanessa saw that the hall was empty. A light burned in the back of the house, but she heard no sound. What should she do now? Should she find the stairs to the basement and risk being made a captive like her father? She hesitated for a moment in the murky darkness of the hallway. How could Cal do such a thing?

When tears gathered in her eyes, she shook her head impatiently. She must be cautious now, very cautious. And somehow she must find out just what Cal meant to do. Much as she hated the thought, she'd have to return to her room before Cal discovered she was missing. She'd have to wait there and pretend to know nothing.

Vanessa silently climbed the stairs to the second floor, feeling along the wall until she touched her own door. Underneath the knob was the key. As her fingers closed around it, she thought of something her father had done once when their cook had taken too many nips of brandy and locked herself drunk in the larder. Papa had removed a sheet from his newspaper and slipped part of it under the door. Then he'd pushed an awl through the lock until the key fell onto the newspaper, pulled newspaper and key to his side of the door, and unlocked it. That was how Cal had taken her key, Vanessa realized.

Very quietly, she unlocked the door, keeping the key in her hand. Once inside, she closed the door and locked it again, then knelt down and pushed the key under the door, trying to get it directly beneath the lock so it might look to Cal as if it had fallen out. She was still on her knees when she heard footsteps climbing the stairs.

Stifling a gasp, Vanessa ran to the bed. She slipped off her shoes and lay down, pulling the quilt up over her. A moment later, a beam of light shone under the door. There was a brief silence and then the key rattled uncertainly before the lock clicked and the door swung open. Cal paused just inside the room.

Vanessa sat up, rubbing her eyes.

"Did I wake you?" he asked gently. When she

nodded, he moved silently across the room and placed his candleholder on the desk, shielding the light from her eyes. "We've heard from your father," he said quietly.

She resisted the impulse to ask if "we" meant William Thornton and himself. It would be folly to give herself away so soon. Her heart thudded in her chest as she stared at him. He looked just the same, not like a man who'd lied to her, who'd deceived her.

"What did you hear?" she managed to ask.

"He's agreed to be exchanged. We'll try to arrange it."

A faint draft blew a strand of Vanessa's hair across her face. With a trembling hand, she pushed it away. "I hope you can," she murmured.

"You've left the window open." Cal walked to the far side of the room and lowered the sash.

"Where's my father now?"

"Still in Libby." Cal's face was grey with fatigue, and yet she thought she'd never seen his eyes look so alive. He frowned at her. "Why do you ask?"

"I thought he might be in a hospital. I do so want to see him."

Cal took a deep breath. "After a few days, we'll know more about what can be done. I'm going now to meet with someone who can help us. I know it's almost morning, but you should try to go back to sleep."

"I will." She pretended to yawn, then tensed. He'd made no move to go. If he approached her now, she knew she couldn't conceal her feelings.

"Nessa . . ."

I'm not Nessa to you, she thought savagely. I'll never be Nessa to you again.

Cal gave her a pleading look, then turned and walked into the hall, pulling the door shut behind him.

There was silence for a moment, and then he called a loud good night.

"Good night," she answered, wondering why he'd waited until he was in the hall to speak. After a moment, she smiled grimly. Of course. He wanted to conceal the sound of the key turning in the lock.

Vanessa lay on the bed listening to Cal's footsteps on the stairs. She heard the front door close, heard the whinny of a horse, the thud of hoofs. Two horses? She couldn't be certain. For a long time, she waited, hearing nothing more. The house was quiet as she stared into the darkness, imagining the minutes ticking away.

At last, unable to restrain her impatience, she slipped on her shoes and went to the bedroom door. Locked, as she'd expected. She could take a sheet of paper from the desk and try to poke the key onto it with the point of the pen, but that would only be a waste of time. Instead, she opened the window and dropped into the alley. As she scrambled to her feet, she saw that the basement window was dark.

At the front of the house, Vanessa retrieved the key from the brick, entered the hall, then hurried upstairs to unlock her door. She reached for the candle on the desk and eased back out into the hall.

Shielding the flame, Vanessa crept down the stairs, staring into the dancing shadows. There was no light in the rear of the house. She cautiously opened a door and walked through a long narrow dining room. Beyond it was a kitchen, and beside the stove was a door fastened with a single bolt.

Vanessa pulled back the bolt and peered down a steep flight of stairs. They couldn't have left a guard with the door bolted—or could they? She descended very slowly, step by step, holding the candle over her head. To her left were empty wooden shelves; to her right all was in darkness. When she reached the bottom, she turned to the right.

Suddenly the light picked out a figure. Vanessa's father, bound and gagged, stared at her, his eyes widening in recognition. With a gasp, Vanessa hurried to untie the gag, then bent down beside him, fumbling with the ropes around his arms and legs.

"Don't waste time," he hissed. "Find a knife. Hurry."

She fled up the stairs, groping about in the kitchen until she found a bread knife. The blade was dull, but somehow she managed to cut through the ropes. When she'd finished, her father slowly stood up, flexing his aching muscles. Then he smiled and reached for her, holding her close, his face buried in her hair.

"Nessa," he murmured, "my darling Nessa." He held her away from him and she saw tears in his eyes. "You're all right," he whispered. "Thank God, you're all right."

It was her father, her dear father, and yet when she looked at him she felt numb. He'd only been gone a few years, but how he'd changed. Now there were deep lines around his eyes, and his hair was completely grey. It crossed her mind that an older William Thornton would look very much like this.

"Thank God they didn't harm you," her father sighed.

"Harm me?"

"That man Preston and his henchmen."

Vanessa shook her head. "I don't understand any of this. I came here to help you, to bring you medicine because a paroled Union officer reported that you were ill in Libby Prison. Cal Preston was to help me get to Richmond, and he did."

Her father nodded. "So that was how they worked it. You weren't held prisoner, as I was told."

"No." She stared at him in bewilderment. "At least not until tonight, when I was locked in my room. But why did they bring you here and tie you up? Where have they gone?"

"To Libby Prison, I suspect." He crossed to the stairs, grabbing the candle on the way. She could see that he limped as he climbed up ahead of her.

"You're hurt!" she cried, running to keep up.

He looked back at her. "What? Oh, my leg. An old wound."

"Where are we going?"

"To the prison."

"But why? You're out, you're safe. Can't we somehow get through the Rebel lines and . . ."

By now they were near the front door. Abruptly, her father stopped and put an arm around her. "Nessa," he said softly, "I'm a Rebel. I have been from the beginning."

She stared, unable to believe what he was saying.

"I was approached before the firing on Fort Sumter," he continued, "by a delegation of farseeing men who understood that we'd need men behind the enemy lines."

Vanessa pulled away from him, tears in her eyes.

He smiled sadly at her. "I couldn't even tell you," he said softly. "Everyone had to believe I was a traitor to the South, that I was a Union officer. I convinced our neighbors in New Market so well they burned down my house."

"Yes, I know."

He took her hands in his. "Nessa, you must forgive me for lying to you. It was necessary . . . for the Confederate cause."

"Everyone lies," she said dully, looking away.

Her father gave her a puzzled glance, then led her out the front door. "We'll talk more of this later," he promised, "but now we'll have to hurry back to Libby. There's no time to waste."

"Libby?" Vanessa repeated, still not understanding.

With a deep sigh, her father turned back to her. "I'm its commander," he explained. "I was wounded on a mission in '61, and when Libby was converted to a prison I was assigned there."

Vanessa stared back at him. Finally, the awful truth was beginning to sink in. Her father a Rebel! How could she bring herself to accept what he'd told her? He'd deceived her. And for what? For the Confederate States of America, the defenders of slavery, the supporters of the proposition that one man could own another. The image of Ancey's scarred back flashed through her mind.

Yet he was still her father, a man she'd always admired above all others, a man she loved. She followed him blindly, not noticing where he led, not caring. Outside, the first light of morning shimmered through the haze. The streets were deserted, the buildings dark. At cross streets, wraiths of fog drifted from the river, surrounding them like ghosts from the past. Her father's boots clattered on the cobbles, echoing unevenly in the mist.

Cal had also lied to her, from the first. And so had William Thornton. Was Robert Jamison implicated too? After all, he'd been the first to give her the news that her father was a prisoner. Vanessa shook her head, recalling what Cal had thought about her relationship to Robert. Most likely they'd used Robert without his being aware of it. How angry Robert would be if he knew.

Ahead of them, a wagon rumbled over the cobblestones of a main thoroughfare, the driver clad in grey. With a shout, her father ran toward the wagon.

Scowling, the driver pulled up and watched them approach, his hand on the grip of his pistol.

"I'm Colonel Woodward of the Richmond garrison," her father called out. "I need your wagon."

The soldier looked him up and down, eyeing his white shirt and brown riding breeches with evident disbelief.

Her father glared up at the man. "What's your regiment?" he demanded.

"Twenty-first Virginia."

Vanessa's father nodded. "Perkins is your colonel. Stocky dark man with greying whiskers."

The driver relaxed his grip on the pistol, but he left his hand on the butt. "Give the password, colonel."

"Death to tyrants."

The driver's hand raised in a salute. "Get in, sir. Where to, sir?"

Colonel Woodward jumped up beside him, pulling Vanessa after him. "Libby Prison," he ordered, "and hurry."

The wagon jounced forward so abruptly that Vanessa had to grasp the seat beneath her to keep from being bounced off. A moment later, her father's arm encircled her, holding her gently.

She turned to him. "I still don't understand. About Cal . . . Mr. Preston. Why did he bring you to that house?"

"I was given your letter wrapped in a message from him saying you'd be killed if I didn't meet with him in secret. I complied because I feared for your life, and when I did he took me prisoner." Her father shuddered. "The man who was with him—when I saw him, it was like looking into a mirror."

Vanessa covered her face with her hands. Lies, lies, so many lies. William Thornton had seemed so pleasant, so harmless. And Cal . . . She began to sob, tears streaming down her cheeks.

"Don't fret, Nessa," her father pleaded. "We'll put all that's happened behind us. When the war's over, we'll build another house in the valley. Not in New Market, perhaps, but we'll manage, you and I. We'll go riding and have parties and picnics, just like we did in the old days."

I don't want the old days, she told herself, rubbing away her tears. I want what I thought I had when I was with Cal in Morton's Woods. Bleakly, she looked up at her father.

"We can't bring back the past," she insisted.

"We can, you and I, wait and see."

Vanessa shook her head. "No, never. I love you, no matter which side you're on, no matter what you've done, but I can't go back to live in the valley."

Her father studied her for a moment, and Vanessa saw the pain in his eyes. "I should have realized," he sighed. "Nessa, you're a grown woman. Have you found someone else to love?"

Abruptly, she turned away. "I thought so," she said hoarsely, "but I was wrong."

The wagon swerved around a corner in the thinning mist, and suddenly Vanessa saw the brick building she knew was Libby Prison. As they rattled to a halt at the back gates, a guard stepped from the sentrybox. When he saw Vanessa's father he stopped short, his eyes widening.

"Colonel Woodward!"

"Yes, Harrington."

"But sir," the soldier stammered, "you . . . you just. . . . It couldn't have been more than fifteen minutes ago that I passed you through this very gate."

"Not me, Harrington, an imposter."

"An imposter? I could have sworn . . . I mean, he looked exactly . . ."

"Was he alone?"

"No, sir. He had a major with him, sir. An officer I didn't recognize."

Colonel Woodward jumped to the ground, stumbling a little on his lame leg. He glanced back at Vanessa, then helped her down. "Preston and his friend," he muttered. He held out his hand to the guard. "Give me your keys," he ordered. "Sound the alarm and rouse the guardhouse. Let no one in or out! Those men plan to release the prisoners!"

The soldier ran back to the sentrybox and disappeared inside. An instant later, Colonel Woodward had unlocked the entrance gate. As he swung it open, an alarm bell began ringing and soldiers spilled out into the courtyard.

Vanessa stood just inside the gate, forgotten, as the men sprinted past her, ranging themselves along the fence toward the river. Shouting at the top of his lungs, her father stood in the center of the courtyard, sending men in pairs into the prison and around the building to the rear.

Suddenly, a shot came from behind the prison, and then another. The men along the fence ran toward the firing and disappeared around the corner. Two more shots sounded, and a cry rang out. At this, Vanessa's father hurried off after his men. Frozen with fear, Vanessa watched him go, then took a few tentative steps before she broke into a run.

Just then a door opened, and a man stepped out of the prison, his face turned to glance behind him. Vanessa stopped, confused. Had her father gone inside so quickly? There he stood, in his white shirt, his riding breeches . . . With a shock, she realized that she was looking at William Thornton.

Thornton hesitated when he saw her, then strode past her toward the gate. When he reached it, he turned and waved to her. The sentry glanced from Thornton to Vanessa and back to Thornton.

Vanessa opened her mouth to shout out a warning, but the words wouldn't come. Cal had told her they hanged spies, and she wouldn't be the cause of anyone's death. Trembling, she raised her hand and waved to William. "I'll wait for you here, Papa," she called.

The sentry gave him one last look and passed him through the gate.

As she watched Thornton stride away, a flurry of shots sounded from behind the prison. Vanessa gasped and hurried around the building, halting just past the corner. In front of her, soldiers crouched behind whatever shelter they could find—piles of barrels, a shed, a water trough—firing from three sides at a row of barrels near the river. From behind it, there came the faint answering fire of a single pistol.

At a signal from her father, the soldiers began to converge on the trapped man, running now from the left, now from the right, kneeling on the ground, firing, dashing forward once again. Then the colonel raised his hand, and the firing stopped.

"Come out, Preston," he shouted. "Don't make us kill you."

A shot whistled from behind the barrels, and the soldiers returned a volley, advancing again.

"No!" Vanessa screamed, racing from the shadow of the prison. As she passed her father, she saw the shock and surprise on his face.

"Cal," she cried, "I'm coming, Cal."

The only sound was the soft thud of her footsteps. Before anyone could catch her, she was at the barrels. As she rounded the row, Cal stood up, a pistol in one hand, his other arm hanging limp at his side, the back of his hand covered with blood. He wore the uniform of a Rebel major.

Frantically, he motioned for her to go back, but instead she ran toward him. He took a step forward, reaching out for her, but before they could touch a shot rang out. Cal spun back, staggered and fell. With a scream, Vanessa dropped to her knees and held him to her, shielding him with her body.

"Vanessa, get away." Her father's voice was firm, angry.

She glanced up to see him towering over her. "If you've killed him, I'll hate you forever." She spat out the words, then turned back to cradle Cal's limp body, tears running down her cheeks.

"He's a spy, Vanessa."

Vanessa looked back up at her father, her eyes filled with fury. "Don't you talk to me of spies and traitors," she snarled. "If he doesn't live, I want nothing more to do with you. You're his enemy, and if he dies you'll be mine."

PART IV

WINTER 1863-
SPRING 1865

Chapter 28

The thirteen stars of the Confederate flag shone brightly, eclipsing the Union's thirty-five, as the Rebels turned back General A. E. Burnside's Army of the Potomac at Fredericksburg in December. And their good fortune continued in the new year as they retook Galveston, Texas, and turned back the Yankees at Vicksburg, Mississippi, in January of 1863.

"If Grant takes Vicksburg," President Lincoln said, "he's my man and I'm his for the rest of the war." But Ulysses Grant failed to capture Vicksburg and was forced to lay siege to the city.

In June, Lee's Army of Northern Virginia invaded the North, crossing the Potomac and marching through Maryland into Pennsylvania. The South seemed closer to victory than it ever had before, and only the Army of the Potomac, with its new general, George Meade, could prevent Lee from striking at the heart of the Union.

"This one'll be a big fight," Brady told Ruth. Then he sighed. "And I've only got the new man, Wilson."

Ruth frowned. "I don't think it was fair for Mr. Gardner to take Mr. O'Sullivan and Mr. Gibson with him when he set up his own gallery."

Brady shrugged. "They wanted to go. I can't blame him."

"But look at all they learned from you, all the money you've paid them. I call it disloyal!"

Brady smiled at her. "I've got one loyal employee at any rate." Then his smile faded. "Ruth, you'll have to go with me this time. Harry Wilson hasn't been to a battlefield before, and I'll need someone I can count on."

Ruth's heart sank. She still had nightmares about Michael's death at Antietam, and she'd never forgotten the horror of Bull Run. Yet Mathew Brady needed her. She knew he couldn't see well enough now to use a camera, could only supervise.

"You're certain there'll be a battle?" she asked hesitantly.

Brady nodded. "If for no other reason than General Meade is a Pennsylvanian, born and bred. And Lee's out of his own territory. Yes, there'll certainly be a big fight, and I've got to be there." He took a stance with his arms folded and sang in a cracked tenor:

Far away in the East was a dashing young blade
And the song he was singing so gaily
'Twas honest Pat Murphy of the Irish Brigade
And the song of the splintered shillelagh.

Ruth mustered up a smile. "What will you do after the war is over?" she sighed. "You'll have to be satisfied with portraits again."

"The fighting seems to go on and on," he replied. "Maybe photographing it will be my life's work. Who knows?"

In the late afternoon of the next to last day of June, still in Maryland and some miles behind the tail of the Union army, Mathew Brady pulled up his wagon before a two-story country inn. "We'll spend the night here," he called back to Harry Wilson, who drove the second wagon.

Ruth jumped down from beside Brady and hurried into the inn. It had been a long, busy day and she was bone tired. In fact, she had barely enough energy to share a simple meal with her two companions before she was back in her small second-floor room. But even though she longed for sleep, she found that it wouldn't come. She finally drifted off, and even then her dreams were troubled.

Ruth found herself surrounded by a dense rust-colored fog. Someone called her name, a desolate cry. She had no idea where she was, but she knew the voice was Jeremy's. She tried to tell him she was coming, but she couldn't speak. The fog choked back her words. She desperately groped about with her hands, first in one direction, then in another, but no matter where she turned, there was nothing to hold onto.

Suddenly, Jeremy's voice grew fainter and Ruth lunged frantically this way and that. She must find him before it was too late. She must! Her heart pounded louder and louder until she could hear nothing else. Finally, she gathered herself for a last effort . . .

Ruth sat up abruptly, the covers falling from her. The room was grey with early dawn, and someone was pounding at her door. Still trembling from her nightmare, she slid from the bed and hurried to the door.

"Who is it?" she asked.

"Open up." A man's voice growled at her from the hallway.

"Mr. Brady?" she whispered, though the voice didn't sound like his.

"Open up." The voice was louder now, threatening.

"No." Ruth backed away from the door. "No."

As Ruth flung on her petticoat, she saw from her

window that the stableyard was filled with horses. Then the whole room seemed to shudder as the man slammed against the door. Catching her breath, she clutched her gown against her body as the door cracked and flew open, the lock smashed.

A man in a tattered grey uniform, a pistol at his hip, strode into the room. A Confederate soldier!

"You've no right to come in here," Ruth cried through trembling lips. "What do you want?" From downstairs, she heard men shouting. Somewhere along the hall a woman screamed.

"You'll have no need for the dress," the Reb sniggered, advancing toward her. With one sharp tug, he yanked her gown away, tossing it onto the floor. His eyes gazed greedily at her breasts, now hidden only by her shift.

Ruth backed away, eyes fixed on him. He was tanned by the sun, a lean man with a ragged blond beard and hair so long it fell past her shoulders.

"Get out of my room," she cried.

He flashed a wicked grin. "I won't be here long," he muttered, reaching for her.

Ruth struck out at him, but he seemed not to notice. Grasping her about the waist, he tumbled her onto the bed, jerking up her petticoat and shift so she was bare to the waist. Frantically, she twisted away from him and grabbed the lamp from the nightstand, flinging it at him.

The Rebel soldier threw up his hand to ward off the lamp, and the chimney smashed, sending shards of glass all over. Without thinking, Ruth snatched up a long jagged sliver and lunged at his face. When he ducked, she threw herself off the bed and raced for the open door.

"You damn little bitch!" A moment later, he was on his feet, running after her.

Ruth half-tumbled down the stairs, darted across the foyer and burst through the front door. On the steps, she ran full tilt into a man who was about to enter the inn. He caught her in his arms, then held her away from him, looking at her with a puzzled smile.

"Let me go!" she cried, struggling to wriggle out of his grasp.

His smile grew wider. "Wait, miss. I mean you no harm. What's the matter?"

Ruth stopped resisting to stare at him. He was a handsome bearded man with pale blue eyes. A Rebel officer with stars on the shoulders of his uniform. For some reason, he looked familiar.

"Sergeant," the officer called out, "have you been troubling this little lady?"

Ruth looked over her shoulder. Standing in the doorway was the Reb who'd broken into her room. She shrank closer to the officer.

"Sir," the man retorted, "I didn't . . ."

"He did!" Ruth cried. And as she spoke, she suddenly realized whom she'd run into. Brigadier General Jeb Stuart. Langston had shown her the photographs he'd taken of Stuart. She swallowed apprehensively. Stuart's cavalry was feared throughout the North.

The general gave a hearty laugh. "Sergeant," he declared, "I suggest you find a gal somewhat more willing than this one appears to be." Stuart released Ruth, then looked back up at the soldier. "What about the medicine? Did you find any?"

"No," the sergeant replied sullenly. "Ain't nothing but bad-smelling chemicals in the wagons. They're photographers."

Stuart scowled. "Then get the others out of there," he ordered. "Tell them to saddle up."

The sergeant disappeared into the inn, and Ruth,

flushing as she clutched her shift, looked up at General Stuart. He bowed.

"I'm sorry you were inconvenienced," he said, his eyes lingering a moment on her full breasts, "though I can understand the sergeant's temptation."

Ruth reddened even further and eased away, hurrying through the door and up the stairs.

She watched from her window as the Rebel cavalrymen vaulted onto their horses and galloped off. She dressed quickly and went back down to the foyer, where she found Mr. Brady standing by the front door.

"I wish I could have persuaded General Stuart to stay long enough for a portrait," Brady sighed. He glanced at Ruth. "You weren't hurt, were you?"

Ruth shook her head, speechless for a moment, knowing it was useless to be annoyed with her employer.

Brady's wagons rode on into Pennsylvania that day, looking for General Meade. They spent the night in Gettysburg after Brady noticed that General Buford's Union cavalry was picketed nearby.

The next morning, as Ruth was drinking coffee with Harry Wilson, they heard the rattle of musket fire. Ruth set her cup down and rose quickly, for the shooting sounded very near. She looked for Mathew Brady, but he was nowhere to be found.

Close by, a cannon fired three times only, like a signal. The muskets' popping continued, and suddenly Brady appeared. "Well, it's begun," he shouted. "Let's get the wagons ready to go."

"Where to?" Wilson asked.

Brady shrugged. "This sounds like a skirmish. We'll wait till a line's established and Meade sets up his headquarters. That's where I want to be."

"The fighting seems too close for comfort already," Ruth cautioned.

"Oh, we may have to drop back for a time," Brady admitted. "All the more reason to be ready to go."

By noon, the What-is-it-wagons were among the other vehicles fleeing from Gettysburg. Behind them, the artillery boomed like thunder.

A mile outside of town, Brady pulled his two wagons into a grove of trees beside a field. As they looked back, they could see smoke rising over the town. The stench of powder drifted toward them on the wind.

They stayed in the grove for the whole day, listening as the noise of the fighting grew louder. By late afternoon, the sounds had drawn closer but they were more sporadic.

"We can't go back to Gettysburg," Ruth said, gazing off to the north. "They're fighting there."

Brady nodded. "We'll camp here."

That night, Ruth slept poorly, even though nothing louder than the croaking of frogs broke the silence. In the early morning, there were Union troops on the road, General Daniel Edgar Sickles' Third Corps. After watching for a while, Brady decided to follow them back toward Gettysburg.

The What-is-it-wagons trundled along the dusty lanes to General Meade's headquarters, a shabby farmhouse behind the Union lines on the crest of Cemetery Ridge. Ruth saw a hospital being set up two fields away and watched as a line of ammunition wagons pulled up in another field, but the big Parrott field guns on the crest of the ridge were quiet. All along the lines, soldiers cooked their meals and smoked, their guns stacked nearby.

Brady started Wilson taking photographs of the silent Parrotts, posing gunners as though they were in action, using first the big Anthony camera and then the smaller stereo double-lensed camera. The negative plates came out clearly, for the sun was very bright. The day would be hot and sultry.

Ruth felt as if she were moving in a dream. All the paraphernalia of war surrounded her, yet no one fought. Not even a musket shot shattered the eerie peace that lay over the hills and fields around Gettysburg. The Rebel sergeant's attack and her rescue by General Stuart seemed to have happened years ago in another world.

"Come, Ruth," Brady called. "We'll photograph the lookout tower."

The log tower was on a rise across the road from Meade's headquarters. Standing at the foot of it, Ruth looked out at the Union troops, deployed with their artillery among the stones of a cemetery on a hill just ahead.

"The Rebs are over there," a corporal told her, pointing in the direction of Meade's headquarters. "You can't see it unless you climb up the tower, but there's another ridge, not even a mile away, where old Bobby Lee's sitting on his white horse watching us."

In the late afternoon, the Rebel artillery finally opened fire. Between the thunderous booms, there was the pop of musket fire. Off to the southwest, a cloud of smoke hung over the battlefield. Soon the Union Parrotts on the crest began to fire, shaking the ground with their roar. Acrid smoke drifted overhead.

Ruth huddled beside the wagons, sheltered from the fighting by the crest of Cemetery Ridge. The noise went on and on, an incessant din that blotted out everything else. Harry Wilson tried to say something to her, but she couldn't hear him. Finally, he simply shrugged and turned away. Eventually, he went off and climbed the slope to the crest of the ridge. Mr. Brady had hurried up there as soon as the first cannon fired.

Ruth was terrified at the prospect of being left all by herself. The sun dropped and blue shadows deepened around her, but still there was no sign of any letup in the firing. Trembling, she stood up, took a deep breath and slowly started up the slope. When she neared the top, she stopped spellbound, high enough to see the flashing fire from the Rebel cannon to her left, the southwest. Clouds of dust and smoke hung over the fields below the ridge, and in the haze there came streaks like summer lightning. After a few moments, she realized it was musket fire.

Explosions suddenly rent the darkening sky to her right, so close she shrank back. The Rebs were firing on the cemetery! Ruth fled back to the wagons, but even from there she could see the shells bursting. Finally, the shooting died down to a mutter, and Wilson and Brady returned.

"Sickles has lost most of the Third Corps," Brady reported. "He's wounded." He took a deep breath. "The Rebs are attacking the middle of the Union line, but they're about through for the night."

"Who's winning?" Ruth asked.

"Looks like a stand-off."

Exhausted, Ruth tried to sleep, but the night was oppressively warm. Clouds covered the stars, so the darkness seemed to press down on her. From the open-air hospital across the fields, she could hear the screams of the wounded. Finally, near dawn, she fell into a deep sleep, only to be roused by the booming of the Union cannon from the cemetery. As she scrambled to her feet, musket fire crackled from her right, the flashes clearly visible in the grey dawn.

Brady and Wilson stayed with Ruth all morning, not venturing up on Cemetery Ridge.

"The Rebs are trying to get around behind the Union line," Brady explained, pointing to the wooded hill that rose in back of them to the northeast.

"What will happen if they do?" Ruth asked.

"I expect we'll be Rebel prisoners."

If we're not killed first, she thought grimly. At her urging, Brady finally ordered the wagons moved farther from Cemetery Ridge, to the shade of a clump of maples. But even there the heat of the sun and the stench of the sulfurous smoke were impossible to escape.

About noon, a silence fell, an unearthly quiet. Unable to contain himself, Brady sprang up and crossed the road, climbing the slope to the crest.

"They're picking up wounded on the field," he reported when he rejoined them. "No fighting at all. If the lull lasts, we'll try to get down there with the cameras."

Ruth shook her head. "Too dangerous—unless the battle's over. Is it?"

"No," Brady replied. "This is temporary. I've seen it in other battles. Both sides stopping long enough to pick up their wounded."

Harry Wilson moved his shoulders uneasily. "I think Ruth's right. We'd better wait till the fighting's over and done with."

"At least we can get ready to move." Brady began to hitch one of the horses to the wagon, and Wilson hurried to hitch up the other.

As Brady climbed onto the wagon, a single cannon roared. The shell screamed by almost over their heads, exploding to their left. Then dozens of big guns boomed in rapid succession, and shells crashed all around them, sending geysers of dirt billowing up in the road.

"My God, they're aiming at us!" Wilson yelled. He leaped onto the second wagon, urging the frightened horse across the field, away from the firing.

Ruth stood frozen with fear. Then she felt Brady's hand grasp her wrist, felt him pull her upward. With a gasp, she scrambled onto the wagon beside him, and they rattled off after Wilson.

"Overshooting," Brady explained calmly. "The Rebs mean to hit the lines on the crest, to soften them up for an attack." He patted her shoulder. "We'll be out of range in a tick. I've not been blown up yet. Don't . . ."

The loud roar of the Union guns behind them cut off his words. Ruth put her hands over her ears in a vain attempt to stop the noise. Now the cannon from both sides were dueling, and the sound was reaching an ear-splitting crescendo. Shells shrieked and burst in the air, hissing in all directions, their explosions marked by puffy white clouds. Despite Brady's words, Ruth was convinced that the shells were aimed directly at her, that the next one would demolish the wagon. She watched in horrified fascination as a shell hung in the air for an instant, then vanished in a flash of fire and smoke. Brady reined in the horse and she saw up ahead that Wilson had halted too.

Had there ever been such a cannonade? Wouldn't the very hills shatter from the noise? Looking back toward the road, she saw a shell explode in a wagon, saw horses and men and fragments of wood blown into the air. Across the field, by the hospital, shells shrieked down and debris blasted into the air.

On and on the cannon pounded until when it finally slowed, Ruth's ears rang with their echo. She shook her head as the sound changed. First it was the rattle of musketry, followed by a strange sound like many men, thousands of men, shouting all together, a vast terrible roar. Suddenly, the cannon on Cemetery Ridge took up again, drowning out the voices. Perhaps the battle would never end, Ruth cried to herself. Perhaps it would continue forever, a kind of purgatory for all who'd been trapped there.

At twilight the guns ceased, but their din was soon replaced by the cries of the wounded. As the full moon rose in the sky, a Union band began to play "Home Sweet Home."

At daybreak, a heavy mist hung near the ground as Brady turned the wagons toward the house that had been Meade's headquarters. Now it was a battered ruin, splintered by Confederate shells.

"Lee pulled out in the night," a sergeant told Brady. "It's over. We licked 'em this time."

Brady turned back to Ruth and Wilson. "We can take the pictures now," he cried, leaping up into the wagon. He urged the horse up the slope to the top of Cemetery Ridge.

Ruth had looked away from the dead horses, the corpses that littered the road, but when they crested the hill there was no way to avoid what lay below. As far as she could see, the fields were strewn with debris. Corn and grain had been trampled flat; where there'd once been an orchard there was now nothing but broken sticks. And lying amidst all this were hundreds, thousands of dead men.

Brady turned the horse and went back down the slope, motioning Wilson to follow. They rapidly circled the ridge until they found an easy way onto the battlefield. In the sultry heat, the dead had begun to putrefy. As Brady got out to set up the camera, blowflies, their iridescent wings flashing green in the sunlight, rose from the bodies. The stench of rotting flesh hung over everything.

Ruth stood by the wagon, clutching at it to keep from fainting. Finally, when she could stand it no more, she bent over and vomited, retching until she could hardly stand. When she was done, she wiped her mouth and steadied her shaking legs. Remember, she told herself, she was here because she believed in what Mr. Brady meant to do. Once enough people saw the horrors of war, surely then it would all end and there'd never be such carnage again.

Taking a deep breath, she squared her shoulders and turned back to the wagon. For the next few hours, she was in a daze, coating plates in the cramped darkroom, waiting until they were properly tacky, dipping them in the chemical bath, sliding them into lightproof holders and handing them to Wilson or Brady, only vaguely aware of the death-strewn field, the rubble of giant boulders where dead men still clutched their rifles.

Then the song Mathew Brady had sung before they started for Pennsylvania began running through her mind, and try as she might, she couldn't keep herself from humming the tune.

Sure the day after battle, the dead lay in heaps.
And Pat Murphy lay bleeding and gory,
With a hole through his head by some enemy's ball
That ended his passion for glory.

Chapter 29

Vanessa stood by her bedroom window on the second floor of the Van Lew mansion. By now she was accustomed to the view of the terraced gardens with their precisely trimmed boxwood hedges and the summerhouse at the edge of the James River. The Van Lews' black servants kept everything in excellent order.

"Jenny Lind sang in my parlor," old Mrs. Van Lew liked to tell her. The parlor did seem a fit place for the singer, with its silk-brocaded walls and teardrop crystal chandeliers, all as sparkling as though Miss Lind were expected back momentarily.

In the fall of '62, when Miss Emily had offered to let her live in her home, Vanessa had heard only the kindness in Miss Van Lew's voice and had accepted numbly, not knowing what else to do. But now she knew why Miss Emily had come forth so quickly, the same terrible day Vanessa had thought Cal was lost to her forever. Emily Van Lew was a Union sympathizer, and for the past sixteen months, Vanessa had gone with her to Libby Prison, helping her to take food, clothing, books and writing supplies to the Union prisoners.

"Vanessa, are you ready?" Miss Emily's high, reedy voice called through the closed door. Vanessa turned from the window, lifting her shawl from a chair as she passed. Despite the sparkle of the sun on the James, she knew the February wind would be chill.

As the two women descended the curving staircase, old Mrs. Van Lew called out from the morning room. "Emily," she rasped, "how much longer must the horse be stabled in our library?"

"Indefinitely, mother," Miss Emily answered with a laugh, "if we wish to keep him."

Vanessa knew that few citizens of Richmond were allowed to have horses, especially now, when the Confederate army's need for the animals had become so great. She'd grown used to the sight of the beast, standing on straw strewn over the parquet of the second-floor library, surrounded by shelves full of Shakespeare, Voltaire and Thackeray in their elegant leather and gold bindings.

"I have a better use for him than carrying a Rebel to fight," Miss Emily added. "You know that."

"I've never doubted you," her mother replied, appearing in the foyer in her black bombazine. "It's just that he stamps now and then, and since the library's directly over the morning room, I'm sometimes startled. But, as you say, we need the poor creature."

Miss Emily kissed her mother on the cheek and started for the front door. Vanessa smiled warmly at the old woman as she passed. She knew she'd never be able to repay either one of them. Not only had they taken her in, but Miss Emily had seen to it that Jonah and Ancey were sent north to Aunt Matilda with a letter from Vanessa.

"We'll have company tonight," Miss Emily remarked as she and Vanessa began the long walk down Church Hill to the prison.

Vanessa tensed with excitement. Another escape! But don't feed your hopes, she told herself. Miss Emily has told you time and again that he's too closely guarded, that she can't arrange to free him.

There'd be a few familiar faces at the back door tonight, men she'd talked to, brought food to. Miss Emily would let them in and hide them in the secret rooms under the sloping rear roof until the uproar over their escape from Libby died down. Then she'd help them slip north through the lines.

But Cal wouldn't be there. He was kept in a single cell deep inside the prison, isolated from everyone except the guards and the doctor. And it was only Vanessa's threats and pleas that had gotten him even this bleak existence.

"If word gets out that Preston is recovering from his wounds," Colonel Woodward had told her, "then he'll be hanged. We'll have to lock him away and hope he lasts until the war's over. That's all I can do."

Vanessa hadn't seen Cal since the day he'd been shot. Miss Emily hadn't seen him either, but she'd assured Vanessa that Cal wasn't dying, that food reached him, at least sometimes. But the guards were determined to keep everyone away from him.

How did a man who loved the western plains as Calhoun Preston did bear the misery of a tiny prison cell? "You should see how big the sky is out west," he'd told Vanessa in Morton's Woods after his memory had come back. "Horizon to horizon. Space to stretch, to live as you like."

Vanessa took a deep breath. "Take each day as it comes," Miss Emily had warned her. "Do what you can for those around you."

That had helped, feeling she was making life a little more bearable for the other Union prisoners. At first, it had been painful to go to Libby, not only because of Cal but because of her father. But as time passed, she and Colonel Woodward had effected an uneasy truce. Her father tolerated her prison visits, just as he accepted the fact that she refused to live with him. In fact, they were to dine together that night.

Over Vanessa's protests, Mrs. Van Lew had recently had her seamstress alter a number of lovely ball gowns for the girl. "Why not?" the old lady had demanded. "Emily insists on looking like a back-country cousin, and I doubt I'll live to see another ball to wear these to. These are perilous times. Must they be drab as well?" So that evening when Vanessa stepped into her father's buggy, she was very well turned out.

He smiled as she settled down beside him. "Charming, Nessa. A real Southern belle."

Vanessa touched her flounced velvet overskirt. "I'm afraid I'm overdressed," she murmured.

"Nonsense. It does everyone good to see a pretty girl. Lifts their spirits."

She drew her borrowed Chinese shawl closer about her bare shoulders, for the wind off the river was raw. "You look tired, Papa," she said quietly.

He sighed. "I've been trying to decide what I should do. Libby is likely to be closed altogether when the prisoners are moved to Georgia."

Vanessa's heart skipped a beat. "Moved?"

"We're sending most of them out of Richmond into Georgia this month. Thousands of men. I've been asked to supervise the transfer, and I've about made up my mind to request that I be allowed to remain in Georgia."

"Why?"

He rubbed his brow. "To tell you the truth, Nessa, I don't like what I do. Other wounded officers lead troops into battle—just look at Hood, with his one leg. And why not me? I think I'll stand a better chance of getting a brigade in Georgia than I will here."

Vanessa clasped her hands tightly together. "Will Cal be transferred with the other prisoners?"

"Probably not. He's supposed to be too ill to travel." He turned to her. "Nessa, give him up. There's no future for you with a man who's locked away in prison."

Vanessa looked away. "I've told you I won't discuss my feelings, Papa. Please honor my wish."

Reluctantly he nodded, then gave her a searching gaze. "You don't object to me leaving Richmond? Leaving you here alone?"

"I'm not alone. Cal is here."

Her father gave a grim laugh. "And the devil take me, wherever I may roam, eh?"

Vanessa laid a hand on his arm. "Papa, I do love you still, but I've explained all this before. It's as though I'm married to Cal, and a wife thinks of her husband first."

Vanessa could hardly wait for the dinner to be over so she could hurry back and tell Miss Emily about the transfer of the prisoners. After her father left Libby, Cal might be doomed, and there was only Miss Emily to help him.

Vanessa rushed up the front steps of the Van Lew mansion. At the door, she was met by Callie, an old black woman who'd been freed by Mrs. Van Lew's husband before he died. "Land, Miss Vanessa," she exclaimed, "we been that busy. My poor old legs is about done for, running up and down them stairs."

Vanessa slipped her shawl from her shoulders. "Can I help?"

Callie blinked at her, then grinned. "You is a fair sight. Ain't been a lady dressed like that in this house for going on three years. But you best put that shawl back on. Miss Emily ain't here, and she says you is to sit in the hall by the back door and wait. I brung a chair for you. No light, Miss Emily says, till you opens the door."

Always before, Miss Emily had tended the door herself, checking who she let in. "Jeff Davis and his men don't trust me," she'd explained. "And I'm often followed. They can't prove anything, but I'm not about to let them try to slip some Rebel spy into my house pretending he's a Yankee prisoner."

Vanessa pulled her shawl back on and followed Callie to the rear of the house. She ought to know tonight's "guests" by sight after all the time she'd spent tending to the Libby prisoners. If she found she didn't, she wouldn't let them in until Miss Emily came back.

Vanessa shifted in the rocking chair Callie'd left for her, shivering in the cold night air. The Chinese shawl had been made more for show than for warmth. She tried not to doze, listening for the tap at the back door. How she wished Miss Emily would return. She must tell her about the plans to transfer the prisoners to Georgia.

Vanessa closed her eyes and tried to bring Cal's image to her mind. Try as she might, she couldn't see him as he'd been when she first knew him in Washington. To her, Cal was the gaunt-faced man of Morton's Woods, the man she'd nursed so tenderly, the man who'd betrayed her.

No more than her father had betrayed her, she reminded herself. Will there ever be plain truth between men again? she wondered. Between people? The war has made us all into spies, has taught us all to lie, even to those we love, for what we're told is a greater good. Will trust ever come back?

She was so lost in her thoughts that she almost missed the quick light tap at the door. With a start, she jumped to her feet, reached her hand to the bolt and pulled it back. Before she eased the door partway open, she hastened to light the lamp beside her.

Outside, a cluster of dark figures hovered on the stoop. Squinting, she opened the door wider, holding the lamp high to see their features. Suddenly, a bearded man stepped forward and the light shone on his face.

Vanessa's mouth opened, but no words came. The light wavered as the lamp slipped from her fingers.

The man grabbed the lamp, saving it from smashing to the floor, then stepped inside, motioning the others into the house. Catching Vanessa's hand, he drew her aside, holding her in one arm as the others passed by. When the last man had entered, he set down the lamp and kicked the door shut.

"Nessa," he whispered over and over again. "Nessa. My Nessa."

She clung to him, unable to speak. After a time, she heard Miss Emily's voice.

"I wasn't certain he'd be here." she said, "but I hoped for the best when I heard the men were digging a tunnel."

Vanessa looked at her, trying to smile.

"Sixty feet of it!" Miss Emily marveled. "And they brought Major Preston with them, God knows how. The Union is certain to triumph with men like these on our side."

Chapter 30

Helena Swane smiled up at the ship's captain, a darkly handsome man with the rakish air of a buccaneer.

"We'll be in Wilmington tonight, without question," he promised. "I haven't spotted a gunboat yet, so I think we'll be home free."

"That's good news."

"In a way." He put an arm around her. "I'll miss you. There's never been a trip like this one. Are you sure . . .?"

Helena leaned briefly against him, then eased away. A romance with a captain aboard his ship was one thing, but what went on when they were safely ashore was something else entirely.

"I'm terribly sorry I can't stay with you," she murmured, "but President Davis insisted I come directly to Richmond on my return. I'm a soldier under orders, you might say." She looked out over the water, grey in the fading light. It would be good to be back home.

Helena had met Rose Greenhow in London, and Rose had introduced her to the right people. "Helena's my confederate, you know," Rose had said. "She took care of things when I was imprisoned, before the Yankees were persuaded to release me. What man can resist her?"

Certainly not Lord Beachnell. He'd even have

married her, except for the fact that he already had a wife. And Beachnell was not the only one who'd taken an interest in Helena. Even Queen Victoria had been most gracious, asking many questions about Washington and the dangers of spying. In fact, the entire court had been fascinated by her, and the weekend parties at their country mansions had been great fun. Yes, Helena had loved England.

Still, after the novelty wore off, she had to admit that she'd been bored. There was no danger in England, no thrill of outwitting a pursuer. When she'd been persuaded to attend a foxhunt, she'd felt a certain kinship with the fox. But, unlike the fox, Helena had never been caught, never would be. She was far too clever.

"The sea's running high," Captain Fanshaw remarked. "Perhaps you'd better go below for a time."

Helena nodded. She wasn't afraid of the weather, but she did need time to pack her trunk. As she turned to go below, she smiled to herself. Even the captain was unaware that the small leather bag she carried everywhere had gold sovereigns crammed into a false bottom. She was careful to make a great show of using the cologne and handkerchiefs it contained, pulling out a small book of poetry from which to read, sharing dainties to eat. Her trunk might need to be put in order, but the leather bag was always ready to go.

By the time Helena returned to the deck, darkness had fallen.

"Wind's come up," the captain called, "but we ought to get into the Cape Fear River with no trouble. I'll have you on solid ground by midnight."

Helena stood for a moment, gazing out toward the shore. Then she clasped her hands before her and began to recite:

'Tis now the very witching time of night
When churchyards yawn and hell itself breathes
    out
Contagion to this world.

He shook his head admiringly. "Never knew a
woman who could say things the way you can. I don't
know how you cram all those words into that pretty
little head."

Helena couldn't manage a smile, for she'd had to
repress a shiver as she spoke the words from *Hamlet*.
A sense of dark foreboding hung over her, as black as
the sky and the water. "Shouldn't we have a last
drink?" she asked, forcing gaiety into her voice. "A
toast to each other and to our futures."

Before they could send for the wine, a shout came
down from the crow's nest. "Yankee!" the lookout
called. "A Yankee ship!"

Captain Fanshaw darted back to the rail. "Full
speed ahead," he ordered, hoping there was still a
chance he could elude his enemies.

But it was too late. The gunboat had spotted
them, and now the chase was on. Closer and closer the
Yankees pressed, and as Helena watched she clutched
her leather bag. If she were captured, the money would
be confiscated by the damn Yankees. And they'd throw
her into a prison besides. How could she bear such a
thing?

It was well past midnight when the blockade runner approached the river mouth. Once inside the Cape
Fear River, they'd be safely within range of the Rebel
shore batteries. Just a few minutes more, and they'd be
out of danger.

"Wreckage ahead!" the lookout cried.

The ship came about quickly to avoid the wreck, then jerked to a stop. Helena went crashing to the deck. Beneath her, wood splintered and groaned, and when she struggled to her feet, the deck was listing.

"Damn. We're aground," Captain Fanshaw shouted.

"Gunboat to starboard," the lookout called. "Another to port."

Two! And they were trapped on a sandbar, helpless. I've got to get away, Helena told herself, trying in vain to curb her panic. She clutched desperately at Captain Fanshaw's arm. "Get me off this ship," she pleaded.

"Lower a boat?" The captain's voice was tense and angry. "Too damn risky."

"I don't care," she countered. "I'd rather take my chances with the weather than the Yanks."

Langston Cook huddled in the blanket, facing the dark waters south of Wilmington. This was the third night of his vigil. When he'd heard the report that a blockade runner was due from England, he'd come down from Richmond immediately. No doubt it'd turn out to be a false rumor, or else Helena wouldn't be on the ship. He'd been disappointed many times in the last year, but still he came.

Suddenly, a shell exploded near Fort Fisher, and Langston leaped to his feet. There was another explosion, then another. They're firing at Union gunboats, he told himself. And if there are gunboats that close, they're chasing one of our runners. He clenched his fists in impotent rage. "Damn you!" he yelled. Leave her alone."

As the bombardment continued, Langston raced down the river bank, heading for the ocean, running until he had enough breath left only to stumble along gasping. Finally, he was close enough to see the bulk of a ship in the light from the bursting shells. She stood two hundred yards offshore, not moving, listing badly. Watching her, Langston strode up and down the beach, muttering incoherently, cursing and praying.

Then a voice came out of the darkness. "For God's sake, help me!"

Langston ran toward the sound and found a man lying in the shallows. When he pulled him onto the sand, he saw that the man wore a sailor's garb.

"Overturned," the man gasped. "Lost my mate. The woman, too."

Over the lap of the waves, Langston heard another feeble cry and he plunged out into the water. "Here! Here!" he cried. "This way!"

A moment later, he caught sight of a figure struggling through the surf. With another shout, he launched himself forward, hands outstretched, slipping and sliding until he touched the rough cloth of a jacket. Grasping it in both hands, he hauled the swimmer toward shore, heaving until they hit the sand.

Langston lay there for a moment, panting, then reached out and turned the body over. In the darkness, he groped for the swimmer's face, then groaned when he felt the stubble of a beard. He'd rescued the lost sailor.

"Where is she?" he yelled.

The man beside him was barely conscious. "Went down," he gasped. "Couldn't hold her . . . too heavy."

Cursing, Langston staggered to his feet. Frantically, he splashed along the water's edge, calling Helena's name. But there was no answer.

Langston found her at dawn, washed up along the shore. A bedraggled leather bag was tied to her waist, and her eyes stared up at the sky. Her golden hair stirred with the movement of the waves, befouled with sand and seaweed.

Langston threw himself down beside her, clutching her cold body, kissing her pale, damp lips. Her leather bag shifted to lie heavily against him.

"Helena!" he cried. "Helena!"

But she didn't respond. Helena Swane would never respond to any man again.

Chapter 31

In March of 1864, President Lincoln appointed General Ulysses S. Grant commander in chief of the Union armies, for Grant had taken Vicksburg on the same day Meade had fought off Lee at Gettysburg. In September, General Sherman seized Atlanta, and in November he began his devastating march to the sea.

President Lincoln was reelected in November in a landslide victory, and General Sherman, as a Christmas present, gave him the city of Savannah. But the stubborn Confederacy fought on. On January thirty-first, 1865, the Thirteenth Amendment to the Constitution abolished slavery in the United States. By March, Sherman had reached Grant near Petersburg, Virginia, south of Richmond, where they were soon to be joined by General Sheridan, fresh from his sack of the Shenandoah valley. In triumph, President Lincoln sailed up the James River to City Point on the Presidential steamer, *River Queen*, to meet with his generals, his winning generals.

On the first day of April at Five Forks, southwest of Petersburg, Langston Cook set up his Anthony camera on its sturdy tripod and surveyed the group of men in front of him. "Remember," he cautioned, "don't anyone move until I'm done or you'll be a blur in the picture." He bent and gazed through the lens at the black troops. Who'd ever have thought the Confederacy would have black soldiers?

Since Helena's death, Langston had followed General Lee's army, and as time passed he'd come to respect the general as much as any man he'd ever met. And for his part, the courteous but reserved Lee had grown so used to seeing Langston Cook's What-is-it-wagon that he'd begun to greet Langston with a wave of his hand. Once he'd even been heard to joke about the photographer. "I can't order the advance," he'd laughed. "Cook isn't here yet."

Langston looked up from the camera. "All right," he called. "I've got it." He took out the plate and hurried over to his wagon, working fast at the processing so there'd be no chance he'd miss the shad bake at the rear of the lines. General Thomas Rossner himself had caught the fish, and he'd invited Generals George Edward Pickett and Fitz Lee to lunch. Cook, busy photographing the officers, had been included as well.

Langston smelled the tantalizing odor of the broiling shad as he pulled up his wagon near Rossner's headquarters. By the time he joined the generals near the fire, the big fish was being served, brown and succulent from the coals. The shad had been split and spread flat across green withes, and Langston thought he'd never seen food look more appetizing.

Whiskey and water went well with the meal, and Langston found himself relaxing. With a contented sigh, he leaned back against a tree and shut his eyes. Time seemed to stretch endlessly before him.

Suddenly, there was a rattle of hoofs. Langston straightened up with a jerk, watching as Rossner, Fitz Lee and Pickett sprang to their feet and ran to a courier.

"The enemy's coming in on White Oak Road," the soldier shouted, flinging himself off his horse.

All the men raised their heads, listening. But there was no sound of hoofs, no thump of marching feet.

"I don't think they're close," Rossner said at last.

"Don't seem to be in much hurry to find us here at Five Forks." Pickett agreed, still listening.

A breeze rustling through the dense woods next to them brought the aromatic scent of the trees to join with the smell of hickory smoke from the fire. But still the wind carried no crack of musketry, no boom of artillery.

"I believe I have room for a touch more shad," Fitz Lee said, sitting down.

The others joined him, but it was soon clear that their relaxed mood had been broken. Abruptly, Pickett stood up and turned to Rossner.

"Tom," he said sharply, "I need a rider to carry a message to Five Forks."

Rossner called up two men, one to ride several hundred yards in advance of the other. Both carried the same message to be certain it got through.

In silence, the officers watched the first rider gallop into the trees, followed shortly by the second. Within moments, gunfire blasted through the woods, and the second rider burst from the pines.

"Woods full of Yanks, sir," he shouted.

Instantly, the generals scattered to their horses. Scrambling behind them, Langston hurried to untie his gelding and leaped onto the wagon box, following them as best he could.

At Ford Road, Langston saw bluecoats swarming all over the woods and the road, with only a handful of grey cavalry opposing them. Pickett ducked his head low onto the neck of his horse, Indian fashion, and raced past. Langston watched in astonishment. He knew he and his wagon could never get through. It seemed a miracle that Pickett hadn't been killed.

Langston turned his wagon as fast as he could on the muddied corduroy and drove his horse back the way he'd come. Everywhere the Rebels were in rout. Finally, he managed to get the wagon to the rear, and by nightfall he was camped with what remained of the exhausted Confederate troops. Five Forks had been lost, and now both the Southside and the Danville Railroads were in danger of being cut by the Yanks, depriving Richmond of supplies.

No one felt like singing that night, but as Langston settled down to sleep, he heard a single tenor voice begin the grim song that had lately become a favorite:

> Stand to your glasses steady,
> 'Tis all we've left to prize;
> Here's to the dead already,
> Hurrah for the next man who dies!

Mathew Brady checked the wooden box of negatives and turned to Wilson. "These are ready to be sent north."

Wilson nodded. "Captain Russell will see to it. He has his army negatives set to go."

Brady looked around at the tent and the canvas-roofed log cabin that he'd had built for his headquarters. "We'll be on the go too by tomorrow," he remarked. "I hear General Grant is pushing ahead again."

Wilson grimaced. "A fine time we'll have with the wagon in that sea of mud they call a road."

Brady gave him a stern look. "If the army can move, we can."

*   *   *

Near midnight, Brady and Wilson were awakened by shouts.

"We've routed Pickett!" a soldier called. "Sheridan's got the Rebs on the run."

"You don't catch me," someone shouted back. "This day ain't over yet! April Fool!"

"You damned knothead, I tell you we took 'em sitting."

Reaching for his shoes, Brady stuck his head out of the cabin. "Where was the fight?" he called.

"Five Forks. You'll get some dandy shots, let me tell you."

By sunrise, Brady and Wilson had the What-is-it-wagon moving, albeit hub deep in mud. They arrived at Five Forks in time to take some photographs of the battlefield.

"This has the feel of a last stand for the Rebs," Brady mused, gazing about. "We wouldn't want to miss anything so we'll have to look sharp."

Wilson shot him a puzzled glance. "For what?"

"For the front line." Brady hesitated. "What would you do if you were General Grant?" he asked.

Wilson shook his head. "There's all those forts between us and Petersburg—Whitworth, Gregg, Mahone. I suppose he'll have to take them."

Brady scowled. "We can't get to the forts yet for pictures, the Rebs won't let us. So keep your eyes peeled for Union troops moving up. We'll follow them."

At dark, when Brady heard that all three of the forts had fallen, he still was nowhere near the action. He camped with a unit of soldiers outside Petersburg, expecting to be trapped behind the lines. But even as

Brady was cursing his bad luck, the fighting drew near him once again. Around midnight, he was startled awake by a series of three massive explosions, each one rattling the glassware in the wagon. Peering out the back flap, all he saw were half-dressed soldiers milling about, looking for an attack that didn't come.

"The Rebs blew up their ironclads in the James," an officer called. "One, two, three. Didn't you hear?"

A cheer went up.

"Reckon they know we got 'em," a private shouted. "Won't be long now."

Brady ducked back into the wagon. "Richmond in the morning," he whispered to Wilson.

Brady's wagon bounced along the Darbytown Road behind the Fifth Massachusetts Cavalry, a black regiment led by Colonel Adams, their white officer. There was no sign of Rebel troops. Their lines and fortifications were all deserted. By mid-morning, Brady was in Richmond.

As the wagon clattered into the city, Brady and Wilson gazed about in amazement. Drunken Union soldiers reeled in the streets, paying no heed to the poorer citizens of Richmond, who were already looting and pillaging. As he rode up, Colonel Adams angrily shouted out orders to his men, putting a stop to the looting and rounding up the besotted soldiers.

Brady pulled the wagon to a halt and scowled. Ahead, he could see that the whole center of the city was in flames. After only a moment's pause, he flicked the reins, heading his wagon toward the fire. "I'll be in at the finish if I have to broil to do it," he bellowed to Wilson. "I'll have pictures of it, the completion of my war views." In his excitement, he pounded Wilson's shoulder with his clenched fist. "Recorded forever, the history of a war, from beginning to end."

* * *

Langston Cook spent two days trying to catch up to General Lee, who'd headed off to the northwest. Finally, in the midst of a driving rain, he lumbered into the town of Amelia Court House, Lee's new headquarters. Early the next morning, he managed to see the general.

"Well, Cook, here you are, determined to put yourself in danger again," Lee chuckled. "Don't you know the entire Union army is on my trail?"

Langston nodded. "It does look that way, sir. But I'd like permission to stay with you."

Lee shot him a swift, shrewd glance, and Langston knew that the general had divined his thoughts. The end was near, and Langston intended to record it.

General Lee sat down, wincing at his rheumatism. He motioned Langston to a seat. "I've seen you staring into that infernal camera of yours, even when so many bullets were whizzing about that my soldiers were beginning to retreat. You're a brave man, Cook. I'm sure your photographs will be of value to the Confederacy."

Langston looked deep into Lee's eyes. "You might remember Mathew Brady, the Washington photographer," he said slowly. "He told me once that he hoped his war views would prevent another war. But I doubt if he really cares who wins this one. To him, everyone loses when there's a war. I've always supported the Confederacy, but this past year I've begun to understand how Brady feels. In the end, only the pictures are important. No matter who wins or loses, pictures can be understood by everyone."

There was a silence.

Finally Lee gave a slight cough. "It's been almost a year since Stonewall Jackson was killed," he said in a low, solemn voice. "He hadn't the slightest doubt that God was on our side. I often envied his faith." He sighed. "Come along with us, Cook. Take your pictures if you must. I wish you luck."

It was clear to Langston that Lee hoped to hold his present position, protecting the Richmond and Danville Railroad, but at noon, the general issued marching orders. Sheridan had cut the track to the south, ending Lee's hope of a retreat to Danville by rail.

Instead, Lee headed north, intending to circle back until he struck the Southside Railroad, which led west to Lynchburg. Langston kept his wagon as close as he could, but soon he fell behind Lee's staff into the slower columns. A motley army trailed after their commanding general: cavalry, infantry, engineers, artillery, even naval battalions from the sabotaged ironclads. Langston stopped to take a photograph of a naval officer shouting orders to his sailors: "To the starboard, march."

Moments later, Langston ducked for cover, his camera clutched to his chest, as Union artillery rained down among the troops. A Parrott shell exploded immediately in front of him, severing a man in two, and Langston hugged the ground, gagging. When he looked up, he saw Yankee troops advancing up the hill toward the road.

The Rebel soldiers turned and fired, decimating the enemy's first line. When the second line wavered, the ragged grey troops rose as one man and rushed down the slope, most bareheaded, many shoeless, throwing themselves at the bluecoats despite a volley of musket fire. Yelling at the top of their lungs, they came at the Yankees with bayonets and the butts of rifles, even with bare fists.

From his vantage point, Langston saw lines of Yankee infantry advancing, row after row of bluecoats. He frantically squirmed away, dragging the camera behind him. Somehow, he got back to his wagon and fled, expecting to be killed or captured at any moment. But he managed to overtake another Confederate unit, and when they turned to battle the pursuing Yanks, Langston rode on toward Farmville instead. He came upon General Lee unexpectedly at dusk. The commander was riding his big horse, Traveller, and the soldiers cheered as he passed by.

"It's General Lee! Uncle Robert!"

"Where's the man who won't follow Uncle Robert?"

The eyes in the begrimed soldiers' faces glowed, lit not only by the glare of burning wagons but by the courage and loyalty within.

Lee smiled and waved, calling to them, but later, when Langston saw him again at headquarters, he was not so confident. "Half the army has been destroyed." Langston heard him tell an aide. "Ewall's been taken and also my son, Custis."

"Have you chosen a place to make a stand?" asked the officer.

Lee shook his head. "No. I'll have to await developments. A few more battles like today's and it will all be over."

The next morning, when Langston tried to take a photograph of Lee's tent, he found that there was no exposure on the negative plate. The Anthony must have been damaged when he'd dragged it over the ground the day before. A poor piece of luck indeed, just when he had the finest seat in the world for photographing the end of the war. Cursing softly, he examined the big camera and spotted a hole in the bottom and another in the side. It looked for all the world as if a minie ball had passed straight through.

By the time Langston had brought out the smaller stereo camera, Lee's tent had been struck. Soldiers bustled all about now, preparing to move on. Langston sighed and went to pack up his own gear. He knew better than to ask these men to pose.

All that day, Lee retreated before the Union forces, fighting only when he had to. From his place in the line of march, Langston looked back on blazing ammunition wagons. All around him, the air was filled with explosions that had been touched off by the flames. The ground was littered with dead mules and dead men. That night, Langston heard that Grant had sent Lee a letter requesting his surrender.

"You may think me cruel," Lee replied when Langston asked him about the rumor. "General Wise wanted me to surrender yesterday. When I refused, he told me the blood of every man killed from now on was on my head." Lee took a deep breath. "Well, it may be true. I refused Grant, too. But I did ask that he let me know the terms of surrender—though I suspect I know them. They're not acceptable while I can still fight."

Langston nodded, remembering that U.S. Grant had long ago been dubbed Unconditional Surrender Grant.

The next day's march was less organized. Now the men straggled along, their officers too dispirited to keep them in line. As Langston drove, he passed a chaplain clutching a musket. When he called out, the man snapped, "I'm the Reverend Harding of the Forty-Fifth North Carolina. I've learned this is no time for noncombatants." Shall I take up a gun? Langston asked himself as he rode past. He knew he didn't want to.

All that day, there were brief skirmishes to the rear, but there were no battles. Before the light faded, Langston took some shots of exhausted men sleeping beside the road, men who trusted that those at the back of the column would rouse them when they passed.

The sun set at six-thirty. Soon thereafter, Langston pulled up in the woods just east of Appomattox Court House. In the tiny village, in front of a small brick farmhouse, he'd spotted General Lee's white horse. As the night darkened, clouds obscured the sky, and the light of campfires reflected ominously from the clouds. Somewhere out there was a ring of enemy fires, closing in on Lee's tattered army.

Langston moved his wagon nearer when he saw Generals Fitz Lee, Pendleton and Longstreet come to Lee's small bivouac fire. There was another letter from Grant, Lee told his staff, a letter stating one irrevocable condition for surrender—laying down of arms—and suggesting a meeting to discuss terms. Lee's reply promised nothing but a meeting and named the place and time.

"I have until ten tomorrow morning before I meet with Grant," Lee said grimly. "In the interim, we'll do our best to break through his lines and escape."

At dawn Langston found himself far back in a column marching raggedly to the northwest. Union artillery boomed behind him, and the rattle of musketry sounded, coming closer and closer. A shell burst in front of him, and Langston's horse screamed and reared. In a frenzy, the animal bolted, dragging the wagon across a ditch and into a field. Langston tried to control him, but it was no good. With a violent lurch, the wagon hit a rock and overturned, tumbling Langston onto the ground. The horse struggled on ahead,

pulling the wagon on its side until another shell landed
squarely on top of it. The explosion knocked Langston
backwards, sending shards of wood and metal flying all
over.

Dazed, Langston picked himself up and stumbled
toward the road, wondering numbly why he'd been
spared. The wagon was totally destroyed, the horse
dead. Vaguely, he looked at his arm and watched as
the blood ran down. He'd not even realized he was
wounded. At first, his head spun as he staggered along,
but soon he felt a little stronger, strong enough to
catch a riderless horse and make his way back along
the column.

When he reached Lee, Langston found the general dressed in a new uniform, his linen snowy white,
his boots, trimmed in red silk, gleaming.

Lee caught his glance. "I'll probably have to become General Grant's prisoner," he said, "and I
thought I must make my best appearance. You've arrived for the finish, Cook."

Langston gave Lee a sad smile. "With no
camera," he replied. He could think of nothing to add
as he watched the general mount Traveller. A lump
came into his throat as Lee and his aides rode past. At
that moment, Langston knew he wasn't like Mathew
Brady. Despite Helena's death, despite all that had
happened, he did care who lost. The Confederacy was
dead, and Robert E. Lee was about to attend the fu-
neral.

Mathew Brady heard news of the surrender while
he and Wilson were still far back behind the Union
lines. As they rushed to Appomattox, a man on horseback hailed the wagon. At first, Brady didn't recognize
him.

"You're too late," Langston Cook shouted.

Brady grinned. "Langston! It's good to see you. Were you there? Did you get photographs at Appomattox?"

Langston shook his head. "No. My cameras were smashed. Like the Rebs."

"A shame. Has Lee left?"

"Gone to Richmond, I heard."

Brady frowned. "Well, I'll find Grant and take a few shots of the house where they met. Perhaps I can catch Lee on the way back." Then he brightened. "It's the finish, Langston, and we're both here for it. Will you come to Washington and see my war views? My completed war views? I always felt you understood what I meant to do better than anyone."

Langston wheeled his horse in and came closer to the wagon. "I understand, but I won't come, Mat. Like Richmond, I'm burned out. Nothing seems to matter."

"But the pictures matter."

Langston looked over at Brady, and there were tears in his eyes. "You take them," he said hoarsely. "Take your goddamned photographs. Develop them, print them, frame them. It's not just the soldiers in the fields who are dead, Mat. Half the country's just died." He kicked his horse to a trot and was gone.

Chapter 32

Ruth O'Neill stood opposite the Willard Hotel in the fading light of late afternoon, staring at the crowded brick sidewalk on the north side of Pennsylvania Avenue. Washington had begun to celebrate on April second, almost two weeks ago, when Richmond fell, and the uproar hadn't stopped yet. That afternoon, church bells tolled, reminding the city that it was Good Friday, a time to mourn, but the men who pushed in and out of the hotel seemed to have jubilee on their minds, not sadness.

Last night, Ruth had strolled with her father up and down the city streets staring in fascination at the glittering City Hall dressed in gas jets, at the flickering shine of candles in almost every window of every house, at the buildings hung with illuminated banners. They'd watched the fireworks at Franklin Square, and later, as her father had walked Ruth back to her rooming house, they'd passed the Capitol. Beaming, he'd pointed to the lighted dome, now completed, Armed Victory in her place at the top.

"You see, our statue has her sword sheathed," her father had declared. "Ah, Ruthie love, it's been a terrible war for us, losing our Michael, but George'll be back with us soon. The war is over, thank God and all His blessed saints. Over and be damned with it."

Ruth sighed. Was she a fool, coming here today?

On each of the past four days, she'd wedged herself into the crowded lobby of the Willard, trying not to be obvious as she stared at every young man who wasn't in Union blue, telling herself it was too soon, that General Lee had given up his sword to General Grant only a few days ago. It was too early for a Confederate to stop being a soldier and come north. But the war *was* over, and so she'd come.

The scent of lilacs perfumed the brisk wind that blew along the side street. The spring flowers were in bloom all over the city, purple and white masses of fragrance. This was the loveliest season of all in Washington.

As Ruth stood uncertainly on the pavement, a carriage drew up in front of the hotel. After a few minutes, a man in uniform accompanied a woman from the Willard, and Ruth watched as he helped her into the carriage, then climbed up to sit with the driver. Something about him seemed familiar, although he wasn't distinguished-looking.

U. S. Grant. Yes, she was certain of it. She'd seen the photographs Mr. Brady had taken of him. General Grant. And the woman must be his wife. The carriage pulled away. As Ruth gazed after it, a young man on a black horse dashed recklessly against the traffic to trot alongside the carriage, staring intently first into the window and then at the general. His rudeness made Ruth wince. He also looked familiar, but she couldn't place him—dark mustache, pale skin, handsome enough. She mentally sorted through the portraits in the gallery, then shook her head. Mr. Brady had never photographed that man, whoever he was.

Ruth turned back to the hotel and took a deep breath. Was she going to cross the street and go in or not? She didn't know if Jeremy was dead or alive. She didn't know whether, if he lived, he'd remember. She wasn't certain that even if he did remember, he'd come. Almost five years had gone by.

She raised her chin and hurried across the avenue, threading her way between the people to enter the Willard. Inside, the lobby was crowded, as it had been each day she'd been there. Looking about, Ruth found a niche between two chairs and leaned against the wall, but a middle-aged major immediately rose and offered her his chair. She smiled and thanked him, feeling only a little guilty as he walked away, for he appeared to be in robust health.

Ruth smoothed the peach silk of her skirt with gloved fingers. The gown had cost more than she liked to think about, this one and the other she'd had made, the green silk. But she didn't want Jeremy to feel ashamed of her, as he must have the first time he'd brought her here, a servant girl, a country bumpkin. Why did she think he'd want to return to the girl she'd been back then, a girl who'd been ignorant, drably dressed, gauche?

You're foolish to wait, she scolded herself. Foolish to waste your time and to presume on Mr. Brady's good nature by leaving the gallery. Ah, but how could she ever forget her handsome Jeremy? Ruth closed her eyes to summon up his blond curls, his blue eyes, the chiseled cast of his features. How arrogantly he had walked, as though he owned the world! She smiled, remembering.

Gradually, Jeremy's fair hair grew dark, his eyes changed to black, his features shifted, he was someone else. Ruth saw, behind her closed lids, the man who'd stared at the Grants in the carriage. Suddenly, she realized that she knew who he was. The handbills had carried his picture early in the year when he'd played Romeo at Grover's Theater. He was an actor. Booth. John Wilkes Booth. And it was rumored that half the ladies in Washington were in love with him. But why had he stared so at General Grant?

Wait. Ruth opened her eyes and gazed straight ahead. Hadn't the *Star* announced just today that General Grant would attend the theater with President Lincoln tonight? Was Mr. Booth afraid the general was leaving the city, wasn't going to his performance? She frowned. No, Mr. Booth wasn't acting this week.

Oh well, it was none of her business. She folded her hands in her lap and glanced at the others in the lobby. So many officers in their blue uniforms. When could they put off those uniforms and wear ordinary clothes, lead ordinary lives?

Outside, she heard music, another band marching along the avenue. As the musicians came closer, they began to strike up "Dixie," a song not heard in Washington until the President, last Monday, had requested it be played, declaring that "Dixie" was now the lawful property of the Union.

> Old times there are not forgotten
> Look away, look away, look away ...

Just then, a man in a black frock coat limped slowly through the crowded lobby, leaning heavily on a cane. Ruth caught a glimpse of a terribly scarred face before she averted her eyes. How must it feel to come back from the battles lame and disfigured? At least George had been spared that, though it must have been terrible to be a prisoner. She frowned down at her hands. Twice, Langston Cook had sent messages to her through Mr. Brady about George, saying her brother was in good health. She supposed she should feel grateful, should forget her bitterness toward Langston. The war was over.

The limping man passed again, and Ruth glanced

at him from under her lashes. He kept his face averted so that all she could see was the scar that puckered up the entire left side of his face, by some miracle sparing the eye, clear and blue, that stared at her, then darted away.

The way he looked at her was upsetting. She turned her head so she couldn't see him, fixing her gaze at a painting of some European field where men bent to their spring planting, a peaceful vista, a scene of promise, of renewal. As this, the Easter season, was a time of renewal, of rebirth.

What would she do if Jeremy never came? There were other men in the world. She knew men were attracted to her. But I can't, she thought sadly. I can't even bear to think about another man. I suppose I'll just go on working for Mr. Brady for as long as he wants me.

When she turned back, the man with the scar had disappeared. She sighed in relief, then stiffened. Twice he'd glanced her way, his eye so blue and bright. No wonder she'd been upset—his eye was like Jeremy's.

She half rose, then sank back. If the man had been Jeremy, he'd have recognized her, spoken to her. She hadn't changed that much. No, he couldn't have been Jeremy. Yet was she sure?

Ruth got to her feet, searching the crowd, but the lame man with the scar was nowhere to be seen. Hurriedly she pushed through the throngs of people, racing through the door to gaze wildly up and down the brick sidewalk. Halfway down the block, a man limped away from her.

"Jeremy!" she cried, running, dodging among the strollers. "Jeremy!"

The man slowed, then stopped, turning the ruined side of his face toward her. Something about the set of his shoulders, the way he held his head, convinced her she was right. Breathless, she ran to him, started to reach out her arms, then stopped, suddenly shy.

The right side of Jeremy's face was as handsome as she remembered, making a cruel mockery of his disfigurement. She stood there staring at him, tears rushing to her eyes.

"Jeremy," she whispered, "why didn't you speak to me in the Willard?"

His mouth twisted in a one-sided smile. "I didn't think you'd want me to."

She held out her hand, and after a moment he clasped it. With a sigh, he tucked it under his arm and led her back to the hotel.

"Why did you come if you didn't intend to talk to me?" she asked gently.

Jeremy paused for a moment. "I promised," he answered softly. "Just as you promised. We've both kept that promise."

"I . . . I didn't recognize you at first," Ruth went on. "Then, somehow, I did. If you'd looked straight at me . . ." Her words trailed off as she realized he'd meant her to see only his scars. "Oh, Jeremy," she cried, "you've been so badly hurt."

She felt his arm tense. "Don't pity me," he said harshly. "I don't hold you to anything you've said in the past. You've kept your promise to meet me. I don't expect . . ."

"Don't be a fool!" she shot back, angry now. "I didn't run after you out of pity. How can I pity you when you're here, you're alive? My brother Michael wasn't so lucky. He died at Antietam."

There was an awkward silence. "I'm sorry," Jeremy said at last. "Antietam was hell. You're right, I was lucky to survive. Though I didn't always feel that way."

He led her through the crowd into the dining

room. A waiter beamed at them as they entered, then showed them to a table, and with a flourish, removed a card that said "Reserved."

Ruth smiled at Jeremy. "This is the table we sat at the first time we came here. You remembered."

There he was, across from her, his eyes the same unclouded blue she'd seen in her mind so many times. "I've never forgotten you, Ruth. Even though I tried. This table—well, it's nothing but a fool's romantic hope."

"And yet you didn't speak to me." Ruth reached out to him, and he took her hands, leaning across the table. "Jeremy, I love you." She loosened one hand and gently touched the scars. "What are they to me? You're still Jeremy."

At that, he looked down, fumbling for the right words. "Ruth, I have to tell you. I fought at Antietam Creek too. Michael and I were both there, but on different sides."

Ruth's voice softened. "The war is over," she murmured. "We can put away bitterness and hatred. What does it matter, now that you're here with me? I never stopped loving you. You did what you had to do, just as Michael did." And just as Langston Cook did, a voice told her from somewhere deep inside.

Jeremy's grip on her hand tightened. "Ruth, my lovely Ruth," he whispered. "My love."

And in that instant, Ruth forgot Langston, forgot everything else. Gazing into Jeremy's eyes, she was no longer aware of his scars, no longer aware of the people at the tables around them, the hotel, the city. There was nothing in the world for her except Jeremy Valerian.